PRAISE FOR

If You Knew, Would You Say I Do?

"I have been working in the field of psychology as an author, reporter, media personality, and psychotherapist for over thirty years and have never seen a more compelling novel that draws you into the story and its characters while simultaneously providing invaluable detailed information about narcissistic abuse and its insidious nature. The stories are riveting as you witness these two women go from seduction to destruction to survivors."

—**Dr. Robi Ludwig**, PsyD, Renowned Psychotherapist, Award-Winning Reporter, and Author of *Your Best Age Is NOW*

"Enthralling and much needed. I was intrigued from beginning to end. Thank you, Laura and Jessica, for sharing your stories so that others may see the light of change."

—**Nicole S. Kluemper**, PhD, Author of *See Jane Fly: A Memoir*

"Authors Lisa Blakely and Tami Parker have masterfully taken readers on a journey [that shows] how . . . [easy] it is to be captivated by someone who is not what they seem. Having been in an abusive relationship myself, this story mirrored my past in many ways, and I felt a kinship in the trauma so many of us have experienced. *If You Knew, Would You Say I Do?* is a book not only for those who have dealt with abuse in a romantic relationship but for everyone. It is essential to see how people fall victim to abusers, especially those with NPD, to prevent it from happening to you or to understand your loved one's trauma and longstanding effects. *If You Knew, Would You Say I Do?* is an important story and a must-read."

—**Dianne C. Braley**, Author of *The Silence and the Sound*, Winner of the NYC 2022 Big Book Award

"*If You Knew* is a powerful, entertaining, and educational work, hooking the reader from the start and never letting go. As a marriage and relationship coach, I so appreciate how the authors, through the art of storytelling, explore and answer the question of why women don't just leave [through] a podcast format, teach about the insidious power of narcissism in relationships, and remind us we all are at risk of becoming a victim of narcissist behavior. I can't recommend this book more highly."

—**Nancy S. Pickard**, Relational Life Therapy Coach, Author of the Best-Selling *Bigger, Better, Braver*

"*If You Knew, Would You Say I Do?* captures the profound complexities of loving someone with narcissistic personality disorder, portraying the poignant and heart-wrenching journey. Yet among the pages laden with trauma and the tumultuous ride of NPD, it delicately weaves a narrative of hope and the possibility of healing."

—**Jessica Noelle**, Author of *Adopting Secrets*

If You Knew, Would You Say I Do?

If You Knew, Would You Say I Do?

by Lisa Blakely and Tami Parker

© Copyright 2023 Lisa Blakely and Tami Parker

ISBN 979-8-88824-213-1

All rights reserved. No part of this publication may be reproduced, stored in a retrieval system, or transmitted in any form or by any means—electronic, mechanical, photocopy, recording, or any other—except for brief quotations in printed reviews, without the prior written permission of the author.

This is a work of fiction. All the characters in this book are fictitious, and any resemblance to actual persons, living or dead, is purely coincidental. The names of some real places appear, but they are applied to the events in a fictitious manner. The names, incidents, dialogue, and opinions expressed are products of the author's imagination and are not to be construed as real.

Published by

3705 Shore Drive
Virginia Beach, VA 23455
800-435-4811
www.koehlerbooks.com

IF YOU KNEW, WOULD YOU SAY I DO?

A Novel

LISA BLAKELY AND TAMI PARKER

VIRGINIA BEACH
CAPE CHARLES

Dedication

We dedicate this book to every reader that sees themselves on these pages.

Prologue

Several months ago, when I launched my podcast, *If You Knew, Would You Say I Do*, I had a basic game plan. I wanted to educate the public about NPD and narcissistic abuse—what it is, how to spot it, how it impacts relationships, and what can be done to minimize the suffering it often brings. It is a subject that has received increased and well-deserved attention. But what was missing, what we needed more than anything, was the opportunity to hear and delve into real stories told through the eyes and hearts and anguish of victims of narcissist behavior. We needed to express professional terms and concepts through a filter of familiar behavior. From my professional background, I knew there existed countless compelling stories that could provide a powerful educational platform. Narcissism is everywhere. It affects countless people. We are well served to understand that insidious disorder in professional and practical terms, and what better way than by opening ourselves up to those who have experienced it firsthand?

The problem, however, is that most people are disinclined to come forward. In part, this is because some don't realize that the chaos, toxicity, and anxiety they've endured is a form of narcissistic abuse. Others fear retaliation, social isolation, or both, feel shame or potential ridicule, cherish their privacy, or don't want the spotlight. It is not easy facing the stark truth of a narcissistic relationship and inviting the public into painful and deeply personal parts of your life.

And then opportunity knocked on my door.

My office received a phone call from two women, Laura and Jessica, who told my assistant, Cassie, they wanted to speak with me about their separate and "horrific" experiences with two narcissistic men, both former husbands. They wondered whether I might have them on the show to hear what they had to say, telling Cassie, "We want to help other women avoid what happened to us." Cassie is adept at screening podcast callers who want to appear on the show, and I give her wide berth to decide whether to politely turn away potential guests. We have received many such calls. And while we have been fortunate to have guests make brief appearances to talk about narcissistic incidents in their lives, we've not had anyone willing to share the full array of details of a sustained narcissistic relationship from start to end, to see the patterns, the recurring challenges, and the full range of risks. Now I had not one but possibly two at the same time. I was all ears.

Cassie arranged a meeting for Laura, Jessica, and me, and a few days later, the three of us sat down for a chat. I was thrilled at the possibilities.

After getting comfortable with pleasantries, Laura and Jessica told me they had only met recently. Both had decided to visit friends and family in New York and wound up not only on the same plane at LAX but also in adjoining seats. After boarding, settling in, and exchanging obligatory smiles, they occupied themselves privately. Laura started watching a downloaded episode of the Netflix series *Ozark*, and Jessica resumed reading a book. It was not until after takeoff, when Jessica nudged her traveling neighbor to alert her to the flight attendant trying to get her drink order, that the two began small talk. It didn't take long for them to realize they shared an obsession for *Ozark*, which led to a passionate exchange about the show's characters and plot arcs.

As their respective comfort levels rose, they dove more deeply into their personal lives, sharing the good, the bad, and the ugly, taking turns to emote about an accumulation of life frustrations. The longer they talked, the more obvious it became that they had profound common ground: both had suffered through relationships with abusive men diagnosed with narcissistic personality disorder (NPD). They couldn't believe the behavioral and emotional similarities in their lives and were even more amazed to learn they both were avid listeners of my podcast. A tight bond and friendship formed, which produced a commitment to share their experiences with a wide audience and, if possible, do it on my podcast. Before they landed in New York, they were on a mission.

Needless to say, I loved hearing this.

From there, Laura and Jessica gave glimpses of various episodes they'd experienced with their former husbands. I told them I couldn't wait to have them on the show to reveal all, and they said they were elated by the chance to share their stories with someone they could trust and who understood what they'd gone through.

They mentioned the healing power of therapy and added that listening to the podcast helped them understand the nuances and layers of narcissistic abuse, giving them hope that more dialogue around the topic and more NPD victims who told their stories would encourage a greater collective understanding of the disorder and a chance to reduce the suffering that targets of narcissistic behavior endure.

What follows, in their words, are their stories—from inception, when their narcissistic partners targeted them, until now—and how the three of us dissected their experiences to illuminate NPD and its traumatizing power.

As you will see in the stories of these two courageous women, the narcissist often appears as a knight in shining armor, a savior, the ultimate soulmate. But that is a mirage, and a temporary one at that, which ultimately will bring harm in one or more forms—psychological, emotional, physical, and financial. If you are with a narcissist, you are in harm's way, one way or another.

How were they to know? How are you to know? Education is the key.

Hopefully, the stories of Laura and Jessica will help dismantle the barriers of denial, incite courage, bring a greater understanding of a disorder that impacts countless people in their daily lives, and help victims find emotionally safer spaces and well-being.

Jules Brennan

APBN board-certified psychiatrist and PsyD, licensed psychologist, and host of the podcast *If You Knew, Would You Say I Do?*

1

Laura

My wedding day was but five months away, so I attributed the unusual emotional distance of my fiancé, Zach, to work pressure. As a drummer for a wildly popular local band in Los Angeles, Zach had his hands full. Every musical club in Southern California coveted his band. Their sound and stage presence consistently drew a full house no matter where they played, and they were about to turn the corner. The band was in negotiations with a record label, which would include a national tour.

On the flip side, the band faced high expectations. Each show drew a music critic, and the nerves of band members, especially Zach, were consistently on edge. They were operating with little or no margin of error. I chalked up his isolation to the wide range of emotions the circumstances brought on.

But after Zach started moaning about his schedule, the incessant demands on him, how he couldn't rely on anyone, and on and on, sometimes with tears in his eyes and on the verge of losing it, different thoughts flooded me. *Is this about the wedding? Is he getting butterflies? Is he reconsidering?* I didn't ask him these burning questions. In truth, I feared certain answers. I called my mother instead.

Mom reassured me that Zach's behavior was normal for men: "He has a lot on his plate. It will be fine. Give him his space. He'll circle back."

I conceded that the motherly advice came from a sturdy foundation. Zach and I had enjoyed more than ten years together. We first connected in New York, where Zach was heavily focused on his music and I on hospitality management. We met at a club where

I worked and local musicians spent significant time, whether playing or not. It was the place to be for local musical talent. And despite our contrasting roots—he was born and raised a city boy and I a country girl from Texas—we bonded straight off, the storybook love at first sight, and quickly melded into two peas in a pod, with marriage our shared destiny. I, of course, knew that even soulmates have issues. A few hiccups before wedding bells were par for the course. So, taking the long view, I embraced my mother's words and gave my beloved Zach breathing room, the least I could do.

But then Zach started coming home late each night. An occasional long night made sense. But this was chronic lateness, well after even two or three encores, and, odder still, Zach avoided explanations for his protracted absences, seeking haven in empty generalities like he "had record or tour stuff to deal with."

Next, he stopped touching me and claimed he was "too exhausted" for sex. He stopped asking about my days. I was a maître d' of the popular Blue Haven restaurant and knew the restaurant business and had stories to tell. We often swapped stories of our respective worlds. Now he was distant, almost bored.

Then, a shoe dropped.

One Friday morning, over coffee in the kitchen, Zach announced that he'd be home close to 2 a.m. When I pressed for details, he stammered with "ums" and "uhs" before saying that the club asked the band to close the show later than normal. Afterward, they planned to meet about the record label situation. It was a sellable explanation.

After cleaning the kitchen as Zach got ready to leave for work, however, I caught a glimpse of my darling fiancé in the bedroom, hurriedly stuffing a pair of underwear into his bag. *WTF. Why is he taking underwear to work?*

I said nothing. I processed.

All day, I fixated on the underwear in the bag, probing for logical explanations, but none came. He had a gym bag, but he didn't take it, which made sense. It was Wednesday, and he met his gym trainer on other weekdays. My suspicion heightened.

I considered calling a friend but rejected that idea, preferring to hide potential dirty laundry, concerned I might be acting a bit paranoid. I made myself crazy all day, and when night arrived, I couldn't concentrate on anything other than waiting for his return home. I asked myself whether I had the nerve to confront him. Would that worsen things? Anxiety swelled inside me. I needed contact. I texted Zach, asking when he'd be home, and got no response. Twenty minutes later, I texted again, with the same result. Agitation enflamed my anxiety.

At midnight, I couldn't stand it anymore. I got in the car and drove to the club. When I got there, I pulled up about fifty feet behind Zach's car, parked in its normal spot in the back of the lot, and stewed inside the car.

Minutes later, Zach exited the restaurant, holding hands with another woman. A surge of vomit rose in my chest, and I covered my mouth with my right hand, keeping my eyes on Zach. He stopped, turned to the woman, and touched her face affectionately. He nestled his head above her shoulder and softly kissed her neck, pulling the woman closer.

I couldn't believe what I was seeing—a surreal, unimaginable scene. My body shook, and panic set in. When the comfy twosome resumed walking toward the car, a streetlight exposed the woman's identity. It was Jemma, a twentysomething sexy bartender. My anger escalated. I felt my head exploding. I watched them slip into his car and reeled when I saw their shadows making out. Despite how paralyzed I felt, I knew my life had dramatically changed forever.

When Zach's car revved, I put mine in gear, rolled fifteen feet behind them, and called him on the cell phone.

"Hi, babe. We are about to play. What's up?" he said upon answering. "I know how much you like the wings at the club. Do you want me to bring any home?"

"That's so sweet of you," I said, doing my best to stifle rising sarcasm.

"Anything for my future wife," Zach said with an upbeat tone that set me off.

"Really? *Really*? You piece-of-shit, motherfucker. Look in your rearview window, asshole!" On "asshole," I planted the palm of my right hand on the car horn, shattering the quiet calm of the neighborhood. Crazed, I maintained the sound for several seconds.

The driver's side door to Zach's car flew open, and a rattled Zach followed. He turned to see me behind him and froze, mouth agape, as I watched him process this unthinkable turn of events. He stared in my direction with a bemused look, at a loss for words, a literal deer in the headlights. I stared back with fury, and his expression morphed from shock to the realization that he'd been nabbed. The blood drained out of his face. He took a deep breath, processed some more, and looked at Jemma as if seeking a lifeline. I couldn't see Jemma's facial expression, but I later told a friend that I'd have paid a serious sum to see the look on "that bitch's" face. Zach shook his head, stumbled into his car, slammed the door, and drove off.

Stunned, I froze. The asshole upped and left me sitting there like a fool. I was devastated. I knew without conceding that it was over. Zach had cheated, with our wedding date fast approaching, an unforgivable act of disloyalty no matter what groveling he might conjure up. We were done.

A week later, while at home, my friend Grace called. She'd dropped by the Blue Haven in the late afternoon for a quick chat before the evening restaurant crowd converged, only to learn that I'd taken a few sick days and "wasn't feeling well." Knowing me as she did, she saw red flags.

When I heard Grace's voice in response to my deflated "hello," I dissolved into tears. "I'm coming over right now," Grace said without more.

Less than twenty minutes later, I opened the door to an eager knock, showing my puffy face. Grace hugged and held me tight for several seconds.

"What happened?" Grace said, pulling away and remaining in the doorjamb.

"The asshole cheated on me. He has a girlfriend."

"What! Zach? Who?"

"Jemma." I turned and retreated into the condo, heading to the living room.

"Jemma? You mean that young bartender with the long blond hair?"

"Yeah, the one and the same," I said and flopped like a sack of potatoes onto the couch.

Grace snuggled close to me and grabbed my hand. We rested our heads on the back of the couch and stared into space. My dog, Shiraz, a French bulldog named after my preferred wine, jumped onto the couch to console his distraught mother.

After a long minute, Grace broke the silence. "You wanna tell me what happened?"

I pored over the painful details of the past several weeks and, as I did, identified the clues that had escaped me. I culminated with the club parking lot confrontation, and then a litany of questions and self-doubt flooded my brain. *How long has it gone on? Why did he do it? Maybe he doesn't love me? Maybe he fell out of love with me? Could I really survive a life without him?*

"The betrayal hurts the most," I said.

Grace affirmed my feelings and assured me all would be good.

"Time heals. Besides, that jerk doesn't deserve you. You'll be way better off without him. And let's not forget, my pretty friend, you are a hottie. I mean, blond, green-eyed, five three, 110 pounds soaking wet, petite, well portioned, and, if I may say, nicely top heavy. A blogger's dream of fashion." She was on a roll. "You will land fine—and before you know it."

Nice to hear, but I felt like shit.

In the aftermath of the Zach debacle, I struggled at work, often in a fog. My thoughts swirled about, taking me down different paths of why, what might have been, and what would be. Several times, I suppressed tears.

But I saw myself as the consummate professional and hunkered down when it mattered. My hospitality training instilled the value of relegating feelings to the back burner in favor of servicing customers the way they deserve. I had mastered the art of the obligatory smile and could dispense the charm with the best of them. I prized my ability to showcase heartfelt empathy to each guest, making them feel they had my undivided attention and were special. I never missed a chance to utter "My pleasure," restaurant-speak that affirms guests. Ironically, food or service complaints became a welcome respite, masking my troubles and allowing a retreat from self-pity. People were passionate about their food, and if their plates didn't live up to expectations, I rallied to make it better—no matter what. I suffered in silence.

At home and alone, I moved in and out of dark moods, finding comfort only when the loyal Shiraz licked my tears or I succumbed to tequila's self-medicative power. The unfamiliar sadness sometimes overwhelmed me, and I continued to struggle with the fundamental question: how did this happen? Sometimes, after locking up the restaurant and bidding farewell to everyone, I longed to go home to see Zach despite how much he disgusted me. I hated myself for feeling that way. I knew it came from loneliness, but I couldn't stop it. In those moments, I yearned for another partner and wondered how long it would take for the pain to go away.

It was a typical busy Saturday night when Carrie, the restaurant hostess, informed me that Mark Corbin, the son of an investor in our restaurant, had plans to dine with four guests. Corbin had dined with us a few times in the past. To provide him and his party a fabulous table, I reconfigured the seating chart, no easy task on the busiest night of the week. Liam Corbin, Mark's father, boasted legendary status in the entertainment law industry. He represented many prominent actors and some major studios in the US and abroad, particularly in France, where he was born and raised.

Mark Corbin, handsome and in his early thirties, was a beneficiary of his father's status and connections and was often featured in "who's who" magazines. Not surprisingly, everywhere he went in public, a beautiful model was draped on his arm. Whether he had a role in the family business, I didn't know.

Once the host seated the Corbin party, I introduced myself and said, "Mr. Corbin, if you need anything, please let me know." He glanced at me for barely a second, as if I'd interrupted him, and said, "Oh, sure, whatever, thank you," and returned to holding court.

The rest of the night was uneventful. Corbin and his guests had a fun time and were elated with the food and service. As the fivesome rose to leave, I sauntered to the front door to bid them a courteous, heartfelt goodbye. Corbin stepped aside to allow his friends to exit single file and, after they did, turned and looked dead at me.

"Where's your ring?" he said with a devilish smile.

I jerked my head back. I had expected something like "We had a lovely evening. Thank you." I glanced at my hand and immediately flashed to the engagement ring buried deep in a clothing drawer at home.

"Oh, that thing," I said. "Yeah, well, my fiancé and I are no longer."

Corbin tilted his head to the side, nodded with a smirk, and said, "Interesting. Enjoy your night." He turned and left.

Interesting? What does that mean? And when has he seen my hand before? The encounter stayed on my mind the rest of the night.

When midnight was about to strike and things at the Blue Haven had wound down, I was alone in the back, reviewing the closing checklist. A voice interrupted my concentration.

"Do you have the bar key?"

I swung around in fright, and there stood Mark Corbin—tall and muscular, his dirty-blond hair swept over his ice-green eyes. He smiled as he ran his fingers through his wavy, tousled hair. *Wow*, I thought, *the guy* is *handsome*. I snapped out of the dreamlike state and straightened my shoulders, reminding myself that he was the son of one of our investors.

He chuckled at my evident discomfort and said, "Get two glasses. Red or white?"

"Red . . . I guess."

I grabbed two red wineglasses, and he asked me to retrieve a bottle of Bordeaux. I gave each glass a generous pour. After a clink of the glasses, we began to chat, mostly about my life story. Mark asked question after question, and as he did, unless I imagined it, he looked at me adoringly. Talking about myself enlivened me. His genuine interest in every aspect of my life numbed the pain I'd been dragging around.

After close to two hours, he rose and said, "It was nice getting to know you," touched the top of my hand, and walked out. I sat there and shook my head. What had just happened?

The next day, Carrie approached me wearing a mischievous smile.

"Mark Corbin called and asked if you were working the rest of the week," said Carrie.

"*Okaaay* . . . did he say anything else?"

"No, that was it."

"Thanks." I shrugged.

I was a mix of emotions. Four weeks into the post-Zach era, Shiraz was the only man in my life. Why would someone like Mark Corbin be interested in me? He seemed to have it all: good looks, an engaging personality, his choice of women, and financial independence.

A few days later, amid a busy Saturday night, a staff member said to me, "You have a phone call, and the person says it's urgent and will not give their name."

"Man or woman?"

"Man."

I picked up the flashing line.

"Hello, this is Laura."

"Hi, Laura, it's Mark. What time are you done today?"

"Probably 9 p.m. I'm not closing tonight." *Why is he asking*?

At 8:50 p.m., I grabbed my purse to head home and stepped outside. Mark was standing next to his car with a smirk. I was bewildered. When I approached him, he reached over, pushed my hair behind my ear, and brushed the back of his hand against my face. He walked me around to the other side of the car, opened the passenger door, stepped back to allow me to enter, softly shut the door, got in the other side, and put the car in drive. The car roared off. We didn't speak. His eyes were fixated on the road while he smiled to himself. I had questions. *Where are we going? What is this all about? What is the catch? Should I be afraid?* I held my tongue.

Mark drove to a secluded cliffside restaurant. When we entered, a team of people greeted us like royalty. Mark instructed the staff in French. He could have been ordering french fries for all I knew or cared; it sounded so romantic. I allowed myself a touch of elation. *I can let go a little.*

Once we were seated, Mark said, "You are such a cutie."

I blushed despite finding the reference odd. A "cutie"?

We dined in the normal course. Mark acknowledged everything I said. What a breath of fresh air to have a man who listened attentively and cared about what I had to say. It was as if he were beholding his muse. His eyes conveyed rapt interest in my every word. I felt an intense connection, noticeably more than in the *best* of the Zach days. When we left the restaurant, Mark held my hand, and I shuddered. In a matter of hours, he had swept me off my feet. I didn't want the night to end.

2
Jessica

Valentine's Day was bittersweet. Three weeks earlier, I parted ways with my fiancé of two years. It was unexpected. He confessed to a major change of heart, that he didn't want children, which he knew did not jive with my lifelong dream to have a family. It was a tough blow. I just wish he'd figured that out before I invested my time, heart, and soul into the relationship. People change their minds—I get that—but this was a deal-breaker that had been simmering for a while and sprung out of nowhere. Thankfully, my career as a real estate agent was going strong, and I had a loving nuclear family and an ensemble of friends. On the other hand, I longed to share my cherished life with the soulmate I knew was out there, one who shared my dream of a family.

That day, however, I was all business when I arrived at the Beverly Hills Hotel, jumped on an elevator, and sauntered to the Heart Healthy Project to attend a fundraiser for a new project in LA. Once inside the ballroom, I absorbed the magical sounds of a baby grand piano amid the animated buzz from countless beautiful people. It was the sort of happening I could get into—a worthy cause and the perfect environment for a promising realtor to network. I grabbed a glass of champagne and mingled.

Before long, while listening to a doctor discuss the merits of the hospital project, I felt a rush of strange energy, the kind of vibe that meant someone was checking me out. I shifted my glance from the doctor's monologue to notice a strikingly handsome and impeccably dressed man in his thirties, about forty feet away, gazing at me. I averted my eyes and returned my attention to the hospital talk. Several minutes later, while checking phone messages, I felt a hovering presence. I turned, and there he was again, this time up close and personal, flashing a beautiful smile.

"May I get you a refill?" he said, nodding at my empty champagne flute and revealing a charming British accent.

"Uh, no, but thank you."

He offered his hand and said, "Collin Worth. Nice to meet you."

"Jessica Wynn. Nice to meet you as well." I shook his hand.

"Pleasure is all mine. . . . Well, it was nice meeting you, Jessica Wynn," said Collin, and with a nod and smile, he casually walked away.

Watching him relocate, I chuckled to myself, wondering if I'd ever see him again. I shook off the tingle of excitement and refocused on my networking rounds. Forty-five minutes later, it was time to exit, and I went to the elevator. Worth sidled up next to me.

"What would it take for a pretty woman like you to have dinner with me?" he asked.

I laughed. "Well, for starters, he'd have to invite me."

"May I have your number?"

"Why not?" I said and gave him my number. On cue, the elevator door opened, and I entered without a word. He waved as the doors closed. *That guy has confidence to spare.*

A few days later, while driving home after a showing, my cell phone rang, flashing an unfamiliar number. Assuming it was a business call, I answered.

"Hello, this is Jessica Wynn."

"Hello, Jessica Wynn." The deep masculine voice was unmistakably British.

As I started to respond, he spoke again.

"Are you free for dinner tomorrow evening?"

"Um, yes, I am," I answered, smiling.

"I'm chuffed to bits! I'll send you reservation details. Cheers." He hung up.

Chuffed to bits? At the first opportunity, a gas station, I researched the phrase, happy to discover it was a popular UK slang term for being enormously pleased. I gave myself a thumbs-up.

That evening, Collin texted to meet him the next night at 7 p.m. at Chez Pallor, a well-known romantic restaurant that local celebrities frequented. For the occasion, I chose a blush-colored one-shoulder, knee-length dress paired with strappy nude heels.

Throughout dinner, Collin played the consummate gentleman, attentive and inquisitive, wanting to know everything about me, my career, family, friends, and background. Conversation flowed easily. Eventually—to get a breath—I changed the focus. "Well, what do you do?"

Collin launched into a long monologue about his career in the spirits industry and his daring entrepreneurial endeavors. He recounted how his ancestors built a distillery business in the UK, which he replicated in the US and other parts of the world. He projected a shrewd, hardworking, and successful businessman with all the personal qualities—smart, stable, fun, active, and attractive—that I prized in a partner.

After dinner, he drove me home to Santa Ana and escorted me to the front door. Turning to leave, he said, "I hope we can do this again sometime."

I responded, "That would be lovely." He was off with a wave—and, notably, without a good night kiss.

The next day, at 7 a.m., as I prepared to hit the gym, Colin texted a breakfast invitation for 7:45 at Marina West, a harbor site where no restaurant existed. Curious and compelled, I accepted, figuring I could survive the loss of a gym visit.

When I arrived, Colin stood at the edge of the docks, and I felt a rush come over me. He looked sexier than I recalled, with his linen shirt, tan shorts, and rimmed light brown sunglasses to match his windswept hair. We hugged, and I couldn't help but notice his firm athletic frame. He grasped my hand softly and led me down the dock, up a ramp, and onto a boat.

"What do you think?" he said.

"Stunning," I said, opening my eyes wide.

"I'm designing this boat. Perhaps you'll enjoy a ride with me when it's finished."

After a boat tour and discussion about boat design and his love of the sea, he suggested IHOP for breakfast, not where I envisioned him eating, but I was ready to go anywhere with him. Again, the conversation flowed seamlessly, and after breakfast, we arranged for him to pick me up at 6:15 for dinner.

At 6 p.m., while putting on the finishing touches for my dinner date, I heard a firm knock on my door. I surveyed my place for tidiness and, once satisfied, yelled, "Coming," and went to open the door.

Collin held a small bouquet of soft pink English roses, my favorite. *How did he know?* I invited him in, but he declined with a nod of the head, palpably eager to get going. I placed the flowers in a vase in the kitchen, grabbed my things, kissed my dog Harper on the head, and off we went.

Colin drove a different car that night—a silver Aston Martin convertible. My look evidently betrayed curiosity because he chuckled and said, "Oh, yes, one of my hobbies is collecting vintage cars."

"Interesting hobby," I said, tongue in cheek.

He grabbed my hand, sending electricity through my body, making me eager for an ice-breaking kiss. Eyes on the road, Collin said, "I could get used to this." He knew what to say.

We pulled into the parking lot of the Cut Prime, a popular steakhouse. Once seated, without conferring, Collin asked for two tequilas on the rocks with limes, ordered food for both of us, and requested the wine list. In minutes, the table displayed a fabulous decanted Cabernet, rare filet, ribs, creamed spinach, tomato with sliced onions, pomme frites, sautéed mushrooms, shrimp cocktail, and a chopped salad. The food frenzy took me aback.

Colin fork-fed me, bite after bite. We resumed sharing our background until he diverted to more delicate matters.

"What about having a family? What does your perfect future look like?" He leaned back in his seat with an earnest look.

"Well, I want my career to keep flourishing, but most importantly, I want to be a mom and have a family—someday," I said, matching his earnestness.

Colin nodded and took a sip of wine.

"That's what I wanted to hear," he said as if teacher to pupil. "Tell me more about your family. How do you get along and all that?"

"I am super close to my parents and my siblings. We've always been close and supportive."

Colin smiled and said, "You know, a good upbringing makes for a sound moral foundation. My family is close, too. My father, in particular, is supremely proud of what I've done for the business."

"Well, how about you?" I said, "What does *your* perfect future look like?"

He squinted and nodded to himself.

"Not sure . . . but marriage and children are in the cards."

That night, in the car in front of my place, we enjoyed our first make out session. Mentally, I checked one box—phenomenal kisser—and longed to move the high school session into the condo. But after several playful minutes, Colin abruptly stopped, exited the car, opened the passenger side door, and bid me good night.

I found the abrupt termination a little odd, but even odder was the next two days—when I didn't hear a peep from Collin. Doubts seeped into my head. The accelerated attention had waned. I retraced the steps. What had gone wrong? I dared not text him, not wanting to appear controlling or anxious. I was perplexed.

As the business week faded, he texted, *Can you have dinner tomorrow night in LA and spend the night?*

Sure, I replied.

I paused to think about what spending the weekend entailed. I had Harper to care for and a real estate showing on Sunday. Not so easy. Still, no way was I letting this opportunity pass. I cajoled my sister into taking the dog and leaned on an assistant to cover the Sunday showing.

Excitement pulsated through me. The upcoming weekend foreshadowed the promised land for the relationship. I could barely contain myself. As soon as I walked into the condo, I packed a bag, fixed myself, and hit the freeway.

Through the double gates where Colin lived in LA, a motor court of different cars, many vintage, lined the driveway. I parked and headed to the front door. The walkway to the entrance featured winding marble stairs above a body of blue water speckled with floating flowers and an eye-popping landscape. A petite older woman opened the entry door and beckoned me in, stepping to the side. "Mr. Worth is in his study. Please follow me." When I entered the study, Collin rose and wrapped his arms around me, kissing me on the cheek. He took a step back and gave me the up and down survey. "Wow, just as I remembered."

A house tour followed, where he showcased his collections of art, wine, cigars, and vintage men's and women's watches. He also introduced me to his perennial house guest, Prince, an adorable Bengal cat.

After the tour, he poured us each a glass of perfectly chilled Dom Pérignon, and after we clinked flutes and took long pulls, he excused himself to order dinner. Thirty minutes later, the doorbell rang, and Collin retrieved a bucket of KFC extra crispy, with all the sides and a mountain of biscuits. Top-shelf champagne and KFC, a romantic formula of a different kind. I loved how he combined sophistication and down-to-earth.

The rest of the night was cuddling and kissing in bed while watching *Wedding Crashers*—until Collin crashed into a deep sleep. It wasn't quite the script I had in mind, so I reset my sights on delightful morning sex.

The next morning, I awoke to breakfast in bed—OJ, coffee, eggs, bacon, toast, a muffin, and a bowl of berries. Collin fed me—one morsel at a time. My mind, however, was fixated on one thing, and it wasn't food. Wishful thinking. After breakfast, Collin got dressed, mumbling something about a haircut and massage. He said nothing about meeting up later. I left when he did. A sweet overnight visit, but the lack of sparks left me wanting.

I spent the rest of the day anxious and confused. I had planned on a weekend away, but as I thought about it, Collin never actually said that, only to bring an "overnight" bag. My schedule opened, and I joined my real estate colleague at the house showing.

Around 5 p.m., Collin texted, asking when I was returning. *Huh?* I shrugged and, without internal debate, replied, *Be there around 7 p.m.*

Did I misunderstand? Thankfully, I hadn't picked up Harper.

The moment I walked through the front door, Collin kissed me passionately, thrusting his tongue into my mouth. Sunday night looked promising. Watching *Unfaithful*, cuddling in bed, inspired Collin, as he demonstrated advanced knowledge of the female anatomy—another box checked—but it went no further. This was uncharted waters for me—a man lavishing attention on me while withholding the sacred act. I suppressed my frustration and elected not to ask for the holy grail. Not my style.

A few days later, after Collin's business trip to Las Vegas, we met for dinner. Halfway through the meal, Collin displayed a black bag from under the table.

"This is for you . . . my dear."

"Thank you. That's so sweet." I untied the neatly wrapped package and opened the box to discover a Cartier watch flecked with diamonds. I exhaled heavily, perhaps too conspicuously. I was overwhelmed. "I can't accept this."

Collin said, "Look, I wanted to get you a gift. I won a lot of money in Vegas. Enjoy it. It's my pleasure. I had a good run. You were on my mind the entire trip. Please enjoy it."

I paused, leaned in, and kissed Collin, strapping the watch onto my wrist.

Collin had an upcoming business trip to NYC and my hometown of Chicago and invited me to accompany him. I was thrilled. Again, I'd need dog and work coverage. I later pleaded with my sister to take Harper, and after hemming and hawing, she relented. The next day, I called in a work chit, sealing that too.

I stayed at Collin's the night before the trip for an easier exit. When I arrived at his place, I left my luggage in the car, bringing in only an overnight bag. The night went as before—enthusiastic lovemaking without penetration on the menu. In the morning, to my surprise, the car took us to the LA County private airport. We were flying private. I was blown away.

The pampered treatment continued upon landing in NYC. A waiting limo at LaGuardia Airport ushered us to a two-bedroom suite at the luxurious Mandarin Hotel on Columbus Circle. Seconds after the valets dropped off our luggage and left, Collin disrobed me. At long last, we had the passionate sex I craved. Another box checked.

Minutes later, Collin directed me to get ready for dinner. But when I emerged from the shower and opened my luggage, I discovered that some of my clothes were soaked in red liquid. I had nothing red in my toiletry bag. What could it be? I picked up my jeans and sniffed. My clothes had been soaked in red wine.

I was mystified. I told Collin, and he acted perplexed.

"Did you happen to leave your luggage in your car at my place?" he said in a somber tone.

"Yes, I told you that. Remember?" I said with exasperation.

"Hmm, not really," Collin said, lowering his eyes.

"It would have been impossible for someone to get through your gate, right?"

"Absolutely . . . well, maybe not for Alli." He shrugged.

"Alli?"

"My ex-fiancé. A psycho . . . and a drunk, with anger issues." Collin turned away and continued to dress.

"I don't get it. How would she get in?" I was incredulous.

"Well, I guess she, um, still has the gate code."

"She still has the gate code?" I said, raising my voice uncharacteristically. "You never mentioned her before. How long were you two engaged?"

"Not long. She wasn't for me. Obviously, she has issues."

I sat down on the bed, not knowing what to think or say.

"Look, forget it. I'll deal with it. She won't bother you again. I'll take you shopping for clothes. It'll be fun."

I didn't know what to make of it, but I let it go for the time being. What I found most odd was that he hadn't mentioned a word about her or his past engagement. We had shared so much about each other in a short time, a free flow of dialogue without any hint of holding back. It was a conspicuous omission.

Once we hit the urban pavement, I put the "Alli" episode behind me and relished the NYC nonstop whirlwind—shopping, restaurants, museums, strolls down Fifth Avenue holding hands, and the theater. Too many exciting things to dwell on something like that.

Next up, Chicago.

Upon our arrival at the Four Seasons in the Windy City, the manager informed Collin that his customary room was unavailable. "I won't tolerate this!" he said, red-faced, banging the counter with the side of his fist. The manager explained that the current guest extended his stay. "I am so sorry, Mr. Worth, but my hands are tied." When his rant subsided, Collin announced, "We're leaving, never to return." We went to the Peninsula Hotel, where Collin scored the penthouse suite.

I had never seen him enraged before. It made me a little uncomfortable. But I was content to let it slide. In the larger scheme of things, it didn't seem to concern me.

The next two days combined a food frenzy and sex. I couldn't believe my good fortune. A little temper and entitlement aside, Collin presented the whole package—a mix of the boy next door and a fine European gentleman. I was in heaven. It was almost too good to be true.

The journey home contrasted with the wonders of the trip. On the return flight, we barely spoke, throwing me off-kilter. Collin was preoccupied. In the blink of an eye, he went from showering me with nonstop attention to virtual silence. When I asked if he was okay, he said yes, just that he had a lot on his mind. Still, I had to wonder whether, somewhere along the line, I had committed an unknowing misstep—maybe a social faux pas that embarrassed him or, worse, that I'd done something wrong. I mined the memory bank and found nothing.

I backed off and gave him space, focusing on ridding myself of anxiety. I'd never experienced such intense feelings with a man I'd dated. He remained silent for the duration of the day, which kept me off-balance and on edge. Once again, I shrugged it off, not taking it personally.

The silence continued the entire next day, with just one obligatory text—*Have a good day*. The sudden halt of attention baffled me. We were moving in such a nice direction; I didn't know what to make of it, but it made me uneasy.

Two days later, Collin asked if I'd make dinner for a client group because he knew how much I loved to cook. I readily agreed, although he selected a day when I had a real estate closing. It would require high-wire juggling.

I conceived a menu of creamy burrata with sliced tomatoes and balsamic glaze, pasta with homemade pesto, pounded, breaded veal chops, baked bread with roasted garlic, and my "famous" Caesar salad. On the day of the event, I hit the market and farm stand for the best ingredients, then converted to realtor mode, fixing my hair and throwing on an off-white suit. The closing proceeded apace until it hit a snag that threatened to scuttle the deal. By the time I fixed the problem, it was coming on 3 p.m., allowing little time for meal preparation.

Once home, I grabbed a change of clothes, put the ingredients in a cooler, and made a mad dash to Collin's place, stopping for the hors d'oeuvres I realized I'd forgotten. At his place, I galvanized into action, but not before getting a kiss on the forehead from Collin, who said, "Hello, my love." *Mmm.* The "my love" thing melted me.

Against the odds, with the help of Marge, Collin's main house employee, I got dinner ready with little time to spare. After greeting the guests and describing what they were about to eat, I went upstairs to regroup and rest. Two hours later, while watching a show, Marge summoned me at Collin's request.

"The fellows want to thank you for the lovely meal," he said, grabbing my hand.

The men clapped to a chorus of "Bravo, bravo," which elated me and made me blush. Collin pulled up a chair next to him and beckoned. When I sat, he put his arm around me. The men asked whether I'd had professional cooking experience. I laughed. "No, just lots of dinner parties and a love for food."

The more the men showed interest in me, however, the more Collin got uncomfortable. His brow furrowed, and his jaw clenched. Finally, he told me, "Dear, please have Marge clear the plates," and "I'll meet you upstairs later." Back in the bedroom minutes later, I fell asleep.

The next morning, Collin shared his plans to meet those same clients in Europe. He wanted me to join him. After a pause, he added, to my surprise, "And bring your friends, Marni and Jon. That way, when I tend to my business meetings, you won't be alone." Thrilled, I said I'd invite them.

There was again the matter of the dog, more problematic because of the length of time away, and more so, the job. Since Collin entered my life, I'd cut some corners at work, and the more cutting I did, the more I was pushing the envelope. When I broke the news to my broker, Anita, a long dead silence followed, and then she said grimly, "Make sure your absence doesn't cost us any deals." *Ouch.*

I sought some risk assessment feedback from Marni. Her response was a question: "Well, darling, has this guy ever said, 'I love you'?" The question caught me off guard, and then I said, "Now that you mention it . . . no."

3

If You Knew, Would You Say I Do?

DR. BRENNAN: Welcome back, everyone, to my podcast, *If You Knew, Would You Say I Do?* I am Dr. Jules Brennan, board-certified psychiatrist and licensed psychologist. I specialize in narcissistic abuse. The aim of the program is to educate the public about narcissistic personality disorder to help those who suffer each day from the trauma of a narcissistic relationship and want to eliminate toxicity from their lives.

As you know, we have begun a new podcast series that features two brave women, Laura and Jessica, who have graciously agreed to share their struggle with long-term NPD relationships. In each podcast, we will hear their stories, in their own words, followed by a discussion with Laura and Jessica of what they've shared. You just heard how their relationships got started—two classic examples of how narcissists target victims.

Laura and Jessica, thank you so much for doing this.

JESSICA: You're welcome.

LAURA: Our pleasure. This is important to us.

DR. BRENNAN: Let's start here. Until you got involved with these relationships, did either of you understand what a narcissist was or have any knowledge about NPD?

LAURA: I had heard the word, of course, but like most people, I assumed it had to do with someone who was self-centered and selfish.

JESSICA: Totally, I agree. I had the same general understanding.

DR. BRENNAN: That's a start, but it is much more. As a reminder to our listening audience, narcissists are people who live only for themselves, think they are better than everyone else, and have little or no empathy for others, even those within their inner circle of family, children, and friends. They don't care. Virtually everything they do, no matter what it looks like, is in service of their power, ego, and self-grandiosity. It is a one-way street way of life. Narcissists with NPD are broken and wired differently. I understand it is a lot to take in, but we will break it down as we follow your personal stories.

Let's focus on when you first met your former partners. Why was it easy to get swept away?

LAURA: Dr. Brennan, when I first met Mark, he wasn't wearing a name tag that said, "Hello, my name is Mark the narc." How was I supposed to know?

DR. BRENNAN (laughing): No, true enough. They aren't easy to detect, especially in the initial phases of the relationship. Most people think that narcissists are loud, arrogant, pushy, selfish, know-it-all types, who stand out. Sometimes that is the case. We see hints of that in Collin Worth. Most of the time, however, in the early parts of a relationship, for example, what we see is magnetic behavior, charm, attention, doting, someone going out of their way to please and seduce you. They are the ultimate manipulators. Most victims don't see the sinister side until after the mask has substantially peeled away, and often it is too late.

JESSICA: When I met Collin, I was swept off my feet. He was charming and seductive and seemed so sincere and genuine. Meeting him was a dream come true, I thought. Like Laura, I was naive about what being a narcissist meant. When I met him, Collin showed none of the classic traits you mention. He was sophisticated, well groomed, quiet, and reserved. Although, I now realize it was facade, a con job mirroring the perfect partner, a critical part of the seductive love-bombing phase. All I knew was that Collin presented himself as a perfect partner who wanted to get married and have children, someone who had similar values and morals. I thought I met my dream guy, an elated feeling after my previous breakup.

DR. BRENNAN: Let's stop there. You used the phrase "love bombing." Let me explain that for our listeners. To many, it may sound like something we'd all want, but it is the opposite. Love bombing is a form of manipulation, a pattern of behavior designed to overwhelm someone with excessive adoration and attention and in the process ensnare them. It isn't genuine. It is used to earn trust and create vulnerability for control. Love bombing doesn't require money or wealth, just the cunning ability to offer endearing words, sweet gestures, supportive listening, great sex, and so on. Don't get me wrong; money and wealth take this to another level, but they are not essential for this behavior to occur.

Keep in mind that narcissists are laser focused on their targets, which are their prey. They full-court press you. Collin lavished you with gifts and exotic trips, showed off his wealth, wined and dined you, and seemed genuinely interested in your hopes and dreams. The scariest and saddest part is that, in the love bombing phase, the narcissist transforms entirely. They alter their demeanor and personality and lie about their interests, family, childhood, and career, willing to do whatever it takes to captivate, mesmerize, and hook their prey. As in both your cases, and so many others, love bombing is like a drug administered to induce dependence, a clever ploy to portray the narcissist as an amazing partner, laying the groundwork for an addictive relationship.

LAURA: That's all sounding familiar. On our first date, listening to Mark speak French was so romantic and intoxicating. He stared into my eyes like no one had ever done. He made me feel I was the only person in the room. We had an instant connection. That had never happened to me before . . . with anyone.

DR. BRENNAN: I should interject an important observation. Jessica, Collin had significant financial resources, whereas Mark did not; he wanted you to think he did. Narcissists present themselves as better than they are, raise their status levels to the highest. In their mind, they are above all. Narcissists come in all shapes and sizes, male or female, and don't need societal power and financial success to seduce their prey effectively. They can be unemployed, live unhealthy lives filled with drugs and alcohol, and lack motivation to work. The game can be played by a diverse population of narcissists. They always overinflate their accomplishments and status to make them appear "perfect" to the outside world—or the victim who was wronged by his family his ex, etc. It is about common methods and behavioral patterns. What you didn't know, Jessica and Laura, when you met Collin and Mark—and what none of us know when we meet our narcissist—is that those first mesmerizing dates and every move thereafter are designed to gain control and assemble worthy *supply*, an entourage of people that serves the narcissist agenda.

Most everything they say is a lie. This is especially true about promises of a future together, what we call *future-faking*—a courtship strategy that promises all the wonderful things you will do in the future together—as you get teased by bits and pieces of the grand plan.

LAURA: Yep, he lied about his family history, childhood, and career, sweeping me up like a knight in shining armor.

JESSICA: Looking back, I was intoxicated. It was hard not to be. He was so attentive and generous in the beginning and seemed to care about me and what mattered to me. I never had someone shower me with such adoration before. He presented himself as everything I wanted in a man. It was like he was inhaling me every time he took a breath. And he made me feel as if *he* had never felt this way before. I was special, the one, what I'd been waiting for my entire life.

DR. BRENNAN: Narcissists move swiftly at the start of a relationship, keeping their prey drunk with excitement, an allure that makes it hard to see the red flags. To get more entrenched, they often reflect what you feel and do, what is called mirroring, which intensifies the connection. Jessica, in your case, Collin gathered information on your upbringing and family and then mirrored similar values back at you, making him seem like the man of your dreams, the perfect mate to assemble a future together.

JESSICA: Yeah, I see that now. His family could not have been more different than he described.

LAURA: The Corbins turned out the same way, as toxic as they come. The apple didn't fall far from the tree. In hindsight, they were the most jealous, meanest, abrasive people I'd ever met.

DR. BRENNAN: Who doesn't want to hear that everything they dreamed of in a partner is standing before them and within their grasp? It is powerful and seductive. Narcissists use mirroring as an effective tool to gain trust. It encourages the sharing of hopes and fears, information the narcissist can file away for control purposes. As we have already seen, narcissists can move swiftly, especially when looking to lock down a relationship. They like to keep you dizzy and confused. Collin was moving at breakneck speed, except for the withholding of sex, another manipulative tactic, making Jessica feel insecure and unsure of her desirability.

More details next time. Thank you to all my faithful listeners and to Laura and Jessica. And remember, listeners, this is not an advice column program. Nothing in this podcast is intended as medical advice for any listener. Each circumstance involving NPD is unique. If you are concerned that someone in your life might suffer from NPD, and you want help, please confer with your doctor or other professional medical personnel.

Until next week . . . *if you knew, would you say I do?*

4
Laura

Mark and I hit the ground running. Each day he told me how beautiful I was, embellishing with "I wish I had met you five years ago," "How lucky I am to have found you," and "I should write Zach to thank him for being a cheating scumbag."

We never lacked in conversation—an early litmus test for compatibility. We talked endlessly about his business in retail clothing and the hospitality business, telling stories in minute detail, no matter how boring the tales might sound to a casual observer. We relished hearing each other's voices. It was less about the words and more about the vibe—the deep stares into the eyes. We laughed hysterically upon learning we both preferred magazines to books, taking potshots at voracious readers of literary works. We shared our favorite Netflix series, each willing to watch the other's suggestions, sharing favorites. We cooked on weekday nights and delighted in rearranging Mark's house to reflect both of us. We had passionate sex, incessantly and prolonged. We were constantly on the move, forever with entwined hands, a weekend here and a boat ride there. Each day melted into the next, a seamless romantic excursion. Mark introduced me to his circle of friends, and everyone treated me like the high school prom queen. And one night, while raising a glass of vintage Barolo at a local restaurant, he said, "Here's to you, the woman I love, like . . . I've never loved anyone before, my future wife." I held back tears, took a breath, and said, "I love you too." I raised my glass to meet his and added, "Here's to us, the perfect couple."

I had found the dream partner and thanked my lucky stars. I had a new life, no longer on the rebound from what's his name. And life was about to get better. After four blissful months, Mark wanted me to meet his parents. Naturally nervous, I was also excited about the prospect. I knew the significance of this step. What I hadn't imagined was the venue for the momentous rendezvous: the family summer home in the south of France. I arranged time off at work and got my mom to take Shiraz, who adored his grammy and feasting on medium rare filets followed by dreamlike walks. Before I knew it, I was on a flight to France, being offered a cheese plate.

Many hours later, we arrived at our destination. Some "summer home." It was an architectural masterpiece, perched on a cliff overlooking the historic city center of Marseille: eight bedrooms, seven full baths, a terrace that wrapped around the entire structure, private gardens, lemon trees, a swimming pool, windows everywhere, parquet floors, and a four-car parking garage. Not to mention original art. I was, in fairness, starstruck. Mark lived so modestly in the US; seeing such a lavish display shocked me. I became even more nervous to meet his parents.

Staff ushered us to our rooms. The family introduction would await an early dinner. After settling in and getting refreshed, Mark and I made our way to meet the family. Beads of sweat formed under my arms, and flutters rose in my stomach. When we arrived at the patio—dinner would be outside—Mark hugged his family members—both parents and two sisters—and turned to me.

"Everyone, meet Laura, my girlfriend." I received obligatory soft hugs from each member of the family, except for Liam, Mark's dad, who shook my hand and nodded with an obvious air of authority. He intimidated me straight off. Everyone took assigned seats, with Mark sitting across from—not next to—me and Liam at the head of the table.

"A *girlfriend*. Ah, you must be, shall we say . . . special. Not a description Mark uses often. We need to know more. Tell us a little about yourself," Liam said.

Mark didn't prepare my expectations. "They will love you. Just be yourself," he said.

An ominous need for a command performance overtook me. I'd have preferred softball questions—"How was the trip over?"— to get rolling.

"Uh, well, I uh," I said, "I'm from Texas. I'm a manager at a restaurant, which is, um, how I met your son."

"I see," said Liam, glancing curiously at Mark. "Married before?"

"Um, no."

"Good. What about your family? Tell us about them."

"My family lives in Texas. We are close, like yours . . . I'm, uh, sure." I regretted those last few words instantly. Liam tilted his head downward in mock disapproval. I forged on.

"My mom's the head of a retail clothing line, and my dad's a math teacher. My younger brother is almost a hedge fund manager. We're a hardworking family."

Liam nodded to himself and gestured with a raised head and wave of his arm, which meant the staff should serve the meal. The "girlfriend interview" was over.

I wondered how I'd done and stole a look at Mark for an indication, at least in the form of a wink and smile. Nothing. Instead, my boyfriend turned his attention to the others, chitchatting with his sisters and parents and leaving me hanging. After a while, once wine got served—with permission from Liam—small talk found a path to me as the sisters engaged me on things to do in France, primarily where and where not to shop, what to buy, and how to haggle. No more personal questions, thankfully.

During the meal, nothing happened without the green light from Liam. When the first course got served, all eyes fixed eagerly on him, and when he nodded in a solemn way, like an army marching band, hands grabbed forks, and the dinner was officially underway. When Sophie, one of Mark's sisters, wanted more water and bread on the table, rather than asking the staff, she said, "Dad, can we get more water and bread?" He gave the nod to a server, and a new jug of water and basket of bread shortly appeared. Each course proceeded in the same manner. From my perspective, as the table energy dissipated, Liam turned to me and said, "You should retire to the guest room. You've had a long journey. You will need your rest for what Mark has in store for you." He nodded at me, like he'd displayed throughout dinner, bestowing permission for Mark and me to leave.

On the way up the marble staircase and snaking banister, past the massive pieces of artwork, I became excited about a night consecrating our French debut. Halfway up the stairs, Mark dropped my hand, and we finished the short journey in silence. At the door, Mark walked in first, leaving me to follow. The door closed, Mark threw his sport jacket forcefully onto the love seat in the room, and he turned to me.

"What the hell was that all about?" he said, every facial muscle tightening.

"Wha-what was what all about? I said, totally puzzled.

"You said your brother is going to be a hedge fund manager," Mark said, wagging a finger in my face. "He's a glorified gopher for a brokerage firm. He doesn't even have a securities license."

"I was just trying to imp—"

"You don't need to impress my father, and my sisters—nothing impresses them."

A sickening feeling filled my stomach. "Mark, calm down. You're overreacting."

"Don't tell me to calm down. Jesus." His voice was loud, and I prayed the walls had good insulation. Mark went to the love seat, grabbed his jacket, and sat down with a huff, like a five-year old denied play time.

I waited until his heavy breathing deaccelerated. It took a while.

"I was trying to make a good impression for you. He will be a hedge fund manager one day."

"Yeah, well, don't do me any more favors. I hardly need you to make good impressions. I mean, really. And don't think ahead too much, will you? Leave that to me." On the last comment, he raised his arm and waved upward in my direction with a look of disgust.

The conversation was over. There would be no sex, not even the makeup variety.

The next morning, Mark flooded me with everything he loved about me, going on about how adorable I was and how I was such a big hit with the family. I was flabbergasted. *What happened to the post-dinner lecture? Did it happen at all? Did I dream it? Shit, I must have dreamed it.* There wasn't a single trace of the prior night's ugliness in Mark's words, tone, body language, or demeanor. He behaved like it didn't happen. So why shouldn't I? Let the day begin.

We took long walks, hand in hand, through the historic streets of surrounding towns, shopping up a storm, buying everything from touristy trinkets to more expensive items. Mark opened the charm spigot full throttle with shop owners and staff, laughing and joking, speaking French, and holding court the way Mark liked. I didn't understand the exchanges, and Mark didn't translate, but I fancied the show. The south of France had become a backdrop to the world we shared, with Mark at the helm.

Later that afternoon, we stopped for some coffee in a town square. Between sips, Mark leaned in to kiss me, saying how much he loved the feel of my lips. He rubbed my bare arm with his fingertips, telling me it felt like an "Egyptian cotton blanket" and that he loved the way I smelled. His attention intoxicated me and left me craving more.

As the day progressed, Mark became increasingly quiet, giving me less attention, almost as if he were brooding about something. I chalked it up to jet lag. Then, Mark vetoed the family dinner invitation in favor of a private meal at a restaurant he described as a "a well-kept secret from pesky tourists," located off a country road. *Hmm, does he have a surprise for me?*

During dinner, after his customary litany of sweet nothings, as we drank another spectacular wine, Mark's face turned serious.

"You're going home tomorrow."

"What? Home? Why? What happened? I . . . did I do something?"

"No. Something major's come up on the business front, and I need to be dialed in." The tone didn't invite debate. It was a proclamation.

"Okay. When will you return to the states?" I said, masking rising panic.

"Not sure. I need time alone."

End of conversation.

That night, we had sex, sort of—more the quickie variety than our usual protracted passion play. After Mark got his, he jumped out of bed and said, "I guess you should pack. A driver is coming for you at 7 a.m."

I barely slept that night, often awakening to ruminate about this puzzling turn of events, plumbing my brain to figure out why Mark had dispatched me summarily to the states. I was shocked and confused. *What the hell was going on? Did the family disapprove of me? Did I embarrass him somehow? Is this the end of the relationship?*

The morning came, and with it, the driver. I looked at Mark, expecting him to help with the bags. He hesitated, rocking back and forth, taking a deep breath, and exhaling heavily.

"Are you really going to leave me?" He tried to smile, but what appeared was a fractured crease that came out creepily.

"Are you joking?" I said with genuine perplexity. "You said you wanted me to leave. You wanted space. I'm at a loss."

"I was heated in that moment, only half-kidding. You exaggerate everything I say. Why wouldn't I want you to stay?"

This was insane. Part of me wanted to leave. The other part thought, *No way. This is too good to toss away. Chalk it up to the mystery of a new relationship, working out the kinks, finding your way forward. Don't abandon ship. It is still upright.* I shrugged—and unpacked. I exhaled, and the panic disappeared.

Mark was the man of my dreams, the odd hiccup notwithstanding. He never mentioned the incident of sending me home again, and I wiped it from my mind. The next day, we took a trip to St. Tropez, had lunch, strolled its charming streets, people-watched, and visited its finest stores. When we walked by Dior, Mark stopped and gazed into the store window.

"Do you want a bag?" he said.

My immediate internal reaction was *Duh, what woman does not want a designer bag?* But I hesitated. Was this another test? Had I become paranoid? I wasn't sure what to say. If I said yes, he might think it was all about the money and lavish benefits for me. I uncharacteristically doubted my instincts.

"Whatever you want is fine," I said.

"Come on, cutie, you need a bag. Let's go in." And in we went. I had to admit, the Dior bag we selected was off-the-charts gorgeous, something I could never afford myself. I felt special. I wondered who was footing the bill for this extravagant trip.

For the next few weeks, we traveled to places I'd seen only in the movies. We shopped, dined, laughed, and drank; well, he drank. Sure, I had my share of wine. We were in France, after all. But I noticed Mark often lacked a shutoff valve and drank until inebriation. He'd slur, walk off-balance, and get short with me. Lunch or dinner. I wondered whether the drinking had to do with me. Did I not make him happy? Was I the problem? No, I countered. There was no problem. Mark shouldered considerable business pressure, and stress came with the territory. Mark owned two trendy men's clothing stores, and it seemed stressful. From my mother, I know how difficult the retail business can be. He deserved an outlet, which placed a premium on my understanding and patience. I needed to work on myself more and see the long game, so I thought. In addition to the stress Mark endured running the stores, Liam looked down on Mark for not following in his lawyer footsteps. Liam rarely missed the chance to make snide remarks about Mark's career choice. He was habitually letting Mark know that he was a disappointment.

5
Jessica

Collin's generosity floored me. It was one thing to treat me to a European trip, but paying for two friends was above and beyond. The invitation induced gleeful disbelief in both Mari and Jon. For his part, Jon was successful and could handle his own freight. He pushed back on Collin's offer, which I conveyed to Collin, and I reported back, "He won't hear of it. The trip is on him . . . except, of course, your indulgent shopping!"

We convened at the private airport in the late afternoon, and introductions followed. I was both excited and eager. I wanted this to be more than a fabulous trip.

It kicked off with slight hiccups.

"What, did you bring everything you own?" Collin said, eyeing my bulging luggage.

In fairness, I packed a lot, poised for any requisite command performance and whatever adventure awaited.

"Better to over than under prepare," I said with a playful smile.

Collin shook his head with mild disgust, exhaled, and led everyone to board the plane.

After takeoff, Collin announced that dinner would be served, and once we'd eaten, he was going to take a sleeping pill, and if anyone wanted to indulge, he had extras. Taking a sleeping pill didn't thrill me. I'd never done that before.

"I think I'll pass on the pill," I said.

"Really? You bring the kitchen sink in your luggage to be *prepared*, but you don't want to get rested for what I've carefully planned?" he said.

Collin had crafted an ambitious itinerary, down to every minute detail. Getting rest in preparation was sensible. I nodded and decided to think about it.

At 10,000 feet, Collin pulled out two cigars from inside his sport coat and offered one to Jon, who politely declined and added, "I have a strong aversion to cigar smoke. Makes me queasy."

"Suit yourself," Collin said, putting one cigar away and lighting up the other.

"Hey, look, Collin, don't mean to overstay my welcome so early, but I don't do well with cigar smoke. Any chance you can wait until we get there?"

"Not to worry, my friend. This plane has a state-of-the-art filtration system. The smoke won't bother you at all," Collin said, taking a long pull from his cherished Cohiba Behike Cuban.

A quiver rose in my throat. Not the easiest thing to push back on Collin, especially when he had a game plan. He captained the ship, and what he said went. I worried how Marni and Jon would adjust to him. I had not fully thought that through, and I feared the prospects of an unmitigated disaster if this trip damaged my relationship with them. I furtively crossed my middle and index fingers.

Collin doled out the sleeping pills after dinner. Down the hatch it went, or I would be left staring at the plane ceiling all night. We got into comfy clothes, all moving quickly into shut-eye mode. Collin and I cuddled during the night, leaving speed bumps behind and resuming our romantic groove. I was excited to land and get the party started.

When we strolled into the lobby of the hotel, staff members separately said, "Welcome back, Mr. Worth." The three of us exchanged looks, and Jon said softly, "Nice touch." The hotel rooms hit the bell, each room appointed with sophisticated French décor and the smell of the sea everywhere.

The first check-the-Collin-trip-box on Collin's itinerary was a European topless beach club. Everyone was beautiful, men and women. We delighted in the ambiance—sipping rosé, chomping on crispy pommes frites, consuming delectable cheeses, and participating in whatever else we desired. Collin left us for part of the day, explaining the call of business. We three enjoyed the balance of the day, taking it all in like a deep breath, returning to our rooms in the late afternoon.

The Collin game plan pegged dinner at 9 p.m. When I returned to the hotel room at 5 p.m., Collin greeted me with a prideful smile and an outfit lay out on the bed.

"I picked this up for you, love," he said.

I noticed that Collin increasingly referred to me as "love" or "my love," rarely using my name. It made me feel special.

The outfit was a stunning silk red dress. I stared at it in wonder, silently hoping that the legion of pommes frites I consumed earlier wouldn't stick out in all the wrong places.

"Thank you for this. It is beyond gorgeous." I embraced him warmly, and he reciprocated.

"Should I wear it to dinner?" I said.

"That's the point, love."

After we got ready, Collin said, "Let's hurry up. We must get going."

"But I thought the reservation wasn't until nine."

"It is, but I decided to take us to an adjacent town. There is also a store I want to stop in before we head to dinner."

I sounded the alarm for Marni and Jon, giving them forty-five minutes.

Collin hadn't commented on how the dress looked on me, a glaring omission. But once our foursome assembled in the lobby—and he had an audience—he filled the void.

"Doesn't she look beautiful in this dress?" he said, beaming.

"Yes, great choice," Jon said.

"I have an eye for fashion, and when I saw the dress, I had to get it for her. I knew it would be perfect. She looks amazing."

"Impressive, Collin. You do have a great eye, and the fit *is* perfect," Marni weighed in.

The car dropped us at a quaint shopping area lined with high-end boutiques. Collin suggested that Marni and I enjoy champagne at a café while he and Jon ran an errand. Later, following the undisclosed errand, Collin and Jon reconnected with us slightly inebriated women, and the driver took us to a beautiful restaurant at the top of the casino. Once we were seated, Collin told the maître d' we didn't need menus—"I know what they serve like the back of my hand. I know what's the best. I'll order for the table." Jon and Marni glanced playfully at each other but said nothing.

After placing the food order, Collin grabbed my hand under the table and gave it a strong, affectionate squeeze. He then leaned in and kissed me gently.

"I have a gift for you," he said, handing me an exquisite ribboned box.

I felt awkward in front of my friends. But what choice did I have? I said, "Thank you," and started to carefully place the box in my purse when Collin raised his hand in protest and said, "Open it now, my love. No time like the present."

"All right," I said, smiling.

I undid the ribbon, peeled back the wrapping, and lifted the top to see a radiating and breathtaking diamond necklace. My jaw dropped and my eyes widened. When I looked up, Collin was staring at Marni and Jon, gauging their reaction. Marni's jaw had dropped. While overwhelmed, I felt like an adored princess and thanked Collin profusely. "A beautiful gift for a beautiful woman. I'm so grateful to experience all this with you."

"It took a smooth operator too," Collin said. He turned to Jon. "I'll let Jon tell you."

Jon pulled back slightly and smiled. "*Okaaay*."

Jon provided a blow-by-blow—how the salesperson greeted "Mr. Worth," that staff offered them a smooth scotch, Collin demanded to see their "finest diamond pendants," and he meticulously studied the batch for twenty minutes before selecting one. Jon then recounted this exchange.

"Please wrap this up and take thirty percent off the price," Collin said.

"I'm sorry, Mr. Worth, thirty percent is more discount than we can offer," the salesperson politely responded.

Collin took a frustrated deep breath and said, "Look, I have neither the time nor the patience to debate this with you. Please get your manager." Jon later confided that *he* added the "please."

The salesperson dutifully retrieved the manager, who Collin pulled aside for a hushed sidebar. Less than a minute later, the manager told the salesperson, "Please wrap it up and give him thirty-five percent off." The conquest complete, Collin stretched out his right arm toward the door and Jon, and they left.

After telling the tale, Jon said, "I must say, it was quite impressive."

"But wait, you left out the best part," said Marni. "What did Collin say to the manager?"

"That I don't know. Out of my earshot," Jon said.

"Collin?" Marni said.

Collin laughed. "My friends, if I told you, I'd have to kill you. Can't reveal the secret code," he responded.

A continuum of indulgence dominated the rest of the trip. As a foursome, we connected well, enjoying many laughs along the food, wine, shopping, and landscape, which pleased me to no end. I was falling in love with Collin, and I felt he was with me. Our evolving bond was powerful and real. True, the lavish attention was over-the-top. I knew that. But I viewed it as a measure of how much he cared for me and his desire to lay a firm groundwork for our life together. Not to mention, the sex was off the charts.

The day of our departure home, Collin suggested I grab breakfast with Marni and Jon downstairs. He had business to oversee. As the three of us reminisced about the trip, Collin appeared and announced we had to go. He paid the bill, and we headed to the car. Like the flip of a light switch, Collin went silent in the car, texting the entire trip to the airport, as if he was the lone passenger. Marni texted me, *Is something wrong?* I texted back, *No idea.* I asked Collin if he was okay, and he didn't respond, keeping his head buried in the phone screen. That behavior continued the entire ten-hour trip to LA, injecting a disconcerting tension among us.

We disembarked in LA, and Marni and Jon expressed their sincere gratitude for the entire journey. Collin replied, "My pleasure. Nice meeting you." He walked toward the waiting car.

His reaction stunned me. We had spent four days partying like rock stars, laughing, frolicking, and getting to know each other. I had felt a budding friendship among us that held the promise of a lasting relationship. I didn't get it. I looked at my friends, shrugged, hugged them, and bid adieu.

Collin treated me no less the same. After Marni and Jon were gone, he said in rapid succession, "Do you have everything, drive home safe, I need to get to the office, I'll speak to you later." He gave me an obligatory peck on the cheek and was off, leaving me mystified.

I rolled my luggage to the car, head down and in a daze, bewildered by the end of the trip dynamics. Once in the car, sitting in the parking lot, I thought deeply about what had transpired, shaking my head for several seconds before turning on the ignition. *Is he icing me? Am I overreacting?* On the drive home, my thoughts raced all over the place—the silence on the plane ride and quick send off. *Did I do something to offend him? Did I act inappropriately in any way? Did I drink too much? Did I not show sufficient gratitude for his gifts? Did I commit social missteps? Maybe it was something with Marni and Jon? Maybe they didn't show sufficient gratitude? Maybe Collin regretted inviting them?* The contrast between the celebratory glory of the trip and Collin's post-trip brooding was stark and alarming. I felt insecure.

Collin didn't contact me the rest of the day except via a late-night text—*Goodnight, love*. Late in the following day, a nauseating dark feeling gripped me because I hadn't heard from him. The longer the silence, the more stuff I made up, my mind playing tricks on me. *It's over. How did this happen? Why did it happen? What did I do wrong?* Negative thoughts paralyzed me. The next morning, not able to take it any longer, I shot him a text—*Are you okay?* He called me.

"Hi, look, I'm terribly busy," he said.

"Okay."

"The trip was nice, Jessica, but I'm behind at work and have to play catch-up."

"Well, everyone, including me, is so grateful you took us," I softly said, thinking this is what people feel when they're walking on thin ice.

"Nice," he said. There was a long pause. "I am going to be busy the entire day," he said.

Something seemed off. And it was clear he didn't want to talk. Nor did I, frankly. We ended the conversation.

My initial confusion deepened. He suggested the trip, not me. He invited my two friends, insisting they come, not me. Yet I got the feeling he blamed me for his missed work. Whatever was bugging him, he was taking it out on me as if I'd done something to annoy him.

I couldn't help but think his feelings for me had changed. Maybe the initial sharp thrill that often fuels a new relationship had dulled, and he was done with me, biding his time to find the courage to end it. I poured over each detail of the trip, looking for clues. I found none, at least none that explained the prevailing mood. That night, I slept fitfully, feeling perplexed—and sad—each time I awoke. The next day, I called a friend, who insisted that whatever was happening had nothing to do with me, and perhaps the relationship had moved too quickly, overwhelming him. The friend added, "He is a guy, after all. Their emotions take longer to find an acceptable home. Give it time and it'll be fine." I so wanted to believe that.

Later that day, Collin called and invited me to come over. He said little on the phone, and, while confused and off-balance, I said, "Okay, see you in about an hour."

When I arrived, Collin acted as if the recent aloofness and brooding never occurred, deleted from the history books. It was the relationship as usual. Apparently, his longing for time apart had evaporated. He embraced me warmly and said, "It's so good to see you, love." Despite the lack of explanation, I was thrilled to have his arms around me. Once I had a glass of champagne in my hand, he said, "Oh, by the way, my closest friend, Stefano di Poggio, from Italy is stopping by. He's in town for a while, and it's important you meet and connect with him. He means a lot to me."

Stefano arrived minutes later, armed with a stunningly gorgeous woman, a good fifteen years younger than him. They made a striking couple. Stefano was LA hip, sharply dressed, handsome, and suave, with a dreamy Italian accent that embellished his natural charm. Collin introduced Stefano and "Francesca" and invited us all into the living room.

We imbibed champagne for an hour. Collin held court most of the time, allowing me to ruminate. Before the couple arrived, Collin mentioned that Stefano had been married for almost twenty years and lived with his wife in their native Italy. I did the math. Francesca could barely be twenty-five, if that. Something didn't jive. When the "conversation" ended, we shared multiple cheek kisses, Italian style, and the guests left. My escalating curiosity bubbled over.

"Collin, how old is Francesca?"

"I don't know." He furrowed his brow, as if to say, *why are you asking me that?*

"Well, she looked awfully young to be married twenty years, don't you think?"

Collin chuckled and said, "She's not his wife. She's his girlfriend."

What? I was appalled—his married best friend had a mistress, and it did not perturb him.

"Are you friends with his wife?" I said incredulously.

"Yes, of course. Isabella is a lovely lady. Hopefully you'll meet her," he said matter-of-factly.

"Umm, is she, um, okay with the girlfriend thing?" I said with caution.

"What do you think?" he said, with palpable condescension, as if he left off "you idiot" at the end. "Of course not, but what she doesn't know won't hurt her. She lives a nice life. You should see the villa they own in Tuscany, overlooking a draping vineyard."

That was more than I could digest, except for a parting statement.

"Well, I'll tell you right now, I wouldn't be okay if that were happening in my relationship," I said with a coquettish smile.

Colin kissed me on the cheek and said, "Of course not, my love."

Collin insisted that we spend considerable time with Stefano while he was stateside. For me, it was suffering. Francesca was sweet and solicitous, but each time I looked at her, I couldn't help but think of Stefano's wife sitting in Europe while he consorted with a girlfriend, going on about taking her on a yacht trip in the Mediterranean that summer. Turned out, too, that Francesca was replaceable. As more dinners with Stefano followed, the guy introduced new women into the mix—his girlfriends, all about the same age, body type, and look. They, however, had different names—Amanda, Julie, Kristen, and Aimee—and I wondered whether each thought she was in line to be the next Mrs. di Poggio. I didn't rock the boat. I made small talk with them all, making mental notes about them so I wouldn't slip up. The whole thing made me feel dirty.

I finally asked Collin what drew him to Stefano. To my mind, the two were opposites, at least when it came to women and values. Collin explained they went "back aways," and he appreciated that Stefano had "his own money." Collin consistently dealt with people trying to use him for his money and connections and not for who he is and what he stands for. As a self-made person, Stefano didn't "need any of that." Their friendship was real, "not built on false, fragile narratives." He blabbed on and on about Stefano's family in Europe and how distinguished his father was, assuring Jessica that "he's a good man."

"Look, love, I know what bothers you about him. I get it. But it's not my place to try to change him. I couldn't if I wanted to, and it would ruin the friendship. The important thing for you to know is that would never happen with us. We are solid and forever exclusive."

6

If You Knew, Would You Say I Do?

DR. BRENNAN: We are back with Laura and Jessica to take a deeper dive into their narcissist relationships. Before we do, I want to point out that acting like a jerk doesn't in and of itself make someone a narcissist. The disorder reveals itself in patterns and recognizable stages that inflict consistent forms of abuse, as we will see throughout this series.

Ladies, let's pick up where we left off. You were both swept away on some seriously extravagant trips with these men.

LAURA: You're not kidding! I had never been out of the country, and having a boyfriend take me on such a lavish trip was jaw-dropping. His family home and lifestyle were surreal. His dad, however, made me strangely uncomfortable. He was the puppeteer, the rest of the family the puppets. I felt thrown back to kindergarten, when I had to raise my hand to go to the restroom. Everyone bowed to him, including Mark.

DR. BRENNAN: NPD can be learned; it often has a family history and gets passed down through behavioral models. There is an early suggestion in your story, Laura, that family dysfunction was deeply ingrained into Mark's psyche. Children raised by narcissists often acquire extreme pathological and unhealthy behaviors to survive the toxic environments that surround them. Mark may be a classic case.

LAURA: Yes, unfortunately, to get what he needed, Mark managed to live by lying, manipulating, cheating, and abusing people. It took a while, but I understood why he drank so much. It was not because of me. Of course, that's not what I thought at the time. I thought everything was my fault, including his excessive drinking.

I know some listeners may be wondering why I didn't leave when he asked me to pack my bags so abruptly. The six months leading to that moment were heaven. It is only now that I understand that Mark was trying to get me to fear the end of our relationship, a constant state of anxiety.

DR. BRENNAN: Yes, the patterns can be a cruel roller coaster of rejection followed by reward, an effective form of abuse. It is known as intermittent reinforcement. It keeps you hooked and addicted to chasing that euphoric response. It helps intensify the trauma bond, which is formed between the abuser and their victim. Mark was punishing and testing you when he said he wanted you to go home. It was perplexing. The reward was that you got to stay and proved yourself worthy because you took the abuse. This is how they slowly break you. Intermittent reinforcement is a strong tool narcissists use to create an addiction to them. When you get inconsistent responses to the same behaviors, it keeps you yearning for more, like the pattern of a gambling addict—winning, losing, winning, losing.

LAURA: What a whirlwind. Within an hour, he said he adored me, told me to pack my bags, and then that I should come back to bed. I went from cloud nine to sheer panic that the relationship was ending, then to relief that he wanted me there with him. Insane.

DR BRENNAN: You had every reason to feel that way because you heard him correctly when he told you to leave; his recount of the events was the opposite. His goal was for you to feel distressed and confused. However, when it came time for you to leave, he acted as if it were a joke, and you were exaggerating. You were a victim of classic gaslighting, an insidious and powerful form of manipulation used to gain full control over you. Consistent gaslighting is a severe form of emotional abuse that causes tremendous psychological damage. It can even cause someone to question their own sanity. Narcissists use numerous techniques to obscure your account of events. Their goal is to destabilize and confuse you, making you question your own thoughts, memory, and ability to produce sound decisions. It is one of the most frequently used tools in the narcissistic toolbox.

First, Mark made you believe you said something inappropriate at dinner with this family and reacted with narcissistic rage. He asked you to leave and then acted as if it never happened, making you doubt your own perception of what took place. You didn't misunderstand him when he asked you to leave, but by the time his gaslighting had done the trick, you not only bought his story but were willing to accept his version of events. These tactics create an atmosphere of coercive control and are often a constant throughout a relationship with a narcissist. They not only cause pain but cause you to blame yourself for what happened, believing the mess is your fault. This pattern of abuse, mixed with sprinkles of love bombing, intensifies the addiction and trauma bond. What you didn't realize at the time was that he was grooming you to put his needs first. Like when he asked if you wanted a new bag, you paused to consider what answer he desired to hear.

LAURA: Yes, yes. I see now it was a test. Instead of thinking about what I wanted, I thought about what he would think. I didn't want to fail.

DR BRENNAN: It's part of a devaluation phase where the narcissist creates scenarios to see whether you will acquiesce to their wishes, using the test results to assess whether you are worthy supply. Keep in mind that everything a narcissist does is calculated to advance their control agenda.

Jessica, you were still getting major doses of love bombing from Collin and getting showered with lavish gifts.

JESSICA: Yes, it is fair to say that Collin seduced both my friends and me by portraying himself as a loving partner who adored me. He created this perfect romantic scenario that deepened our bond—and it worked! I was falling in love and believed that he was as well.

DR BRENNAN: This kind of love bombing is like a fairy-tale—and blinding. You don't see the cracks until it's too late. What people don't understand about narcissists is while you are authentically and genuinely falling in love, they are infatuated with acquiring new supply. They are excellent at feigning romantic love and compassion, but they are incapable of feeling genuine unconditional love. Their love is a means to an end, void of empathy, compassion, support, and nurturance. The only love they know is love of themselves.

I want to focus on the gaslighting you went through, Jessica, in this part of your story, with doses of ghosting thrown in.

Starting with the last day of the trip, Collin hit you with a severe silent treatment, which struck me as a premeditated tactic to throw you off-balance after a magical trip, manipulate you by making you feel insecure, and force you to take the blame for his altered mood. What a better way to make someone feel insignificant than to pretend they don't exist.

JESSICA: Yes, I was totally confused and felt I'd done something wrong. Honestly, I thought maybe he didn't want to see me anymore.

DR. BRENNAN: Which is precisely what he wanted to happen. It's a form of abuse that brings a range of negative emotions, including anxiety and fear of losing the relationship.

JESSICA: Exactly. After such intense love bombing and attention, the sudden shift in his behavior mystified me. I felt insecure, invisible, and unimportant without him ever saying a word.

DR. BRENNAN: Exactly, Jessica. Collin knew what he was doing. He wanted to destabilize and gain control over you. It gave him power. He didn't want you to get too comfortable at this stage in the game. He waited for you to break, grovel, or apologize for something you didn't do.

JESSICA: I hated that I was at his mercy to relieve my anxiety and fear. I wanted him to help me feel emotionally okay, to love me and adore me like he did on our trip. Looking back, it was a horrible place to be—and a huge red flag. It was a pervasive pattern that continued throughout our entire relationship, causing me to feel guilt and shame and responsible for his dismissive behavior . . . as if I had done something wrong.

DR. BRENNAN: We will need to hear more, but this type of behavior can be the onset of a pattern of trauma bonding, common in narcissistic relationships, where the abused craves validation and attention from the abuser as time goes on, deepening emotional dependence. The cycle can be treacherous. The more frequent the abuse, the more validation the abused seeks and the greater the control the abuser has.

JESSICA: How about Stefano bringing in a new woman every other week while his wife was in another country raising their children? It confused me that Collin wanted to be around someone who seemed, from a moral standpoint, 180 degrees different.

DR. BRENNAN: Thanks for raising that. Narcissists tend not to have real friendships. Everyone in the circle they assemble around them is considered supply. You are kept close if you are benefiting them, and if not, you are disposable. Relationships are nothing more than transactions. Collin presumably perceived many benefits in Stefano as a companion. Stefano was from a wealthy European family. He owned numerous homes and often had a harem of women.

Please understand that narcissists have no defined personality of their own, so they steal attributes from people they revere, both good and bad, making them their own. Collin envied and admired Stefano and adapted his friend's behaviors as his own.

JESSICA: That is so true because when I first met Stefano, I couldn't believe how different they were. But in reality, they were one and the same. Collin wanted to be like Stefano.

DR. BRENNAN: Every person in a narcissist's life, including romantic partners, friends, coworker, siblings, and even their children, have designated roles to benefit the narcissist. Stefano is but one example.

JESSICA: Like my friends on that trip?

DR. BRENNAN: Absolutely. Remember how Collin got Jon to sing his praises for him? Collin is heavily into self-glorification, but he's clever. Rather than always advocating for himself, like he did with the silk dress, he enlisted Jon to sing his praises, who, as a guest of Collin on that extraordinary trip, was in no position to refuse. It was quite shrewd . . . and effective. His agenda included Marni and Jon, wanting to make sure they were love bombed by him so they could remind you that he was an amazing catch. Narcissists surround themselves with what we refer to as flying monkeys—people who admire and are devoted to the narcissist, sing their praises, or do their dirty work for them.

That's all the time we have today. Thank you to my faithful listeners and to Laura and Jessica.

Until next week . . . if you knew, would you say I do?

7

Laura

After our US return, Mark and I spent virtually all our spare time together, and when not together, Mark endlessly texted sweet messages. For the first time in the relationship, I felt safe; we had turned a corner and were on the path to something special and enduring. It was a storybook—how it was supposed to be.

Then an odd thing happened—not all at once but in trickles. Mark began issuing behavioral commands, which struck me as stylistic preferences. He started to dictate what I should wear when we went out. "No more looking like you work at a library," he said with a high schoolish laugh. I paid no mind to the condescending remark, his peculiar if uncomfortable way of showing attention and caring. Another time, while we were window-shopping and I fell slightly behind, he said, "No, no, not good. Sweetie, you need to walk on my side, always."

"Okay," I said with a nonchalant shrug. When at a dinner with friends, I voiced a different point of view regarding restaurant etiquette, based on my well-honed maître d' perspective. Later, when alone at home, he lectured, "Never disagree with me in public on matters relating to my business. It makes me look bad." I shrugged again.

One day, when I tried several times to ask about meal preparation for that night, he said not to call or text him at work "from two to five—too much going on." And to top it off, while our sexual escapades continued to ring the bell, Mark began insisting, implicitly, that I play a more submissive role, leaving him in charge.

In no time, we'd compiled a set of relationship rules, unilaterally mandated, covering the wide expanse from the public arena to the bedroom. While the rules could irritate and be counterintuitive, I dismissed them as a cluster of adjustments in the care and feeding of the male ego. Life isn't perfect.

Mark tended to drink in excess, and when he did, he'd stay up to the wee hours. Sometimes, during late nights, slurring his words, he'd go off on my appearance, wondering if it had changed. "Was your hair always that thin?" "Your skin used to be so silky smooth. What happened?" And the lead balloon: "Honey, have you added a few lbs?" When I expressed annoyance, he'd laugh and say, "Don't be so sensitive. I'm joking. You take everything so seriously." I struggled to see the humor and wondered whether I was being overly sensitive. *Maybe I am too serious sometimes.*

Occasionally, I'd push back, testing the waters, trying to set some boundaries. In those moments, rare as they might be, Mark invariably retreated, bringing flowers or modest gifts home and morphing into his charming persona like nothing untoward had happened. Sometimes, he'd go the extra mile, springing a surprise experience to smooth things over. He knew how to rise to the occasion, which he did after the "lbs" remark.

The fix was a trip he arranged impulsively to Napa Valley to meet his friends from France for a weekend of wining and dining. While not an apology—Mark did not apologize—I accepted the gesture as sufficient contrition, excited to make the trip and meet new people.

That Friday, we took a short flight to Napa Valley. Mark shared biographical snapshots of the people we were joining, giving conspicuous attention to his friend Felipe's girlfriend, Elena, who he described more than once as "hot and beyond gorgeous" and who "always dressed to the nines!" A constant subliminal theme that haunted me was owning up to the appearance standards of Mark's social circle. Very French and very fashionable. I lacked the resources to stockpile the kind of wardrobes Mark and his friends took for granted and didn't need reminders about my shortcomings in that regard. The Elena comments stung in the wake of the "dressing like a librarian" remark weeks before.

Once there, Mark introduced me to the other three couples. No surprise, Elena lived up to the advanced billing—and then some. She was singularly striking, a 5'7" brunette with beaming green eyes, flat-out gorgeous. And, yes, she dressed to perfection, sporting a glamorous style.

The group started the night with a toast of Cristal champagne at the hotel and shared friendly, low-key chitchat. The bubbly consumed, the entourage packed into a Mercedes-Benz Sprinter that transported us to the Castello di Amorosa winery for evening festivities.

The long farm table that formed a dividing line down the center of the vineyard was set like a wedding: rustic flowers, flickering candles, and beautiful place settings and wine glasses, everything perfectly exhibited. The setting sun added a fairy-tale touch. His friends knew how to set up a beautiful party. It couldn't have been better: the vineyard, the budding sunset, Mark, and beautiful people. The food flowed, each dish scrumptious and paired with wine a master sommelier chose. Paired with a light red pinot noir, the group's favorite was the smoked salmon terrine.

Mark took center stage—the life of the party—and his friends treated him as such, the fun guy holding court. As I watched him play master of ceremonies, I noticed how much everyone wanted to engage him. The guy had no off switch, and he ingested the attention like a drug. The more he got, the more energized he became. He paid rapt attention to those he favored, and as for the others, he doled out polite lip service. I saw the patterns, the different degrees of approval that depended on his personal social hierarchy. Elena ranked high on the list. He laughed heartily at her not-so-hilarious jokes.

The night went from sublime to borderline raucous. The wine poured nonstop. Mark got sloppy, and a few hours in, people in small groups excused themselves in a parade back and forth to the bathroom, leaving me alone. Eventually, Elena whispered to me, "Are you going to have fun tonight?" I glanced at her and smiled equivocally, which prompted her to grab my arm and lead me to the ladies' room, where she lay out two lines of cocaine on the counter. Using a rolled-up twenty, Elena snorted one line in a swooshing inhale. Elena, it was clear, had done this before. She nodded her head toward the remaining line and said, "All for you, sweets." Drugs weren't my thing, and I wasn't about to start. When Elena disappeared into a bathroom stall, I wiped the coke into the sink and ran the water, and when she reemerged, I rubbed my nose like she did.

Mark's excessive drinking was one thing, but habitual indulgence in cocaine—and who knew what else—was quite another. It disturbed me, and I didn't know how to handle it, except that if I was going to raise the issue, I'd better find a more opportune time—if ever there was one.

The night became early morning, and the group relocated the bash to the hotel. I was exhausted, and the more tired I got, the more energy the others had. They were partying like there was no tomorrow, and I struggled to stay awake, receding slowly into the background. Bored, I excused myself politely to get some rest. Mark said nothing. I fell asleep almost immediately.

I awoke at 9 a.m. to find Mark sprawled and crashed on the bed next to me. I went for a stroll and had breakfast alone, and when I returned to the hotel room, Mark remained out cold. I showered, put on a robe, grabbed a book, and climbed under the covers, eagerly awaiting his rise. Mark slept until noon. When he awoke, I expected him to reach over and make passionate love to me. The setting demanded nothing less.

Stirring into consciousness, Mark rolled halfway off the bed and sat on its edge, looking away from me.

"You should pack up," he said groggily and gruffly.

"Pack us both up?" I said.

"No, just you."

My heart dropped into my stomach. Tears slowly slid down

my cheeks. I exhaled deeply and spoke in a quivering voice. "This is . . . crazy. What . . . the hell . . . is wrong with you?" I struggled to maintain composure.

He turned to face me, his eyes half shut, but he said nothing. I shook my head in disgust, said no more, got out of bed, dressed, and left. After getting water in the hotel lobby, I bumped into Mark's friend Felipe, who said, "Why the sad face?"

I explained what happened. Felipe shrugged and said, "Yeah, that's Mark."

That's Mark? Is that how he treats all his women?

I meandered to the room and found Mark in the shower. My bag packed, Mark emerged from the bathroom, a towel around his waist.

"I think things with us aren't working out," he said robotically, as if reading a script.

"Well, if they aren't working out, why the hell did you bring me here to meet your friends?"

He didn't answer.

"*Why?*"

When he didn't respond, I said, "You'll never get another chance to do this to me."

"Stop overreacting, Laura. Just calm down. Enough with the drama."

"Overreacting? Drama? You just watched me pack up all my shit!" I had never raised my voice with him before, a role reversal that Mark's surprised look corroborated.

He said, "Okay, okay. Look, just stay. I'm tired and cranky. Just forget it."

A truce of sorts. Despite my disgust, I had no appetite for leaving. I shook my head, and for the balance of the weekend, I went through the paces of playing the girlfriend, polite and conversational, while simmering inside.

Back in Orange County, the relationship resettled, and normal patterns took over, except I was less vibrant, more staid than normal.

A few days later, during the afternoon, while I was food shopping, my cell phone blew up with pictures of Mark smiling in front of a gorgeous home. Then this text: *I hope me, you, and Shiraz can live in a house like this one day.*

Mark consistently paid loving attention to Shiraz, always playing with him. He treated the dog like his baby—like our baby—and for me, watching Mark display genuine sweetness with my dog augured how he'd do as a father.

Mark brought me to a house near Laguna Beach. It was beautifully landscaped and charming, with three bedrooms, three bathrooms, a small courtyard, and a backyard with a splash pool. The floors were wood, with a simple kitchen. There was a balcony off the kitchen and enough space for a tiny table and two chairs. The BBQ grill was next to a round outdoor table. I pictured us eating with friends and Shiraz running around on the grassy area near the pool.

My belly fluttered with butterflies. Less than one month ago, Mark told me we weren't working out. Now, this. *What did it mean? How do I process all this?*

The next day, Mark took me back to the house, and as we stood in front of the front door, he said, "I have an offer you can't refuse."

"Oh, and what might that be?" I said with a coquettish smile.

"Sell your house, quit your job, and you and Shiraz move into this house with me."

It didn't sound like a marriage proposal, at least not how I had envisioned. *Is this as close as Mark could get?* I was ready for one. I was twenty-nine, with a man I loved, who had professed a desire to marry me and raise a family—and who often treated me like a queen. Despite the speed bumps, he had professed his love and smothered me with attention. So far, so good. But his "proposal," such as it was, struck me as tentative and risky. Upend my life without an engagement? And what about my career? I wanted to become a teacher, which Mark knew. My musings kept coming back to one thing—why not propose marriage in the good old-fashioned way?

I could do without the bended knee, content to hear four simple, traditional words. Why ask so much of me before making that overt commitment?

"Well, what about my career? Can you afford this?" I said with caution.

"Plenty of time for the teacher thing. Can't raise a family with two parents working all the time." His tone was soft but firm, with a touch of a fait accompli. He nudged closer to a proposal, sort of.

"Hmm, big step, don't you think?" I said.

"Uh-huh" was what I got back.

"Need to think about it, get some girlfriend time. Fair, don't you think?"

"Sure, sure, how's twenty-four hours sound?" Mark said in a way that I couldn't tell if he was serious or joking. I shot him a look to convey, *Surely you jest.*

He laughed. "Just kidding, just kidding."

I plunged into the deep water. "When would we be married?"

"Married?" he said inquisitively, as if a new thought. "First things first. Much to do before that, you know, all the legal stuff. Blame my family. They're very protective of me. All in good time."

And that was that, for the time being, at least. The next day, I called my friend Grace and arranged happy hour drinks and dinner. I texted Mark with my general plans, not revealing where Grace and I planned to gather. He didn't respond.

Grace and I spent an hour catching up, each aided by two martinis, before I put my newly dealt cards on the table. Amid the details of the recent conversation with Mark, Grace tapped me on the knee. When I flashed her a quizzical look, she tilted her head upward, indicating something or someone was behind me. I swung around to see Mark with a big smile. First instinctively happy to see him, I then thought, *Wait a minute. How did he know where I was?* I awkwardly introduced him to Grace. Mark was polite but barely gave Grace a glance.

"Sorry to barge in like this, ladies, but Laura and I have a dinner reservation across town in thirty minutes," said Mark, opening his arms wide, apologetically.

"I don't recall you mentioning that. Grace and I were about to order some food, Mark," I said, grabbing the menu off the table.

"Oh, damn, my bad. Maybe I forgot to tell you. So sorry, Grace. I am getting forgetful lately. Working too many hours. Hope you don't mind," Mark said, doing his best faux mea culpa.

"Not to worry, Mark. It's nice to finally meet you. Laura and I can have dinner another time." And with those parting words, Grace gave me a big hug and whispered in my ear, "More to discuss. Love you, sweetheart."

As Grace walked out, I said, "How'd you know where to find me?"

"Oh, didn't you tell me?" he answered with exaggerated innocence.

"Nope. Don't think so," I said firmly.

"Lucky guess. Hey, we need to get moving."

After an unremarkable dinner, walking out of the restaurant, Mark casually said, "Oh, by the way, forgot to ask, when are you listing your place?" I didn't want to engage him on the subject, so I said, "I'm looking into it." That was true only insofar as I had discussed the possibility with Grace in our aborted get-together.

The next morning, I called Lindsey, a casual friend, a real estate agent who had sold and purchased homes for other friends and who came highly recommended. After a preliminary chat, I asked Lindsey to list the house. Within seventy-two hours, Lindsey had three bids over the asking price. The positive response flooded me with excitement—and unease.

I called Grace to bring her up to speed and get assurances on my newfound direction. We met at a bar in the late afternoon. Grace and I transformed into serious mode when our second martinis hit the table.

Grace said, "What's your instinct? Your internal GPS is the best way to figure things out."

"I know, I know. I want it to happen, but it's going so fast," I said anxiously.

"I understand. Let's start here: do you love the guy?" Grace said, tilting her head down and raising her eyebrows.

"Yes," I said, nodding a few times.

"Does he love you?" Grace said, widening her eyes.

"Yeah, pretty sure," I said, with a blended nod and shaking like a figure eight.

"Pretty sure?" Grace said, wincing.

"Well, he tells me often enough," I said as if trying to convince myself.

"Okay, let's go with that for now," Grace said and tilted her head. "And he wants a family, correct?"

"Definitely," I replied.

"Laura, he's not perfect, but how many guys out there are?"

"Point taken."

"I mean, we all have flaws, right?"

"Don't I know it."

"Flaws don't make us unworthy."

"For sure."

"He has a career."

"Yes, he dresses nice . . . as he should, owning clothing stores."

"And here, my gorgeous friend, is the pièce de résistance: he loves Shiraz, correct?"

"Undeniably."

"Okay, then, am I in the bridal party?"

I laughed aloud. "Goes without saying!" We clinked martini glasses.

As the holidays fast approached, nostalgia consumed me—family and the cheerful prospect of watching favorite holiday movies, imbibing spirits, and indulging the waistline. I hoped Mark would join me. He had not met my family or, for that matter, my friends, other than the summary exchange with Grace.

That night, Mark was in his office, going over samples from a new designer, when his father called. Mark put the call on speaker. The door was ajar.

"Hey, Dad."

"Hi, Son, what're you doing?"

"Looking at pieces for next summer season for the store."

"Let the manager handle that." His father didn't wait for a response, although none was expected. "I am calling about the holidays. What are your plans?"

"I do not know. I have to ask Laura."

"Ask Laura? Why? Her opinion doesn't matter. The girl is white trash. Face it. She should thank her lucky stars she gets to use the Beverly Hills Hotel bathroom."

Mark took the phone off speaker. It was too late. I had heard it all, and Mark knew it. I was floored and speechless. When Mark emerged, he couldn't ignore the tearful eyes.

"Look, he was only joking, and at this time of day, I can assure you, he had more than his fill of wine.... I'll buy you an Appalachian-style trailer next week." Mark laughed uncomfortably.

Yeah, Grace, I thought, *he's not perfect. He just doubled down.* I shook my head at the insensitive attempt at deescalating humor.

"Do you expect me to let that comment roll away?" I said, holding down more tears.

"Well, you'll learn, like me, that when it comes to my dad, you need a thick skin and to bury your emotions," Mark said with exasperation. "You are wasting too much energy on this, always with the drama. Let it go. Be a grown-up."

He started to walk away. As he did, I said, "Your dad calls me white trash, and you're annoyed at me?"

Mark drank heavily at dinner that night. After his fourth glass of red wine—after prolonged silence at the dinner table—he said, "I think this may be moving too fast."

I froze—and then fear overcame me.

"What's moving too fast?" I said.

"Us. Maybe we need a break."

"Why? Did your *dad* say something to you? Did you tell him I heard his comments?" I leaned toward him with a look of defiance.

"I'm not discussing this with you tonight. I'll talk to you when you calm down."

"Calm down? I listed my home and quit my job, and you want me to fucking calm down!"

Mark shook his head, got up, went upstairs, and instantly fell asleep, staying that way until one in the afternoon. Awake for several hours by the time Mark awoke, I remained anxious and pissed. He slept like a baby while I tossed and turned, stumbling out of bed exhausted, with puffy eyes.

When Mark came downstairs, he poured himself a cup of OJ.

"Good morning. What are you doing today?" he said as if last night's scene hadn't happened.

"Gee, I don't know, Mark, trying to figure out the rest of my life maybe."

"Jesus fucking Christ. Will you just chill? You are so dramatic."

I went upstairs to shower, anxious and confused. Thirty minutes later, Mark joined me.

"Let's call a truce. I'll take you to lunch. I know a spot on the water's edge you'll love." I suppressed the rising temptation to refuse and nodded.

The rest of the day, Mark doted on me, doing his best to sweeten the sour pot. And that night, we had the best sex we'd had in weeks. As we lay in bed, draped over each other, he said, almost to himself, "Our babies are going to be beautiful." Then he whistled, and Shiraz jumped on the bed and cradled between us. "Mrs. Laura Corbin sounds much better than Ms. Laura Blazer, don't you think?"

8
Jessica

One morning, while strolling through a public park, Collin announced, "The time has come for you to meet my parents." His earnest tone implied a turn-the-corner moment for the relationship. It was a major step—a step I'd been eager to take. Collin went on and on about his parents and their wonderful relationship with him. I was both excited and nervous to meet them.

The inaugural event would be dinner at his parents' stateside Malibu home. The Friday of the dinner, en route to meet Collin for the connecting drive to his parents, I stopped by a local florist known for wildflowers, selecting a stunning bouquet of pink peonies and white alstroemeria.

Pulling into his driveway, I spotted Collin waiting outside, looking his typical handsome. He walked briskly and hugged me tight, and after a prolonged and passionate kiss, he stepped back and said, "You look so beautiful . . . my parents are going to adore you . . . and wow, the flowers are perfect . . . and so thoughtful!"

Upon arrival at the parental home, I stayed to the right and slightly behind Collin as his father opened the door.

"Greetings, Dad. Meet Jessica. Jessica, meet my father, Oliver Worth."

I stepped forward and said, "Hi, Mr. Worth, it's so nice to meet you," offering my hand, which Mr. Worth shook. He dropped his eyes away from me, uttering "Hello" in a perfunctory manner. He then said, "Please come inside," and turned to lead the way.

The mother sat in the living room, looking pensive. Collin said, "Jessica, this is my lovely mother, Alice. Mom, please meet Jessica."

She surveyed me up and down and stayed seated. I broke the awkward silence, offering my hand. "Pleasure to meet you, Alice."

Mrs. Worth grabbed my hand limply, and I handed her the bouquet. "Thank you for having us over this evening." She took the flowers, placed them on the end table, and said, "Hello," as if it took all her energy to mouth the two syllables.

Hmm, baby steps, baby steps.

Once all were seated in the living room, Mr. Worth began talking to Collin in a rat-a-tat-tat nonstop sequence. I found the display quite extraordinary, an unpunctuated stream of consciousness I'd never heard before. Sitting next to the mother in an adjacent chair, I tried to strike up a conversation. Mrs. Worth was pleasant enough but reserved as we endured a painstaking process to get acquainted. About twenty minutes later, Oliver Worth said, "Well, let's eat," and he ushered us unceremoniously to the dinner table, where, once seated, he picked up where he left off, talking incessantly, this time mostly about himself and criticizing or putting down people outside the family. Neither parent asked much about me or my family, treating me like the flowers that remained lying on the end table, as if they'd never see me again. Alice Worth remained stoic, hardly uttering a word, and when she tried to get a word in edgewise, her husband shut her down, either directly—"You don't know what you are talking about"—or interrupting to provide his thoughts while she floundered in mid-sentence, keeping the conversational spotlight on him. Collin held my hand most of the night and paid as much attention to me as he could during the one-man show.

On the car ride home, I craved a debriefing.

"Collin, maybe it's me, but I got the impression your parents didn't like me."

"Nah. They're old-school British conservatives, set in their ways . . . and protective. They know how I feel about you, so they're anxious. Don't let it bother you."

"Okay."

"They can be jealous when I focus attention on someone new. Give them time. They'll come around."

Baby steps.

What he said made some sense, but I couldn't help but feel wanting. I had imagined a joyful gathering with enthusiasm, natural interest, and, of course, approval along the lines of "She's a keeper, Collin." Instead, I experienced ambivalence at best and disinterest at worst. And the frank disclosure of parental possessiveness gave me pause.

As the weeks progressed, however, the relationship blossomed, prompting me to request that Collin meet my family. I knew that meeting would be light-years from what I'd experienced with his. My family was close-knit and caring, and they had expressed keen interest in meeting the new man with long-term prospects. Collin initially put it off, with seemingly credible excuses, but he eventually relented, and I arranged a restaurant assembly.

Collin and I arrived first and took up seats at the bar, nursing drinks, while I briefed him on family background. My oldest sibling, Adam, and his wife arrived first and joined us at the bar. Adam was a consummate family guy with three kids and traditional values. I had always dreamed of a family like Adam had. He was my role model for what life can and should be. While I enjoyed the role of aunt, I yearned to be a mom. I hoped Collin and Adam would hit it off, and, sure enough, from the get, they did. Adam had long enjoyed business success, and he and Collin shared a common language and entrepreneurial spirit.

When my parents ambled into the restaurant with palpably eager eyes, my sister-in-law and I greeted them like magnets, telling the host we were ready for the table while Collin and Adam closed the bar tab. The six of us were fiddling at the table with menus when my older sister, Alessia, and her husband showed up ten minutes later, fashionably late as usual. Alessia looked displeased at her assigned seat, which I implicitly knew meant Alessia couldn't easily interrogate Collin. No question, Alessia wanted the lead in testing whether Collin aligned with the dizzying accolades her younger sister had used to describe her new love.

It would be hard for Collin to ignore how well we got on together and how stable and grounded we were. My parents had been married for more than thirty-five years and still looked lovingly at each other. Everyone showed interest in what the others were doing and wanted to know more about Collin. Collin noted privately how the family sweetly doted on me. I was, after all, the baby of the sibling trio and the only one without children, a fact left unsaid.

Collin charmed and engaged everyone on matters far and wide, especially business topics with my dad, a successful real estate investor. The night was filled with laughter, toasts, and stimulating conversation, and Collin fit right in. My father paid the bill, and as they exited, he and Collin set a lunch date. The night exceeded my expectations.

In the car ride home, I looked for the customary debriefing.

"So, what did you think?" I said, my voice full of eagerness.

"About what?" he said, eyes on the road.

"The dinner. My family," I said, as if to say, *What did you think I meant?*

"Oh, it was nice. Your family's nice. Good people. I had an enjoyable time."

"Are you okay?" I said.

"Sure. Just beat. Been a long week."

We continued in silence for several minutes until Collin broached a new topic.

"I'm thinking about charting a yacht to meet Stefano for the summer. We've been talking about it for some time."

"Uh-huh," I said guardedly, asking for more.

"Yeah, well, when we were younger, he and I spent many a summer together, boating through the Mediterranean on his father's yacht. Been a while."

Collin talked about the trip, always in the first person, recounting the conversations he and Stefano had.

"Sounds amazing," I said, masking the rising tightness in the pit of my stomach, as there was no mention of me in the plans.

"Is his wife going?"

"His wife?"

"Yeah, you know, the woman he's married to that I've yet to meet."

Collin tightened his mouth at the sarcasm. "Uh, no, not that I know of."

Just like that, the night went from an engrossing dinner with my family that held the promise of a delightful future to significant summer plans that left me waving goodbye at the dock as if I were an afterthought. The logical misstep in the sequencing was more than bothersome. I saw a pattern: one day, things went well, and the next, doubt about the future of the relationship consumed me. I gazed out the window, lost in thought. *Why is there no consistency? Don't I deserve the comfort and security that we are heading in the same direction with our relationship?*

As summer approached, Collin mapped out his plans. Not once, however, did he mention me joining him, even for a part of the trip.

One morning over coffee, Collin's head submerged in the *LA Times*, I couldn't hold my tongue any longer.

"Can you please pass the almond milk, and, oh, yeah, am I going to join you this summer when you meet Stefano?"

Passing the almond milk without looking up, eyes still on the newspaper, Collin said, "I'm not sure."

I softly exhaled, gulped what remained in my coffee mug, got up, and said, "I need to go. Early meeting."

I kissed his cheek goodbye. He lifted his head in an upward nod, leaving his eyes down.

Once in the car, I called my friend, Samantha, and gave her a summary.

"I have no clue where this is headed now. Up and down, up and down," I said after the prologue. "I don't always need to be included, but for most of the summer . . . that's bullshit."

"I get how you feel," Sam said. "I'd be the same way. Is it possible, though, that you are reading too much into it? Maybe he wants to finalize his plans before he asks you to take off work and everything. He is a little odd . . . I get that, too. Guys are strange creatures sometimes. But he does seem super into you, and you are together twenty-four seven."

"That is exactly the point, Sam. You don't go from twenty-four seven to zero during the summer. That is why I'm confused. I mean, shit, how does he go from being by my side nonstop to jetting off for the summer without me?'

"Don't torture yourself. Discuss the future with him. Lay it on the line. It is important to you, and make no mistake, you deserve that much."

That night, I agonized and didn't sleep well. In the morning, I felt no better and entertained the possibility of ending things. I became angry and frustrated. I had fallen in love with this man and thought he felt the same about me. But his actions didn't always add up. Worse, Stefano wasn't high on my list of masculine role models. The two of them galivanting around in the Mediterranean didn't sit well. How could this man—who showered me and my family with attention and charm, always going on about a future together—spend a summer without me and with an unabashed giglio?

Should I end it?

The next day, I ignored Collin. *Let him stew*, I reasoned. That night, he called.

"Hi, love. Been missing you," he said sweetly.

"Do you want a future with me?" I said.

"What the fuck is that about?" he said, taken aback.

"Really? Do I need to draw you a relationship map? How about leaving me for the summer to hang out with a serial cheater . . . for starters?"

"Whoa, whoa. Calm down, calm down." Collin spoke with uncharacteristic anxiety.

"I *am* calm. Maybe you can explain why you are planning your summer without me."

"That's not true. I'm looking forward to you joining me. I've been trying to figure out scheduling and all that. My business life has been over-the-top insane, but it's also what brings the perks and makes trips like that possible. Be nice to have the space to figure things out . . . so we both can enjoy it."

I was torn. Part of me felt relieved. Another part not so. Did he have a change of heart when confronted, or was that his honest, albeit poorly shared, plan all along? Is this a game? Did I overreact and reveal deep insecurities? Was I being unfair to him?

On balance, I was inclined to trust and put my faith in him. I so wanted this to work. All the other pieces fit. But I had lingering doubt.

"Why, then, when I asked you if I was in the plans, did you say you weren't sure?"

"What are you talking about? I never said that," Collin said defensively. "You're making things up. I told you I was working on my plans and would let you know."

"That's not what you said."

"Spare me the drama. I don't want to argue. That's not what I said. You're coming. No more to discuss."

I wasn't satisfied. I wanted to continue the conversation but knew, when it came to Collin, sometimes the path of least resistance was the best way forward. He'd come around. He always did. We were on the same page, and that is what mattered most. And, again, I had to allow for the possibility that I mishandled the situation, that my insecurities overshadowed my judgment, that maybe I was too anxious about the future, rushing things in my heart and pushing him to want distance. I had to own my own stuff.

In the next few weeks, things went back to normal. We'd ride around the neighborhood in a golf cart while Collin gossiped about his neighbors, always putting them down. He'd go on about how one "cheats on his wife and lives off his daddy's money," another "has a gambling addiction and a striper for a wife," one family owns "three houses in a row, with the three siblings living off the inheritance," and he can't even "keep track of who is sleeping with whom." Not to mention the "daft man who married that rich bitch just so he can play golf four times a week and drive fancy cars."

That's a lot of neighborhood gossip!

I asked how he knew all that information.

"Boys know what boys do. Go to one poker game and watch their lips flap unfiltered after a few drinks!"

"Well, are you sure you're not guilty by association?" I said.

"Me? Are you kidding? I'm not like those people. I'm the opposite. You know better."

One thing is for sure, by all indications: Collin was an industrious, self-made person with an unwavering desire to build a traditional family based on "good morals and values." That fit snuggly into my ideal picture of a future with a man I loved, making him irresistible.

We will get there, I reassured myself. *It is but a matter of patience and time.*

9

If You Knew, Would You Say I Do?

DR. BRENNAN: Welcome back, everyone. Today, Laura and Jessica are here to explore what we just heard about their stories. Let's talk about the mixed messages these ladies were getting from Mark and Collin.

Laura, share your mindset when Mark asked you to leave what was supposed to be a gloriously romantic trip. Again.

LAURA: Confusion was the immediate emotion, quickly followed by overwhelming anxiety and self-doubt. We were in love, or so I thought, enjoying a romantic trip, and again, he banished me from the kingdom as if I'd done something horribly wrong. While I tried my best to push back and stand my ground, I scrambled emotionally. I was devastated. It happened again after his father called me "white trash," and somehow, I was to blame as he started to back off from the relationship.

It's easy to see how crazy it was now, but at the time, when my emotions were a wild, swinging pendulum, getting an objective handle on things was hard. Looking back, I see how masterful he was at pushing me away and rapidly pulling me back before I had any chance to process the abuse.

DR. BRENNAN: Mark was using intermittent reinforcement to control you. He put you on a roller-coaster ride of punishment and reward, a back-and-forth that allowed him to mold future behaviors to his liking and exercise dominance. He is all in one moment, raising questions about the relationship the next, and then faking the future the next, playing you like a yo-yo. For instance, you could make his favorite meal, and he tells you he hates that. The next week, he asks for his favorite meal again and loves it. Inconsistent responses to identical behavior keep you hooked, chasing positive feedback.

Narcissists often couple intermittent reinforcement with gaslighting to create an unstable atmosphere and allow coercive control, which can cause severe cognitive dissonance. This can erode self-esteem over time because the inconsistent behavior and contrasting thoughts cause anxiety and self-doubt in a fight-or-flight state. Not taking accountability for their actions or owning their part—and putting the blame on you—is gaslighting! For instance, you are on a romantic trip when the person you love abruptly asks you to leave as if it's over. Confusing, to say the least. And, worse, you accepted these occurrences as part of the relationship. Make no mistake, that's abuse.

LAURA: Yes, I was disoriented and heartbroken, and he labeled me dramatic and overly sensitive. I kept questioning whether I was the cause of it all. As in the story with his drinking. He'd drink to excess, put me down incessantly, tell me I had no sense of humor when I took offense, and then charm his way back into my good graces when sober. It was maddening.

DR. BRENNAN: Yes, Laura. What we are seeing is how pervasive gaslighting can be in a narcissistic relationship. It trivializes and dismisses the feelings of the other person, as if they were illegitimate or false, and attempts to reverse responsibility for what occurred. Over time, you learn that when you speak up, it only makes matters worse. No one ever wins an argument with a narcissist. Getting conditioned to accept the abuse prepares you to slowly lose your sense of self, your voice, and ultimately, the loss of your spirit. It feels like being erased. This is how the narcissist gains control.

I should add, though, that gaslighting is not the exclusive province of the narcissist. It can happen in other situations. But it is an essential narcissistic weapon and commonly manifests in a pattern. Mark and Collin, it seems so far at least, often resort to gaslighting. It can be a powerful control mechanism.

JESSICA: I have learned that gaslighting is the narcissist's first language. Not only was Collin a pathological liar, but he constantly told me I did not see what I saw and hear what I heard. Gaslighting 101. He dismissed my emotions as overly sensitive or dramatic or that I was simply crazy. I knew what I heard when Collin wanted me to think I wasn't invited for the summer trip with Stefano; then he lied, claiming he had invited me or was considering taking me. To add insult to injury, he minimized my feelings and shut down the conversation, not allowing me to be heard. That sort of thing became pervasive in the relationship. As the relationship progressed, the lying and gaslighting really ramped up, and I was practically living in a fairy-tale state of mind.

DR. BRENNAN: Unfortunately, gaslighting is not as obvious as it sounds. It is an insidious abuse tactic that builds over time, causing the victim to gradually doubt themselves, feeling foolish, confused, and unworthy. It has devastating effects on the human psyche. The narcissist constantly denies the emotions of their victims, and, in response, victims adapt their behavior, burying emotions and silencing themselves. It can be a vicious cycle.

JESSICA: We aren't stupid, but the manipulation is so subtle and sneaky that you don't realize it is happening. Both men came on strong. It was dizzying. They did an amazing job mirroring everything we wanted in a partner. I suppose, in hindsight, we were easy prey.

DR. BRENNAN: Please don't blame yourselves! The highs of seduction, especially when love bombing is at its peak, can be a powerful inducement, nurturing the thought that negative behaviors are temporary and rough spots in building a long-term relationship are natural. Hope for change can spring eternal. You were both hypnotized and mesmerized by professional liars. Narcissists have an abundance of manipulative tools for systematically gaining emotional, psychological, physical, sexual, and financial control.

JESSICA: Yes, Collin wanting to be with me twenty-four seven made me feel loved and desired, like I was the one, his soulmate. He told me I was everything he'd waited for his entire life.

DR. BRENNAN: That's a natural feeling, entering an exciting new relationship. Looking back, however, we see Mark employing an assortment of control mechanisms in Laura's life, from annoying little things—what she should wear or where she should walk with him—to more troubling things—like not contradicting him in public or calling him only certain times of the day—to the more disabling—like isolating her from friends and cajoling her to assume a position of financial dependence. In hindsight, it is a collection of powerful red flags.

LAURA: You know, at first, I found it sweet that he wanted the future mother of his children to stay at home and raise them, assuming he'd support me when I wanted to fulfill my long-standing dream to teach. Instead, it was the beginning of his financial abuse. My condo and job were gone, and I was substantially dependent on him. I had some money from the sale of my condo, but not for long, as you will see.

JESSICA: How are any of us to know? It can happen so quickly. I've never had someone love me so intensely before. It was like I was under a spell. Honestly, I thought he was damn near perfect. I look back to when he was driving me around on his golf cart, telling me how awful his neighbors were; he was projecting his negative characteristics onto them. It's creepy!

DR BRENNAN: Good observation. Narcissists are the most contradictory people you'll meet, and a good thing to remember is that the accusations they levy and judgments they make regarding others are normally self-confessions.

JESSICA: Yes, I think we will see that as the story unfolds. But how can you protect yourself? I have to be honest. If someone had told me that Collin Worth was a fraud, I would have never believed them. I would have thought they were jealous!

LAURA: I did warn Mark Corbin's next victim, but she didn't believe me. More on that for another day.

JESSICA: How do you know he's not just an asshole but a narcissist? We all are vulnerable to these predators.

DR. BRENNAN: Great question. How does anyone know? Well, you certainly don't want to be dating a jerk either [laughing], though they are far less dangerous. A lot of narcissistic behavior mimics a normal healthy person, those who are excited about a new relationship. Keep looking for the patterns, like twenty-four seven contact, over-the-top gifts or attentiveness, mirroring your hopes and dreams, words not matching actions, gaslighting, and silent treatments. As we delve deeper into your stories, I am sure we will see more of them.

Truth be told, narcissists don't show up wearing a ski mask, with a knife in their hand, telling you the many ways they intend to abuse and destroy you. They are masters of their craft, skilled in gaining trust and grooming their prey as they stockpile power and control in the relationship. So much more to learn.

Don't miss the next podcast. We will hear more from Laura and Jessica and continue to clarify what differentiates narcissistic from healthy partners and identify the various red flags.

I am your host, Dr. Jules Brennan. Until next time. *If you knew, would you say I do?*

Thanks for listening.

10

Laura

"What's wrong now?" Mark said, making no effort to suppress his condescension.

"Huh, wrong, oh, nothing," I lied. "Just a little tired. Why?"

"You've been sulking, acting like Shiraz went missing or something."

The truth was that I continued to struggle with the turbulent ride of our relationship, and at times, it preoccupied me. But I had to give Mark credit; he was paying attention and got the message. Thank God for small things.

"Well, I tell you what. How about we go to Hawaii and kick back for several days?" he said after a prolonged silence. "It seems what the doctor ordered. I have a friend who has a house there, and I asked if we could stay there for a week. They owe me a favor."

Hawaii? Why not? No argument there.

And off we were. Aloha!

We arrived at a house on the Northern Pacific Ocean side of Kauai. While we'd be there only five full days, the setting couldn't be better. Arriving at the entrance, Mark placed his luggage on the ground and opened the front door. He grabbed my luggage and placed it on the ground next to his. He turned to me.

"Come on. I wanna lay ya," he said, laughing at his sophomoric humor.

I shook my head with a smile, and he swept me up and carried me into the place. Rose petals coated the bed, and on the night table stood a chilled bottle of his favorite champagne. We unpacked, shared the bubbly, and dove into the sack for mid-afternoon sex.

After taking showers, we frolicked on the beach half-naked and grabbed a poke bowl from one of the local food trucks. The Hawaiian people were so down-to-earth and chill. It was so welcoming. We ate and drank and had lots of sex. The next four days followed suit—nonstop indulgent fun.

On the last day of our stay, I took a nap after a mind-blowing scuba diving excursion. As evening approached, Mark awoke me with a gentle nudge, and when I opened my eyes, he said, "I have a surprise." Groggily, I sat on the edge of the bed. He smiled ear-to-ear, grabbed my hand gently, and took me to the backyard—a table set for two, draped in crisp white linens and adorned with Hawaiian flowers. It was breathtaking, all of it: the table, the mood, him, and us.

We had a lavish meal, drank exceptional wine, and reviewed the fascinating details of the trip and the wonder of the Hawaiian Islands.

After we knocked off dessert and I moved to get up from the table, Mark raised his hand like a traffic cop.

"Do me a favor. Stay here. I'll be right back."

"Okay," I said lovingly and with a shrug. I leaned back and relished how happy I felt—a full flush of contentment I hadn't enjoyed in a long time—or come to think of it, ever.

He was gone over ten minutes. I got anxious and rewound the trip. Not a single hiccup had tainted the entire trip, not even a moment of frustration or disagreement. It had been a dream trip in every respect, the kind of experience you expect from a honeymoon. *No way*, I told myself, *is an issue lurking around the bend.*

Then Mark returned, took my hand, and led me down a path to the beach, and as we neared the beach shoreline, I saw a sailboat bobbing near the water's edge. My confusion rose, and my heartbeat accelerated. *What is happening?* I looked at Mark, and it was like he'd won the lottery. I'd never seen such excitement in his face. My heart beat faster.

He dropped to one knee, and in as smooth a move imaginable, he slid a little red box out of his right pocket, flipped open the top with his thumb, pulled out an antique ring, and grabbed my right hand with his left one. He said, "Will you marry me, cutie?"

I brought my left hand to my mouth as tears of unbridled joy trickled down my cheeks. *It's happening!* Stunned and overcome, I forgot to answer the question.

"Ahem, I think there is a pending question," he said, summoning all his charm.

"Yes, yes . . . yes, of course I will," I blurted out in excitement.

We hugged for a long time. After we moved back a step, he put the ring on my finger.

"Honey, this is my grandmother's ring that belonged originally to her mother. It is a cherished family heirloom."

Wow.

"I am honored to wear it. I love you."

He hugged me again, with a warm, full embrace, and while the *I love you* return didn't follow, my head spun so fast that it didn't matter. I was over-the-top ecstatic.

"Come on, the future Ms. Corbin. A ride awaits us."

We ran down the beach, holding hands, to the boat with sails snapping whimsically in the warm breeze. Once we boarded and took seats, the boat captain served us a glass of champagne, and we headed out on a sunset cruise. We absorbed the setting in silence for a few minutes, both tongue-tied from the grandiosity of it all and needing our systems to recalibrate.

"Mark, I am so happy right now. This is what I had dreamed of."

"It was so hard to keep this a secret—I can't tell you. I wanted it to be as special as it could."

"Well, future husband, you hit the ball out of the park," I said, raising and tipping my glass toward him in a toast. He reciprocated, and we clinked our gold-lined vessels.

"I am so looking forward to building a family together," Mark said as we watched the sun and the edge of the horizon inching closer to each other. "We'll make beautiful babies, don't you think?"

"But of course."

My life and our relationship were back on track. I was thrilled to the core.

Danielle, Mark's oldest sister, and her husband hosted a Fourth of July dinner gathering, the first time I'd been around the entire clan since our Hawaii engagement. I enjoyed how her family related to each other. More normal behavior and seemingly drama-free. I looked forward to the event, but I was a little nervous.

Her children created place cards for everyone. Mine read "Aunt Laura," the first public recognition that I was about to become a bona fide member of the Corbin family. My heart fluttered, bringing a warm smile to my face. Adjustments can be tough for some people, especially with a tribe ruled with an iron fist by a patriarch like Liam. My patience was paying off.

The dinner table was spectacularly set, as if *Architectural Digest* collaborated with Johanna Gaines (of HGTV's *Fixer Upper*). Each detail exuded perfection. The perfection, however, didn't last too long.

The first odd episode involved the behavior of Mark's sister, Sarah, toward her husband, Jack, and the collective family reaction. Jack struck me as genuinely nice. He certainly treated me kindly. He radiated a laid-back laissez-faire aura. I liked him. Sarah, on the other hand, had all the markings of a partner from hell. She treated him like a whipping post. She pelted him with little put-downs, digs wrapped in faux humor, which revealed more about the misery of the bully than the target. I checked Jack's reaction—he took things in stride with head shakes—and rolled my eyes internally. But one episode blew my mind.

Jack placed a water glass on the wrong side of the place setting, and you'd have thought he'd ruined the entire dinner, as if he'd dropped a platter of all the grilled food on the floor. She criticized him unmercifully—"What in God's name is wrong with you? Have you learned nothing from me about etiquette?" Neither seeing the irony in her words nor being satisfied with the public upbraiding, she threw a wooden serving spoon in his direction, which, owing to her evident lack of athleticism, went flying right by my head, barely missing me. The toss was so bad that Jack, standing a few feet from me, didn't have to duck. I did.

And that was that. Sarah stopped the maniacal rant, someone retrieved the missile, and people continued what they were doing. And this was the kicker: no one spoke a word to me even though my face almost met an airborne utensil. The Corbin family simply moved on. Just another day in wacko land.

That occurred before other guests had arrived, thankfully. When people trickled in, the ambiance became more subdued and formal. The dinner party ensemble consisted of Mark's parents, his sisters' entire families, and a friend of his parents, a man named George, who arrived with a much younger girlfriend.

Things proceeded normally until Mark's mom became visibly shit-faced. That was a new one. I had never seen her drunk before, but it reminded me of Mark's excessive drinking, a habit he kept under wraps in front of his family, never wanting his dad to see him tipsy. He'd wait until we got home to supplement his libation intake. I was learning more about the apples falling from the family tree.

And then there was this conspicuous omission. I expected someone—Mark, his parents, or his sisters, a bevy of eligible candidates—to toast our engagement. I mean, it was the right thing to do. But other than the "Aunt Laura" place card, the fiancé thing didn't happen. It was one step forward, two back with this family.

The evening ended, and Mark and I went to a local hotel. He beelined to the bar and ordered a whiskey to bring to our room—"a double," he instructed the bartender. We shuffled to the room in silence. I awaited a mention of the wooden spoon "airplane" that nearly clipped my ear. Nothing. I let it go. Learning to pick my battles.

The next morning, Mark's phone blew up, and I let him know his dad had called several times and maybe something was wrong. Mark shot up, dialed his father, and listened, nodding and saying nothing. Then he hung up.

"What was so urgent?" I said.

"Oh, a close friend of my dad hung himself . . . in the guest bedroom," he said without emotion.

"Who?"

"You know, George. You met him and his girlfriend last night."

"Oh, my God." I started to tremble.

Mark shrugged.

"What . . . um . . . whose guest room?" I said, trying to stay calm.

"My parents," Mark said.

"Are you kidding me? Oh, my God. That's so awful. What happened? What can we do? How are your parents?" I put a hand on his shoulder, trying to console him. It evoked no response.

"My parents? They're fine," Mark said. "My dad said the guy's girlfriend drove him to do it."

"What?" I said, putting my hand to my mouth. "This is horrifying."

Later, when at his parents' home, if you didn't know what had happened, you'd never know something so tragic had occurred hours earlier, other than consistent remarks that blamed the tragedy on the "annoying hag" of a girlfriend. When the poor thing arrived later, distraught and a basket case, they consoled her like a best friend. I needed a playbook to figure these people out.

I was beyond perplexed. We had enjoyed dinner with this man the night before, after which he returned to the parents' home, retired to their guest room, and killed himself—and so far as I could tell, no one in the Corbin clan seemed fazed. Despite my efforts, I couldn't process any of it, except to wonder whether members of the family I'd soon inherit by marriage came with beating hearts.

11
Jessica

Our summer excursion to the Mediterranean fast approached. I prepared meticulously, cashing another chit at work—thankfully, summer work demands lessened substantially—and lining things up for Harper, courtesy of the dog-sitting generosity of my older brother.

On departure day, I met Collin at the airport, lugging two bulging suitcases. He shot me a familiar look.

"Let me guess," he said, the sarcasm dripping from his mouth, "you are relocating to Europe," and then he bobbed his head in mock comparison between his single bag and my gargantuan ones.

"Well, in case you haven't noticed, I'm a woman, and here's a news flash, Mr. Handsome, we women come well-prepared." I couched my words in feminine sass to inject a healthy dose of levity into the tit for tat. It didn't work.

He shrugged. "I just don't get it. Why so much stuff?"

"*I* don't get it. What does it matter? It's just us on a private plane," I said with some frustration, extending and opening my arms wide to reinforce the "who gives a shit" retort.

"Just seems a tad excessive is all." His way of retreating.

I loved being with Collin, but the little digs grated.

Once we arrived abroad, Collin went to the boat while I surveyed a local market for essentials. We unloaded and got ready to meet Stefano at a jewelry pop-up, which was the buzz around Portofino.

It turned out that Stefano's wife, Stella, was the most sought-after jeweler, and I finally got to meet her. As we exchanged the three cheek Italian kisses, I felt compromised, knowing like I did the girlfriend harem Stefano harbored in the States. I was also bemused. Stella was drop-dead gorgeous and had a body to die for, with thick, long, medium-brown hair that hung in loose curls around her face. And her jewelry designs were exquisite. Why on earth did the guy need girlfriends when he had this talented beauty? I couldn't stop thinking about the whole sordid situation and clung to an internal mantra—*Mind your own business; it's their life, not yours.* It wasn't easy. The whole thing sickened me.

The first day on the water approached perfection. We sipped chilled rosé virtually end to end and basked in the warm sun and magnificent views.

Things took a sharp turn on day two.

Collin channeled his best Jekyll and Hyde as his mood swung from charming and attentive to agitated and preoccupied. He spent most of the day on the phone and most of that screaming at some poor soul. I assumed it was business-related, which I normally steered away from, but it had become so distracting that I asked what was up. His cold stare and squint meant only one thing: *mind your own fucking business*. Okay then. I let him be, and for the balance of the day, he went AWOL, and I rode solo.

The next day introduced a new tension. The boat had engine trouble, which turned Collin inside out. In fairness, he'd doled out considerable funds for this trip and had a reasonable expectation that the boat would work without a hitch. But he berated the captain in a way no one deserves. I mean, shit happens, and you deal with it the best way you can. Collin dressed the guy down badly. And while the engine got fixed without fanfare, Collin continued to operate at a low boil, allowing each wrinkle to trigger frustration. He was a swell of combustion, and the promising extraordinary trip teemed with stress.

Paranoia set in, putting me on guard. I flashbacked to an aunt of mine who, in bemoaning life with her former husband, my uncle, said within earshot of my receptive teenage ears that life with him was "a procession on eggshells." I was starting to understand what she meant.

Collin had planned a special dinner at a nearby port. He insisted, however, that we take the tender—a small boat that provides transportation to and from a larger vessel—as part of the romantic experience. It sounded wonderful until the captain weighed in, with no trace of ambivalence, that it was not a good idea. "I strongly advise against using the tender. The seas are way too rough." *Good enough for me*, I thought, but the nautical pushback enraged Collin, who went off in a full-tilt rant in our cabin about how the captain was a "full-fledged moron."

"I don't give a shit what he thinks. We are taking the tender." I was unpersuaded.

"We have a chef on the boat. Let's enjoy our evening here. It'll be fine, honey. There is always tomorrow." I could not have spoken with more sweetness.

"Look," he said, with a dismissive headshake, "I want to take you to this amazing island, and that's that. Get ready. We are going."

And that *was* that. As the tender got lowered into the choppy waters, my heart started beating like a rock and roll drum solo. Collin jumped in first and offered his hand to help me. Anxiety built inside me.

The captain was spot-on correct—no shocker there. In seconds, the waves crashed over the bow. I squeezed the rails on my seat, envisioning what it would be like to drown in these deep blue seas. We weren't out five minutes when I suggested we retreat to the boat. Collin didn't respond; his knuckles gripped tightly on the wheel as the tender pounded through the surf full speed ahead. I dropped my head, not bearing to look at the water. Each second seemed an eternity. One time, I took a peek. Big mistake. The port looked so far away, as if we'd made no progress. It was insane, and fear overcame me. I convinced myself we were not going to make it and began to pray. I didn't look up again.

The next word I heard was "Voilà." I looked up, wide-eyed, and by the grace of God, Collin was steering us into the port a lifetime after we had left. I was an emotional mess and furious, not to mention soaking wet with windblown knots in my hair. I tried to get it together but remained worried. We had the return trip to make.

I barely ate while thinking about the return—in the dark, no less. I drank more than usual, hoping to get numb for the wild ride home. Thankfully, with the sun setting, the sea calmed enough that I didn't freak out and could relax a little. When we reboarded the boat, Collin threw his shoes demonstrably on the deck and berated the captain for allowing us to leave on the tender in the intense seas. *Huh?* Evidently, Collin thought the captain—notwithstanding his clear advice *not* to go—should have physically prevented us from leaving. For a moment, I thought Collin had gone certifiably mad. The captain had the same thought. He shook his head and walked away without comment. *Good for him*, I thought. I was happy to close my eyes and sleep the experience away. It had drained me entirely.

The next day, we were set to meet Stefano in Sardinia. The boat sailed throughout the night, and we awoke in the new location. Collin and I went on land to have breakfast and enjoy a little shopping. I was stunned when he bought me a Birkin bag, which I never imagined hanging from my arm. I was in shock. The rest of the day, he texted and chattered on the phone, and I took in some rays and read a novel. We enjoyed lunch on the deck. By then, Collin had returned to earth, paying attention to me, professing his love repeatedly, and saying how thrilled he was that we were a couple, eager to see what the future holds. The music to my ears washed away the craziness of the tender experience and his frustration-induced rants. Hearing his words and connecting with him made me happy. I could see the loving husband he could be and the family life we could have.

I got ready to go to dinner in an all-white, three-quarter-length flowy dress and sandals, my skin warm and slightly bronzed from the day. Collin looked handsome when I met him on the deck. We disembarked the boat. *No tender today, thankfully!*

We walked two blocks and entered a beach club to meet Stefano. When I saw his arm around another woman, "Angela," it turned out, my jaw dropped. Two days ago, I'd met the guy's sweet wife. Now I was about to dine and party with his mistress. I didn't know how much more of this covert intrigue I could stomach. Worse, I was on a slippery slope. The deeper I got, the more complicit I'd be. At some point, I'd be a conspiracy member, if I weren't already, co-opted into a web of deceit. I felt grimy and guilty.

The beach club was decorated wall-to-wall with thirty-something beautiful people dancing with passion and enthusiasm and imbibing mixed drinks at an alarming rate. To help us catch up, Stefano placed an oversized vodka bottle in the middle of our table and poured shots. This was Stefano's playing field. He could party with the best of them. I couldn't leave, and I wasn't about to sulk, so I joined the merriment, doing my best to keep pace with the wildness. In truth, I had a wonderful time. It was fun. But I couldn't shake thoughts of Stella. It tore at me. I was grateful Collin was not like Stefano when it came to relationship loyalty. We might have had a few rough seas, but we had a relationship based on mutual morals and trust.

The next day, I woke up around 9 a.m. to the sounds of Collin yelling on the phone. It was the wee hours in the States, and I wondered what could be that important. During a long listening segment, he cupped the phone to muffle his voice and softly mouthed the words, "It's my dad." I whispered in return, "Is everything okay?" He put his hand up and continued to talk. I lifted an index finger upward, indicating I was headed to breakfast, got dressed, and climbed the stairs to the deck level. Collin didn't join me.

For most of the day, Collin chatted on the phone, barely speaking to me. I gave him space. At around 4:30, he joined me on the deck and released a week's worth of frustration and energy.

"People are idiots. The world is crawling with them. If I'm not on top of them twenty-four seven, everything goes to hell in a handbasket. I always get the blame, that's what happens when the buck stops with you, but the incompetence is mind-boggling. It pisses me off that they have the nerve to blame me for the problems they create. Fucking unreal."

I wanted to show support by asking some open-ended questions. But the vibe suggested that I limit myself to affirming nods. He was venting and not asking for my two cents. Venturing into the fray might worsen things. *Pick your spots, girl.*

The trip continued, and Collin resolved some of the business issues. Each port was more beautiful than the next. Things started to flow when the main cabin air-conditioning stopped working. Once again, shit happens, but coming on the heels of the engine failure and the nonstop business problems, the latest hiccup ignited Collin, who went ballistic. I thought he was going to throw the captain overboard—if he didn't suffer a heart attack first. I'm no betting person, but I'd wager a handsome sum that this captain will never book a trip with Collin again. As they say, life is too short.

That evening, Collin wanted to take a walk and vent about what was going on back home. I listened and consoled him. As I chose my words carefully, he squeezed my hand. I was glad I could be there for him. I felt special that he confided in me. Despite the magnificence of the trip, that short walk became the highlight.

After the trip, we returned to the States. In many ways, it was a trip of a lifetime—despite the chaos. The beauty of the seaside ports mixed with Italian villages was picturesque. Still, I was excited to see Harper, and Collin was eager to get back to work.

We landed around 3:30 p.m., and I told Collin I was headed straight to my brother's place in Orange County to retrieve the dog. He didn't comment. I asked if he'd heard me.

"Yes, I heard you. But I want you to stay with me tonight."

"Collin, I need to get Harper; it's been weeks."

"Okay," he said, like a disappointed and vulnerable little boy.

I knew that Collin didn't like to hear "no" and wanted me available on demand. When he didn't get his way, he either threw a tantrum or sulked. This time, he sulked. Strangely, I felt guilty. We had been on an amazing trip, and he was preoccupied most of the time, and now, it seemed, he wanted to make up for lost time. I got it. And, in truth, I wanted to be with him too. But I had things to tend to, most especially my dog. If we were to have a thriving relationship, we had to respect our respective space and needs. Playing the wounded child when you can't have your way won't cut it, and I hoped that sort of behavior would diminish over time.

After picking up Harper, my phone buzzed in my purse. It was Collin.

"Hi, there. Just picked up Harper. What's up?"

"Come back to the house and bring Harper. We'll have dinner, watch a movie, and cuddle."

"Collin, I really need to check on my place and get ready for the work week."

"Okay, see you tomorrow," said the wounded child.

The next day, in the late morning, while I was at a real estate showing with prospective buyers, a barrage of Collin text messages rattled my phone. I silenced the phone, but not before a client said, "Whoever is trying to reach you is relentless!" I apologized.

When the clients walked outside to inspect the pool area, I checked my phone to discover ten texts from Collin, each a variation on a theme—when am I coming to him? I couldn't decide whether to be flattered or bothered—or both. I texted back. *I'll see you tonight. Clients here. At a showing.*

Why can't you meet me for lunch? he responded.

Can't. Gotta go, I returned.

That evening, I loaded Harper in the car and drove to LA. I arrived to find Collin waiting in the doorway, looking eager.

Looking me lovingly in the eyes, he said, "I want you here with me all the time. No more two places. It's time."

I kissed him softly and said, "Collin, sweetie, I want what you want, but that's a big step."

"Don't you believe we have a future?" he said, taking a short step away from me and sounding a little hurt.

"No, no, of course, I do. I just have my house and a job. And my dog." I reached out and grabbed his arm.

"I know all that, but we have a home here—together."

The tenacious Collin had emerged, although I took to heart what he was saying. The problem was, we weren't engaged, and, without that, it would be a huge leap into uncertainty. I tried to process, mindful I still stood in front of the house.

He squared his shoulders, exhaled, and said, "Yes or no?" *That . . . I didn't expect.* A line in the sand?

"Let me have a day or two to gather my thoughts."

He looked annoyed. "Are you for real? What thoughts do you need? I love you. You love me. We are a great couple with an amazing future ahead. What more is there?"

"Collin, yes, I know. I agree—"

And he grabbed me, swung me around, and said, "Welcome home, my love."

I got swept up in the moment and said, "Okay, okay, yes." We got giddy and gave each other a big hug. After dinner, we made love all night, after which he held me tight, and we fell asleep that way. I had taken the plunge. I was all in.

The rest of the week, I commuted back and forth to LA, which was exhausting. "Let's have a family dinner on Sunday. Invite your family, and we'll barbecue. I don't want you slaving in the kitchen, even though I love your food. We can have a chef come or have it catered."

"You know I love cooking. Not a problem. I'll prepare a menu."

"Okay. But make sure you get someone to help clean. You tend to tear up the kitchen, and I don't want a mess." I ignored the dig.

My family arrived to see an outside farm table adorned with flowers and candles. The weather was amazing, and the wine was flowing. Collin insisted on sitting next to my older sister—a tough nut to crack, as they say. I assumed he wanted to check her pulse on how she felt about our relationship. We all laughed, ate, and drank until late in the night. I was so happy my family seemed to adore Collin like I did. It was working.

My sister left first, and I walked her to the car. We exchanged small talk for a few minutes. Then she disclosed what she really wanted to say.

"Are you really moving in?" she said, delivering her trademark big-sister protection.

"Yes, why?" I said, with no hint of doubt.

"Why? Here's why. No ring, little sister. No ring. . . . Look, I wouldn't sell my house." The last comment barked "buyer beware."

Later, Collin asked me what my sister and I chatted about since we were outside "forever."

"She's my big sis and nervous about me moving in without a traditional commitment."

"Oh, please. She's just jealous."

12

Laura

Mark and I set the wedding for May 15, 2006, and began planning. Like all brides, I wanted everything to work as seamlessly as possible, aware that a hitch or two might happen, as they always did, but otherwise, I expected smooth sailing.

The first item on the planning agenda was selecting a location. We wanted the ocean as our backdrop, but financially, that was a stretch, so we settled on a beach ceremony and a reception at one of the beachfront restaurants where Mark's dad was an investor. That turned out to be easy. We quickly identified nearby hotel choices for guests and the bridal party. One major box checked.

Well, not quite. There was the matter of the location deposit.

"What about the deposit?" I asked.

"What about it?" Mark said, incredulously.

"Um, it has to be paid now."

"So, you've got proceeds from the sale of the condo, right?"

"Uh, yeah."

"There you go."

I had assumed, however, that Mark would be contributing. But I didn't push back. As the bride, I knew the tradition. I handled the deposit.

The next hurdle was the guest list. We agreed on a modest size, one hundred, but got derailed by how to divvy it up between us. Mark had a far more extensive network, but I thought that meant that I should get to invite a greater proportion of my smaller world and share equally in guests. It wasn't his wedding; it was ours. The negotiations, which is what they became, didn't go well, and rather than prolong them and create angst, I relented, and we settled on a 75-25 ratio.

Mark delegated the job of picking out invitations to me. "I don't have the time and don't really care. You handle." Not a problem, my love. Because time was precious, I jumped on it and selected the nicest format I could get in the shortest time. The vendor sent a proof. I showed it to Mark, and he said, "Fine," spending all of five seconds glancing. We had another box checked. Well, except, again, for one thing, the same thing—money.

"We need to pay for them right away," I said. "We're late getting them out and can't dally."

"So, what's the problem? Pay them," Mark said, his eyes buried in his laptop.

"How?"

"What do you mean, *how*? Use your condo money. I thought we discussed this."

Okay, we had, but was he saying that the entire financial burden for the wedding rests on my tiny shoulders? Apparently. But was that so bad? Mark promised to keep our family financially secure for the rest of our lives. Wasn't this the least I could do? And again, I was the bride. The condo proceeds it was.

Next was the planning crème de la crème: picking out a wedding dress. I had long envisioned what I'd look like on my wedding day, and I aimed to fulfill that dream. After several consultations and Grace's valuable input, I came upon a perfect design. Elegant, traditional, and feminine. Not stark white, antique white, with beautiful handsewn ornate designs across the strapless top and long train. It was exquisite. When I showed Mark the design, he said, "Looks fine." *Looks fine? That's it?* I get that most guys aren't into bridal gowns, but Mark had taken such a keen interest in *everything* I wore. I wondered where his head was at regarding the wedding. The "looks fine" comment didn't sit well, especially for the next comment I had to make.

"I'm running out of funds. I can't pay for the dress. And we haven't even talked about the live band you wanted. I need some help here." I leaned back in my seat, eagerly inviting a response, and not just any response, a "No problem, honey, I got this" response.

He stopped what he was doing—looking at his phone—and gazed at me with a look of mild exasperation.

"I don't understand. We've discussed this . . . how many times? Have you talked to your dad?"

"No, actually. I don't want to put that kind of pressure on him," I said meekly.

"Pressure? His daughter is getting married. This is what dads do. He is probably wondering why you haven't asked for help. He probably feels excluded, even slighted."

Maybe Mark had a point; maybe I was overprotecting my dad and making decisions for him. I knew his resources were limited, but come to think of it, I didn't know the details, and why should I deny my parents the opportunity to participate? Later that day, I called my father. After updating him on the state of planning, I revealed the buried lead.

"Dad, I hate to ask, but I am wondering, you know, whether, um, you and Mom might be able to help out a little."

"Sweetheart, of course," he said without missing a beat. "We were wondering how you want to handle that. It'll be easy. We'll refinance the house. Your mother and I have already discussed it and were going to raise the subject with you ourselves."

Refinance the house? I wanted to cry. It made my bones ache.

"No, no, Dad, if that is what it takes, I'll find another way. That's not acceptable." My voice quivered, and I held back tears.

"No. It's not that big a deal. We want you to have your day, and I am sure Mark's family will help as well."

He thought wrong.

"Mark will handle the finances once we are married. I want this handled traditionally, but not if you have to mortgage the house . . . unless we can consider it a loan. I'll pay you back."

"The important thing, Laura, is that you are happy and with the man you love. Let's not worry about the loan thing. We can deal with that down the road. Let's get this taken care of now. I love you, sweetie."

"I love you too, Dad."

Then, a shoe dropped. A big, heavy shoe. We were alone, having dinner at home, when Mark got up, went into his office, and returned with a document, which he handed me.

"This is a prenuptial agreement that the family attorneys need you to sign." He handed me a pen. "Take a look and sign where it indicates." He sat back down and poured a healthy dose of wine down his throat.

"Right now? I need to read this carefully. And shouldn't I have a lawyer look at it?"

"Look, get an attorney if you want. Just get it signed. And don't ask questions, or this won't happen. We have no choice." He picked up his wineglass, and down went another ample gulp.

My head was spinning. On one hand, I would be spending the rest of my life with Mark, *So this a mere formality, right*? On the other, *Who knew what was in this thing?* I needed to slow down the train.

"Okay. Give me a few days to find an attorney."

The next day, I called Grace for attorney references, and in two days, I sat across from one in an office. I had sent her the agreement in advance of the meeting. After some chitchat and background, she cut to the chase.

"If you sign this document as it's written, you need to have your head examined." She tilted her head down at me and waited for a response.

"But I assume this is just a formality. I'm not getting a divorce."

"Not now, you're not." That comment hurt and, frankly, pissed me off, and she saw it.

"Let me try a different way. Please understand that I'm not commenting on the nature of your relationship or the character of your future husband. Nor am I predicting dark days ahead. But my job is to protect you if things go south. And statistically, they go south a lot. This is not a formality, Laura. First, teeing up this agreement during wedding planning is coercive and in bad faith. The timing is no coincidence. It is designed to force you to sign a one-sided agreement without question because of the impending wedding and the money you've invested in event planning. That's for starters. More so, the contents of this agreement deny you everything in the event of a divorce, leaving you nothing but little more than the clothes on your back . . . and your dog. He generously carves out the dog. I mean, if a divorce happens—let's say twenty years later—you even have to return the engagement ring to his family. But much worse, you waive all your rights under California law in the event of his death. You don't even get the house if he dies. It goes to his parents. In other words, if he dies the day after the wedding—God forbid—his parents can kick you out of the home. It is clear that Mark doesn't have much in his name as of now but stands to inherit significant wealth when his parents expire. It is also clear that they do not want anyone outside of their lineage to have access to it. Mark's current earning power is not substantial. And for someone who has left her job, sold her own place, and used the proceeds to finance this wedding, it's offensive. It is the worst prenup I've ever seen."

I sat back, feeling overwhelmed. I lowered my eyes in thought. I hated this. I wanted to cry. I dared not. She continued.

"I am happy to try to negotiate a better deal. But this is so one-sided that I will only represent you in that effort if you acknowledge my legal advice in writing. If the shit hits the fan down the road, I don't want to be responsible for your decisions. It is that bad. You'd have to acknowledge you were forewarned."

I got up, thanked her for her time, said, "I'll be in touch," and left.

When my head cleared, which took a few hours, I saw that the prenup situation boiled down to handicapping two distinct options: signing the agreement with the assumption that the marriage would not fail—or negotiating the prenup and risking a wedding cancellation. As I saw it, the first option gave me a husband in a few months and a good shot at a happy life and family but risked a disaster if, in the words of the esteemed counsel, things "went south." The second option virtually assured my single status for the foreseeable future, a current life with no money, job, or home, and the loss of a boatload of money invested in wedding planning, including my parents' money.

I opted for optimism and a successful marriage and signed the damn thing.

To my surprise, Mark insisted we stay together the night before the wedding. I was okay with it. Tradition has its flaws.

We had dinner at the hotel, and from the start, Mark drank rapidly and excessively. I politely asked him to limit his intake, as I always did. "Please," I implored, "it's the night before our wedding. We need to be sharp and clearheaded." In one ear and out the other. He got drunk.

That night, we had uninspired sex. Mark seemed agitated and distant. I told him I loved him. He didn't reply. While we lay in bed in the silent aftermath, he jumped up and got dressed, donning a pair of jeans and a perfectly ironed button-down shirt.

"Where are you going?" I checked my watch. "It's almost midnight." No response. "Remember, I have the makeup artist coming at eight, and you are supposed to go to your parents until showtime."

"Yeah, I know, I know. I'm restless. It's all good. I'm going to the bar for a nightcap. Be back in thirty." And in a flash, he disappeared.

I fell asleep and woke up around 3 a.m. I reached out to graze Mark's side. He wasn't there. I sat up. "Mark?" Nothing. *Where is he?* I trembled. *What should I do?* I jumped up, threw on some clothes, grabbed my phone, and left the room.

I didn't know where to look. I dialed his number—repeatedly. Straight to voicemail. I went to the lobby. There was only one staff member there. For some reason, I didn't want to ask him for help. I went to the bar. I surveyed—not a trace. I even looked behind the bar on the floor. Same result. *Should I call 911? Not yet.* I went outside and found the valet. This time, I asked. He hadn't seen anyone. Then, I started having different thoughts. *Did Mark have cold feet? Did he just leave me at the altar?* I panicked. No, no, couldn't be that, couldn't be. There had to be an explanation. I walked to the back of the hotel near a veranda and saw the outline of a man sleeping on a bench. I hesitantly took a step forward and then two steps more. Unreal. Mark was sleeping on the bench.

I felt relieved, horrified, and confused. I shook him until he awoke. He opened his eyes, trying to recognize who I was, sitting up when he did.

"Why did you leave me here?" he said. The guy was incorrigible. His instinct in a stupor was to blame. I escorted him to the room for what remained of a night's sleep, this time in a bed.

The sun rose before I preferred. I was exhausted. It was 7:30 and our wedding day. I awoke Mark, an undertaking. The bridal party and makeup person were thirty minutes away, I had to clean the suite, and Mark had to be gone forthwith. Miraculously, he got the message, rose from his daze, did what he had to do to get his act (somewhat) together, and stumbled out of the room.

Grace arrived first, like a ray of sunshine. I was dying to share the drama of hours ago, but I was too embarrassed, and, besides, we had bigger fish to fry, getting me ready for my glorious day. A makeup session with girlfriends was a fabulous way to kick-start the day.

The makeup artist was an old friend. I loved his sense of humor. I knew he'd make me laugh, and he didn't disappoint. He had us all in stitches, filling the room with love and laughter as Grace zipped me into my gown, and I was poised to become Ms. Mark Corbin. Mission accomplished, the ladies went elsewhere for photos. I walked them to the door and bid them adieu. Grace lingered a few seconds. She turned to me as the others walked down the hall.

"I love you," she said.

"More," I responded, as I always did.

She started to leave, stopped, exhaled, and turned around. "One more thing," she said, "you don't have to do this."

She knew me like a book and sensed something wrong. My eyes teared up. *I'm happy, right? I'm only having normal wedding day jitters, right?* My mind reeled. I could feel the looming excitement of my dad corralling my arm as he led me down the aisle, giving his daughter away to the man of her dreams. I could see my handsome husband smiling ear to ear as we ambled toward him. I basked in the beaming faces of the assembled guests and absorbed the magnificent setting amid the Santa Monica Mountains. I could hear us read our vows and tingled from the security of the ring slipping onto my finger. I imagined the prolonged kiss we would share after they pronounced us "husband and wife" and anticipated a swell of pride as the master of ceremonies said, "Let's all raise a glass for the first time to Mr. and Mrs. Corbin."

I smiled at Grace and said, "Yes, my friend, I do."

13

Jessica

I rented my place and moved in with Collin in record time. I was homesick at first. I had left a cute house in a vibrant neighborhood where I'd lived for years. I had routines and the usual familiarities. Change isn't always easy, but it passes. I once saw a sign by construction roadwork that said, "Temporary Inconvenience, Permanent Improvement." That, I hoped, summed it up. Harper, on the other hand, didn't bat an eyelash despite the loss of a well-established walking route. Dogs are like that—resilient and adaptable.

Collin made me feel at home. But when I started floating ideas about changing a few things here and there, he pulled the welcome mat away. This, I quickly realized, was the first hurdle. I appreciated that he saw the home as "his" place, and understandably so, and that it reflected "his" sensibilities. But to me, while respectful of his legal ownership, I saw this as "our" living space, and it should reflect, to some extent at least, both our preferences and styles. I wasn't thinking of a fundamental overhaul, only a few touches to reflect that I lived there, too. It was, in fairness, early, and I realized that he, too, had to adjust to sharing his space. I decided to give him some rope and bide my time. I was thrilled to be with him on a regular basis. It was a step in the right direction.

A week in, Collin complained about the "energy"—meaning the noise—of the animals frolicking together. Prince and Harper enjoyed each other's company and loved to tear around the house in a never-ending cat and dog chase. I found it funny. Collin didn't. So, I proposed, "How about some boundaries for them, like no balls inside?"

"Good," he said. Problem solved.

The next night, while watching a movie, I noticed Collin rubbing his eyes.

"You know, ever since you moved in, my eyes have itched," he said. "You think it's the perfume?"

"I wouldn't think so. I've been wearing the same brand forever."

"No, it's not you. I think it might be Harper."

"But you aren't allergic to Prince."

"Yeah, but Prince is a cat, and I'm not allergic."

"Ah, true . . . well, you'll get used to it, I'm sure."

"You don't get used to a dog if you are allergic to it!"

"Okay, okay, down, boy. I'll pick up allergy medicine tomorrow. Not a problem."

"Absolutely not. I have no interest in taking medication for a dog that isn't mine," he said with a petulant tone that intimated *this discussion is over*.

Was he insinuating what I thought he was?

I was up first the next morning. When Collin came down, I asked if he wanted coffee. No answer. I followed up with "Are you upset?" Silence again. I shook my head in disgust, and not wanting to engage in his childish playground theatrics, I left for work.

After I eased into the workday and my head cleared, I decided not to stand on ceremony. I texted Collin around 10 a.m., asking to meet for dinner in Orange County at a new restaurant that had garnered rave reviews. No response. Around noon, I texted, "Are you okay?" Nothing. At 2:30, I called and got sent to voicemail, a Collin black hole since, for reasons I didn't quite get, he almost never checked it. I left no message.

The longer he ghosted me, the more anxious I became. I reviewed the situation. Our issues in our brief cohabitation were of one type: who controls the living space, him or us? I couldn't help but think Collin might have second thoughts about the move-in, along the lines of *be careful what you wish for*. The more I thought of it, the worse I felt.

I texted Collin's housekeeper, seeking his whereabouts. Her quick response was *He is here, been here most of the day.* Not a good sign. He was for sure ghosting me, and I hated when he did that. But the more momentous question was whether he was revisiting the initial decision that we live together. Were we done before we started?

I finished work at 6 p.m. and headed to LA. By this time, I had cascaded down the slippery path of self-doubt. *Is any of this my fault? Am I not being fair to him? Did I not show sufficient empathy regarding the allergy? Did I move too fast, wanting to change things in a home where he'd lived for many years? Am I being insecure or, worse, dramatic, overreacting to his initial reactions that, in time, might smooth over?*

I arrived at our (his?) place and entered through the garage. I found Collin on the couch, reading his phone. He didn't look up.

"Hey, what's up? Been trying to reach you all day," I said, trying to sound cheery.

He said nothing, not even hello, and got up and went to his office. I followed him.

"Collin, we need to be able to communicate. Please talk to me."

"I tried to talk to you last night, but you didn't seem to care that I'm allergic to your dog." He shuffled some papers on his desk.

"Of course, I care, but what do you want me to do?"

"Here's an idea. How about taking Harper to your brother's? He loves being there, and they have a dog." He had given this some thought.

"Are you seriously suggesting I give my dog away?"

"That's just the thing. You wouldn't be giving him away. It's your *brother*, Harper *loves* Lefty, and you'd be able to see him *all the time*. What's the big deal? I mean, if you think about it, it's a small sacrifice for our future."

Ouch. *Good one.* I took a moment to measure my next words.

"What if I asked you to relocate Prince? How'd you feel?"

"I'd miss him, but I'd do what was right to make you happy. You'd be more important than my dog, especially since Prince would still be in my life. It'd be like creating a win-win out of an unfortunate situation." Another nice play, I had to admit. I took a breath.

"Well, what'd make me happy is keeping Harper."

"Well, then, I guess you have a decision to make."

Wow. Tears streamed down my face. Collin dropped his shoulders in recognition.

"Look, I don't want to argue, but I'm allergic, and I can't change that."

He left the room. I sat in the chair in his office, my head spinning. I couldn't believe this. My home is rented. I just moved in with a man I love. Harper is my baby. And I don't even know if my brother would consider taking him. I needed time to digest this. Right now, giving Harper away—and that's what it would be—was inconceivable.

I went for a run with Harper. When I returned, I sat outside, and Collin came out and squeezed my shoulder affectionately.

"My love, I love you, I want a family with you, but I can't feel sick in my own home. I can't get comfortable with it. It's not the end of the world."

"Collin, I understand your situation, but it *is* a big deal, a *major* deal."

"Listen, don't be so sensitive. It's not as if he'd be going a shelter. He'd go to your brother's place to hang with another dog."

"Please, Collin, have a little empathy. This is my dog we're talking about."

And around and around we went.

On the way to work the next morning, I stopped at my brother's. He wasn't there, so I explained the situation to my sister-in-law. She said they'd been considering a companion for Lefty, and if I wanted, they'd be more than happy to take Harper, with "unrestricted visiting rights!" The kids would be overjoyed, she added. She gave me a big hug. I slept on it.

The next day, with a heavy heart, I delivered Harper to them and cried all the way home.

The loss of Harper pushed to the front burner the idea of building a family. We both wanted one. I was anxious. During lunch one Saturday, out of the blue, the topic came up.

"People shouldn't get married unless they want kids," Collin said.

"Well, that fits us fine, I'd say. We both want a family."

"Uh-huh, at *some* point."

"At *some* point? Keep in mind," I said, "I'm not getting any younger."

He chuckled. "You are so young."

"Well, thank you. That may well be, but don't forget my issue."

Collin nodded and squinched his mouth as if he'd forgotten, but he knew of my past surgeries, which skewed the odds of getting pregnant and delivering a child. And, worse, the older I got, my personal problem compounded, drastically lowering the odds. My biological clock had its own handicap.

"Jessica, I want to have a child with you. I love you, and you are going to be an amazing mother. Let's focus on this."

I made an appointment with my OB-GYN, Dr. Glen Simmons, to discuss the chances of a pregnancy. While I was in the waiting room, a woman arrived with the cutest baby bump and sat next to me. It gave me shudders. I was excited to explore my situation with Dr. Simmons. When we sat down, we reviewed my history. He kept his cards close, wanting to run tests, and once the results were in hand, we'd reconvene to assess.

Later that evening, I told Collin about the Simmons visit.

"Great, that's exciting."

"Will you come with me when we go over the test results?"

"Sure."

A week later, Collin and I arrived at Dr. Simmons's office. I was nervous; Collin was cool and collected. After I introduced them, we got down to business. Dr. Simmons peeked at my file as if biding his time, and several seconds later, he exhaled and raised his eyes.

"Jessica and Collin, unfortunately, because of the gynecological history, as things stand, you have less than a ten percent chance of conceiving."

I looked at Collin. He showed no reaction, staring straight ahead. I cried. Dr. Simmons waited until the sobs ebbed and said we could try a few things "to improve the odds," but it would be, "in the best of cases, an uphill battle." We discussed the options. Collin and I both thanked him, and I closed with "Collin and I have some thinking to do."

I spent the evening in a major funk, not wanting to discuss the dreadful news. Collin gave me space. The next night, we explored the treatments Dr Simmons recommended, which were designed to stimulate my ovaries, which timed attempts to conceive precisely with ovulation. The game plan was to start the program when my next cycle began. I remained hopeful. I hadn't given up. Collin was supportive.

A week later, Collin and I reviewed the game plan while lunching in LA. As we did, he stopped, smiled, and looked lovingly at me.

"You have beautiful skin. I love holding your hands. I'd like them even better with a beautiful emerald-cut diamond looking back at me."

I smiled and said, "No argument there."

After lunch, we went to a jewelry store. After scanning the goodies, Collin asked them to size my finger. Then, Collin said, "Step outside, my love. Let me finish up." The excitement inside of me escalated. I started having visions of Collin getting down on one knee and asking me to marry him. *Is this happening?*

He exited the store with a bag and said nothing. Nor did I. When we got home, he went into the office, returned without the bag, and poured us each a glass of wine. My heart pounded. He took a deep breath and said, "Jessica, I love you so much. I'm so happy with you." He raised his glass and said, "To us." I raised my glass to his, we clinked, and I said, "Yes, to us." He responded, "KFC?" At this point, I was expecting a ring, not a bucket of chicken. *Perplexing. But was he just waiting for a special moment to make the proposal more memorable?* So I went with the flow and waited for that special day to come . . .

14

If You Knew, Would You Say I Do?

DR. BRENNAN: We are back with Laura and Jessica, with some major developments since we last spoke. Laura, a ring! Jessica, you moved in. Tell us more.

LAURA: The way he planned the engagement was nothing short of perfect. He set up this spectacular proposal; it was a night I will never forget. To say I was excited is an understatement. I had no reason to believe this was going to be anything other than happily ever after. It was a dream moment.

DR. BRENNAN: Laura, I hear you. It certainly sounded like a magical night. At this point, the last thing you were looking for were red flags and reasons to say no. It is understandable that you were swept up in the moment with the man you were in love with—and who you believed loved you. Any observer would be hard-pressed to see any major hiccups in the relationship, never mind signs of mental illness. I see this daily, and truthfully, it takes education, training, and experience to discern the difference between poor relationship behavior and inappropriate, unhealthy—and worse—dangerous behavior. Things like gaslighting, the need for twenty-four-seven contact, isolation, the silent treatment, obsessive control, and major future-faking are all reasons to pause. They sometimes masquerade as caring, doting, or enthusiastic attention. But the truth is, in the beginning, when the love bombing is intense and the connection at its highest, it's nearly impossible to see your partner as a nefarious monster. He had you where he wanted you.

LAURA: You are so right. I didn't think to hit the pause button because I was all in. Knowing what I know now, I wouldn't just pause;

I would slam on the brakes and jump out of the car!

JESSICA: Oh, my God, me too. I was intoxicated by Collin's attention and future-faking. I believed every word he said. In fact, his sweet landscaper tried to warn me and said, "How do you live with Dr. Jekyll and Mr. Hyde?" I looked at him like he had three heads. I thought *he* was crazy.

Only, he knew! He had worked for Collin for twenty years and knew what he was capable of.

DR BRENNAN: Most people starting new relationships are on their best behavior. The reality is, however, that the narcissist enters a relationship on high alert, with a completely different agenda than a healthy person. They are looking to consume and condition you so they have full control over you. The fast pace they use to prove their commitment is a warning sign.

LAURA: I was on such a high from the engagement. Then we went to his sister's, and I'm expecting his family to at least acknowledge our commitment to each other. Instead, his other sister throws a spatula by my head while berating and belittling her husband. To make matters worse, his father's best friend kills himself later that evening, and they blame the girlfriend like it was a normal occurrence. They didn't miss a beat! Can someone pass the croissants, please? Bunch of freaks.

DR. BRENNAN: That's a good point, Laura. We tend to excuse behaviors because of the way narcissists groom us to hold them in high regard. We have little reason to disbelieve what they tell us. By this point, you were embedded in a cycle of abuse, which made you ripe to believe anything he told you, and if you expressed doubt, you got gaslit and told you were crazy or too sensitive or wrong. The skilled narcissist has targets coming and going emotionally. Mark's family asserted that the girlfriend drove the friend to end his life, and you believed it. Mark grew up with toxicity, so it was normal for him. As you said, "Please pass the croissants."

JESSICA: Can we talk for a minute about the whirlwind trip I was on with Collin? One night dining with Stefano and his beautiful wife and the next swimming in oversized champagne glasses with Stefano and his girlfriend du jour. None of my business, I know, but I kept coming back to that phrase: "If you want to know who someone is, take a hard look at their friends."

DR BRENNAN: Remember, everyone in the narcissist entourage serves a purpose and fills a role. None of the relationships are genuine. No accumulation of your time or loyalty matters to them. It is only what you can offer them today. They will cut out a person who has stood by them for twenty-five years in a nanosecond, without a second thought or looking back. It's eerie stuff.

LAURA: Yep, when was the last time Collin spoke to his best friend, Stefano?

JESSICA: Exactly, they no longer speak. One of the saddest parts of this addictive love-bombing and devaluation phase is that I was so hooked that I made major sacrifices to prove my loyalty, which I see now was exactly what he wanted. Not unlike Laura, I moved into Collin's home and rented mine without an actual commitment other than his words. But worst of all, he had me give Harper to my brother, convincing me that his dog allergies, and thus my dog, stood between us and future life together.

DR. BRENNAN: Sadly, Jessica, narcissists slowly take everything you love away until there is nothing left, not even yourself. Your sacrifices only serve to intensify the trauma bomb, and in that instance, it enhanced Collin's power and control. Trauma bonds are formed much like addictions to drugs, following a pervasive pattern of highs and lows. When the abuser pulls their love away, the victim obsessively longs for attention and approval again. Once the narcissist serves that hit of validation, the anxiety and pain are washed away.

JESSICA: When I didn't immediately agree to see if my brother would take Harper, Collin felt I was defying him and not putting him first. Essentially, I was intimidated and convinced this would jeopardize our future.

DR. BRENNAN: When you defy or slight a narcissist, punishment is warranted in their eyes. Collin used the silent treatment, a powerful tool that invokes insecurities, including fear of losing the relationship. Being shut out is painful and not much different from when kids ignore you on the playground when you have done nothing wrong. It hurts and makes you question whether you are worthy or lovable. Over time, you become conditioned to expect to be erased when you defy the narcissist, so you avoid it as best you can, putting the narcissist in a position of power. Make no mistake, the silent treatment is a form of abuse.

JESSICA: Exactly how I was feeling. I felt so vulnerable. He was able to shift the blame and make me feel guilty for not prioritizing his allergies over my relationship with Harper. To make it more intense, he dangled the hope of marriage and children. The kicker is, as it turned out, Collin never had a dog allergy. How cruel? As I agonized over giving my dog away, Collin just didn't want two animals running around the house making noise. Sick!

DR. BRENNAN: Blame shifting is a common gaslighting tactic. It occurs when narcissists commonly twist situations; you ask yourself, "Am I to blame?" They love it when you make sacrifices for them. It gives them a feeling of control. They know that the more they break you and the more you do for them, the harder it will be for you to find the strength to leave. Laura, when you sold everything, you were under Mark's complete financial control, and similarly, Jessica, your place was rented, so you were at Collin's mercy to a considerable extent. All these behaviors just served to intensify the trauma bond.

LAURA: Imagine how bad I felt, asking my hardworking dad to help pay for my wedding when Mark certainly could have contributed more. Looking back, it kills me. It took me years to pay him back, and later, you'll see the spell he had on my family as well.

DR BRENNAN: This was the beginning of Mark's financial abuse. His agenda was to deplete your savings from the sale of your condo while you and your family paid for a fabulous wedding—so his family and friends could be impressed. When a narcissist reaches their goal of financial dependence, it is much more difficult to leave. Financial abuse can leave someone desperate and dependent, and slowly but surely, he was achieving his goal. The narcissist is always ten steps ahead. Each move they make is a means to an end, often through manipulation and abuse. Those caught in their web have no idea until it's too late.

That's all the time we have today. Please don't miss our next podcast with Laura and Jessica; it's going to get even more intense.

I am your host, Dr. Jules Brennan. Until next time. *If you knew, would you say I do?*

Thanks for listening.

15

Laura

Mark was a creature of habit. A particular kind. He liked to reprise experiences whenever people treated him like a rock star—with unconditional adulation. I didn't mind the back seat. It suited me. Besides, I was married and in love, and we were in Italy on our honeymoon. My heart was whole. With the way I felt, we could have been anywhere on the planet.

The morning of our first full day, we went to a car rental company to get us to Milano. We first surveyed the lot for options, and Mark, to put it mildly, was none too pleased with what he saw. Before I knew it, he and the manager were deep in a theatrical debate. I tried to get a word in edgewise to lower the temperature, but that further inflamed Mark.

No surprise, Mark prevailed, and we wound up driving away in a beautiful black Mercedes that had not been visible when we arrived. I didn't ask how he did it. I went along for the ride.

En route to Milano, we stopped for lunch at a seaside pizzeria. By that time, Mark had decompressed. He had conquered. He was good.

Out of the box, he ordered a bottle of Chianti, which he pretty much drank by himself, and then ordered another bottle. I was never a fan of daytime drinking. Mark? Well, he didn't need a watch to remind him it was five o'clock somewhere.

As we enjoyed the lunch—the thin-crust pizza was off the charts—Mark held my hand softly, and we talked about building a family. To think that I was watching Zach betray me with Jemma only two years ago was crazy. Time can be an ally.

"Come on, cutie. Let's go make a baby," he said, pouring the last of the wine down his throat.

"I think that is a swell idea," I said with a giddy girlish smile.

I had dreamed of being a mom since I was a little girl.

Mark got up, removed the car keys from his pocket, and wisely handed them to me.

"You drive."

I nodded. No debate necessary.

It was my first rodeo navigating the Italian Brenner Autobahn, which, unlike the German Autobahn, claimed to have speed limits. It became readily apparent that the Italians never got the memo. As soon as we hit the freeway, I felt I was in the middle of the Indy 500, near automobile anarchy. I became tense.

Mark was no help—a gargantuan understatement. He criticized whatever he didn't approve of, every adjustment I tried to make. As he bitched and moaned, I gripped the steering wheel tighter, flushing the blood out of my fingers; cars in both directions whizzed by in a blur. I tried to concentrate. I had to manage this. No way did I want to yield the wheel to Mark. The man had more than forty ounces of Chianti coursing through his bloodstream—and his agitation was rising.

Suddenly, my right arm got slammed by something. I thought an object had come through the window. But it happened again and again, three times in all. *Holy shit!* Mark was punching me. I jerked my neck around to look at him and quickly returned my eyes to the road. Tears seeped from my eyes. My driving got erratic. I wanted to pull off the road but feared making sudden movements. I began to panic.

Mark grabbed the wheel and pulled the car to the shoulder. I braked, and we came to a stop.

"Put the car in park and get the fuck out!" he said.

"What?"

"You heard me. Get out and go it alone. You're going to kill me," he said, contorting his face as if acting in a horror film.

"Please, don't do this. Don't leave me here." I kept my voice low. A screaming match was not the way to go.

"Fuck you, cunt!" he said, eyes bulging.

Woah. He had never spoken to me like that. Nor had he ever hit me. What in God's name was going on?

"Get . . . the fuck . . . out," he said, with a new calmness that frightened me.

I got out. My entire body was as numb as the arm he had viciously struck. Standing there in shock, I watched him pull away. As soon as he did, I realized my phone was in the damn car. *Shit!* I had no means of communication, didn't speak Italian, and had been hit by my husband on day one of our honeymoon.

I looked around, dazed. The world spun around me. Anxiety overwhelmed me, a nightmare in broad daylight.

As I tried to process this astonishing turn of events, I looked up and saw the taillights of the rented Mercedes. It had stopped. Then, it reversed toward me. *Is my husband going to run me over?* As he got closer, he slowed, backed into the same spot as before, and rolled down the passenger window.

"Get in . . . now!"

I battled two competing fears—getting in the car with a maniacal man or staying on the side of a foreign freeway alone, with no sense of what to do. I said nothing. My mind raced. I peered down the road, searching for an answer, and exhaled.

"I barely hit you. Don't be so dramatic. You're acting like a toddler."

His hurtful words floated past me. I was trying to gauge. I was in a potentially explosive situation. I didn't want to provoke him.

I returned my eyes to him, shook my head, and got into the car. *Path of least resistance?*

We drove without a further word, the atmosphere in the car as thick as chilly fog, arriving in Milano thirty minutes later. As we pulled into the hotel driveway, he broke the silence.

"Get yourself together before we go into the hotel. I don't want them to think we are unruly Americans. We're in Italy, remember?"

I wiped my eyes, gathered myself, and grabbed a wrap from my bag to cover the red, swelling part of my arm. I had packed the wrap to wear during what I presumed to be a cool but romantic evening in the city, strolling the streets of Italy and sharing plates of homemade gnocchi and gelato. Now it was dressing for my husband-inflicted bruises. I was stunned.

We weren't in the room five minutes before an inebriated Mark was asleep on the bed and snoring. *What should I do? Pack and leave the country? Call someone?*

I decided to do nothing and let the incident simmer. I would see where my emotional compass took me. I went out on the balcony to watch the street action; couples went to-and-fro, happy and in love, holding hands, mimicking a mood I had enjoyed hours ago—now dashed. *Could that be recaptured?* About an hour later, I heard the French doors open behind me. A shiver ran up my spine. I didn't turn around. I kept my eyes on the bustling street. Mark leaned down and kissed my head. I sighed, doing all I could to fend off a barrage of tears that begged to flow from inside.

"Come inside, cutie. Let's practice making that baby we talked about at lunch," he said boyishly, without a hint of acknowledgment as to what happened after lunch.

What the fuck? I wanted to vomit. He brushed my damaged arm, and I winced in pain. A blotch of dark blue had started to emerge.

"Mark, you hit me, not once but three times. What is happening to you?" I said firmly. I had reclaimed my sanity.

"Cutie, come sit on my lap. I'd never hurt you intentionally. You know that."

"I do? . . . You did!"

He dipped his head and scrunched his eyes.

"Look, remember when I told you I don't do drugs? The truth is, I sometimes take prescription drugs, and before getting in the car, I took a Xanax. I am guessing it didn't mix well with the wine, and I kinda blacked out." His voice got increasingly lower, and tears formed in his eyes, which he wiped away. "Sweetheart, I honestly don't remember. I truly don't. You are my soulmate," he said, pleading.

I wanted to believe him but wasn't sure I could.

Mark rubbed my back and held me tight, whispering all the things you'd crave to hear on a normal honeymoon. Those lovely "sweet nothings" rang hollow.

It was the first time anything like this had occurred. I wondered if his words held any glimmer of truth. I wanted this to be a freak aberration, a ghastly one-off. I wasn't ready, however, to embrace the explanation.

"Let's talk tomorrow" is all I said.

We went through the paces the rest of the evening—having dinner, avoiding the breaking news of the day, and trying to focus on the wonderful Italian culture. To my surprise, I slept well that night. I needed it.

The next morning, at breakfast, Mark could see I was still recovering. After making my coffee and serving me a pastry, which he'd never done, he tried to resuscitate the relationship.

"Look, I love you. I need you to forgive me. I guarantee what happened will never, ever happen again. It will be the last time I combine alcohol and drugs." I nodded and waited for more. "Forgiveness and love should be the glue of our marriage. You need to show me you want that kind of relationship. Are you up to it?" He sounded like a shrink speaking to a patient. "I love you"—that was twice—"and that is all you need to know right now—and that I'll never mix those things again."

Mark started moving in his seat uncomfortably. I continued to say nothing. I stared at him, trying to find the truth in his eyes. "Damnit, Laura, you need to forgive me. If you can't, we should end this now. You can tell your dad his stubborn daughter wasted his hard-earned money on a marriage that can't work."

That was a low blow. The thought of the marriage not lasting seventy-two hours horrified me, but it seemed a real possibility. I felt guilty. Had I dug my heels in too deeply? Was I being, as he said, "stubborn"? I kept thinking of my family. Mark had pushed a button, tilting the focus toward me and away from his insane (maybe) drug-induced behavior. *Rescuing the marriage was my job now? Okay*, I told myself, *he apologized, sort of, the way Mark does. Accept it and move on.* I couldn't let the marriage falter so early. I had to give him a second chance. I had to hang in there. "Okay, I forgive you . . . this time."

"Excellent. Let's go enjoy this incredible country." And we did. Mark was affectionate, loving, and attentive for the duration of the trip. We visited many cities and restaurants. We ate, drank, visited iconic tourist sites, and stared into each other's eyes like the newlyweds we were. Believe it or not, but for the early speed bump, we had a spectacularly normal honeymoon.

And we worked on having that baby.

16

Jessica

I accepted the exceedingly low odds of getting pregnant. It didn't get much lower than 10 percent. Still, I wasn't giving up. It was too important to me and, by all indications, Collin. Maximizing our remote chances required time management. The medical strategy contemplated taking medications to stimulate ovulation and having sex within a narrow time period thereafter. The windows were fleeting. We had to stay loyal to the system.

Not so easy with Collin.

His attitude was, well, if the stars are aligned, meaning *his* schedule—terrific. If not, we could opt for another time. His business schedule reigned supreme. So, we bounced around without consistency, extending the existing intolerably long odds. One step forward . . .

But then, early on, something unexpected happened: my period was late. *Could it be?* I was supposed to pick up my first round of medications on the third day of my cycle, but it never came. I called Dr. Simmons to explain, leaving a voicemail that my cycle hadn't started. As we awaited a return call, Collin weighed in. "Why don't you take a pregnancy test?" I was about to remind him of mathematical reality but elected to humor him. I grabbed my purse and bought a supply of pregnancy tests at the local pharmacy. I wasted no time taking a test on my return.

The line turned pink. I went flying down the stairs. Collin lay on the couch.

"Collin, look, pink, pink! I'm pregnant!"

"No way, false positive," he said, not moving a muscle.

"Stay here." I ran upstairs and took another test.

"Test two is positive!" I screamed from above.

"Take another one," he screamed back. So, I did.

"Three for three!"

"Holy shit!" He bounded up the stairs and gave me a huge hug. We were excited. No way could all three tests be wrong. *Could they?*

The next day, I called Dr. Simmons's office to relay the news. The nurse said I should come in for a blood test, explaining that over-the-counter tests are not always accurate, bringing me down a few emotional pegs. I went in and had the office test.

Two days later, the nurse called. Yep, the tests were accurate. I was pregnant. After relaying the amazing news, she said that Dr. Simmons wanted to monitor me closely because I was high-risk. I hung up, called Collin, and told him he was about to become a father. He was thrilled. Then I called my mother and shrieked into the phone. "Mom, I'm pregnant!"

The pregnancy news nudged the get-married issue to the back burner, at least for the time being, comforted as I was by Collin's earlier comment that "the only reason to get married is if you're having kids." We were having one, ergo . . .

For the next few months, Collin was his most attentive and sensitive. He doted on me like he'd never done before. At sixteen weeks, we went for a routine amino and were over the moon when we learned we were having a girl. I started to pick out cute little pink onesies and pictured her room painted like an English garden. Collin was supportive and let me nest and adorn her room just the way I wanted it. I was so happy.

Then, as the end of month six approached, he became distant. He stopped touching me. He no longer wanted to have sex—even though I was "the sexiest pregnant woman the world had ever seen." He was, to his credit, open about it. He said he couldn't get over the stomach. It zapped his sex drive. Hmm. Was I "too fat" for him? Was he afraid he'd hurt the baby? I was hornier than a teenage boy with hormonal superpowers. The no-sex thing was a problem. I also worried about what it portended for getting married. And the daily rejections made me feel unattractive and undesirable. Negative thoughts overwhelmed me.

The marriage proposal limbo tortured me, and I assembled the courage to get into it. I first asked about the ring he'd purchased.

"Don't you recall? It was an investment, and it is long sold, and for a pretty penny, I might add," he said, sounding like he had made a major conquest.

"You mean the ring *we* picked out that day?"

"No, I mean the ring *I* picked out... for an investment." He shook his head with a look that said, *What's not to understand?*

"No, no, you said it was our engagement ring." My voice was screechy.

"Jessica, sorry, your memory fails you." He shook his head again and rolled his eyes like he was dealing with a child.

"Collin, what are you trying to do here?"

He blew out a big belt of air and pronounced, "This conversation is over."

Later that night, I curled up in bed, scrolling through my phone with a heavy heart, wondering what my future looked like. With or without Collin? Single mom? As I tormented myself with a litany of "what-ifs," Collin peeked inside the door, a small bag in his hand and a devilish smile. He opened the door wide and tossed the bag softly onto my lap.

"I don't want you to suffer any longer!" he said, broadening his smile.

I looked at him sideways, opened the bag, and found a box that held the same diamond ring I'd picked out. I didn't rejoice instantaneously. I was happy, of course, but why the misdirection and months of keeping me in limbo?

I rebounded. While a far cry from a traditional proposal, I had the ring. We were getting married. Progress.

Three days later, Collin told me the family attorney had a prenuptial agreement for me to review and sign. "You'll need an attorney to review it for you." I was not surprised. I had expected to sign one, given his assets. I called friends and got a strong recommendation for an attorney. I sent her the prenup and got a call to meet in her office a few days later.

Once we exchanged pleasantries, she didn't mince words.

"Jessica, there is no way you should sign this without significant changes." I told her I was confident Collin wouldn't permit any. She shook her head.

"Let me explain," she said. "First, the financial terms are horrible. There are many horrors, but the worst is that Collin has zero obligation to provide financial support, including child support and alimony if you get separated or divorced. In either scenario, you'd be on your own.

"And here is another nonstarter: in the event of any legal action regarding the marriage, you are solely responsible for your attorney's fees—and *his*!

"Then there is a collection of truly bizarre clauses.

"For example, it gives Collin sole discretion to decide various things, including what religion to raise the children, where the kids will attend schools, how the children will spend their summers, and what vacations you two may take.

"If you commit infidelity, you lose all custody rights, *all*, a one-way clause that doesn't apply to him. Think about *that*."

She had legally flogged me. I didn't want to hear any of it.

"I know all this. I have read the agreement," I said with exasperation.

"Listen, Jessica. Please understand. This is the worst prenup I have ever read, and I have been doing this for almost forty years. It stinks to high heaven. While some of it might not be enforceable, getting a court to declare any provisions illegal is a costly undertaking—and not guaranteed to succeed.

"I cannot advise you unless you let me renegotiate this piece of garbage. If you won't . . . and that is absolutely your choice . . . I must decline the representation."

I reported the meeting to Collin.

"If you don't like it, don't sign it, but unless you do, as is, with legal advice, we can't get married. It's out of my hands."

I called another attorney and forwarded her the document. She called me four hours later and delivered the same message as the first attorney. I told Collin, and he said, "Well, you'd better call a third. A lawyer must sign off on this." I called a third. Déjà vu all over again.

I called a friend and reviewed the situation with her. She said, "Jessica, a man of his resources naturally will want to protect premarital assets. His family is pressuring him. He loves you, you want to marry him, and you are having his baby. Play the game if you want to be married. Find an attorney, anyone, and persuade them to do what is needed."

I called a college pal, Ari Cooke, a real estate attorney at the time. I explained the situation. He cut me off in mid-stream, seeing where I was headed, and said he couldn't advise me on a prenup. It was way out of his league. I pressed him. I didn't want legal advice, I told him. All I needed was for him to sign off on the deal, a literal flick of the pen. I explained that if I tried to change one thing, Collin would not marry me. I was eight and a half months pregnant and wanted our baby to begin its precious life with a traditional family, a mother and father. The thought of giving birth out of wedlock because of a document struck me as absurd. I loved him, and he loved me. True, the whole thing intimidated and scared me to death. But I knew the way forward. There could be no negotiations and changes. Otherwise, a personal disaster would ensue. He said he'd think about it.

A few days later, Ari called.

"I'll do it," but he added the caveat that our lawyer-client agreement had to provide that under no circumstances would he be responsible if this thing blew up down the road.

"No problem. I love you, Ari. Thanks."

The next day, I told Collin I had an attorney. After a phone call, he directed Ari and me to convene at his attorney's office the next day at 9:15 a.m. for the signing. When Ari and I arrived, we learned what awaited was more than a ceremonial "signing." Before we put ink to paper, I had to undergo a videotaped deposition to ensure I understood the agreement.

I couldn't believe what he—or his *family*—wanted me to do. For the next five-plus hours—yes, count them—his attorney grilled me on every word in the prenup agreement to make sure I understood everything and fully consented of my free will and without coercion to each of its terms. Ari had to be present for the entire ordeal (for which I paid)—or else no deal, which would set the stage for me becoming a single mom. I was sworn in, and then the questions kept coming, a drumbeat of little blows to my heart. Here is but a sample:

Attorney: Jessica, I want to direct your attention to paragraph 3(d) of the agreement, which we've marked as exhibit 1. Do you see that clause?

Jessica: Yes, I do.

Attorney: Have you read that provision before today?

Jessica: Yes.

Attorney: More than once?

Jessica: Yes.

Attorney: Please read it aloud for the record.

Jessica: "Jessica agrees that in the event of a marital separation or divorce, under no circumstances will she be entitled to any financial support from Collin, whether in the form of alimony, child support payments, or any other financial benefits. By signing this agreement, on the advice of her personal and independent attorney, she expressly acknowledges she will never request any court to award her any support and that by making such a request, she will be in breach of this agreement and forfeit any other rights it provides her."

Attorney: Do you understand that provision?

Jessica: I guess.

Attorney: You guess? Is any part of that provision unclear to you?

Jessica: I don't think so.

Attorney: What is your understanding of that provision?

Jessica: I get nothing if the marriage doesn't work out.

Attorney: And is that acceptable to you?

Jessica: It doesn't make me happy.

Attorney: Jessica, I am not interested in whether it makes you happy. I only want to know if you understand and accept the full impact of the provision you read into the record. Do you, or do you not?

Jessica: I do.

Attorney: And you accept that under this agreement, you may never ask the court . . . not so much as *ask* . . . to award you, for any reason, any financial support, correct?

Jessica: Correct.

Attorney: Not a dime, correct?

Long pause.

Attorney: Do you need the question read back?

Jessica: No, I heard it the first time, loud and clear.

Attorney: Do you care to answer?

Jessica: Yes, not a dime.

I endured this professional torture from 9:30 a.m. until 3 p.m.

while more than eight months pregnant, in a windowless room, with no food or water—except a single Diet Coke—pouring over the minutia of each provision, including legalese standardized terms, in a twelve-page, single-spaced prenup, while being recorded on video.

I told Collin during a five-minute mercy break that his attorney had treated me like a homicide suspect. Collin said, "Listen, it has to be this way." He grabbed my hand, squeezed it, and then kissed me on the cheek. "We'll get through this." *We will*?

Once done, Ari and I signed the deal, which cleared Collin and me to get hitched. Collin asked the attorney to please marry us on the spot, but the fang-tooth counselor refused, explaining the "optics" wouldn't be great if we got married moments after signing the agreement. *Really? How about the video optics, a chapter straight out of CIA interrogation training materials?*

Collin and I left together, first stopping at In-N-Out-Burger because I was famished after six hours in captivity. After, we went to the courthouse to get married, racing to get there before the window closed and managing to get decreed Mr. and Ms. Worth at 4:55 p.m.—smelling of french fries. Now that's an optic! Not how I pictured my wedding day. But a baby was due in ten days. I could breathe again.

We met my parents the next night for dinner. My mother joyously wrapped her arms around me and my father the same around Collin. We discussed staging a ceremony after the birth. My parents were thrilled.

The next day, Collin and I called his family to let them know we wanted to plan a small ceremony. They were pleased and supportive, but for one evidently major scheduling wrinkle: his sister wanted to plan the celebration around her nail appointment and her kid's soccer games.

17

Laura

Back from the revived honeymoon, we transitioned to the routines of our lives. There were no more rants or diversions into crazy land. We enjoyed the house, our lives, and each other. The good times were back. We were both so excited at the prospect of our first child. We explored baby names and agreed if a boy, Mason, and if a girl, Mia, paying tribute to Mark's insistence that each begin with "M." I loved the names, so there we were, except no child of yet.

Then, I missed my period, prompting an excitable appointment with my OB-GYN to find out whether it was our lucky day. Mark joined me, and sure enough, I was pregnant. Voilà!

Mark was beyond excited, and together, we shared the news with our respective families, both of which were ecstatic. For the next several weeks, Mark made sure I ate well and felt fine, each hour on the hour. The energy in our home was electric. We had turned the corner on the marriage. Each day was bright. I couldn't have been happier.

At sixteen weeks, when the inevitable baby bump showed, we visited the OB-GYN for an ultrasound. During the routine ultrasound, the nurse said, "Do you want to know?" We looked at each other, smiled, and nodded enthusiastically. She said, "Okay, then, you should paint the room blue."

I was ecstatic. A dream soon a reality. Mark looked disappointed.

We went to have lunch at a restaurant he favored. Once seated, Mark asked the waitress to bring "us" a bottle of rosé, "the color I wish the room was going to be." Mark went on and on about how he wanted to have a "daddy's little girl."

"Shouldn't we just be happy to be having a baby?" I said.

"Of course, you're happy. You'll get the little baseball player you always wanted."

"True, Mark. I love sports, but girls play sports, too. Let's just hope for a healthy baby. That's what's most important."

He shook his head with a mild look of disgust and said nothing.

"Why not order a glass? I can't drink now," I said.

"Worry about yourself and *my* baby. I'll worry about me. Thanks."

He drank the entire bottle and half of another. It was 1 p.m.

Mark criticized my driving most of the way home. I ignored him, relegating his voice to background noise, preferring to savor the fabulous news. Once home, he uncorked another bottle of wine and dove in, my cue to take the dog for a walk and get some exercise. Before I could leave, he insisted we watch a movie. Sure. Predictably, twenty minutes in, he fell asleep. I changed clothes, laced up my sneakers, grabbed Shiraz's leash, and bounded out the door. The outside air refreshed me, and Shiraz engaged in the futile but joyous exercise of chasing every bird and squirrel in sight. After about fifteen minutes, my phone buzzed. It was Mark.

"Where the fuck are you?"

"I'm walking Shiraz."

"Please come home."

"Okay, almost done. Be back soon."

When I returned, Mark grabbed my arm and swung me toward the kitchen island, like tossing a Frisbee.

"Mark, get a grip. I was just walking the dog."

"We were watching a movie. . . . You don't get up and leave me."

"Correction. *We* weren't watching a movie. *I* was. *You* fell asleep, and it was your idea. And, one other thing, be careful touching me; I am carrying *our* baby."

"Okay, okay, drama mama." *Drama* had become his go-to label for me. I evidently missed a career in the theater.

We returned to the movie, and lo and behold, Mark passed out again. I made tea and went to lie down, pulling a warm blanket up to my neck, with Shiraz by my side, and thought about what it would be like as a mama to the tiny boy in my belly. He'd be my world—that I knew for sure. I was giddy with excitement.

Mark vanished the entire next week on business, freeing me to figure out how to set up Mason's room. I favored antique white, with soft baby blue and a pop of yellow.

When Mark returned, he had a cheerful bounce in his step and announced he wanted to go baby shopping. Twist my arm. We spent several hours the next day in and out of stores and, among many decorative incidentals for the room, found a crib I adored. I imagined Mason sleeping cozily inside, which filled me with love. It was a glorious day. Everyone we ran into wished us the best for our new family. Shop owners commented about my cute baby bump and what an adorable baby we'd have. "What a striking couple." That evening, armed with a horde of purchases from Target, we relaxed and enjoyed a takeout Chinese dinner. I was consumed with happiness. After eating, exhausted from one of the best days of my life, I told Mark I was going to bed, with an "I love you." I got a nod in exchange.

At about 11 p.m., loud banging awoke me, and I dragged myself out of bed to find out what was happening. The kitchen was strewn with remnants of a wild party, bottles of alcohol everywhere, but no Mark. I called him and got no answer. I discovered him in the living room, talking loudly on the phone. He didn't notice me. I shook my head and went upstairs to a guest room to take advantage of a quieter space. I quickly fell asleep.

I don't know how much later—it seemed like a few minutes—but I felt someone jostling me awake. I opened my eyes to see Mark standing over me, his eyes wild, his forehead glistening with sweat.

"Get downstairs, dammit; you don't sleep in another room," he said like a lecturing parent.

"I was trying to get some rest, and you, uh, were . . . so loud," I said groggily.

"You have a fucking excuse for everything," he said, intensifying his voice.

I inhaled, stayed focused, and said nothing more. It was late. I was pregnant. He was drunk. I rolled off the bed, shuffled toward the stairs, and headed down to the master bedroom.

I took a few steps when something struck my head, and as I cringed, I saw a book crash onto the steps below and tumble down to the bottom. Mark grabbed and dragged me to the top of the stairs and onto the landing, ripping my T-shirt.

"Mark, stop! You're fucking hurting me!"

I tried to get up. He pushed me toward the tile floor and kicked me in the side, glaring at me. His eyes were black and empty. He bounded down the stairs, leaving me there, with the parting words, "Go to fucking bed." I felt moisture on my neck and reached back to discover a trickle of blood running from the back of my skull. My heart pounded. My only thought was my baby. *Is he okay?*

I stumbled to the bathroom, turned on the shower, and curled up in the corner, trembling. I had to get away from him. That much I knew. I had to save my baby and myself. My mind whirled, trying to patch together how the day went so sideways. How did we go from baby shopping and buying a crib to him striking me with a book, drawing blood, and kicking me? Was there too much focus on the baby and his arrival? Did he feel left out? It was too much to dissect. I remained in a fetal position until I was sure the madman had passed out. Shiraz licked the blood off my hand and gave me a look that dog lovers know well—he wanted to help. I held Shiraz tight and cried some more. I decided not to call 911. I didn't know where that would lead. I had to think. It was almost 1:30 a.m.

I quietly strolled to the bathroom door to see if Mark was sleeping. He was. I grabbed Shiraz and went to the garage, got in the car, and locked the door. I felt momentarily safe. Emotions and thoughts flooded me. I was filled with fear, shame, intimidation, self-doubt, and desperation. I couldn't think clearly. I was broken and confused. I was newly married and pregnant. My family should be starting, not ending.

I cried myself to sleep—until the sound of the garage door startled me out of my peace. I had so much fear that I could barely breathe. I thought, *What would he do if I didn't open the door?* I struggled with the intense, immediate decision of appeasing him versus the consequences of not opening the door. I pushed the door open slowly.

"Come inside . . . please," he said sheepishly.

I saw the Mark I thought I knew. I also saw a sick person, someone who swore to protect—not hurt—me. I couldn't find words.

"If you acted like you loved me, I wouldn't have done this," he said mechanically. *What is he saying? What more does this man need from me?* I didn't respond; I couldn't. In the face of my silence, I watched his initial somber expression change to mean.

"If you tell a single person about what happened, I will make sure you never, ever, get custody of that baby." I began to tremble, still sitting in the car. I didn't want to lose my shit. I wanted to stay dialed in as best I could. I wanted to get some control over the situation.

"Mark, what has happened to you? You pushed me down a flight of stairs!" I said firmly.

"Bullshit, Laura. You slipped. How can you say that? I'd never push you with my baby inside your belly." He spoke as if he believed what he was saying.

"You need help! This is *not* okay." I was operating with controlled anger.

"Laura, I love you. Please come inside. You are fine. The baby is fine. Don't make a big deal out of everything. You know I'd never hurt you." He was back to pleading.

Fear grabbed my throat. I felt trapped. *Is he psychotic?* I pondered the possibility of losing my baby to him. As one of the most prevalent and highly regarded attorneys in LA County, his father wielded considerable local power and was connected with people in the system. The idea horrified me.

I got out of the car, ending the discussion, but I slept in the guest room. He didn't protest. When I awoke in the morning, I decided to do two things: visit my OB-GYN to check on the baby and consult a family attorney.

When the doctor saw the gash on my head and bruise on my ribs, he said, "Wow, what happened?" I started to cry softly. I wanted to say, "My husband is beating me. Please help." But if I did, I knew the doctor would summon the police, triggering a legal morass that would risk Mark trying to take the baby or, worse, kill me. I was scared to death of what this man might do. I wiped my tears and said, "I slipped on a wet step and fell to the landing." He urged me to get an X-ray. I asked him to please check the baby first. He obliged, hooked up the ultrasound machine, did his thing, and declared, "The baby is fine." I later got X-rays. I was fine, too—physically.

I researched family law attorneys, finding someone affordable, at least for an initial consultation. I made an appointment for the following day.

Mark came home around 4:45 p.m. with flowers and a beautiful necklace—a diamond with *M* hanging from it—for the "mommy to be and our little Mason."

"Let's get you and my baby some food," he said, putting the necklace on my neck.

"Mark, we need to discuss yesterday. What you did isn't okay on any level."

"Laura, I love you more than life. It was a little book. You are so tiny that a sheet of paper could send you flying. Please, Laura, forgive me. Don't we want Mason to have the best life?" Dr. Jekyll had returned.

He grabbed my hand, looked into my eyes, and again professed his deepest love for Mason and me. I even saw a tear. He went off about all the places he couldn't wait to show him and how excited he was to teach him French. I let his words hang in the air without comment, hoping they'd find a permanent resting place. That night, he rubbed my feet and back until I drifted off to sleep. I woke up to a fresh cup of decaf at my bedside and a chocolate croissant from the French bakery, my favorite.

Please, God, give me strength. I want this to work.

Mark knew what he did was wrong, and maybe when little Mason arrives, he'll revert to the old Mark. Maybe. I couldn't, however, find comfort in any positive scenario.

Mark skipped work that day, creating a dilemma. How could I get to my appointment with the attorney? I contrived a promise to meet a friend to help her with career issues. He whined but took the bait when assured I'd be home soon.

An hour later, I was at the law offices of Joshua Kline. Tall and bespectacled, Mr. Kline sported a bow tie and a stiff and formal professional demeanor. He rose when I entered his office and invited me to take a seat. My heart and head buzzed about the room like a deflating balloon. Before we even got to it, I started to cry, and he pushed a box of tissues in my direction. I wiped the tears, gathered myself, and regaled him with my life. Down deep, I hoped he'd get up, come around the table, and give me a reassuring hug. But I knew that wasn't going to happen.

"Let me be honest. You live in a no-fault state, and if you go to battle, based on what you have so far, your husband will get fifty-fifty custody of your unborn child. Not because it would be right but because you have little proof of abuse other than your word, which, while valuable, will be neutralized by his, especially if it is revealed that you gave a different story to your doctor. It would become a classic case of he said, she said."

How could this be? I implored that my husband was beating me. I have bruises to prove it. I was speechless.

"The best advice I can give you, at this juncture, is to go home, and the next time he hits you, call the police to create a paper trail. You need to build a case."

Are you kidding me? Wait for the next beating? He might kill me. I was utterly distraught.

What should I do? I began to convince myself that I needed to build on the positive. Yesterday, we had a good day. My baby deserved a mom and dad. I know the "good" Mark is in there—the Mark I fell in love with. *And I loved him*, I thought.

No, I wasn't giving up. I had to solve this myself. I can fix this.

18
Jessica

Near the due date, the doctors found a fibroid obstructing my birth canal, which meant our best-laid birthing plans yielded a C-section delivery. Happily, that went well, and into the world came Alexandra Emily Worth, registering at eight pounds, eleven ounces and sporting a hearty mass of dark black hair. I had never known love like I did that day. The first time Alexandra put her tiny finger on mine, I melted into love tears. It was the most beautiful moment in my life.

That night, the C-section pain became distracting, and I had Collin summon the nurse. She appeared right away, examined me, and upped the meds in my IV to increase my comfort. I begged Collin to stay the night. He resisted, preferring a peaceful sleep at home. He finally caved and stayed. The nurse said, "I'll bring some sheets for the couch. If you need anything during the night, just let us know. We are here to help."

When the nurse returned, she plopped the sheets onto the couch. "Here you go," she said and turned to leave, drawing a quizzical look from Collin.

"I'm sorry. Can you please make the bed for me?" he said.

I couldn't tell if she didn't hear or was ignoring him.

"Can you please make the bed up for me?" he said with an exasperated voice.

She smiled politely and, in a professional voice, said, "Sir, I am a nurse. I don't set up beds for visitors."

"I don't do sheets. At home, someone does that for me," Collin said haughtily.

"Well, I'm sorry, but you're not at home anymore," she said. No ambiguity there.

"Honey?" Collin said, turning toward me.

Honey? I couldn't tell if he wanted me to intervene on his behalf or get out of bed and do the sheets for him. I looked at the nurse, who had turned her head, and as she was leaving, she flashed me a look that said, *is this for real?* I shrugged and smiled for her benefit, and she left shaking her head.

I was mortified. Collin had treated the night nurse—there to take care of me, to make my life more comfortable—like hired help.

"Maybe I should go," Collin said weepily.

"No, you should stay. I want you to stay," I said, my eyes rolling figurately in my head.

He exhaled deeply and plopped onto the couch, tossing the sheets aside. There, he stayed until I fell asleep and, as I'd learn later, for the rest of the night. He never removed his clothes or shoes and never made a bed for himself, sleeping through the night, sitting with his legs crossed on the small coffee table in front of the couch.

Over the next two days, Collin was in and out of the hospital, and most of the time, he complained about the length of the hospital stay. It didn't take long to see his lack of patience to keep me company, constantly agitated by how busy he was and all the things he had to do. I shared his eagerness to leave. I wanted to start my life as a mother, but I would have appreciated some attention and support, not to mention excitement about the start of our family.

Collin hired a nurse to help with adjustments at home. I was grateful for her, especially since Collin made it clear he didn't want the presence of his daughter to intrude on his own time and with the dynamics of his life. For example, after getting a dose of what it looked like in the hospital, Collin railed against my breastfeeding the baby. He found milk coming out of my breasts "offensive." I didn't stop, despite his protests, searching for places in the house where he didn't have to look.

Days after I returned from the hospital, Collin announced that he had a client dinner in two weeks that he wanted me to prepare. Thankfully, I talked him into using caterers. "I might have to breastfeed during the dinner, Collin." That did the trick.

Collin also did not want a crying baby disrupting his sleep, meaning there'd be no alternating sleepless nights. I slept with a baby monitor tucked under the pillow so I could bounce out of bed on red alert at the first signs of a whimpering Alexandra.

This was hardly the shared family life I had envisioned. I tried to persuade myself that we were in an adjustment period, that once things settled down, Collin would settle in, find a warm space as a father and husband, and become an integral part of the family unit—instead of spending most of his time on a remote island. But week in and week out, I didn't see promising signs, turning my hopeful thoughts into naïve wishful thinking. When I tried to raise the issue as kindly as I could, Collin took refuge in the "grave issues" his business faced, highlighting his role as savior of the business for "us." That is why, he explained, he was often gone, on the phone, or zoned out in thought. However you sliced it, since our daughter arrived, Collin was reduced to a stranger in his newly constituted family.

Imagine my amazement when Collin dropped this pearl of an idea. "Alexandra needs siblings . . . and there is no time like the present." The smile that accompanied the comment displayed how oblivious he was.

I recoiled in astonishment. The prospect scared the shit out of me. I was parenting alone. Adding one or two babies to the mix didn't seem prudent. On the other hand, I wanted more children, and to that extent, I had his attention. Besides, what were the odds of it happening? As far as I was concerned, we had won the baby lottery the first time, defying odds that bordered on the medically impossible. *So why not try? What's to lose?* Collin may have been flip in his comment, but medically speaking, there probably *was* no time like the present. And the worst case, it would improve our sex life, which had recoiled into hibernation. *Strike while the iron was hot* seemed an apt cliché.

I met with Dr Simmons. He said what I knew I'd hear. While the odds were against us again, we'd have to engage in the same process suggested before. It would include injections during the period cycle to induce ovulation, followed by lots of unprotected sex. It was all about the timing.

Six months later, I was not pregnant. Collin's consistent refusal to have sex when the medical odds were at their best, in contrast to when he felt like it, lowered the odds all the more. I had battled my way back to my pre-baby weight, but his desire had shifted. He often made disparaging comments like, "Why are you never in heels anymore?" or my favorite, "Are you sure you lost all your pregnancy weight?"

Then, this default mantra. "I am a businessman. I have to take trips for us to enjoy the lifestyle I provided. I am trying to sell my business. It is vital. I can't plan my life around your menstrual cycles." That speech typically brought the curtain down on further dialogue.

I stopped taking the drugs. His response: "Sounds fine. What is meant to be will be."

Collin insisted I quit real estate to devote all my time to Alexandra. His wife didn't need to work. I was content to devote myself to raising our daughter. It made sense at one level. But the reality was that Collin's life had not changed with the birth of our daughter, only mine.

Collin often blurted out how proud he was about having a daughter and being a father, but his actions didn't align. For one, he lacked an instinctive way with kids; he seemed oddly uncomfortable. More than that, he treated his daughter like a prop that bestowed bragging rights, a symbol to exploit in his social world. *Look at me. I'm a daddy.*

He had odd rules. He refused to install a car seat in his vehicle out of concern for damaging the leather upholstery. He wouldn't add child protective devices to the house that compromised its aesthetics. He opposed safety measures, like a pool fence and child locks, rationalizing that if I dutifully kept an eye on Alexandra, they'd be unnecessary.

I enjoyed his time away on his incessant business trips. For one, it spared me the constant refrain about things I did wrong. His absence did not rob me of affection. When Collin was around, I only got whiffs of love when he wanted something. I didn't necessarily expect our relationship to be what it was when we first started dating, but now he looked at me as if he didn't like what he saw, as if he had made a huge mistake.

He also stopped sharing information about his business. In the prior days, we'd shared our business experiences as a matter of course. Now, when I inquired about the imperative of selling his successful business, he said, "Let me worry about the business. I have my reasons. It's something I must do, or I'll be in trouble down the road."

"Trouble?"

"Don't ask a million questions, Jessica."

Once perched on a pedestal in Collin's world, I now felt unimportant and dismissed.

19

If you Knew, Would You Say I Do?

DR. BRENNAN: Welcome back, everyone, to my podcast, *If You Knew, Would You Say I Do?* A lot has happened since we last engaged with our listeners. Laura, your relationship has taken a turn, so let's start with you today.

You are a newlywed and questioning whether you've married your knight in shining armor or a villain.

LAURA: It was no secret that Mark drank too much and maybe dabbled in street drugs in his past, but after the marriage, it never crossed my mind that he had any sort of addiction problem. Nor had he been physically abusive. In hindsight, I see the pattern of emotional and psychological abuse that led to this, but he was so skilled at seducing and grooming me; I was blinded to what was really happening. I believed we were in love. *I* at least was, and he made me think he was as well. Looking back, by the time I said, "I do," I had already been financially and physically isolated. I had no money, and my friends were Mark's friends, except for a few women I barely saw anymore, like Grace. I chalked it up to lives taking different directions.

JESSICA: I'm sorry, Laura. I can't imagine what was going through your mind at that time, and you had no support system to lean on.

LAURA: I felt fear, shame, and embarrassment and wasn't sure how to reach out to anyone. I was a little bit paralyzed.

DR. BRENNAN: Exactly where he wanted her! Abusers isolate and control. Mark worked hard to weaken your connections to your friends and family, making it harder for you to leave. Once narcissists know you are hooked, loyal, and dependent on them, their masks start to slip, and the evil self unveils. Welcome to the Devils' Playground!

LAURA: I prayed every night for the good Mark to return, completely unaware that he never existed. It was a facade. A Mark masquerading as good made special guest appearances to keep me on the hope train.

DR. BRENNAN: Mark and Collin were adept at injecting you both with consistent amounts of reward and punishment, what we call intermittent reinforcement, to control you and intensify the trauma bond. No one can be prepared for how shrewd and manipulative the narcissist can be. With their pathological lying and constant gaslighting, they will confuse you and distort your version of what took place. They are forever the victim, never taking accountability for their actions and always armed and ready with a version of events that fits their narrative. Exactly how Mark justified physically abusing you with a logical explanation.

LAURA: Maybe I was naïve, but I had never seen nor heard of anyone abusing their partner. I was trauma-bonded, for sure. I made constant sacrifices to meet his needs and excuses to justify his poor behavior. I believed that if I just loved him more, I could change him. I wanted a family, we had one, and I wanted it to work.

DR. BRENNAN: Laura, that makes perfect sense, and most people in a relationship would think the same way. Facing consistent abuse, victims of people with NPD rarely stand a chance. The narcissist's slow, deceitful grooming makes you feel unworthy, confused, ashamed, not good enough, brainwashed, and seek their approval. Their needs always come first, and yours never matter. The abuse is insidious, and oftentimes, people don't know what is happening until it's too late. If he punched you on your first date, you wouldn't answer his text for a second one.

LAURA: Yes! I was so shocked when he punched me! It was surreal. I was stunned; my thoughts raced with disbelief. I was so vulnerable, and he immediately began damage control and entered what I now know as the "honeymoon" phase in the cycle of abuse. His apology and reasoning were plausible, and so I justified the behavior. He had me convinced that the drugs mixed with alcohol made him act out. He seemed sincere and genuine. His intense love and affection afterward made me believe he was telling the truth.

DR. BRENNAN: Narcissists are notorious for future-faking, making false promises, and pathologically lying. Their strategies are effective. One out of four women and one out of eight men are abused by an intimate partner in their lifetime. Listeners, remember, abuse is not only physical; it is emotional, psychological, financial, and sexual. I can't stress this enough: you don't need to be hit to be in an abusive relationship!

JESSICA: True, Collin had not hit me, but he cruelly stripped me of my dignity, broke my spirit, and almost took my soul. He had almost full control over me.

DR. BRENNAN: Yes, at this point, you are carrying his child and struggling with your upcoming nuptials. Listeners must understand that if you have a child with a narcissist, it gives them ultimate control. They will own a piece of you through your child for the rest of your life.

JESSICA: Looking back, Collin knew once I was pregnant and not going anywhere, there was no rush to give me the ring we'd picked out a year prior. I now know he enjoyed watching me squirm every time I opened a gift, hoping for a proposal. My anxiety put a skip in his step. He got a charge out of seeing me deflated and desperate.

DR. BRENNAN: Narcissists love to ruin special occasions, and he got a lot of traction out of that ring. They know how to keep you walking on eggshells to make sure you never feel completely safe. Narcissists exist based on other people's energy. Of course, they prefer adoration and adulation, but a negative, distressed response will serve them as well. A narcissist would rather have you spit fire at them and hate their guts than make them feel insignificant.

JESSICA: Just like he knew that I'd sign anything he put in front of me, no matter how detrimental it was for me, two weeks before my due date. At that point, I struggled with such cognitive dissonance that I wasn't in the right frame of mind. He wanted to marry me, he didn't want to marry me, he loved me and said I was the sexiest woman ever, but then he wouldn't touch me because my stomach was in the way. He had me where he wanted me, so I'd sign something not only detrimental to me but to our unborn child. The scary part is, he knew exactly what he was doing! It was well orchestrated.

DR. BRENNAN: Yes, Jessica, those were a few conflicting, opposing messages from Collin that caused anxiety and confusion and served to strengthen the trauma bond. The trauma bond is a main ingredient in the narcissist pupu platter of abuse that keeps you in the relationship much longer than wanted.

JESSICA: To add insult to injury, I was held captive in that attorney's office, and—one thing I failed to mention—his family then caused such chaos regarding our "wedding" dinner that we cancelled it because they were so controlling and toxic. Collin chalked up their pernicious behavior to jealousy, something Collin accused everyone of.

DR BRENNAN: Nothing the narcissist does is by accident—whether they marry you, don't marry you, have a baby with you, don't have a baby with you—everything they do is calculated, and their ultimate goal is to break you down, giving them full control. It is their way of grooming you to continuously succumb to their commands and demands, ultimately silencing you into accepting whatever you are given. Their needs are all that matters, and you are expected to continue to give them your everything for nothing in return.

JESSICA: Exactly. Collin insisted we have another baby and wanted to start the fertility medications right away, but when it came time for him to do his part, he became difficult. I was injecting my body with drugs, and he was unavailable when I was ovulating. I realize now that he did that to make me feel confused and anxious, like a game. After months of injections, I stopped, and he couldn't care less. *Whatever will be will be.* It was one gigantic mind fuck.

DR. BRENNAN: I see how that made you feel confused and anxious. Narcissists have kids for different reasons than emotionally healthy people. For them, it is the gift that keeps on giving because it ties you to them forever. They get to groom new little humans for certain required outcomes, the child becoming a pawn in a giant narcissist chess game. Children become insurance that guarantees their ability to abuse you forever. Especially if the child has distinguished talents, like a standout athlete or student, which renders them showpieces. Collin punished you during the fertility process—for precisely what we don't know—but it was cruel and calculated. It could be something as simple as him not getting enough attention from you as you were understandably preoccupied with tending to Alexandra or your pregnancy.

Well, that is all the time we have.

I'm your host, Dr. Jules Brennan. Until next time, *if you knew, would you say I do?* Bye for now, and thanks, ladies. Thanks for listening.

20

Laura

Counting the days to my fast-approaching due date, I shoved the situation with Mark into the deep background and bubbled with joyous anticipation. I couldn't wait to meet my precious baby boy, imagining the thrill of holding him for the first time. His room was ready, and my hospital bag was packed, including the sweetest little onesie in pale blue and a tiny matching Texas Rangers cap. His arrival consumed all my thoughts. I was in love already.

Monday night, as I got ready for bed, I had cramping like nothing I had felt before. I was two weeks away, dismissed it as normal body transitions, and went to sleep.

At 5:30 a.m., I awoke to a gush of liquid all over my legs. I shook Mark.

"Mark, get up. My water is breaking. I think this is it!"

He rolled out of bed, looked annoyed at the water pool gathering below me, rushed to grab a blanket, and shoved it under me.

"I don't want this disgusting shit on our mattress," he said, making the kind of crunched-up face a child makes when tasting food they can't stand.

Disgusting shit? Did he really say that? What planet am I on?

No time to deal with his antics, though. I got out of bed and called the doctor's office to report. The on-call doctor said, "Go directly to the hospital. You are having a baby today." I felt lightheaded, barely able to focus, and overwhelmed by a mix of emotions. I got dressed and grabbed my bag. Mark, however, took his sweet time grooming himself.

"Mark, we need to get going," I said with urgency.

"First, a shower and a shave. I can't go to the hospital like this."

I peered into his face to make sure he was serious. He was. After he emerged from the shower and dressed, he brewed coffee. I stood there, leaking water, dumbfounded.

By the time we were in the car, I was on the edge of panic, and when Mark stopped to buy an espresso and a toasted croissant, I nearly lost it.

"Have you lost your fucking mind, Mark?"

"Hold the drama. This'll take a second." *Will anyone believe this?* You couldn't make this shit up. A human being was inching out of my body, and this guy was ordering extra strawberry jam for his croissant.

By the time we arrived at the hospital, the baby had started to crown. The nurses hooked me up to a battery of monitors, and because I was not dilating, they gave me Pitocin, a natural hormone that induces labor. By mid-afternoon, my contractions had brought me close. I was half-giddy, half-delirious. If I looked like how I felt, I was quite the sight.

Meanwhile, Mark had summoned friends to our room and, ever the host, ordered pizza, sushi, Chick-fil-A, and an assortment of munchies, turning my hospital room into a food court. He tried to command the room but couldn't compete with the enveloping energy directed at me, which made him antsy. After the nurse left for a few minutes, he tried his hand at humor, at my expense, saying that when he took the wedding vow, "for better or worse, who would have thought the worst would look like this," pointing at me. His sycophants chuckled, but the nurse, who returned during the "joke," shook her head with disapproval and evicted his prized posse.

"I think you are ready to go. Let me get the doctor," she said sweetly, squeezing my hand.

Three intense hours of pushing and mind-reeling pain later, I heard the cry of my precious baby. *I love you so much, Mason!* A nurse brought him to the nursery for cleanup. Mark and I waited in the room alone, which had deescalated from frantic to quiet. I was drained to speak but in heaven. Mark said nothing, off somewhere else.

A nurse returned Mason to us, introducing his impressively strong lungs. He cried piercingly for hours. Not a problem for Mark. Prone on the pullout lounger, he slept through it all, snoring without a care in the world. The next night, the nurse asked if I wanted Mason in the room or the nursery. Conflicted but exhausted, I said the nursery and asked Mark to go home "to get some rest."

Mason and I were set to leave the hospital the next day at 10 a.m. I was overjoyed to start my new life as a mother. Ten o'clock came and went. Mark arrived at 11 a.m.

Mark hired a cleaning lady, Maria, for a few weeks so I could tend to Mason. At first, I thought, *How sweet*, until he disclosed that he hired her to make sure his clothes were clean. *Okay.* I was happy to have another person in the home, even someone I didn't know. Frankly, I felt safer with a stranger than my own husband and the father of my child. And better still, my mother was visiting for two weeks, flying from Texas. I was thrilled to have her and Maria in the house.

My mom's stay flew by, and before I knew it, she was headed back to Texas. I still had another week of Maria, which comforted me. When Maria's final day closed, I walked her to the front door, cradling Mason in my arms. Maria kissed Mason goodbye and hugged me. She had tears in her eyes.

"Take care of your mama, baby boy."

"I'm sad, too, but we will stay in touch," I said.

"I do this for a living. I'm not sad about leaving; I'm sad that you and Mason are living with someone like Mark."

"What? What do you mean?" I was stunned.

"He's a sick person. Something's not right with that man. I feel bad for you two." She shook her head with a stern and disapproving look, and out the door she went. My jaw dropped as I watched her walk to the car. *Where did that come from?* She hadn't witnessed any abuse. I was unaware of anything Mark said in her presence to warrant those comments. Was he *that* obvious?

A few days later, a crying Mason interrupted my sleep. The clock read 1:30 a.m., out of sync with his feeding schedule. But I supposed that happened. When I picked him up from the bassinet, he felt like a baked potato fresh out of the oven. He was on fire. I grabbed the baby thermometer: 101.8! I shook the dozing Mark. When I picked him up, I noticed a lump under his arm.

"Mark, Mark, get up. Mason has a high fever and a lump. We need to get to the ER!"

"For Christ's fucking sake, I'm not going to the ER in the middle of the night!" he said, rolling the other way in bed.

With no time to argue with him, I gathered a few things, put Mason in his car seat, and drove to the hospital without him.

By arrival, his fever had risen to 102.2, and within minutes, a team of doctors and nurses were attending him. I waited outside, feeling helpless and alone. I started to cry. About thirty minutes later, a doctor came to see me.

"We aren't sure, but we need to rule out soft tissue carcinoma, cancer," he said somberly.

"Okay" was all I could get out. My eyes asked for more.

"We need to do an MRI and run more tests to see if that's it," he said without emotion.

"May I come in?" I said between sobs.

"No, I'm sorry, that's not possible," he said softly.

"Will it be painful?" I was keeping it together by the narrowest of threads.

"Honestly . . . yes, at least a little . . . but we will do our best. It won't take too long."

It was a nightmare. They took my tiny little baby. Fear gripped me. I gathered what was left of my wits and called Mark. He didn't pick up. Unreal. I leaned against the wall across from the room where the procedure would take place. Three doctors and a nurse walked in, dressed in full surgical regalia. I held the urge to throw up and strained my ears to hear the banter behind the closed door—a low, indecipherable rumble, competing with Mason, screaming at the top of his lungs. I got wobbly, struggling to stand, and slid down the wall and onto the floor, where I remained, head down, crying softly.

A few minutes later, a hand placed softly on my head. I snapped upward, thinking I'd see Mark. It was, however, an elderly woman whose eyes riveted me, emoting pure love. She smiled and said, "Sweetheart, I felt your presence from my room. I was sent from above to tell you everything will be okay. Don't worry. Bless you." Before I could respond, she walked away, causing me, mouth agape and eyes lowered, to do a double take on reality. *Yes, that just happened.* I looked up in search of her. She'd disappeared. *Am I going mad?*

Minutes later, the doctor burst through the door with good news. "We don't think it's cancer, but we need to keep him here." He also brought some unwelcome news: they didn't have a diagnosis. I asked for Mason. They declined. I couldn't touch him for now. Nor was he allowed to wear clothes because of the high fever. Each second tortured me.

Several hours later, Mark sauntered in, disheveled and stinking. The first thing out of his mouth, literally, was whether the doctors were doing their jobs correctly. I answered with an eye roll, lacking an ounce of capacity for him and his childlike me-me behavior.

We waited forever for diagnostic information. It was maddening. I was so drained, so distraught; my entire being throbbed from stress. Mark filled time on the phone or took leave to go who knows where. I had virtually nothing to say to him. He provided no comfort.

That night, when Mark was doing his disappearing act, a nurse came over and, without saying a word, hugged me. The words that followed blew me away.

"I feel bad for you. Your baby will be okay, not to worry, but your husband needs serious help."

I pulled back and said, "What do you mean?"

"He's mentally off, and I'm not positive, but I'm betting he is on substances."

I defended him, focusing on the stress of dealing with all this. She said nothing; her crunched eyes and mouth conveyed skepticism.

After nine days in the hospital, Mason's fever broke, and he took a turn for the better. The doctor diagnosed a viral infection and the lump as a neuroma, not common in infants but not a major issue. The lump would go away without treatment.

That was the longest nine days of my life. Mark was useless. He didn't even bring a change of clothes for me. I had a friend do that. I craved freedom from relationship misery. I wanted the family of my dreams. I wanted normalcy. *Is it possible?*

Three weeks passed, and things went smoothly. Progress? To build on the momentum, I surprised Mark with a steak dinner—bone-in rib eye, his favorite. He arrived from work at 5:30 p.m. as planned and said, "Hi, darling," gave me a kiss, and, seeing the set table, said, "Wow, everything looks yummy."

Mark sliced into his steak, took a bite, made a face, and spit it out.

"Do you expect me to eat this shit?" he said angrily.

"What are you talking about? That's your favorite." I was mystified.

"Yes, medium rare, not this overdone leather crap you served me."

I stood and angrily said, "Suit yourself," grabbed his plate, and tossed the entire meal, plate, steak, steamed broccoli, and all into the garbage. I walked away.

"Why, you fucking cunt! You didn't pay for those dishes. Get your fat ass over here, and get the plate out of the trash . . . NOW!" He was screaming.

"Go fuck yourself," I said.

He stood up, pushing his chair aside so hard that it crashed onto the floor. His bulging eyes were menacing, his face beet red. He came toward me, and I ran. I dashed to the stairs, bounded up to our room, and tried to lock the door, but he wedged his body into the doorjamb, came in, and shoved me against the closet door. Towering over me, he picked up a bottle of cologne and threw it at me. I ducked. The bottle whizzed by my head and struck the edge of my shoulder, shattering, covering me in glass and men's cologne, drawing blood. He shoved me to the ground and left. I used my T-shirt to wipe the cologne and blood. Tears streamed down my cheeks.

I pulled myself up and locked the door. I examined the cuts, and despite the blood, it didn't look that bad. Miracle. Petrified, I thought to call 911. I remembered the legal advice I received. I had to build a record with a police report. But then I thought, *If I went there, would I unleash a process that risked losing my child to foster care or child services?* It seemed unfathomable. But at that point, my ability to discern reality from fantasy was severely compromised. I could not imagine any judge giving him custody rights. He was a certifiable madman and probably an alcoholic. Indecision held me captive.

When I heard the front door close behind Mark, I cleaned up and examined my injured neck. Not as much glass as I feared. I heard Mason crying. I went to him, leaning over the crib while tears washed off me and onto him. I promised him I'd do whatever it took to get away from Mark. He continued to cry. Concerned about exposing him to shards of broken glass, I jumped in the shower and rinsed as fast as I could, threw a towel over my arm, and then picked him up, tightly holding and singing as tears continued to drip down my face.

Thirty minutes later, I heard the front door open and Mark's unmistakable footsteps. When we faced each other, I backed up and tightened my arms around Mason. Mark thrust his arm and hand into the air, his way of saying, *I won't hurt you.*

"Can we talk?" he said.

"There's nothing to talk about," I said. "You need to leave."

"Laura, please, I want to fix this." He'd been crying.

"It's not fixable. You need serious help," I said, turning Mason away from him and watching his every muscle carefully.

"I'll do whatever is needed. I need you and Mason in my life," he said.

"You need to see a therapist . . . and when you do, you need to be honest about the drinking and abuse." He nodded a few times, looking down, processing.

"I'll do whatever it takes," he said, raising squinty eyes to me. "I promise."

I wanted him to disappear into the ether and allow Mason and me to live peacefully. I knew, however, down deep, that would never happen.

21
Jessica

After considerable delay, squabbling, bouts of drama, and many road shows, Collin found a buyer for his business, reaping enough money for him to retire at forty. For him, it was a new dawn, and from my perspective, it gifted Collin an uncluttered calendar to enjoy time with Alexandra and me.

The first few weeks featured a celebration of his brilliance, accomplishments, and business savvy. There were dinners, lots of sex, trips, and more family time. I had, however, counted my chickens prematurely. Not having a business to run made Collin palpably uncomfortable, a fish out of water. He lacked purpose and structure and became restless, searching for hobbies to fill the time. For a while, he drifted aimlessly, but then he fixated on a vocation of choice: offshore fishing and the hunt for big game in the deep seas. He began to charter fishing boats, his new life passion. He asked friends to join him, preferring an old childhood friend, Derek, a fellow entrepreneur. The Derek reconnection wreaked a troubling déjà vu. Derek had a thing for women half his age—à la Stefano—and like Stefano, he collected a harem of nubile candidates, alternating among them day-to-day, like a restaurant's daily special.

As with Stefano, Collin's preoccupation with Derek didn't sit well with me. Whenever I expressed disapproval of Derek's lifestyle, Collin invariably commented that if he wanted to cheat on me, he'd divorce me instead, always ending with "I love my life, I love my wife, and I'd never divorce you," topped off with a kiss on the cheek, the signal that ended the conversation.

Collin immersed himself in the new hobby, purchasing his

own fishing boat, a top-of-the-line sports offshore fishing yacht. He named the vessel *WORTH IT* and fancied himself the "sexiest captain," holding the power to dangle excursion invitations in front of a wide berth of friends, a coveted social perk. It meant that Collin left home for long stretches, sometimes as many as ten days. And the more seafaring miles he logged, the less interest he showed in me and Alexandra. In fact, what spare time he had was spent investigating new businesses to acquire and investment opportunities. He downgraded his family to barely an afterthought.

To the world, we had all the markings of a "normal" family. I cheerfully mothered our first child, and Collin presented as the successful entrepreneur who provided for his family. We lived in a beautiful home. We traveled to exotic places. We entertained socially and shared blissful moments with friends and family. On social occasions, Collin displayed heartwarming sentiments and uncommon generosity, professing love for his "beautiful" wife and "incredible" daughter.

Behind closed doors, a starkly different story held court. Pins and needles dominated each of my days, worrying, moment to moment, if Collin would ignore, belittle, or rage, an assortment of ways to make me feel small.

If, for example, I prepared breakfast, I anxiously awaited one of two reactions—a lecture about what I did wrong or praise for what I put in front of him. Flip of the coin.

When I made dinner, he wanted to go out. When I didn't have anything prepared, he wanted a home-cooked meal. If I made steak, he wanted chicken. If I made pasta, he wasn't eating carbs. Which way was up?

The house had to be in tip-top shape whenever he deigned to be present—no kid toys or bottles lying around. When I'd hear the garage door open, I went on red alert, surveying quickly that everything was in its proper place and hoping he was in a tolerant mood. If not, he'd fly off the handle and berate me for being "sloppy" and "lazy."

If I brought up anything related to my needs or concerns about our relationship, he shut it down quickly. "I'm not going to discuss this with you. Stop bringing it up." Or "What in your life is so bad? Do you know how many women would die to have your life?" If I displeased him for any reason, he'd punish me with the silent treatment or blast me with rage.

As time went by, silence became the safest course.

I never put the lie to the public facade he relished, suppressing urges to poke the tiger and tell the world I lived with a bully, an emotional terrorist, hoping things would change. I prayed each night for the old Collin to return.

For a long while, Collin restricted his disdain to the privacy of our home. But then he expanded his reach. For example, we once invited twenty people over for a midday weekend brunch. I handled virtually every detail, including the food preparation. It was a major effort, and I toiled tirelessly. I must say, it was phenomenal. About two hours in, however, barely having lifted a finger to help, Collin said in front of everyone, "Jessica, you are a hot mess. Look at the kitchen. You have become such a slob." That comment triggered a familiar feeling of inadequacy, a sense of being washed over, and I retreated emotionally inward.

If I confronted him about his mean comments, he'd deny they spilled from his lips, dismissing me as "crazy" or "delusional." Getting him to take responsibility for his words, to be accountable for their impact, had become a fool's errand. He could do no wrong.

In a span of six years—starting when Collin first flirted with me at the hospital fundraiser—my life had gone full tilt topsy-turvy. My personal world went from bright optimism and hope to dark clouds hovering over a state of hopelessness. Pervasive gloom eclipsed the initial joy that captured my heart. The man who had once drenched me in praise and adoration and treated me like his queen pulled a 180, kicking me to the curb, bombarding me with hurtful put-downs, and making me captive to his whim.

Yet I didn't give up. I toiled to create an amiable atmosphere to overcome the negativity and return our relationship to normalcy, like the early days. I dressed better, cleaned more, and was a better "assistant," more attentive, a better chef, and a more eager lover. The more I tried, the more he put me down and withheld affection and sex.

I operated from a position of weakness—financial dependence. Collin never let me forget that I didn't contribute financially to the family while, at the same time, not wanting me to work. When I decided to pick up a few clients again and get a listing or two to regain financial ballast, he'd find a way to occupy my time, making it difficult to regain ground in my real estate career. I was entrapped in the vise Collin customized, a catch-22.

Collin's behaviors fluctuated from one extreme to the other—like how Collin handled sex. He'd withhold sex for weeks on end. When I complained, he'd flood me with physical attention, which never lasted long, dashing flickers of renewed intimacy and returning me to the hamster wheel, confused and frustrated. Over time, the gaps in attention widened.

Then Collin fired a shot off the bow.

One morning, Collin left the house without a word about where he was headed, acting secretive. He promised to return for lunch so I didn't dwell on the oddity of the morning exit. As noon approached, I prepared salads for us and lunch for Alexandra.

When Collin arrived, he said, "Hi," and we sat down to eat. I awaited a report on his morning activity. Head down, his eyes darted about as if he was unsure or concerned about something, fiddling with the salad. He finally lifted his head, exhaled, and said casually, "I think I want a divorce."

I wasn't sure I heard him correctly. But he kept staring at me with palpable anticipation, his eyes eagerly inviting a response. I realized my hearing was fine. Fear pulsed through me, and tears flooded my eyes. I didn't know what to say and kept looking at him. He didn't flinch. I took a deep breath and gathered myself.

"How long have you been thinking about this? What happened to 'I love my life, love my wife?'"

He tilted his eyes down and didn't reply.

"Do you have a girlfriend?" My mind rapidly filled in the blanks.

"No, Jessica, this has nothing to do with another woman. I am not a cheater." He spoke proudly, as if it were a badge of honor. He shoved a generous portion of salad into his mouth.

"Do we have any iced tea?" he asked nonchalantly, as if we were discussing the weather.

I flashed him a look I hope conveyed, *you have to be kidding*. Visibly disappointed in my nonresponse to his question, he shook his head, got up, and retrieved a bottled iced tea from the refrigerator, returning to his seat. He opened the beverage and took a swig. He looked at me. I stared at him, expecting more.

"Look, let's face it. We have no passion. I want a soulmate and that passion we used to have." He raised his eyebrows and gave me a wanting look, expecting me to agree.

Part of me was not surprised. How could I be? Another part, however, said this was bullshit.

"We are a family. We should try to work on this, go to therapy." I tried to sound firm but knew equivocation coated my voice.

"Jessica, I like the family thing. That's why I stay—it's cute."

Cute? "Collin, do you love me?" My voice cracked.

"Yes, I love you, but not like a soulmate." Like a knife in my heart. I was devastated.

"Collin, please. Let's try to do something to salvage this. I know you love me, and I love you." I felt the pleading of my voice in my heart.

He shook his head. "I don't need some idiot therapist trying to convince me we should stay together." Anger had seeped into his voice.

"Therapists help, Collin. They see both sides. They are educated and trained to help people save relationships." My pleading had turned into begging.

He looked away for several seconds, deep in thought. Then he looked at me.

"Okay, if you find someone you think is good, I'll consider it . . . maybe." He rose, patted Alexandra on the head, and left. I sat there, immobilized. I dropped my head to my hands and cried. After gathering myself, I cleaned the kitchen, went outside, and called my friend, Skylar. I gave her a summary.

"Jessica, take a deep breath. So many things can be going on here. Maybe he's having a bad few days, or there is some other explanation. He said he may go to therapy. Keep that alive. Channel your energy toward finding a well-regarded therapist."

"Okay." I was struggling.

"How about calling Patricia Sherman? A friend of mine used her to deal with her husband's NPD. Sherman was hugely helpful."

"NPD?" I asked.

"Yeah, narcissistic personality disorder. I'm not saying that is what Collin has, but Sherman is a great therapist. She knows her stuff."

I heard what Skylar was telling me. I tried to pull myself together. I was shaken. I was also thrown off by the NPD reference. Later that day, I researched NPD and discovered some parallels. It gave me much to think about. For the time being, I needed to find a therapist—and pronto. I called Patricia Sherman and Howard Slock, another therapist recommended to me, and made appointments with them both. The next day, I met separately with each, grilling them to get a read on how well they might understand Collin and how easily Collin would accept them.

Both were qualified, but I decided to book two more appointments to provide a stronger decision basis. One was a nonstarter. He was too good-looking, which would trigger Collin. The other was an older woman with gray hair that gave her a matronly and mature look. I liked her a lot, but Collin disrespected his mother, and the paternal reminders would likely be the death knell. I selected Dr. Slock and told Collin I wanted to talk.

"I spent the last week interviewing therapists for us."

"Uh-huh," he said, his eyes fixed on the iPad.

"We have an appointment next week to meet with a gentleman named Howard Slock."

He looked up. "What do you mean *we*? *You* can go if you like. I went to one this week, and he said I am completely normal. There's nothing wrong with me," he said triumphantly.

"What? Why didn't you tell me? I have been calling and going to appointments all week to try and find someone for us to speak with. I thought we agreed to marital therapy." I spoke with a raised voice, which jerked his shoulders back. He shook his head, displaying a condescending smirk.

"Once again, your memory fails you. I didn't agree to anything. I just needed to get my head straight, Jessica, and move on from this for now. My head is straight."

He got up and went to his office and didn't mention divorce again. I returned to walking on eggshells while his life continued as before. I was baffled. *Why did he mention divorce? Why did he shut down the discussions? Is divorce off or on the table? What is really going on?* I was afraid to stay, afraid to leave, afraid of Collin. I was too scared to address it again. What was happening to me? I reinserted my head back into the sand. I had become a shell of the woman I once was.

I continued going through the motions of living with him, receding further into an emotional shell. I wanted desperately to leave most days but felt paralyzed. I was losing myself.

Alexandra was my priority. I had to focus on my daughter and find value and contentment. Alexandra was about to turn six, and I looked forward to celebrating the birthday with family and friends. I relished coming up with a memorable theme party for her friends and her. I loved being involved in kids' games and watching them with big smiles on their faces, hearing the sounds of their laughter. The party was an enormous success.

When it came time for Alexandra to blow out the birthday candles, Collin receded into the background to smoke a cigar. It portrayed his relationship with his daughter. He rarely did anything with Alexandra. He didn't swim with her or take her to playgrounds to enjoy the play structures and mingle with other kids. He rested on his inexhaustible inventory of "hi, my sunshine," passing comments and pats on the head, the sum and substance of his fatherly love. It broke my heart. Whenever Alexandra needed attention, I provided it, sometimes prompting Collin to say with derision, "Look at you, all mom all the time." *Yeah, and Dad none of the time.*

Collin continued traveling in search of business opportunities, vying to make deals here and there. When not traveling, he was out and about, networking, he'd say, to land new clients. He rented a beach house in Malibu, which he justified as a write-off and a suitable place to entertain clients. I helped decorate the place, but he declined to give me a key, claiming he only had two and needed the spare for clients. I rolled my eyes and figured he'd give me one soon enough.

The night before an overnight trip, I had a nightmare. I awoke in the morning to profuse sweating and a heart beating through my chest. I reached for Collin next to me and woke him up.

"What's up, Jessica?" he said with crunched eyes.

"I had a nightmare. You were on a boat, making out with a twenty-something girl in flip-flops and a bikini. You said you were leaving me for her, and then you both laughed at me."

"You're batshit crazy, Jessica, my God." He laughed, turned over, and went back to sleep.

I nodded. *Maybe I am.* The dream kept recurring.

22

Laura

Much to my surprise, on his own, Mark booked an appointment with a therapist, who, it turned out, had worked with him before. I liked the sound of it, but it raised questions. How did the earlier sessions go? For how long and why did they stop? I chose not to ask, content he took the step and fearful of rattling the hornet's nest, especially after unsolicited assurances that he'd "be one-hundred-percent honest."

After his first therapy session, as soon as he entered the house, he pillaged every nook and cranny where he had nestled alcohol and wine and poured the entire inventory unceremoniously into the sink. When done, he said, "One box checked."

For the next two weeks, Mark continued his therapy sessions—with tangible results. He wasn't drinking. I was cautiously optimistic—emphasis on *cautiously*.

The first major challenge was a BBQ at a friend's home. The prospects made me nervous, and I asked Mark if he felt up to it, knowing there'd be an array of drinking. Calmly, he said, "No problem, cutie."

The party was the most fun I'd had in a long time. Everyone was sweet and friendly, kids ran around having a ball, and the best, Mason was the center of attention. A perfect day for a new mom, and more than that, it was a window into future family life. I was beaming and had a surge that we might be turning a corner.

A couple of hours into the party, Mark sauntered over to me with an affectionate smile—and, to my dismay, an open beer in his clutches.

"Mark, what're you doing?" I said in a whisper.

"Calm down, calm down. Beer is like water . . . and I'm only having the one. Not to worry."

History—if not respected—can repeat itself.

Keeping a wary eye on Mark, I counted two more beers, making it a grand total of three. Ordinarily, in the scheme of things, three beers over a few hours at a social event were no cause for concern. But we weren't in ordinary waters. I had a pang in my heart.

For the next few days, Mark resumed his sober streak, and while I hoped the three beers were a one-off, a party-specific indulgence among friends, I didn't trust him. I couldn't. He had an unreliable track record, and any slip, given the behavioral patterns, could precipitate a regression. I had to insert myself more directly into the situation. I couldn't let him do this alone. Too much was at stake. I begged him to let me see his therapist. I told him straight up that I couldn't stay in a marriage like this, worrying each day that my entire world might implode any moment, that it wasn't healthy for any of us. He looked at me with sheepish eyes and said, shockingly, "I agree."

Days later, I was sitting alone in an office across from Mark's therapist. We hit it off. I liked her demeanor, and I thought she understood what I had to say and, more importantly, believed me. She seemed motivated to help us get through this.

"My advice is that you arrange an intervention."

"Okay. Did Mark admit to alcohol abuse?" I said with some surprise.

"Yes," she said. "He acknowledged he has a problem."

"Great . . . but I, um, don't know about an intervention. Mark lives behind a well-polished image. It's what he's about. An intervention would shatter that. I'm just not sure he'd be willing to go there. In fact, I am quite sure he wouldn't. It could backfire."

"I understand, but remember, there's more here than alcohol abuse, as serious as that is."

"What do you mean, 'more here'?" I assumed she meant the physical abuse.

"Your husband is also a drug addict," she said as if I should know. *What?* I almost fainted.

"I, um . . . I mean, other than one time at a big party with friends in Napa, where everyone. . . except me . . . did cocaine, I've never seen him do drugs. And he has told me more than once he never uses drugs. The drinking I know all about, trust me, but drugs, no, never."

"Well, he uses, and regularly, according to him." She was studying me.

"Wow," I said under my breath. I paused, nodding to myself. "Okay, look, he'll flip out if I raise drugs as part of any intervention. If he is using drugs like you say, he has managed to keep it a secret, certainly from me, and I suspect from others as well. Going there will be like walking onto a field of landmines. Isn't there a better way?"

"Well, how about this? In the next session, let me suggest he go to AA and get a sponsor. That is a small step, more private, and you can build from there."

After I left, many thoughts swirled in my head. Before I went to see the therapist, while hopeful, I felt boxed into the worst imaginable situation. Now, I saw that my imagination shortchanged me. It was worse. How had I missed the signs? Would he go to AA? Where would that take us? Should I consider the intervention? What should I do? It seemed odd that she was sharing this information. I felt overwhelmed, ill-equipped, and sick to my stomach.

When I got home, Mark didn't ask me about my session, and I kept my newfound knowledge to myself and started observing him more. One day at a time.

Sometime around midnight, flashing lights woke me, as if I were in a dance club. I opened my eyes to find Mark turning the bedside lamp on and off rapidly.

"Mark, what in God's name are you doing?" I said, shaking the cobwebs out. He said nothing. "Please stop," I said.

He laughed deliriously and walked out of the bedroom. *Am I dreaming?* I rolled away from the lamp and went back to sleep.

Not long thereafter, I awoke again, this time to Mason crying. I got up, walked down the hall, and as I entered his room, I saw Mark doing the same thing to Mason's room. *What the hell is going on?*

"Mark, stop it. What is wrong with you?" I was at a loss.

He laughed demonically and said, "Now he's awake, and you will have to get up." He walked out of the room and went to bed. I stood there, shaking my head, trying to fathom what was happening. *Is my husband having a nervous breakdown? Is he insane?* I didn't know what to do. I comforted Mason until he was asleep and returned to bed, curling up with tears and praying to God that I'd find a way out of this alive—and sane.

The next day, I sent Mark a text at work, saying we had to talk about the night before. He didn't reply. I managed anxiety all day, and when he came home after work, I confronted him.

"Did you get my text?" I said, begging for a reply.

"Yep, sure did," he said, walking away from me.

"You have nothing to say?"

"Yeah, bitch, I have something to say. If you want to leave, get the fuck out, but you will not take my baby. He belongs to me." *Wow.* I knew immediately that I had to keep it together. I could hear the time bomb ticking.

"Um, no, Mark, he is *our* child."

"You aren't hearing me. If you leave, you are gone, forever, and the baby is mine. I'll bury you and make sure you'd never see him again, and that, bitch, is not a threat—it's a promise." He continued walking away, leaving me trembling.

I put Mason in the stroller and went for a walk, crying the whole time.

Things got worse. While only four months old, Mason seemed slow to do normal things, like rolling over on his own and smiling. He often had this blank stare and cried a lot—*a lot*. When I took him to the pediatrician to get her thoughts, she said Mason was "developmentally delayed," and we should keep a watchful eye on him and report back in four weeks.

I shared the medical report with Mark that night. He ignored me, preferring his TV show. I grabbed the remote control and paused the program.

"What the fuck . . ." he said, looking up at me for the first time.

"Mark, dammit, the doctor said Mason is developmentally delayed. I am worried."

"Look, if he isn't one-hundred-percent normal, he is getting sent away."

"Sent away? What are you talking about?" I said, astonished.

"We can send him to one of those homes that treats kids who aren't one-hundred-percent normal. There is a place in France that my friend's cousin went to. He'll love it there. No way will I be embarrassed by a kid who isn't"—he made quotation signs with his fingers—"*normal*. Besides, it'll be good for him."

He yanked the remote out of my hand and resumed his show.

Mark had a way of leaving me speechless. I was stuck at a crossroads. I couldn't leave and couldn't stay. I went back and forth. The competing options were beyond awful. If I stayed, my life would be a daily disaster, and if recent occurrences were any guide, it would get worse. Before this latest turn of events, I had passing bouts of fear. Now I lived constantly in fear. Every day. I feared for my sanity. I feared for my life. I feared for my baby.

If I left, taking Mason with me to Texas, which I continued to ponder, Mark would undoubtedly unleash the full power of his family and resources to make my life miserable and try to take Mason away. He'd spare no expense, and I'd be virtually defenseless. He'd probably make up a pack of lies about me, say I kidnapped Mason, or other crazy stuff.

Mark got meaner. He made it a daily occurrence to approach Mason, lean down, and say comments like these:

"Mommy wants to leave me, and when she does, you'll be living with Daddy and never see her again."

"Once Mommy is gone, I'm going to send you to a special home."

"Mason, Mommy is a bitch and wants to leave Daddy, and you will suffer."

"Mommy is a bad person; only I can save you from her."

It got worse.

A woman I'd met through Mark's larger social circle called me out of the blue and invited me to coffee. It felt out of place, but I didn't want to push back, so I agreed to meet. At the café, we each ordered lattes and sat at an outside table. We exchanged innocuous pleasantries for about ten minutes before her face went from genial to grave.

"Look, Laura, I don't know you well. But I do know Mark. And you didn't hear this from me. Okay?"

"Okay."

"Rumors are circulating, within his family and social group, that you have severe postpartum depression and—"

"What? What are you talking about?"

"Mark keeps saying you've gone off the deep end since the baby was born, and he is doing everything he can to help you."

"Help me? Are you serious?"

"He's telling people you aren't a good mother, and he's trying to find a therapist to help you."

I wanted to scream. My mind was about to burst. I took a deep breath. I wanted to defend myself and tell her everything. But I thought better of it. I kept it simple.

"Look, I appreciate what you are doing, I really do, and your confidence is safe with me. But none of that is true. *None*. It is the opposite. I'll leave it at that."

The entire ride home, I processed. I had inside information. How could I use it? I didn't know. I didn't have much time, I figured, but I had to be smart about this. Mark knew I was on the brink of leaving and, playing the long game, had decided on a preemptive strike. It was undeclared war. I decided to play it close to the vest.

When I got home, he was there. I asked him how therapy was going, and he said, "Great." Then, I saw an opened bottle of tequila and a half-filled glass with a floating lime. I should have ignored it. I didn't. It enraged me. I grabbed the tequila bottle and emptied it down the drain. In seconds, I was on the kitchen floor, with Mark's hands around my neck. He cleared his throat and brought up a ton of phlegm and spit in my face. I tried to get free. He was much bigger and in a rage. I didn't have the strength. Then he let go and stood up.

"You know what, just go and take your wacky kid with you. Leave. But remember this, bitch, next time, you might not be so lucky."

The next day, I got ready to leave.

"Mark, I'm going home to Texas with Mason. We'll be gone a week."

"Bullshit," he said angrily. "Absolutely fucking not. You think I'm going to let you go home and tell your white-trash family that I'm a psychopath and steal my son from me. Think again."

"Look, Mark, we need time apart. It's only a week. We each need to clear our heads."

"Fuck you, speak for yourself. My head is clear, and my family isn't going to Texas without me—if you know what's good for you."

I had to stay the course as long as possible, not trigger him if I could help it, and come up with a way forward. I needed a military-style escape plan. I was a prisoner of domestic war.

From then on, Mark watched me like a hawk. He feared, justifiably, that I might bolt for Texas with Mason surreptitiously and brace for a custody fight.

A few nights later, a screaming Mason woke me up. It was 11 p.m. In between his belts of anguish, I heard adult voices, at least two. One was Mark's. I went into Mason's room, and there was a stranger staring at Mason, with Mark behind him.

"Who are you?" I asked the stranger.

"Herman, meet my old lady," Mark said, slurring his words.

I gazed at Herman, trying hard not to show my internal reaction.

He had teeth missing, looked like he hadn't showered in weeks, and stunk of booze.

Mark poked me in the arm and said, "Cutie, meet Uncle Herman," and laughed.

I picked Mason up, left, put him in bed with me, and locked the door. Two hours later, Mark banged on the bedroom door violently and said, "Open this fucking door now, or I'll break it down." I opened the door to see Mark alone.

"Who was that man?" I said.

"We met at a bar, and I was too drunk to drive home, so he drove me home in my car."

"Did you know him?"

"No, he happened to be there and free."

"Jesus, Mark, he could have killed us!"

"Calm down, drama queen."

"Calm down? I find a stranger in my house, staring at my baby, in the middle of the night, and you don't see a reason to get a little riled?"

He said nothing.

"Has your new friend left?"

"Yeah, yeah, the boogie man is gone, in a cab," he said with a jittery laugh.

"I'm done with this, Mark. You are putting our baby in danger. Please leave."

"This is my house, bitch."

He grabbed my forearm tightly and yanked me to the ground. I felt his foot connect with my back. The kick was so hard that I gasped for air. He said, "Please, get the fuck up, and quit the drama."

He detoured to the bathroom. I picked up Mason, grabbed Shiraz's leash, and sprinted to my car in the garage. Behind me, I heard Mark yell, "Where are you, you little cunt?" I put Mason in his car seat and Shiraz in the passenger seat. I remotely opened the garage door, and as it lifted, I floored the car in reverse and sped out of the driveway. I drove to the police station.

On my way, Mark called over fifteen times. Then the phone rang, showing it was my mother. It was 2:30 a.m. I picked up, thinking the worst.

"Mom, are you okay?" I said without saying hello.

"Yes, sweetheart, I'm fine. Mark just called and said you are having a nervous breakdown, and I should call the police to help you. He is afraid you're going to harm yourself or Mason. He said he called the police station and told them you are driving around recklessly with your infant child and are drunk."

"Mom, I am fine. Mason is fine. Mark is lying. He attacked me, Mom, and we are escaping to the police station. I'll call you later. I have to get there."

I called Mark.

"What's wrong with you, calling my mother and telling those lies? You are beyond sick."

He laughed. "She believes me. So will the police. You're done." He spoke nervously. I said nothing.

"Laura, if you go to the police, I'll kill myself, and I'll have someone kill you and Mason." I continued to say nothing. After a long pause, he continued.

"I will leave the house for a week. Please come back." I hung up.

I pulled into the police station and went inside with Mason and Shiraz. I explained everything to the person at the front desk. She had me take a seat while she summoned someone to talk to me. About ten minutes later, I sat in a room with an investigative officer. He patiently listened to my story. When I finished, I leaned back, exhaled, and waited.

"Here's the situation, Mrs. Corbin. We can arrest your husband, but he'd likely be free in twenty-four hours. There'd eventually be a court hearing, where he'd tell his side of the story and you'd tell yours. Who knows what that would bring? It's a crapshoot. The system isn't kind. You might want to rethink this."

For real? I am alone in this? Get him arrested, and he'll be free to make good on his threat to harm us. So much for creating a record. I got up, thanked the officer for "his time," and left, disgusted, depressed, and desperate. I drove home, unsure what to do when I got there. When we arrived, Mark's car wasn't there. I pulled into the garage and entered the house. He was gone.

Shortly thereafter, Mark called to say he was headed to the therapist first thing in the morning and would admit the abuse. I thought he had already. He begged and pleaded. I listened, and when he stopped, I said I had to feed "our son." I fed Mason, put him to bed, and curled up in the fetal position on the couch. I wondered what it would be like to not wake up.

My mother called at 5:30 a.m. and woke me.

"Laura, are you okay?"

"I'm fine, Mom. Mark has a drinking problem, and I am trying to get him help." We talked about that for a bit, but I limited the conversation to the drinking, rationalizing that my mother wouldn't understand the depths of what I was going through, nor know how to help. I also wanted to save her from the stress of it. She pushed back.

"Mark said you are not well," she said with a broken heart.

"Mom, trust me. It's Mark who isn't well. He was smashed last night when he called, and I took Mason out of the house to be safe. Everything is now fine. Don't worry. He is seeing a therapist."

"Okay, please be safe, sweetheart," she said ambivalently. We exchanged an "I love you" and hung up.

Later that day, Mark said he disclosed his abuse to his therapist. "She recommended anger management classes, and I should be okay." He promised to stay away a week, but two days later, he showed up with a dozen roses.

"Cutie, I'm going to get better. It's just a process," he said cheerfully.

I nodded and said nothing. He ordered food. When the doorbell rang, instead of the food delivery person at the door, there stood Mark's therapist.

"Um, uh . . . hi," I said with equivocation. "Nice to see you again."

"May I please come in?" she said eagerly.

I pushed the door open further and stepped back as she entered. I called to Mark that his therapist was here to see him. She corrected me. "Actually, I'm here to see both of you." I showed her to the couch and offered her a glass of water. She said, "No, thank you. I won't be staying long." Once we were all seated, she cleared her throat and leaned slightly forward.

"I'll be direct. You have six weeks to get help with this situation, or I am calling child services and suggesting that Mason go to foster care." She leaned back, waiting for a response. I was flabbergasted. *What is this woman saying? What did Mark say to her? Did he threaten her? Is she completely on his side now?*

Shaking, I said, "I'm . . . I'm totally confused," struggling for more words.

"I have said what I needed to say," she quickly interjected and got up and walked out without another word. Mark said nothing. Once the door shut, I turned to Mark.

"Why is this woman threatening to take our baby? What is going on here?"

"I don't know. Fuck her."

Law enforcement had proven worthless, and now the therapist, the one person I thought knew the reality and could be instrumental in helping us find a workable solution, had become an adversary. Who the hell knew what Mark told her? But considering the lies he'd spread about me, it wasn't hard to imagine. I had only one more place to turn—the judicial system. I found a different attorney and made an appointment. I knew I'd been there before, and while that was a complete bust, I had to give it another shot. If an attorney couldn't get it done, if the court system couldn't save me, I might have to resort to extreme measures.

23

Jessica

"I want to experience heli-skiing in the Swiss Alps." Those were Collin's first words when he came home. I didn't conceal my bewildered nonverbal reaction.

"I want to go away, just you and me, a second honeymoon. . . . Remember how much fun we used to have skiing? Find someone to take care of Alexandra. We'll be gone three weeks, so line up someone good. Let's have some fun."

I nodded with a tight smile to buy a few seconds. I wanted alone time with Collin and was pleased he wanted the same with me. Not to mention the prospects of reigniting the marriage. But by this point, I was off-balance with him, so confused about us; I wasn't quite sure what to make of this idea. I was also apprehensive about leaving Alexandra that long. Until that point, we'd only been apart a night or two.

"Sounds great, Collin," I said, doing my best to show enthusiasm.

My friends were optimistic and supportive, reasoning that this was exactly what Collin and I needed: alone time. I bought into the narrative, feeling a glimmer of optimism that Collin genuinely wanted to reconnect.

I researched heli-skiing, and, as suspected, it is off-trail, downhill skiing, usually only accessible by a helicopter. I'm an avid skier, but as amazing as it looked, it commanded a greater degree of execution and a higher comfort level for adventure. It was also, so far as I could tell, potentially dangerous, underscored by the consistent advice I'd read that heli-skiers should "pay attention to your guide."

I shared my fears with Collin, and he calmed my nerves by saying he'd hire a private guide so we'd never be unattended.

I started to get excited. It wasn't so much the destination—although the trip sounded incredible—but that Collin wanted to spend time with me again and do some work on our relationship. The rest was icing on the cake. My parents happily agreed to take Alexandra.

When the day to leave arrived, Collin looked like he fell out of a styling magazine. He wore a tailor-made ski outfit suitable for the torchbearer in the next Winter Olympics. Of course, I didn't feel my outfit was up to snuff.

We arrived in Zermatt, Switzerland, and hooked up with the private guide, who escorted us to our pilot at the outskirts of the mountain range. We headed to the first of several impressive resorts Collin had reserved. The pilot was eager to get moving. He explained that the weather would soon take a bad turn, and we needed to get in the sky quickly. We had some administrative work to do regarding passports, which the pilot stressed we do immediately. We returned after a slight delay to a grim pilot.

"I'm sorry. I think it's best if we stay put and let the weather pass. We can leave early in the morning. The skies are not safe." His professional tone didn't invite discussion. He didn't, however, know Collin.

"That's not acceptable. Either you fly the plane, or I fly the plane. Either way, we're leaving as agreed. Okay?" Collin was adamant, not inviting discussion.

Despite what I knew about Collin, under the circumstances, I was surprised at how resolute he was. His whole body tensed up. I looked at the pilot. He looked amused, and then, when he realized Collin wasn't joking, he looked stunned and confused.

"Sir, my advice to you . . . and your wife"—he turned to look and nod politely at me—"is to wait until the morning . . . for your . . . and her . . . um, safety." I became frightened. I knew this discussion wasn't over. I knew Collin. But getting in a small plane with a pilot who didn't want to fly during lousy weather lacked all semblance of sensible.

"Collin, it's okay. Let's have a nice dinner and leave in the morning," I said, coating my words in as much sugar as I could muster.

"Goddammit, Jessica, don't tell me what to do!" Collin said, swiveling his head toward me for barely a moment before returning his furious gaze to the pilot.

"You're getting paid a ton of money. You are either going to do your job or not, get paid or not. Which is it?" Collin said, staring with fury into the eyes of the pilot.

The pilot said nothing. His face turned grim. Then, he nodded toward the plane, and Collin briskly boarded. I couldn't believe it. But I followed. Collin had successfully intimidated the young pilot into going against his better judgment.

We squeezed into the six-seater with our guide and pilot, strapped up, and in less than ten minutes, the tiny plane was slicing upward through dense, black, ominous clouds. Once at the desired elevation, the plane flattened, and we began to bounce up and down as if we were on a trampoline—so violently that I worried I might eject from my seatbelt. Fifteen minutes into the flight, the pilot wanted to put the plane down. Flying had become too risky to continue. But he struggled to locate a landing strip in the middle of the mountains, searching frantically for a valley, relying on his visual and spatial awareness. The guide kept gazing at me reassuringly, doing what he could to make me feel that everything would be okay. Then, amid the pilot's efforts to find safe ground, the plane's alarm system shrieked—"pull up, pull up, terrain, terrain,"—with red lights flashing so bright that I couldn't see up front. I ducked my head between my trembling knees and prayed I'd see my daughter again. Collin squeezed my hand, which didn't diminish the rage I had toward him. We continued like this for what seemed like an eternity but probably spanned fifteen minutes until, finally, the pilot, dripping with sweat, landed the plane at our original destination. After disembarking, my legs were so weak, I could barely stand, and the guild helped me walk. When the pilot got out, he bowed down on both knees and kissed the ground! Collin said, "We made it, didn't we?" He looked around and added, "Well, what should we do for dinner?"

We arrived at the resort and checked in. Collin wanted to eat, but the adrenaline from the flight still surged through me, killing my appetite. He ate alone while I curled up in bed and tried to sleep. It was a rough, fitful night, and my nerves took time to settle.

In the early morning, we awoke to a room full of smoke. Collin was fit to be tied and started screaming into the phone. When the resort manager appeared minutes later, I thought Collin was going to strike the poor guy, who assured us they'd solve the problem by our return from the day's skiing. There was a problem with the fireplace's back draft, which caused smoke from the prior night's fire to rechannel into the room. I tried to calm Collin and ushered him out the door and toward the base lodge.

The skiing exceeded my expectations. The view was breathtaking, like gliding atop a soft bed of clouds. It was magical, and to my surprise, the terrain was not as difficult as I'd envisioned. We left the drama behind.

At dusk, when we returned, the manager informed us that they had cleared the room of smoke smells. When we opened the door, however, the room wreaked of a gross blend of smoke and air freshener. Collin ignited like a set of firecrackers. He berated staff in sequence as we passed them en route to the manager. It was like shooting apples in a barrel, and it mortified me. He threatened everyone he saw, unbridled in his rage. He demanded a plane so we could leave. A voice screamed in my head. I wanted to go home. He threatened a lawsuit and said he would bill them for ruining his clothes. I had never seen him that incensed. It was dizzying. Out of his earshot, I apologized for his behavior. Far from rekindling our marriage, the trip had disclosed the darkest side of Collin—his maniacal side—setting us back significantly.

They gave us a new room for the night, which calmed Collin down. We enjoyed a nice dinner and left the next day for a new resort. Nothing like starting over.

The new resort, known for its exquisite, mind-blowing heli-ski excursions, was even more beautiful than the previous place. Collin was salivating at the adventurous prospects ahead. Me? I worried silently that I lacked the experience and confidence to handle the remote, challenging, and restricted slopes, seriously uncharted territory for me. My stomach tied up in knots. When my jitters spilled out of me, Collin assured me that he would be by my side and that I should not worry. It didn't help. I worried.

The next morning, at sunup, we went to the helipad to board for the day's adventure. The resort dropped us on a remote mountain top, with views that went for miles, with the most spectacular peaks I had ever seen. Collin told the guide that we would meet him at the bottom, that he wanted to be alone with his wife to experience this surreal moment. The guide hesitated, but Collin assured him, with a calm but authoritative voice, that it would be fine. We started down, and in less than a minute, I could see that the slope from the prior place was child's play compared to this mountain—many times more difficult. Panic began to throttle my heart. Then it got scarier. It started to snow, and not mere flurries but thick mounds of moisture, a downpour of white-on-white snow that induced snow blindness. I started to freak out.

Collin was an expert skier, unfazed and emboldened by the course difficulty; the blizzard-like conditions slowed me down. He raced forward, and I steadily downshifted; he got further and further ahead. As the terrain got steeper and more treacherous, my entire body began to shake. I was paralyzed and came to an abrupt stop. I screamed for Collin to help me—so loud it burned my throat—but he either couldn't hear me or didn't care. His black figure became a speck on the white mountain. I attempted to traverse sideways across the hill and started to roll, my feet flew over my head, one ski fell off, and my ski-less leg buried deep beneath the fresh, wet snow. I was stuck, and ice tears rolled under my helmet. I got spacey. My head filled with thoughts of Alexandra. I wondered whether this was Collin's plan all along to get "rid" of me—an unfortunate ski mishap, he would tell everyone.

Is this how I am going to die?

I managed to get my buried leg out of the snow. I couldn't see much in front of me and lay there, unmoving, watching the downpour of snow—normally the most beautiful sight, and now the blanketing of death. I began to dream and go in and out of consciousness. I became numb. After what seemed like hours, I heard the whirl of a helicopter and looked up to see a safety rescue basket coming toward me. Our guide held a megaphone, instructing me on what to do. I had to grab the rope until I could strap myself in. I was so cold that I could barely move my fingers to snap the clasp to hold me while the basket lifted. Collin was in the helicopter—smoking a cigar!

After I got lifted into the helicopter, I lay down on the stretcher. The guide covered me in blankets. Collin put his hand on my leg, his way of comforting me. He said nothing.

After I got warmer and more comfortable, I felt a surge of anger rising in my chest, rattling me into awareness. I sat up and looked at Collin. He smiled.

"You okay?" he said, his first words since abandoning me.

"You asshole. Are you trying to kill me?"

"Come on. I thought you were right behind me. Why did you stop?"

"You uncaring bastard."

"Calm down. You're here, you're alive, and you're fine." He shook his head with a patronizing smirk.

"Fine? No, I'm far from *fine*. I'm upset, and I'm pissed and freezing cold, Collin. If it's no biggie, how about we have the guide lower you in the snow, and we will be back in an hour, fucking asshole." I looked at him with as much fury as I could. He shook his head and took a long puff from his cigar.

We traveled in silence until we arrived at the resort. As we walked toward our room, Collin slowed his pace close to a stop.

"Well, if what you said is how you feel, then leave." He shrugged, displaying that same patronizing look, and picked up his pace, getting ahead of me. I stopped walking.

"This trip or our marriage? Because I'm ready to leave both!"

He stopped and turned, replacing his smirk with a glare. I stopped in the hallway as well, and there we stood, facing off, several feet apart.

"If you try to divorce me, I'll make sure Alexandra lives with me. I'll paint you as a mentally unstable mother, and she will be mine. I'm taking a wild guess that is not an outcome you want. Just calm yourself and get some sleep. You are always so fucking dramatic!" He turned and walked away, his steps loud and full of angst.

I desperately wanted to go home. I wanted to cradle Alexandra in my arms and never let her go. For the remainder of the trip, I refused to do anything that made me uncomfortable and stayed as close to the guide as possible. Collin spent the entirety of the trip in his own little world and, when not in activities, on the phone texting and taking "urgent" calls.

After the trip, I kept to myself and shielded Alexandra from Collin as much as possible. I was lonely, scared, and confused, now my new "normal." My birthday came, and Collin did all the right things—flowers, a gift, and a birthday card with this inscription: "I look forward to fifty more years with the love of my life. I can't imagine doing life with anyone but you. Forever and always, Collin." Dr. Jekyll reporting for duty.

Those words brought tears. If only his actions lined up. While I wanted to believe what he said and hoped our marriage could find its way back, each time I saw specks of light, darkness overshadowed, and the pain cut deeper. It was a vicious cycle, and I needed to be free.

24

If You Knew, Would You Say I Do?

DR. BRENNAN: Welcome back to my podcast, *If You Knew Would You Say I Do?* Today, we are going to take a deeper dive into the lives of these two courageous women, Laura and Jessica. There is a lot to unpack here. Laura, can I give you a hug?

LAURA: Of course!

DR. BRENNAN: In fact, you too, Jessica. How about a group hug? You have both endured so much, and sharing your stories is not just brave but will undoubtedly help listeners escape their abusive relationships and encourage hope for a life free of abuse.

Having a baby should be a time of celebration, but as we see from your situation, Laura, it was tainted by many traumatic events.

LAURA: You're not kidding. I was beyond shocked at Mark's reaction when Mason was sick. He was less than six weeks old. I felt so alone and helpless. He provided no comfort. His lack of concern was astonishing. Our baby had a lump, a biopsy, and a high fever, and he was useless. While I lay on the hospital floor without even a change of clothes, he was evidently busy drinking and using drugs, which was apparent to one of the nurses. My focus was on Mason. All I knew was, he wasn't present, and I felt alone and afraid.

DR. BRENNAN: The narcissist's lack of empathy doesn't discriminate. It can be difficult for people to process that a narcissist can act so callously toward their own children. Mark showed no concern for his newborn baby, who was in the hospital with an undiagnosed illness for nine days. He put his needs above everyone else's. It was clear, Laura, that Mark didn't intend to end the cycle of abuse, and what followed was a barrage of future-faking, false promises, lies, and intensifying physical abuse.

LAURA: At the time, I was grateful to be home, knowing Mason would be okay. I tried to bring normalcy to our home with dinner, but the overdone streak triggered Mark, and he attacked me.

DR. BRENNAN: You had no way of knowing what would trigger him. Narcissists thrive on reactions, both good and bad; they need them to live, like we need air to breathe. Mark knew what he was doing by spitting out the meal you made. He knew it would set you off. He was angling for it. He needed his fix. Narcissists have contempt whenever you are at peace and feeling good. Narcissists have a knack for interfering with the good moments of other people. They can't bear to see others happy. They are notorious for ruining holidays, special occasions, birthdays, and anything that seems to bring others pleasure and where the attention is not directed at them.

And they have all the power. They created the reality the two of you lived in. If you question it, they become punitive and vindictive. You learn to be silent and navigate landmines.

JESSICA: Believe me, I was on that battlefield in perpetuity. Colin said whatever he needed to get his desired response. When he sold his business, for weeks, it was a giant love affair—how amazing our future looked, no more stress of the business. I thought the old Collin had returned to me. However, that was short-lived. Alexandra and I quickly became invisible once again a mere one month later. I could do nothing right.

DR. BRENNAN: Narcissists have no attachment to whatever spews from their mouths. Their words are calculated manipulations to control you. Collin gave you a hefty dose of the honeymoon phase when he sold his business. And just like that, you were back to the discard phase, where, unbeknownst to you, you had been for some time and where you would remain for eternity.

JESSICA: I called it the "divorce phase," but I see now that it was the discard phase. Collin had me constantly fearing the loss of the relationship, and throwing out the "D" word put my anxiety in overdrive, exactly where he wanted me. Casually proclaiming he wanted a divorce and that I should find a therapist had me running around to find a professional who could help us. Only to find that he'd been to one on his own and purportedly got told there was nothing wrong with him.

DR. BRENNAN: Narcissists aren't good therapy patients. They don't follow through with what is covered in the sessions. They think they know more than everyone else and that whatever problems exist are the fault and responsibility of others. They think everyone else has the problems, not them.

JESSICA: I was relieved when he seemed to bury the idea of a divorce. However, I was living under extreme psychological tension and in a constant state of denial, cognitive dissonance, and disconnect from those in my life. I was rationalizing, justifying his behavior, holding tight to the good times, and assuming the responsibility to bring them back. What came next was the never-ending cycle of blaming myself—maybe if I lost weight, was more fun, kept the house cleaner, showed more attention to him, was more supportive, and on and on. Maddening. I could have parachuted from an airplane, naked, delivering a cake to celebrate his birthday, and when I hit the ground, his first comment would have been, "But the candles blew out."

DR. BRENNAN: Of course, you were experiencing cognitive dissonance. One day, he was telling you he wanted a divorce, and another, taking you away on a romantic second honeymoon. They are two opposing beliefs happening at almost the same time. Your mind is simply not able to handle the inconsistency. Narcissistic tactics are designed to leave you in a constant state of anxiety and confusion, which is what happened to you. Their demands are exhausting and infantile. And narcissists constantly move the goalposts, making it impossible to satisfy them. Loving and serving a narcissist is like pouring water into a strainer. With narcissists, the other person endures most of the responsibility to fix the relationship and gets blamed for whatever is "wrong." It's a constant lose-lose. Once you resolve one problem, before you can take a breath, another is close behind.

JESSICA: At this point, I felt shackled to the hamster wheel, forever seeking Collin's approval, constantly afraid of disappointing him, and making sacrifices I never thought I would.

DR. BRENNAN: You had entered the devaluation and discard phase, a vicious cycle where the narcissist goes from an intense interest in you to total disregard and disrespect. It can repeat itself and even last a lifetime. Narcissists assume the right to control you forever, whether you're together or not, and will do so if you let them. Pain and destruction are the consequences of life with a narcissist.

LAURA: I know the cycle well. I, too, was in the devaluation/discard phase. After the escalating physical abuse, with a two-month-old to take care of, I was in a state of exhaustion and disbelief that my life had become a nightmare. I was being abused by my husband—and at the risk of losing my baby to a madman. I held tightly to the hope that the therapist would help him and our marriage. Sadly, that was not the case. Remember, at this point, I didn't know Mark had NPD; I assumed it was *only* an alcohol problem.

DR. BRENNAN: How would you know? How would anyone know? Narcissists are clever chameleons. They move in and out of persona to suit their agenda. It's like getting blindsided. You don't see the next persona coming until it's too late. That is why education about this disorder is vital. It helps people spot the red flags at the outset and begin to appreciate the sheer danger of a relationship with a narcissist.

LAURA: The abusive cycle intensified throughout the relationship when he started taunting Mason—waking him up in the middle of the night and threatening to send him away if he wasn't perfect. And let's not forget the smear campaign I was ignorant of—Mark telling people I had severe postpartum depression and was crazy! He had isolated me from friends and family and had their utmost attention.

DR. BRENNAN: Narcissists set the stage by smearing their victims before they are even aware. The narcissist paints the picture of how others will perceive you long before the discard. When things fall apart, which they inevitably do, they need others to believe you are the crazy one and they are the victim. Mark could sense you were on the brink of leaving, which meant exposing his truths. He needed to go into overdrive and sway his *audience*. He had already laid the groundwork, which you were completely unaware of. People like Mark can be remarkably persuasive; a case in point is how he had your mother thinking you were something you were not. This is a setup that undermines your side of the story because people will have formed an opinion based on the narcissist's pathological lies about you.

JESSICA: How about my skiing disaster? I thought I was going to spend eternity as a human popsicle.

In hindsight, I foolishly thought Collin wanted to rekindle our marriage in a honeymoon of sorts, but it was just another hoovering attempt to pull me back in. Instead, I was nearly killed. Collin seemed to enjoy putting me in dangerous situations. First, the plane experience, and then losing me in the snow-covered mountains. I had never felt so unsafe with Collin.

DR. BRENNAN: Let's address hoovering for a moment because this happens throughout abusive relationships, particularly when you have entered the discard phase. When narcissists feel they are losing control over their victim and that person is threatening to leave the relationship or expose them, they hoover so effortlessly, trying to con you and regain control and continue the cycle of abuse. Hoovering can be grand gestures, like a trip, or small, like words you want to hear while rubbing your feet. The outcome is always the same; it's a form of manipulation to validate you and make you feel important. They want you to hop back on the hope train. Keep in mind, hoovering can be as insignificant as a text of a happy emoji after no contact for a length of time. Any response at all lets them know you are still in the game, and it gives them a sense of control.

Regarding your trip, no one is ever safe with a narcissist. They are characteristically reckless. They often deem themselves above the law and are intimidating. For instance, the young pilot knew better than to fly, but Collin bullied him. People like Collin like to watch people squirm in dangerous situations they don't fear. Collin had a sadistic side and enjoyed watching you panic and suffer. Your pain and fear were a great supply for Collin and energized him. I am certain we'll see more of that side of Collin as the story unfolds.

Before we sign off, I wanted to mention Mark's therapist, who makes a professionally questionable, unannounced visit to your home, Laura, and threatens dire consequences if you and Mark don't fix things between you. There is something familiarly eerie about that in your story.

LAURA: Yes, what I described turns out to be the tip of the iceberg. I don't want to spoil things at this point, but your listeners will be amazed at how that whole thing plays out. It was beyond anything I could have ever thought possible.

DR. BRENNAN: Okay, again, thank you both for sharing your stories.

I'm your host, Dr. Jules Brennan. Until next time, *if you knew, would you say I do?* Thanks for listening.

25
Laura

The first lie was to my mother. I needed to pay the lawyer and didn't have access to any money without asking Mark and raising suspicions. Telling my mother that I needed funds for therapy did the trick. She didn't question me. "Of course, honey."

The second lie was to Mark. Anything I did out of the ordinary was sure to draw his attention. Rather than meet with a lawyer, I had "to attend a mommy and me class." No questions asked. He couldn't care less.

The lies made me feel dirty. But I was desperate, and you know what they say about desperate times and measures.

When I arrived at the law office, with Mason asleep in the portable car seat, the office manager politely shuttled me to a large conference room decorated with live plants. I smiled. I could use the extra oxygen. After a few minutes, a man who looked like a defensive lineman for the Las Vegas Raiders entered. I stood to shake his hand, facing his belly button. He had kind eyes and a sweet smile. A gentle giant. After pleasantries, I emoted my life story, illustrated with photos of the abuse and voicemails I'd saved.

He looked at Mason sleeping peacefully, and when he turned back to me, tears were in his eyes.

"Laura, I'm so sorry. This is awful. You and your baby will be safe. I will do what I can to protect you."

I wanted to hug him.

"What happens next?" I said eagerly. "I don't have much money."

"Let's discuss the financial part in a second," he answered, lifting his hand like a traffic cop. "You have enough evidence to get protection. You want a restraining order. First, gather the evidence to support the application. Get all your ducks in a row."

I nodded, waiting for more.

"You can prepare the forms at the courthouse without me. You don't need me for that. We'll have you manage as much as you can without me to save money. I will monitor everything."

It was Thursday. We planned to file the following Monday. I was about to draw a major line in the sand. I was petrified.

I arrived home to Mark asleep on the couch. I fed Mason and put him down for a nap. The two of them asleep gave me a window to get my "ducks in a row." I backed up all my domestic abuse evidence. I made sure I had all of Mason's files—birth certificate, medical records, and Social Security number—scanned to my laptop. I needed to cross every T and dot every I to prepare for the major battle that loomed. I had to be ready and strong.

Mark had arranged a dinner with friends for two days later, the last thing I wanted to do with him. But I played along. I had to. We met at a French restaurant. When we arrived at the table, Mark pulled out my chair and proceeded to pour compliments all over me. I flashed my best faux smile. Sitting at dinner was torture. I burned to tell these people how their bestie was a wife beater and recount in uncomfortable detail that the man they admired and bowed down to was a monster. Each time he touched me at dinner, I shuddered inside and wanted to crawl out of my skin. I existed alone in an alternate universe.

After dinner, when we were in the car, Mark turned to me.

"What the fuck is the matter with you? You never learn," he said angrily.

"Learn what, Mark?" I said without flinching.

"If I've told you once, I've told you a thousand times. It makes me look bad when you get up from the table before I do and walk five feet ahead of me to leave."

"I mean, really, Mark? That's what's important to you?"

He started the engine.

"And another thing," he continued, "where the fuck were you tonight? You sat there most of the night like a mummy. So disrespectful to our friends."

"On the contrary, Mark, your words, as always, enthralled me," I said.

We drove in silence the rest of the way home.

When we got home, he poured himself another glass of wine and began to flirt. I knew where that was going, but the last thing I wanted was to have sex with him. I snubbed the advances.

"What's up with you? Where is your affection?" he said.

"Affection? I am still dealing with the last incident."

"That's your *problem*. You can't forgive," he said. "I can get laid anywhere. I don't need you, bitch."

"Go ahead, Mark. Go fuck whoever you want. Have at it, big shot." I flipped my hand at him.

"Oh, really? Let's be clear. You are my wife, and you will fuck me on demand."

He pushed me onto the bed and held both my hands over my head with his left hand, glaring at me. I froze in horror. I screamed and cried. His eyes bulged.

"Shut the fuck up," Mark commanded.

He whipped out his dick and proceeded to masturbate while holding me down, smiling wildly the whole time. I closed my eyes. He came all over my face.

"You liked it, you slut. Don't lie." He stood, laughed, and went to the couch.

I lay there with tears rolling down my face, unable to get up.

"You filthy animal. You sicken me!" I grabbed the side of the bed to help me up. I felt frail.

He laughed and refilled his wine glass. I ran to the shower and let hot water wash over me for several minutes, trying to dissolve the nightmare. It was Saturday; I had twenty-four more hours to get through. *You can do it.*

Mark spent the rest of the weekend on the phone. I cared for Mason and counted minutes. Finally, Monday morning came, and I was ready. Mark slept late. I woke him, and he said he wasn't going in that day and went back to sleep. I needed to collect a ton of stuff before going to the courthouse. I needed him out of the house. I clanged what I could in the kitchen to disrupt his sleep. He appeared groggily, mumbling something about a doctor's appointment. Perfect. Once he left, I stuffed a trash bag with materials I had secretly assembled. I dropped Shiraz at a dog day care place—with arrangements to pick her up no later than five—and Mason and I hustled to the courthouse. As I drove, I glanced at my baby in the rearview mirror and said, "Baby boy, Mama is in the fight of her life, but I will do everything in my power to protect you." My eyes filled with tears as he held his blue bear and bit his nose.

Once in the courthouse, I found the room for filing restraining order applications, with its array of cubicles and legal forms. Mason thankfully slept in the portable car seat. I got to work, writing up a storm. Mason never slept for long, but that day, he slept, well, like a baby. He was doing his part.

Four hours later, a clerk came over and said, "We close at 4 p.m."

"Thank you. I know. I'm doing the best I can. I'm almost done."

Meanwhile, my phone vibrated nonstop. Mark's texts started out nice and steadily regressed to threats. Nothing unusual there. I ignored them.

I finished and provided my submission to the clerk. She explained that the court would review the papers, and if approved, a sheriff would serve and evict Mark from the house until the next court date.

I called my attorney and said, "I did it."

"Okay," he said, "I'll keep checking the status."

Outside the courthouse, I found a place to sit, holding Mason close and crying on his little head. From him, I drew the strength to take this step.

While still sitting there, my attorney called.

"Did you really write seventeen pages?"

I said, "Yes, and that wasn't all of it."

"Well, nice work. The court granted the TRO [temporary restraining order]. The sheriff should serve the papers by 6 p.m. Do me a favor," he added, "drive by his retail store to see if his car is there. That way, they know for sure where to find him. If they miss him the first try, they may not return until tomorrow."

"Shit," I exclaimed. "He has to be served today. I can't go back if he's in the house." The stress of the legal process I had unleashed hit me hard for the first time. I couldn't imagine what might be in store. For how long would the nightmare that had become my life continue?

I drove by the store. His car was there. I reported the finding to my attorney. He said he'd notify the sheriff's department. I waited a few parking spots down, with a view of the front door, my heart pounding. Ten minutes later, the sheriff arrived, stopped in front of the plaza, got out, and slowly walked to the door of Mark's store. He entered the store, paper in hand, and less than five minutes later, he walked out empty-handed. A minute later, Mark walked out with papers partially crumpled inside his fist. My heart skipped a beat. Mark walked to his car, his jaw clenched, his eyes bulging, got in, and peeled away down the street in a fit of fury. I exhaled, relieved and afraid at once.

Before driving off, I called the day care place for Shiraz. It was closed. I had lost track of time. I left a message, and after a few minutes, the lady from the day care called me back.

"You were supposed to pick him up at five."

I burst out, bawling. I couldn't talk or stop sobbing, as if a wall protecting my heart had crumbled. Once I regained control, I gave her a synopsis of my current woes.

"Look, I have Shiraz. Give me your address, and I'll bring him to you," she said.

"Thanks, but I can't pay you today. Later this week, but not today."

"Not a problem. Don't worry about it."

"I can't thank you enough." I was so grateful.

I just wanted a divorce. I fed Mason and put him down for the night. I sat on the couch and absorbed the many texts and voicemails from Mark, threatening me if I did not return home. I was afraid. I worried that a restraining order wouldn't stop Mark Corbin. Who knew what he was capable of? I had thrown down the gauntlet. Losing wasn't in his playbook.

Still, despite the rising fear, I felt a warm sense of comfort knowing I had taken a major step to reclaim and rechart my life and save my son. I went to bed and slept through the night for the first time in over a year. When I awoke the next morning, I focused on the tasks at hand. I had more work to do. The restraining order had a fourteen-day shelf life. I had to prepare to request an extension. I fretted about how Mark would respond.

26

Jessica

Collin left for a two-week trip to London to reconnect with a former business associates and play golf. I cherished the separation. A major dose of self-care was overdue, and who knew, maybe the time away would throttle his good senses.

The first night of his absence, while I was immersed in a comedy movie, the iPad connected to the TV emitted a pinging sound. I assumed it was technology gone amuck and paid it no mind. When it happened a second time, I investigated, and after trial and error, I discovered that the iPad and Collin's iPhone were linked. On deeper discovery, I detected text messages between him and a 305 (Miami) area code number. I put the movie on hold.

> **Collin: I'm in our favorite hotel in London, where we stayed that time, in "our" suite. Missing you terribly.**
>
> **305: Are you crazy? YOU broke up with ME. Otherwise, I'd be there with you. Do you think I'd rather go to the beach with friends than be with you?**
>
> **Collin: Could be worse. The beach in Malibu sounds amazing, and you look hot in a bikini.**
>
> **305: What do you care? You left me.**

My chest tightened. My body shook. My head ached. *Who the fuck is this? His girlfriend? Two years ago? He has a mistress? Is this real?* It was all I could do not to scream. Riveted, I inhaled deeply and read on.

Collin: Short memory. You created so much noise and said you didn't trust me. How am I supposed to live with that?

305: For years, I told you over and over that I wanted to be with you full time, and you kept saying, "In time." Time is up, Collin.

Collin: Remember the videos we took? Wishing you could be with me right now.

305: You know I want to be there. All I have are our sex videos, reminders of what it's like to feel you inside me! I can almost feel you now.

Collin: You and I had what people dream of. I am going to masturbate to the videos now. Facetime me. LOL. Pick up.

I started crying. Then I stopped suddenly and became furious. *Fucking lying, cheating hypocrite piece of shit.* A girlfriend for years! Making sex videos while withholding sex from me. No wonder he was content to withhold sex. He was fucking someone else. My heart pounded in my chest. I began sweating. My mind jumped into the fast lane, questions coming at me rapidly. *Where did he meet her? When? Do I know her? Where does she live? How many lies did he tell me? Did this bitch ever come to our house? Did she ever see Alexandra? Were there others like her?*

Ping!

Collin: I needed that. Love you. Sleep well.

305: XO love you too.

My phone buzzed. Collin texted.

Collin: Love you. Going to bed. Give Alexandra a kiss for me. XO.

I didn't know what to do. I wanted to unleash a barrage of venom on the asshole. I inhaled deeply again. Another part of me said, *No, hold off, play along, think this through.*

Me: XO.

I wanted to vomit! An internal mantra consumed me, *You fucking piece of shit!*

I hardly slept that night. Whenever I awoke, I'd start crying. The betrayal scorched my stomach. And this had to be the tip of the iceberg. I fixated on all the times he must have been with her. Years? How many? I flashed to the trips he took for "business," imagining all the lies, the pervasive infidelity. Each time he texted me *love you*, was she lying next to him? My life had been a massive heap of lies built upon lies.

The torture of reconstructing my fraudulent life continued in the morning over coffee, with tears running down my face, only to be interrupted by the now infamous "ping." I grabbed the iPad. Texts had resumed, a series of business-related messages. And then, these:

305: Hey, baby, I'm so horny!

Collin: Of course you are, baby. I'll call you soon. Got some business to take care of.

305: Love you.

Collin: XO.

Another dagger to the heart. I put my hands over my ears, trying to close out the world, remaining there for fifteen minutes. I struggled to think clearly. What should I do? I called my friend, Skylar, a very savvy businesswoman and mother, and gave her a blow-by-blow. She offered a straightforward perspective.

"Don't confront him," she said. "Not now."

"You have no idea how much I want to," I said.

"I have an idea. It's understandable and normal. But be strategic. Hire a private investigator and gather evidence. You'll need to have your shit together. Remember the prenup you signed. Once you call him out, it will be declared war, and you need to be prepared."

I nodded. She was correct. I had to play my cards smartly. Her brother knew a PI named Hank Rivers, who was highly recommended. Rivers and I talked, and I hired him. I had him first trace the 305 phone number. Less than an hour later, Rivers called.

"Her name is Danielle Lurie. She is from Miami Beach but lists two LA addresses as well. She's twenty-nine but lacks any notable employment history. She has a son."

I froze. *Is that Collin's child? Is that boy Alexandra's sibling?* I paused to breathe.

"What are the other addresses?"

The first was nearby, a few miles from where we lived. The second—*holy shit*—was the Malibu place he had rented *for clients*! No wonder he tightly controlled my comings and goings there and wouldn't give me a key. *How stupid was I! What a fool I was.* I wondered, *Does the asshole travel with her and the son? Is she living there with her son?*

I explained it all to Hank.

"If you'd like, I can stake out her place and see what more I can learn."

"Yes, do it."

I dissolved into tears again. My breathing was agonized. After a few minutes, I gathered myself, called Skylar, and updated her. She doubted the kid was Collin's and theorized that Danielle Lurie was "probably an escort."

"I don't know how I will be able to contain myself when he comes home. How will I face him and not explode?"

"Not so easy, Jessica, but you have to. He has money and power. Consider him dangerous. You need to keep gathering information to save yourself and your daughter. This is war."

Ping!

"Hold on, Sky. It's happening again."

Collin: I LOVE LOVE LOVE YOU YOU YOU. I want to taste you right now!

305: I wish you could, baby! When you come back, let's take a trip. Let's be the two of us like we used to be. We are soulmates.

Collin: I'll book our favorite villa in St. Barts.

305: We'll recreate our favorite video!

"Wow."

"Read it to me," Skylar said anxiously.

"Wow," Skylar said.

"Is this my fault? What could I have done to prevent this?"

"Stop it, Jessica. Just stop it. This has nothing to do with you. He is a lying, arrogant piece of shit, an awful person. This has nothing to do with you. You are an amazing wife and mother. I mean, shit, who knows how many times he's done this? Guaranteed, she isn't the first, and bank on this: she won't be the last."

Still, I couldn't hold back the floodgates of self-doubt—if I were thinner, younger, better in bed, less consumed with motherhood . . . would things be different?

The texting continued—hundreds, a babbling parade of mutual obsession. Skylar had halfway convinced me not to turn the whip on myself. But bearing witness to their intimacies and expressions of love and desire devastated me. The hardest to swallow were the comments about me—the "crazy X" and "haggard housewife" (HH).

The day Collin was set to come home, the following text exchange came across the transom:

Collin: Home to the HH in 15.

305: Will I still be seeing you later?

Collin: See me? Here, see me now (dick pic)

305: See you and see you inside me (vagina pic)

Collin: XO, I need you. Love you!

305: Love you!

Rage and desolation consumed me. I wasn't sure how I was going to contain myself. Before he was due home, I put the iPad on silent mode, undoing his prior mistake.

The garage door opened, sounding like rumbling thunder, and seconds later, the lying piece of shit strolled through the door.

"Hi, honey. I'm exhausted. How are you?" he said cheerfully.

"Oh, just fabulous," I said, with a slight edge. The sarcasm eluded him.

"Great, sweetheart. I'm going to shower and relax." No hug or kiss. Like a roommate.

I watched him slog to our bedroom, presumably with thoughts of his nasty girlfriend and undetected double life, cool and collected, whistling all the way, so smug and arrogant. At that moment, I felt morally grounded. Superior. He was a lowlife.

Maintaining composure was the most difficult challenge I'd ever had. I followed him into the bedroom and said, "I want to hear about your trip."

"Jessica, I'm exhausted. I told you I need to relax. Can you give me that much?"

I turned, went to the kitchen, poured a glass of wine, furtively snatched the iPad, and went to the yard. Like clockwork, a minute later, this appeared:

Ping!

Collin: Getting in the shower. Wish it were with you. The HH is outside, probably walking again. Lol that's all she ever does.

305: Tempt me.

Collin: Call you in 5. I want to hear your voice while I masturbate.

305: I'm ready when you are.

Collin: (pic of him masturbating and finishing)

305: You didn't wait, baby.

Collin: Just the thought got me so excited. See you in the morning.

305: Can't wait to taste you.

My husband was in my bathroom masturbating to his girlfriend. This can't be happening. He has led a double life since I met him. How fucking stupid was I?

I called Hank and asked him to surveil Collin starting first thing the next day.

When Collin left in the morning for "a business meeting," I alerted Hank. Less than an hour later, Hank reported. Collin drove to the Danielle Lurie address near our home and knocked on the door. A woman answered, and they exchanged a prolonged, passionate kiss before moving inside.

An hour later, they left together in his car and landed at The Parlor, a lunch place Collin and I had been before. Hank secured a table relatively close to them.

Hank called later to say he couldn't hear much other than this: Danielle planned to accompany Collin to Puerto Rico next week on another business trip.

Over the next few days, I waited eagerly for Collin to disclose his impending "business" trip, largely keeping my distance from him. Each night, we slept in the same bed, alone. One morning, I awoke to him rubbing up against me, looking for a morning quickie. I jumped up and said, "Alexandra is crying. Got to go." An effective getaway.

That morning, he revealed the Puerto Rico trip. I said nothing. By this point, I only wanted him to vanish into the atmosphere, never to return. The next morning, after breakfast as a "family," he left, kissing Alexandra and me goodbye. I took the iPad off silent mode.

Several hours later, that now-familiar sound pierced my ears.

305: Call me.

305: HELLLLOOOOO.

305: Please call me, Collin.

305: Did you block me? Your phone is going right to VM.

Collin: Calm down, Danielle. Shit.

305: Why aren't you answering me?

Collin: I'm in that same villa where we filmed many of our sex tapes, watching them now.

305: I'm supposed to be there, but you keep pulling and pushing. Told you from the beginning that I wasn't in this to be your mistress of convenience.

305: Crazy-making is your MO.

Collin: You know I'm going through a lot with business stuff. I need your support, not your noise.

305: What about my needs? They are as important! You made me promises.

Collin: What more could you need? I support you and your son. I love you, we are together all the time, and no one eats your pussy like I do.

305: I want to be your wife, Collin. Like we discussed. You promised you would leave her.

305: Hello???

305: Collin, answer me!

Collin: I have to go, meeting someone.

305: Better not be someone from Diamond Girls. I still have friends there.

Collin: Stop. Call you later. You need to trust me.

305: My friends say you'll never leave your wife.

Collin: Stop listening to your jealous loser friends. I hardly speak to my wife. My business is my first priority.

305: Then leave her.

Collin: If you are that unhappy, then go back to Miami.

305: Trying to call you.

305: Collin!!!!

305: I can't take this anymore. If you don't tell her, I will.

305: You will regret this.

Collin: Don't you EVER fuck with my family.

Collin: Do you really want to go back to where I found you? I can call Diamond Girls and get you back in. I'll give you a strong recommendation. LOL

305: How dare you? I did that work to support my son. You know that.

Collin: Don't you ever threaten me.

305: Fuck you, you cheating lying piece of shit.

305: IM TELLING HER.

I called Skylar.

"Sky, Collin is coming home tomorrow. I'm going to confront him. He and his whore are fighting big time, and she's threatening to expose the affair to me. She's enraged, and who knows to what length she'll go? Can you please get Alexandra tomorrow and keep her for the night?"

"Of course."

When Sky arrived the next day, she gave me a long hug. I needed it.

"This isn't going to be easy, Jessica, but whatever you do, try not to let on about the iPad. That thing may be your best ticket to the other side. If you confront him, figure out another way to tell how you know. An anonymous call, even."

"I'll try my best, Sky, but no promises."

27

Laura

With the TRO in hand, it was time to tell my family. I first called my brother. He listened with admirable restraint, and when I paused to say, "That's it," he responded.

"I am going to break every bone in his body," he said. "I'm coming out there, and I'm going kick his ass." Before I could suggest that that might not be the best approach, he rechanneled his frustration.

"Why did you lie to me, Laura? You lied. When you came to my wedding, I asked why the brace on your wrist, and you said you tripped down a set of stairs. I can't believe you shut us out. This is what family's for."

"I understand how you feel. I do. I was too scared and ashamed to tell anyone. In hindsight, maybe it was a mistake. But, I needed time to formulate a safety plan for Mason and me. I feared doing anything that risked losing him. I tormented myself about how to handle things."

He said, "Okay, okay. I understand. I love you. We got this."

I called my mother. She became hysterical within a minute, which I should have expected, especially after keeping my parents in the dark. She didn't call me out about lying to her about the money. That would come later. I let her rant until she turned the phone over to my father, who kept saying I should return to Texas at the earliest possibility.

As much as I appreciated the heartfelt concerns of family, as I saw it, no one could grasp the depth of the mess I was in or what barreled down the road next. Everyone had opinions and emotional reactions—as they were entitled—but they couldn't possibly appreciate how immobilizing it had been for me and how insane it would likely continue to be.

I prepared for the upcoming court hearing to address whether the court should extend the TRO for two months. I organized the supplemental evidence to assist my counsel, although he assured me the hearing would be straightforward. Two weeks before the hearing, Mark agreed to the sixty-day extension, rendering the hearing, as my attorney described it, "pro forma," meaning we should be done in less than five minutes. He added, "Your presence isn't necessary, but be there to show the court you care."

I arrived at the courthouse with Mason to find my counsel outside, pacing and agitated.

"They pulled a fast one," he said nervously.

"Who? What fast one?" I said with mounting anxiety.

"They reneged. Mark will only agree to extend the TRO if you sign Mason over to him. If you don't agree, they want a full-blown evidentiary hearing."

I was confused—and began to shudder.

"I don't understand. What, um, what does that mean?" I finally said.

"It means, first, they will oppose the extension of the TRO, and second, they want to explore custody issues. It also means you may have to testify."

"Testify? What? I'm not prepared to testify. I mean, look at me. I'm wearing jeans, a T-shirt, and sandals! I'm not prepared. You didn't warn me about this!"

He didn't respond. Panic gripped me.

"How much time do we have?" I asked.

"Less than an hour."

I called Grace and explained the situation in a rapid-fire, trembling voice, begging her to get Mason. Bless her. She dropped everything, and thirty minutes later, she showed up and swept Mason away to her place until further notice.

The cool, suave, caring advocate of mine, my knight savior, had begun to show kinks in his shining armor. He wore a frantic look and was unraveling, which didn't help me, as I was coming apart at the seams. What the hell was going on?

I soon found out.

When we opened the courtroom door, I received the shock of my life. A sea of people, buzzing aloud like an active beehive, had assembled in the pews on the left side of the courtroom: three attorneys, an ensemble of Mark's sycophant friends, and his entire family. They looked primed to attend a Broadway production. I became nauseous. My attorney kept running his hands through his hair. We'd been lured into an ambush.

As my mind spun and I clung to my composure, the bailiff stood and said, "All rise," and out of the front of the room, like the Wizard of Oz, a judge appeared in classic black robes. It was a woman. *Good sign*, I thought. *She'll see through Mark and his bullshit.*

To start, Mark's attorney pulled out three photo albums. He provided one to my attorney, and after getting permission to approach the bench, he delivered the other to the judge. My attorney objected to the evidence, arguing that the hearing was a "garden variety matter to extend the TRO only two months," and, in any event, he'd not had "time to review the surprise evidence." To no avail. The photos were deemed admissible. A favorable ruling in hand, Mark's attorney began to plow through the photos, page by page, moment by moment, providing descriptions here and there as "offers of proof." It was as distorted and selective a portrayal of our life together as imaginable. When the attorney finished the revisionist pictorial history, he closed the photo album and addressed the court rhetorically.

"Your Honor, do these pictures look like an unhappy family? Does this family man seem like someone who'd lay a hand on his wife? I mean, we need to get real here."

He then asked permission to call witnesses. I was flabbergasted. We were getting steamrolled. Again, my attorney objected on the same grounds as before, with the same results. The court permitted a procession of Mark-lovers to the stand to testify on his behalf. One after another, people I hardly knew smeared me, labeling me variably as "unstable," "insecure," "drunk," "lazy," and "spiteful." Mark, in contrast, was "loving," "family-oriented," "a kind soul," and "a dedicated father."

I'd be cast in the leading role of a *Twilight Zone* episode. A TRO hearing featuring his abuse had mutated into a referendum about me. I was utterly sickened. I prayed for my attorney to turn this around.

My attorney cross-examined the Mark-lovers on the fly. He made a few points, I thought. Most witnesses admitted they had only seen me with Mason for short intervals, and some not at all, and those that did couldn't identify anything untoward. Further, none had seen Mark with Mason alone—ever. Half of them sheepishly conceded that Mark was their "boss," working for him at different retail stores. None could explain the photos that showcased my injuries, although one pathetic disciple said, "Maybe she did it to herself." Unreal.

I couldn't imagine the judge buying any of it.

The best was Mark's father. He testified, "My son is the type of guy you see at a homeless shelter, serving food on the holidays." My jaw dropped, and I restrained an audible groan. Mark didn't have a charitable bone in his body. He scoffed at the downtrodden and unfortunate, calling them "weak" and "inferior." He hated them.

His father had the gall to testify, "As a youngster, Mark was a dedicated athlete who lived a clean life and was admired as an inspirational leader, receiving MVP awards in multiple sports." In his next breath, he said, "He was, I might add, also a studious kid." Really? Mark was a mediocre athlete at best and hated school. In fact, he got suspended from school for allegedly attacking a teammate on the basketball team. And I never once, not once, caught him with his nose in a book. He could barely sustain interest in a newspaper article.

Mark took the stand briefly. He played it close to the vest. He denied ever hitting me. He denied ever threatening me. He said I had a drinking problem and that I suffered from severe bouts of postpartum depression, often flying off the handle at the slightest frustration. "Sometimes I think she is mentally ill."

My attorney did what he could, so far as I could tell. Mark stuck to his story. He denied everything and professed his undying love for me. He worried about me. He thought I needed professional help. The photos? Well, Mark said that after the baby was born, I suffered from lightheadedness and imbalance and fell a few times, especially after consuming wine, which I apparently did in copious amounts.

Other than stating "his full name for the record," everything that gushed from Mark's mouth was a lie. He perjured himself for thirty continuous minutes.

The crème de la crème witness for the Corbin clan was a psychologist. He testified that he spent a full day with Mark and "under no circumstances could he hurt a woman. The guy is a big teddy bear, a loving and caring individual." He had no explanation for the photos. And he got jittery and looked foolish when admitting the obvious, that he formed his conclusions without interviewing me or seeing the photos.

It was noteworthy that the therapist we both visited, who showed up unannounced at our door to threaten me, didn't testify. I had to find out about that relationship. Something wasn't right. It smelled.

Then, another surprise.

My attorney informed the court that he had not planned on an evidentiary hearing; his son was in the hospital, and he was expected there. Was he really leaving? He was sweating profusely.

I had yet to take the stand. Was he going to stay long enough to ask me questions? Could he seek a short continuance so we could prepare? I knew the truth, but I assumed preparation would help. I begged him to stay long enough for me to say something. He agreed, "ten minutes max," and he winged it. *We* winged it.

I told the judge that Mark was a drug addict and an alcoholic and gave brief examples. I told her about the physical attacks and the recent sexual abuse. That was about it. I kept it together, but I was a mess inside. The opposing attorney "waived cross-examination, for now."

A few hours in, the judge excused herself to chambers. Ten minutes later, she returned.

"I am granting the requested sixty-day extension of the TRO. I am, however, ordering that during the TRO period, the minor child, Mason, may spend weekends with his father, and the petitioner shall cooperate in making that happen. No excuses, no games."

As the courtroom emptied, my attorney said, "Not bad, but I have to run. I'll call you." And he was gone.

Not bad? I couldn't believe it. Sure, I got the extension, but Mark and his expensive legal team had defamed me in the eyes of this judge, and who knows what that might mean down the road? Worse, exposing Mason to Mark and allowing time with him alone was a travesty. An absentee father, he knew nothing about childcare. He was a reckless drunk and addict. He posed a danger to his son. *Not bad? No, not good.*

Mark brandished an ear-to-ear smile. I glared at him. He pumped his eyebrows in response, the symbolic gesture of the psycho conqueror. At that moment, I hated him, every part of him, and I hated his family. They sucker punched me. They made a fool out of my attorney.

Once alone in my car, I broke down in a flood of tears. I called Grace to arrange Mason's return to me. Grace wanted a report. I could barely speak and wasn't in the condition to review the debacle. "I'll tell you another time." She insisted on bringing Mason to the house to make it easier. I was a zombie the rest of the week.

Friday came, and I had to give Mason to Mark at 5 p.m. The thought of them alone together continued to freak me out. I couldn't eat. Every time I looked at him, I cried. I packed everything he could possibly need for the weekend. I didn't relish seeing Mark, even for a minute.

At five sharp, an authoritative, loud knock shook me from my daydream. When I opened the door, expecting to see Mark, I found instead a large muscular man in a black suit, all buttoned down, with a white shirt and red tie.

"Can I, um, help you?" I said, my confusion evident.

"Yes, I am here to get Mason Corbin," he said with a deep tone.

"Excuse me, but who are you?" I stepped back and shielded Mason.

"The Corbin family sent me. I work for them." He was stone-faced.

I took another step back, shut the door, leaving him outside, and called my attorney. After getting my report, he said, "Let me make a call." A minute or so later, he called me back and said, "Laura, you must give Mason to the gentleman. He is an employee who works for the Corbin family. He's authorized."

Unreal. I had to turn over a one-year-old to a person I didn't know. I felt like Mark and his family were ripping my child from my womb. When I handed him over, Mason cried so loud, and his little face turned crimson red. The pickup man was nonplussed. He turned and toted him away, and as he did, Mason thrust his tiny arms and hands toward me in a "please save me" desperation. He kept crying and reaching for me the whole time he walked toward his car. I stood there, helpless, dying inside. I have never felt such heartache. Mason disappeared into the car, and I felt a thick pain in my chest. I thought a heart attack might be underway.

When the car slipped out of sight, I shut the door, collapsed to the floor, curled up into a fetal position, and stayed there, unmoving and silent, for over an hour.

I shuttered myself the entire weekend. And when Monday morning came, ending my weekend torture, I waited outside for Mason, starting at 8:30 a.m.; he was due by nine. A few minutes after nine, a black suburban pulled up, and the driver opened the side door. I went to reach for Mason inside, but he stepped in my way.

"Please stand back, ma'am," he said in a deep voice.

"Stand back? I am his mother, goddammit." He said nothing

and reached to get Mason and his belongings. He placed the bag on the ground and handed Mason to me. I held him tight, feeling his moist little breath on my neck. He buried his head on my shoulder. I wanted to hold him like that for the rest of my life.

Once inside, I inspected him, head to toe, for bruises or other issues and then fed him breakfast. I put on his favorite show, and we sat on the couch as I spooned the cereal into his mouth and laughed at Elmo. My heart hurt badly.

Then, an amazing thing happened.

Mason said, "Mama," his first word. My heart melted. He kept repeating it. "Mama, Mama, Mama." I cried softly and hugged him tight. "Yes, baby boy, Mama is here." For the first time in many months, I felt pure joy.

The days passed quickly, and the next court date loomed. This time, I was prepared for the fight, as was my counsel. We met on the courthouse steps and entered together. I ignored Mark and his entourage. I braced for the fight.

Someone in the clerk's office, however, forgot to docket our matter, meaning the case was not scheduled with the court. A clerk suggested we wait to see if calendar space opened later. We sat for hours until the attorneys learned a mediator they knew (and respected) was in the building and might be available to try to broker a resolution. Mark and I consented to try.

Once in the conference room, the attorneys bantered back and forth. It became clear that Mark wanted me to move out of the state. I wanted that, too. But Mark had to win. So, I played it differently. I pushed back on the idea of leaving California. Mark said, "You are moving." I resisted. *I have friends in California. I have more job opportunities. I am comfortable here. I like the weather better. Maybe, if we can reach an agreement on custody, I'll leave.* If I moved to Texas, he would get to see Mason once a month for two days (as opposed to every other weekend). He took the bait. We agreed. I'd move in about a month. In the meantime, Mark had two more visitations.

I spent the next few weeks packing and taking care of Mason. Mark's next visitation was coming up, and the thought of it sickened me. I had to survive two visitations before boarding a one-way flight to Dallas.

During the first pre-move visitation, I called Mark, the one call I was allowed, to check in on Mason. Mark didn't answer. I waited another hour and called again—again, no answer. My heart pounded through my chest. I made several frantic calls—to his family, his friends, and on—and no one knew where he was. Knowing Mark, he was likely at a hotel, and I eventually tracked him down at one of his favorites. I called him from the lobby. He answered.

"Mark, is Mason with you?" I said tensely.

"Maybwee." *Drunk.*

"Please stop this. Where is he?" I pleaded.

"Not sure," he said, sounding like he really didn't know.

I started crying.

"I'm in room 420." He hung up.

At the hotel, I bounded up the stairs in a panic.

I knocked, and no one answered. I pounded on the door, and Mark opened it. He was noticeably shit-faced. The room reeked of smoke. I screamed, "Where is Mason?"

"Calm down. He's in the other room," he said.

I found Mason in a crib, with no clothes on, face down. The room was cold, and the crib had no mattress. When I rolled him over, feces smeared his belly.

Mark followed me, smoking a cigarette.

"See, he's fine. Calm down. That is your problem. You are always so hysterical."

I picked Mason up, pressing his body against mine to warm him. He cried and grabbed my hair.

"I'm taking him home," I said.

"No, this is my weekend. If you do, I'll call DCF [Department of Children and Families] and tell them you've stolen him." He laughed.

"I guess your choices are to leave him or stay with me. Which will it be?" He laughed again, manically.

Ironically, and sadly, he was correct. I couldn't leave him alone with him. I had to stay. I hated that I was there, but I was not going to leave Mason alone with him.

"I'll stay."

When he heard those words, he converted to the good Mark. He professed his love for me and went on and on about how he'd do anything to have our family together. He claimed he was reading books on divorce, trying to figure out how to win me back. He begged for forgiveness. He ordered my favorite dinner—chicken parmesan and Caesar salad.

I desperately wanted this nightmare to end. I didn't know what to do—other than play it cool and close to the vest. For now, and most importantly, Mason was safe, and I was with him. I tried not to buy into his words. It was everything I wanted to hear *before* we got to this point, but I knew that the outcome would be the same.

I slept with one eye open and waited for the sun to rise. In the morning, even though it was Sunday, Mark said I should take Mason home. He must have had a social agenda for the day. Rumors had him hanging out with a twenty-two-year-old. I gathered his stuff and left.

I had one more visitation to survive before boarding a plane to the Lone Star State. The night before that visitation, Mark texted that he would not take Mason for the weekend. He wished me safe travels and ended with "I love you, cutie, forever."

28

Jessica

The garage door opened, kickstarting a rush of adrenaline through my system. Collin walked in, kissed my forehead, and said he was going to unpack. He returned to get a glass of water. I stood at the stove, fiddling with how to start, my heart pounding, my body vibrating, as I grasped the counter to keep me steady.

My phone vibrated. A 305 number. *The* 305 number. She was texting me! Collin was oblivious, chomping on pineapple.

> **305: Collin has been living a double life and is a lying piece of shit.**
>
> **305: This is his GF of 5 years.**
>
> **305: He said how you trapped him by getting pregnant. I know ALL about you. He said he never loved you.**
>
> **305: I have proof of everything if you want to see it. We have traveled the world.**
>
> **305: BTW, he had a GF when you two started dating, all the way up until he met me.**
>
> **305: Her name is Katy Rhodes.**
>
> **305: He said you were never in love, and you are a crazy alcoholic and addicted to pills.**

I struggled to breathe. I couldn't believe what I had read. Knowing about the sick relationship helped me process this latest craziness. But I was still beside myself with fury. I looked at Collin, shook my head, and jutted my phone in his face.

"You animal! Your lowlife girlfriend is texting me like crazy!" I screamed. He betrayed no emotion. He sat there, unmoving, like a smirking sculpture.

"You've had a girlfriend for the last five years?" I screamed again.

"So what?" he said. "You cheated, too."

"I cheated? Are you fucking crazy! What kind of human being are you?"

"Look," he said, with an unsettling calmness, "don't listen to that crazy bitch, Danielle. She is mad because I want to end it with her."

"You're ending it with her?" I said with a blend of curiosity and skepticism.

"Jessica, I've been trying to. She just won't go away quietly."

"I don't give a shit, Collin. You disgust me. You two made sex videos?"

"Big fucking deal. I'm not running for president, am I?" he said, laughing.

"You sick bastard. I am the mother of your child. How could you do this to me? If you are ending it with her . . . call her . . . now . . . in front of me . . . and *tell* her."

"Stop, Jessica. Don't tell me what to do. I told you it's over, and it is."

"You're a fucking liar!"

I left and got in the car. I wasn't on the road for ten minutes when the phone rang. It was her.

"Hello. Yes, I know who it is. Why the fuck are you calling me?"

She unleased a stream of consciousness, as if emoting to a close girlfriend, about what a jerk Collin was, as if I needed the tutorial. She wanted to join forces against him. I was incredulous. But I let her talk. The woman had no filter. I figured she might cough up something helpful. I tried to get some questions in edgewise, not so easy, but I learned a few things. Neither she nor her son had met my daughter. She hadn't even seen a picture of her. Collin often labeled me as "crazy"—"you sound nothing like that, Jessica"—and painted me as a manipulative woman who not only tricked him into marriage but also withheld sex from him "to punish" him "for working hard to provide for the family." She refused to say how they met—fueling the suspicion that she was an escort—and clamped down on providing information about the trips they'd taken together. She kept bringing the "discussion" back to how Collin was a habitual liar and could not be trusted. I finally finagled my way off the call.

I returned home, went to the guest bedroom, and staggered into the shower, standing motionless under the stream of water and staring at the walls. I was numb.

After the water cleanse, I went into the bedroom, put a pillow over my head, and screamed. I was going mad. Moments later, Collin entered, sat at the end of the bed, and started the cry.

"I am so sorry, Jessica," he said.

"You should cry until your eyes fall out, you piece of garbage." I got up and went into the guest room, where I stayed the rest of the night. I didn't sleep for more than ten minutes at a time, constantly waking up hysterical. It was a horrible night.

Collin lurched to hug me in the morning. I forearm-blocked him and said, "Don't you dare touch me." He started to leave.

"Where are you going?" I said.

"Jessica, I'll be home in an hour. We can talk then . . . and I won't be interrogated about where I am going."

"Interrogated? *Interrogated*? You don't think our situation . . . and what you've done . . . deserves a thorough conversation? You don't think we have some work to do here?" I felt like I was talking to a child.

"Jessica, everything will be fine. I will work it out, and we will talk about this later." He turned and left.

Why did I even care where he was going? I should have said right there and then, *Get out and stay out*, but the fear of losing my daughter crippled me, and I clung to the hope that, somehow, if she was out of the picture, things would get better. I was a mental mess, in a complete fog, running on anxiety.

I grabbed the iPad and waited.

Ping!

Stefano: You okay?

Collin: My girlfriend just spoke to my wife.

Stefano: Damn, man, that's a major downer.

Collin: I'm so depressed. You know how it is when you lose your slut.

Stefano: Been there many times, lol. Don't humiliate the lady at home, though.

Collin: Too late, lol.

Stefano: Plenty of pieces of ass out there.

Collin: Yeah, well, my wife hates me.

Stefano: She'll chill, give it some time, and be smart.

Who the fuck is this person? This is not the Collin I married. He is speaking like a thug, degrading both me and his girlfriend. Is this who he really is?

Collin came home in the afternoon and implored me to talk. He talked. I listened. He apologized repeatedly, claiming he "never meant for this to happen." He had ended it and wanted "terribly" to keep his family together. He moaned about how he became "lonely" when I spent so much time with Alexandra. And when he sold his business, he became depressed and needed something to "fill the void." (He forgot he had met Danielle before he sold his business, not to mention how many others.) I had to "move past" this and trust when he said, "It's done." He reprimanded me for accrediting her lies. He closed with "I want to make this work."

I said virtually nothing. I kept looking in his eyes for glimpses of genuineness. Hard to see through the darkness. *Is it over? Can I forgive him? What about how he treated Alexandra and me on a daily basis? Is this salvageable?*

The next morning, Collin asked if I would have breakfast with him at his favorite spot. He told me he wanted to talk about us.

Before touching my food, I poured my heart out and shared my agony.

"I assure you," he emphasized, "the Danielle thing is over. We'll get through this."

"Collin, I don't know if I can. The betrayal is so deep. How can I trust you again?"

"You'll have to let go of the past, Jessica. That's the only way it can work."

"No, Collin, we need therapy."

"Sure, sure."

"Why did you do it, Collin? What made you choose her? How could you do this to me?"

"It's not about you, Jessica. I was going through tough times, and you weren't there for me. She was. You think I wanted this to happen, but when I met her, she was hypnotizing."

I started to cry. "Hypnotizing? Are you kidding me?"

"Jessica, I know we'll get through this."

"I will find a therapist and make an appointment, okay?"

"Okay."

For the next several weeks, Collin swarmed me with attention. We went for walks and played with Alexandra. We had sex, although it felt like an out-of-body experience. At night, he held me tight, staring into my eyes and telling me how beautiful I was. And, by all indications, his communications with Danielle ceased. We were on the right track, and I desperately held onto the hope that maybe, just maybe, things might change. I so wanted the pain to go away.

As we moved slowly but steadily toward normal, one afternoon, I popped into the house earlier than expected after taking Alexandra on a playdate. As I neared the bedroom, I heard groaning, as if Collin were about to orgasm. I peeked in the bedroom to see Collin lying on the bed, his pants around his ankles, masturbating while FaceTiming Danielle.

I couldn't believe what I was witnessing. My heart beat so loudly; I was sure he could hear it.

"Oh, baby"—he moaned as he came—"felt like I was inside you."

"I hope you will be soon," Danielle said.

I stormed to the bed, shrieking. "Collin, I'm fucking done! You are a pathetic, sick, selfish bastard." He tried to stand, tripped on his pants, and ejected the phone from his hand into the air. As the phone crashed into the carpet, I could hear Danielle's muffled voice scream, "Collin, Collin, is everything okay?"

"You betrayed me, Jessica. I can't believe you were reading my texts."

"I betrayed *you*? You lowlife piece of shit." I walked away. He continued to rant.

"You want a divorce? You'll get it, Jessica." Get ready for a war you'll never win. You're a crazy, unstable bitch, and everyone will know it when I'm done with you!"

"Fuck you, Collin," I yelled from the hallway. "Do what you gotta do."

Later that night, I found a forlorn Collin sitting at the end of the bed in pitch-black, staring into space as if comatose. He didn't move or say anything.

"What are you doing, Collin?" I said as if talking to a teenager.

"You and Alexandra would be better off without me. I have caused irreparable damage; you are a good mother, and you will raise our girl just fine on your own."

"Okay, that is fine. But let's follow up on the therapist idea, get some professional help," I said. "No matter what our futures hold, we will need it."

"Okay, please make an appointment for tomorrow if you can," Collin said. "I'm ready."

29

If You Knew, Would You Say I Do?

DR. BRENNAN: Welcome back to my podcast, *If You Knew Would You Say I Do?* Today, we have my guests, Laura and Jessica, to discuss the next installment of their past relationships with two narcissistic abusers. Remember, abuse is not just physical; it is emotional, psychological, sexual, and financial. Ladies, I commend you for sharing your story with the world to help save lives. Let's get started with you, Laura.

LAURA: Hi, thanks for having us back.

DR BRENNAN: Today's discussion could be triggering, so if I dig too deep, please let me know.

LAURA: Okay, but I want people to know that I am sharing my path so, hopefully, listeners can avoid becoming a victim of narcissistic abuse. It's sinister, but the more educated you are, the better chances of survival you'll have when targeted. Leaving was hard, not because I didn't want to get away from him, but because I was trauma-bonded, and I knew it would be the fight of my life. I wish I had left earlier, but I did the best I could at the time.

DR BRENNAN: Yes, people should understand that the difficulty in leaving is completely normal. Most victims in these situations don't leave the first time, the second time, or ever, unfortunately. The question always arises, though. "Why didn't they just leave?" Well, there are many reasons—fear, shame, guilt, hope, financial stress, and the ultimate threat of losing their children. However, one of the most powerful psychological reasons people don't leave is that they are trauma-bonded to their abuser. The trauma bond is developed between abuser and victim, similar to what occurs between a prison keeper and a prisoner. The victim has often lost all sense of self, and they become dependent on their abuser, much like a drug addict to a drug. Toxic relationships are addictive because of the constant reinforcement of punishment and reward. Frightening as it may be, the addiction is difficult to break. Please be mindful of those you know who are in abusive relationships. It is an extremely difficult and dangerous situation to escape from.

When you try to leave the narcissist, it sets off their panic bells, awakens an intense fear of abandonment, and causes them grave personal injury. Narcissists will do whatever it takes to get the outcome they desire, even if it means destroying you, your family, and your children. It is frightening. They crave control. It is their lifeblood, and the prospect of exposure, abandonment, and losing control of their supply can drive them to desperate measures. Statistically, victims of abuse are at greater risk after they leave their abusers.

It is important to have a safety plan in place, which national and local domestic violence shelters can provide. Not everyone has a strong support system, people who understand the danger, depths of pain, and additional barriers when escaping an abusive relationship. Often, victims are unintentionally revictimized by family and friends because they lack a depth of knowledge about these situations. And worse, sometimes, family and friends align with the abuser, which can be devastating.

LAURA: I desperately wanted to believe the restraining order would keep Mason and me safe. I was certainly glad I had one, but it didn't take me long to realize a TRO wasn't going to deter Mark from trying to get what he wanted. One thing I didn't mention in the last episode but learned later was that he paid a woman from yoga class to impersonate a therapist. That whole thing with her was staged—a carefully crafted charade. Yes, he actually paid off an employee from "Crystal Harmony," where she bought and sold healing crystals and minerals, to impersonate a therapist, with whom

I shared my heart and soul and innermost fears. How sick is that! At the time, I thought his behavior was because of drug addiction and alcohol abuse. I didn't know he had a personality disorder, NPD, which added an entire new layer to his behavior, injecting a cruel, manipulative dimension.

DR. BRENNAN: Wow. I have heard many a story about the lengths to which narcissists will go, but that ranks right up there with the most outrageous. But it is not surprising in the scheme of things. Nefarious manipulation is their MO. That is one reason the restraining order was necessary because no one knows to what lengths narcissists will go when they feel humiliated, abandoned, or exposed. They will do anything not to lose their well-groomed, beaten-down supply. After all, it took a lot of work to bring you psychologically and physically to your knees. Narcissists need to win; losing is not an option. Ringling brothers has nothing on the circus acts that take place when going to court with a narcissist. It is their grandest arena, an uneven playing field, where they can legally abuse you and put on their greatest phony performance.

LAURA: I quickly understood why family court has become known as the "unjust" system. For starters, you are surrounded by other narcissists in the legal system, including some judges, psychologists, attorneys, and others in positions of power who can alter your life and the lives of your children.

DR. BRENNAN: There is truth to that. But in their defense, most legal system professionals are not educated about NPD or cluster B personality disorders, what they look like, how they work, and especially how they affect the victim and their children. It has taken me years to understand the depths and nuances of these disorders. The justice system has an acute need to become educated about them.

LAURA: Unfortunately, politics, money, and power go a long way to influence the family court system. Mark's family connections gave him ready access to powerful pit bull attorneys, experts, and, in some cases, friendly witnesses. Mark heavily relied on his family to orchestrate my ambush in court, and guess what? It was effective. Judges have discretion, and in my case, after watching the Lifetime movie *The Happy Corbins* and other false narratives they spewed, she fell for it, and days later, Mason was taken out of my arms by a security guard and transported to his abusive father. To add insult to injury, that judge was removed from the bench three weeks later because of heroin addiction. I mean, you can't make this shit up. The drug addict judge let my drug addict ex have access to my baby.

DR. BRENNAN: I can't imagine how devastating that must have been. I agree; you don't want to end up in the court system with a narcissist, but unfortunately, most cannot avoid that scenario.

JESSICA: I have to jump in and say that family court is like a bad circus act run by the clown, with the animals out of control. For a narcissist, the courtroom is the "greatest show on earth," a stage where they can shine bright.

DR BRENNAN: That is so true. Other than immersing yourself in the education of NPD, I can't emphasize enough the importance of finding an attorney who understands NPD in high-conflict divorces. Otherwise, victims will be repeatedly revictimized by the court system.

Jessica, you experienced your own sting of betrayal on what you uncovered. I am so sorry for what you had to endure.

JESSICA: The sting of the betrayal was astounding! I know this sounds crazy, but I was utterly shocked. Collin was quick to call other men losers because they cheated on their spouses while doing the exact same thing with hookers and escorts. In a million years, I would have never thought Collin would pay an escort for sex.

DR. BRENNAN: Yes, narcissists are notorious hypocrites. Always keep this in mind: their accusations are their confessions.

JESSICA: Truer words were never spoken. I repeatedly go over how it was possible that I didn't know he had a girlfriend for so many years—and the others since the day we met.

DR. BRENNAN: It is common for narcissists to have full-on relationships while with a partner. They have a constant need for supply, adoration, sex, and money. Like a child, they continuously require a shiny new toy to fill their emptiness. No one toy promises more than the other, and they all wind up in the same junkyard. You were consumed with trying to appease Collin to avoid his wrath; you couldn't think clearly, Jessica. You were living in a persistent state of fear and self-doubt, which he sustained with gaslighting, lying, abuse, manipulation, and the most effective, hoovering. He was busy convincing you that he wanted his family together, Danielle was in the past, and he was ready for professional help with a therapist.

JESSICA: Of course, at first, I thought Collin had found the love of his life in Danielle, but after time, I realized he had merely replaced me with a new supply, a set of fresh, new, adoring eyes who also did not see beyond his mask and who he groomed and brainwashed like he did me. He love-bombed her like he love-bombed me. He lied to her like he lied to me. And she became addicted to Collin as I did and joined me in the discard phase.

DR. BRENNAN: I can say comfortably that she wasn't getting a better or different version of Collin. She was getting the same abuser with the same methods to secure her as supply. He controlled and abused you both simultaneously. He may have executed each scheme differently, but his motives and tactics were identical—intermittent reinforcement, brainwashing, trauma bonding, gaslighting, triangulation, silent treatments, future-faking, and hoovering. All built on a flimsy bed of lies.

JESSICA: Oh, my God, when I read those texts, I thought Danielle was his soulmate, getting a different Collin, the good Collin, the one I longed for day after day, the one I thought I met. I was devastated, my heart shattered. Their exchanges were intimate, sexual, and intense. I was watching my husband speak to another woman in a way he had not spoken to me in years. It was mind-blowing.

DR. BRENNAN: I'm sure that was enormously painful to see and process. Everyone thinks that the new girlfriend, a.k.a. supply, is getting a better version of their husband or boyfriend, and that is *not* true. Narcissists don't change for *anyone*. They may change costumes or masks, but what lies beneath remains the same. Don't sit around thinking their new supply is getting the *good* him—and only the good. I can promise that they are not. The good him, in whatever form it appears, as with you, is a vehicle to gain complete control and secure supply. It appears only when necessary to advance the narcissistic agenda. Over time, less and less of the good version shows. Each new supply suffers the same cycle of abuse, from love bombing through cruel devaluation and ultimate discarding.

JESSICA: I was obsessed with the nature of their relationship and how sexual it was. I was riveted by the exchange of them masturbating with each other and the constant exchange of naked pictures. I studied their texts for hours, searching for answers to what it was they had and we didn't. It seemed she was getting the attention and affection that I longed and begged for, but the more I read, the easier it was to see a similar pattern of abuse, manipulation, and crazy-making behavior like I had endured for many years.

DR. BRENNAN: What you didn't understand at the time, Jessica, is that to gain control, Collin simply adapted his personality to mirror that of a twenty-five-year-old escort who spoke like a millennial and used sex as her power to create that "soulmate" connection. Narcissists have an uncanny ability to mold themselves to fit any circumstance for the desired outcome. They could tell one victim who begs for a puppy that they hate animals and post pictures of the rescue dog they have with a new girlfriend who loves dogs months later.

JESSICA: Oh, yeah, Danielle was in the devaluation phase, but it took me some time to see it because the sting of betrayal blinded me. He had future-faked her and made her believe she'd be the next Mrs. Worth. Danielle obviously grew impatient and felt the need to take matters into her own hands by exposing their affair to me, hoping

I'd leave, and he'd keep his word and marry her.

DR. BRENNAN: Remember, narcissistic plans never include anyone's happiness but their own. They lack sincere connection or loyalty to anyone or anything, even when they call you their soulmate or phone you a hundred times a day. It is all about control!

Thank you both, again, for sharing the details and intimacies of your life.

I'm your host, Dr. Jules Brennan. Until next time, *if you knew, would you say I do?*

Thanks for listening.

30

Laura

I returned to Texas with a blend of conflicting emotions: the relief of putting many miles between Mark and me, a finalized divorce in record time that limited his Mason visits to once a month, the pain of leaving good friends, familiar haunts, and a state I loved living in, the odd feeling, bordering on embarrassment, of living with my parents in the room I occupied as a teenager, and the daunting reminder that I was unemployed, with no prospects and limited resources. But what mattered most, what kept me emotionally afloat, was that Mason and I were together and safe. I breathed easier.

The sense of peace didn't last long.

No longer subject to a restraining order, Mark called me incessantly. If I didn't pick up, he'd harass my family. If they didn't cooperate, he'd threaten them. He told my brother, then a hedge fund manager, that it'd be a shame if the SEC got an anonymous call from a client about the Ponzi scheme he was operating. He told my mother that her boss would be none too pleased to hear she'd threatened Mark in response to his request for basic information about his daughter.

It was hard to find the baseline for normal, but somehow, I had to find a way back there.

I enrolled in a medical assistant program and, after an exhausting search, found a permanent sitter for Mason. The days were long as I charted a new life one step at a time. I needed patience and lower expectations, finding joy in little moments, at least for the short haul.

The problem, however, was that no matter how much I tried to focus on that precious light at the end of the tunnel, thoughts of

Mark alone with Mason tormented me. I could deal with how he treated me. That had started to roll off my back. But I couldn't ignore the risk he posed to our son. He was dangerous and troubled, and until he got serious professional help, I'd be incarcerated inside his madness. How long would that last?

Three days before his first Texas visitation, Mark requested I bring Mason to him at the airport car rental agency. I didn't argue. Not worth it. When I arrived in the car lot, I spotted Mark waiting for his car. My heart pounded, and my hands rattled. I had not seen him in several weeks, and the sight of him sickened me. Spotting me, he beckoned me to drive toward him. I obliged. As soon as Mark picked up Mason, he started crying and arching his back.

"You sure fucked this kid up. Hope you're happy. Can't leave his mama for a second," he said. I shook my head, helped with the car seat—another fundamental parenting skill he forgot to master—and watched him drive away in a huff of disgust. Anxiety clogged my throat. *What might go wrong with him alone with Mason? When would the next shoe drop?*

That night, I couldn't sleep. I lay awake, staring at the ceiling. At 1:30 a.m., my phone rang. The caller ID said "Mark."

"Hello?" I answered with tense curiosity.

I heard loud music in the background but didn't get a response.

"Mark, are you there?" The music blared, and the phone silence continued.

"Mark?" Nothing.

I disconnected and called him back, with no pickup. I called his hotel room, and after three rings, a woman answered.

"Hello?" she said, with a frustrated voice.

"Who's this?" I asked.

"Who's *this*?" she abruptly answered.

"This is Mark's ex-wife. The mother of the child I am praying is in the room. Who are you?"

"I'm Debbie, the hotel babysitter. Your Mark isn't here. He was supposed to be back by 12:30. I have to be at work at nine. I tried calling him. He doesn't answer. I can't stay. I was about to drop off the baby with the hotel staff when you called. I have to leave. And, frankly, your child has cried the entire time. This has been a disaster."

"Please, please don't leave. I'll drive there and get the baby. Just wait until I get there. Please."

"Look, I have to get some sleep. I can't stay any longer."

"If you don't stay, I'll call the police and tell them you abandoned my child in a hotel room," I said, raising my voice. "I'll be there in less than an hour. Just stay." I heard a deep exhale.

"Okay. One hour. Not a second more. And bring an extra forty dollars."

Forty-five minutes later, after miraculously evading the Texas Highway Patrol, I arrived at the hotel. As I pulled into the hotel parking lot, the phone rang. It was Mark.

"Why did you call me so many times?" he said in a slurred, angry voice.

"Are you serious? The babysitter was about to leave Mason with the hotel. Where *are* you?"

"I was out, having fun. Is that a crime? . . . Anyway, I'm back at the hotel. Everything's fine. Mason is fine. Life is fine. Except you, of course, the drama queen, aren't fine."

"Mark, you haven't seen your son in over a month, and you go out to party all night?"

"Fuck off, you jealous bitch." And he hung up.

I stood there, mummified. *What should I do?* I needed to stay close, in case. I couldn't afford a room, so I parked behind the hotel and slept in the back seat. That morning, Mark called and said, "Mason is still fine, in case you stayed up all night worrying about him. I'll bring him back tomorrow." I felt a part of me gone forever. I drove home in a daze. When I arrived, I drew the drapes of my room, crawled into bed, and lay there in darkness, listening to my breathing and wondering if I was going mad.

The next thirty days passed in a blur. Each day, I went through the motions of living—a shell of who I once was. But I kept telling myself that, in time, things would get better. They had to.

The day before Marks's next visitation, I noticed a lump around Mason's belly button, which prompted an immediate visit to a pediatrician. On visual inspection, the doctor diagnosed an easily reparable small hernia. I scheduled the outpatient surgery and informed Mark. I was loathed to communicate with him, but the medical release form required his signature. When he got the form via email, he responded with a rant about how my "neglectful mothering" caused the hernia. I couldn't believe I had to tell him that "umbilical cord hernias aren't anyone's fault. They are normal." He remained fractious, refusing to sign the form despite a few requests, forcing me to reschedule the surgery three times. When I wrote that his "dereliction of parental duty is endangering" his son—admitted hyperbole—he caved, with a caveat: "I'll sign if you have lunch with me."

I chose the path of least resistance.

When we arrived for lunch two days later, Mark had a box of truffles (my favorite) and flowers. He said, "My two babies. I miss you both so much." He told Mason that the flowers were for him and handed me the truffles. Flowers for Mason?

Mark was subdued during lunch. At one point, he promised to get "real" help and go to a rehab facility and a therapist of my choice. He worked me hard, skillfully triggering prospects of a normal family. His swarmed me with provocative entreaties—"Please . . . you are the best thing that ever happened to me," and "I know I have a problem. . . . I want you to help me build our family. . . . We can do this together. . . . Let's get back to what we once had."

I'd been free of him long enough, however, to appreciate the sobering differences between a Mark-less life and a life if I returned to him. His stories all had the same ending. I had danced to those familiar tunes often before. It was time to get rid of the dancing shoes in favor of running shoes. So, while his words were enticing and tugged at my heartstrings, my instincts steered me in the opposite direction. I trusted my internal bells and whistles. I reclaimed myself.

On the other hand, I feared rejecting him. Mason would be in his care the rest of the weekend and for years to come. I had to manage him as best I could. He was volatile and unpredictable.

I told him I'd "help" him, which appeased him.

During this period, I noticed bodily changes. I was often fatigued. I didn't sleep well. My face sometimes twitched. I lost track of things. I struggled to listen well in conversation, often wandering in thought. Hives formed on my arms and legs. I had intermittent headaches.

Doctors uniformly offered the same obvious explanation: "stress" or "anxiety illness."

Friends urged me to pamper myself more—an appealing idea. I figured I'd start with a pedicure at a local place aptly called Lovely Nails. On arrival, I picked a color, sat down, and put my feet into the bubbling hot water. Sublime. *I need to do more of this.*

As she started to massage my feet, my phone rang. Mark. I hesitated to answer, but with him, you never knew, and I took the call. He was frantic, screaming. I couldn't make out his words at first, but then I heard "lost." *Mason is "lost."*

I bolted from my seat—my feet dripping wet, my calves covered with lotion—and ran out the front door like a mad woman. I kept trying to talk to Mark.

"Mark, please calm down so I can hear you. What is happening?" I had gone from sheer delight to utter panic in thirty seconds.

"I'm in Neiman Marcus on Main and looked up and couldn't find Mason."

"Call 911 now!" I screamed.

I jumped in my car and sped to the location.

Tears rolled down my cheeks the whole way. *Where is my baby boy? Is he in danger? How could he let this happen?* I became dizzy and almost fainted while driving. I kept envisioning a pedophile scooping Mason up and never seeing him again. Forty minutes of terror.

When I was five minutes away, Mark called and said "they" found Mason. He had wandered off and lay down under a clothing rack. I pulled onto the shoulder of the road, turned off the ignition, and sobbed with great heaves. *Co-parenting with this maniac will be the death of me.* Finally, I restarted the car and returned home. I had barely enough energy to exit the car on arrival. I went inside, crawled into bed, and cried myself to sleep.

Around 4:30 p.m., my phone rang again, jolting me out of a deep slumber. It wasn't Mark, thank God. It was a good family friend, Max, who'd heard I was back in Texas. He called to have a drink and dinner. I resisted, he insisted, and I relented. We met up at UNI Sushi in Plano. I found him at the bar. We ordered drinks and caught up. The more we talked, the better I felt about the world. I was having a normal life experience.

Then the phone buzzed. It was a text from Mark. I ignored it, as well as a few more. Less than a minute later, the phone rang. It was my mother. I let it go to voicemail. She called back. I took a deep breath, apologized to Max, who said, "Not a problem," and answered.

"What, Mom?" I said, not concealing my annoyance.

"Mark just called me and said there was a major emergency and had to reach you. But you weren't answering his text messages, so he called me. Then he hung up."

"Shit." I hung up without saying goodbye. "I have to go," I said to Max.

"Is your mom okay?"

"She's fine. I'll explain later. Welcome to my bizarro world."

I tried calling Mark. He didn't pick up. I got in my car and, before driving off, called repeatedly. I drove toward the hotel. On the way, I pulled over, got out of the car, and threw up. I got back in the car and resumed the drive. Ten minutes later, Mark texted.

Mark: All is fine.

Me: Pick up! I'm calling you.

Mark: Don't tell me what to do. Next time you go out with someone, you might find a real emergency to handle. For now, hope I ruined your date, you cheating bitch.

Me: You asshole. It was a family friend. And in case you forgot, we're divorced.

Mark: You've been warned.

My mother later explained that she'd told Mark I was out with a friend, which, in light of our recent discussion over lunch, no doubt set him off. In his fragile mind, we were on the road to relationship healing, and I was on a date—in violation of some implied pact. The man was a human house of cards.

Sunday came, and I offered to pick Mason up at his hotel, an offer I knew he wouldn't refuse. From my perspective, it meant less time for him with Mason, a form of risk management. We didn't say a word to each other when I arrived. *Chilly.* As I pulled away, I peeked into the rearview mirror to see Mark glaring at me.

Once settled in at home, retrieving strawberries from the refrigerator, I turned to see Mason slumped over and rolled up in a ball, unable to straighten his body. I screamed. My parents weren't home, and I felt a rush of helplessness. I snapped out of it after a few seconds and called 911, begging for assistance. The paramedics arrived quickly. They lay his tiny body down and concluded that he needed hospital care. In minutes, we were off in the ambulance, Mason on a mini stretcher, me panic-stricken next to him. Once underway, I noticed trickles of blood on his leg, but I couldn't figure out the source. I started freaking out. The female paramedic assured me that Mason was "stable." Stable? He didn't look it. I asked what was wrong, and she said, "Probably a gastric bleed, but he'll be okay. To make sure, the ER doctor will check him out." I started praying.

As soon as Mason got wheeled into the ER, a nurse inserted an IV, and before long, Mason woke up. The ER doctor confirmed that

Mason had suffered "a gastric bleed," likely due to food poisoning. He'd be fine and could go home once he was adequately hydrated.

I called Mark to update him. "You're in a fucking *hospital*?" he said with feigned shock.

"Yes. I had to bring him to the ER. Our son had food poisoning."

"Maybe you forgot, Laura. You're required to get my approval before bringing our son to any hospital. It's in the marital settlement agreement," he said smugly.

"*Really*, Mark? It was a serious situation. He needed immediate medical care. I didn't have the luxury of fishing you out of some bar."

"Rules are rules. You will learn . . . the hard way." He hung up.

When Mason settled down, the hospital green-lighted me to bring him home, and my dad collected us at the hospital. En route, I revisited the brief conversation with Mark, how he resorted to a legal power play and showed zero interest in Mason's well-being. He never even asked how he was. Not once. *Who does that? What kind of human being is he?*

31

Jessica

Silence filled the car during our late morning drive to see Kira, the therapist Collin and I agreed to consult. My eyes on the road, Collin fixated on the passenger window.

"Jessica, why do you think you are here?" Kira asked. Collin and I had settled into adjoining seats a few feet apart on the coach directly across from her.

"Our marriage is on the brink . . . and I think Collin is suicidal," I said a little too fast.

"Collin, is that right? Do you feel suicidal?" she said with no hint of point of view.

"No, that's ridiculous. She's overreacting, as she always does. I have a ton going on in my life. Incredibly stressful. It's a challenge for her to grasp that. No one is killing anyone. We are here because Jessica has issues with me that she needs to work on."

Kira didn't betray any reaction.

"Jessica and Collin, scale of one to ten, how committed are you to working on the marriage?"

"A ten, of course, or I wouldn't be here," Collin said as I gathered thoughts.

"Jessica?"

"Hmm, well, I'd, um, say about six . . . or something like that." Not exactly an unequivocal response. Truthfully, I was closer to a one than a six, but I didn't want to quell things at the start. I wanted to provide some encouragement while being relatively forthright.

"Are you joking? A six?" Collin said, standing in protest. "Why are you wasting my time? Why are we even here?"

"Collin, forgive me, but trusting you and believing anything you say is difficult. Can't you at least see that?"

"Jessica, you better get to a ten soon. I'm not wasting my time and money on this." He remained standing.

"Are you listening, Collin? I need time. This isn't something you fix overnight. It's a process."

Collin flashed the same smile at Kira that he did at me that fateful day I gave him my phone number outside the elevator. He could turn it on like no one I ever knew. A crease of a smile slipped onto Kira's face, barely discernible, as if she couldn't help herself. It sent a chill up my back. Collin plopped back onto the couch.

Kira moved the discussion to background information, steering us away from angst and controversy and keeping the therapeutic ball in the air. Collin charmed, smiling and nodding at Kira, affirming whatever she said, floating effortlessly through all emotional moments as if he were equipped with evolved emotional intelligence. Each time a small hiccup occurred about something he did or didn't do, he trotted out an excuse, always at the ready, deftly painting himself as a well-intentioned husband who was the victim of circumstances. I provided my perspective in measured tones, almost as if speaking "for the record." If I had any doubt before, I no longer did; Collin would blame me for all that went wrong in our marriage. His persona couldn't tolerate any personal reckoning or admit any accountability. I had tired of it and paid more attention to Kira, trying to read her, hoping she wasn't buying the Oscar-worthy performance playing out in her midst. We agreed to meet again.

While our initial session left me wanting, it inspired me to research narcissism, and I voraciously perused popular works on NPD. The self-education empowered and helped me understand the disappearance of my self-esteem and my inability to extract myself and stand up for myself. One book became my go-to, *From Charm to Harm*. Each word described Collin to a T, convincing me that he suffered severely from NPD. He met every criterion, a classic case study. The eye-opener came with a price, too—that my entire relationship, from the start, lacked a genuine romantic and loving foundation, that Collin was a manipulative, uncaring person, my marriage a sham, and I'd been living a lie all these years. At bottom, I was a mere prop in a man's narcissistic, dramatic performance.

I kept asking myself two related questions: *why do I still cling to the relationship, and why do I want to take care of a man who abused me?* It was crazy. For goodness' sake, I consoled him over the loss of his girlfriend. Why? There was nothing healthy about that. The man I loved and trusted with my life presumably never loved me and extracted pleasure from the pain he'd caused me. *Maybe I am demented, too?* It all seemed incomprehensible. I had to read more. I had to understand how this happened and what I could do to protect both Alexandra and me.

We hung in with the therapist, and Collin even went alone a few times. Things improved on the home front. We were civil to each other. And while our life did not return to exciting, it tilted toward normal for a longer period than ever before.

One day after therapy, Collin suggested we visit an Apple store, where he insisted we each get Apple watches. "I can tell you how much I love you all day right on your wrist. You won't need your phone all the time." Indifferent, I said fine. His came with a navy band, mine pale pink. He spoke to his at least ten times before we returned to the car—"Text Jessica. Tell her I love her." They came across as sweet gestures and, in the moment, washed away some of the pain I carried around with me.

The next few days, Collin showered me with a degree of attention that rivaled our early dating days. It was flirty and sweet. The difference was how I processed it. Armed with newfound enlightenment that Colin Worth was a cunning fraud, I filtered everything he did and said, taking nothing at face value, always searching for hidden meanings.

On the other hand, I felt weirdly bonded to him from years of abuse. I was whipsawed between accumulated emotional scars and a new cognitive understanding of the underlying causes. I had a personal stake I couldn't quite shake or understand.

I wanted to believe that the Collin I loved and adored—and who I thought felt the same about me—had returned to stay, like the biblical prodigal son. But my heart resisted those spells of optimism, falling prey to the view that the fluctuating feelings I had were part and parcel of an invisible man's latest calculated manipulation. I lacked trust at the core. I gravitated to the realization that Collin couldn't love me or anyone else, that—as a deeply flawed human being—he was fundamentally incapable of love. His words of presumed affection were empty expressions, a collection of syllables patched together with no meaning, unattached to any genuine emotion, a vehicle to get what he wanted.

One late afternoon, while circulating within a market's produce section, my watch started pinging off the hook. I glanced down, expecting the umpteenth insincere love message of the day from Collin, but it was the dreaded 305! I halted the cart and yanked my phone out of my bag to see seven texts from Danielle—no words, only an inventory of videos.

I dared to venture, so I pushed play on one, and when it started, the bag of lemons I was holding parachuted to the ground. It was a sex video of Collin and her. *OMG*. I relocated the cart near a wall, darted outside to my car, and watched all seven videos—a few from St. Bart's, one in London, and one from his "boys' trip" to the Dominican Republic. The camera was so graphic that I could pick her vagina out of a lineup. Watching Collin orgasm while mouthing how much he loved her was beyond anything I could handle. It is—deep down—something I will never unsee.

That rogue of a woman was hell-bent on destroying my marriage to remove me from the picture. She'd waited years for him, moved her son countless times to keep the plan alive, and came unglued and went ballistic when he discarded her—and stayed there. Losing Collin wasn't an option for her. God only knew what she'd resort to next.

I drove home like a mad woman.

"I have something for you to watch on Apple TV, Collin," I said, bursting into the house half out of breath.

"Can we watch it later, honey? I'm working," he said innocently, eyes down.

"No, we can't. You have to see this. Your jaw will drop." I must have looked crazed because when he looked up, his eyes bolted open.

"Okay, okay."

I turned on the Apple TV and pushed play. There was Collin and Danielle in the flesh, going at it without inhibition, prime-time porn.

"Jessica, turn this shit off. Where did you get these?"

"Where do you think? Your personal whack job sent them to me. The question is why?"

"I don't know why, Jessica, except that she's pissed. I cut her off and ended it. She's a nutjob, and these are old videos. The problem is that, by engaging her, you encouraged her."

"Are you kidding, Collin? She was your girlfriend for years. You think I'm not going to want to know about your double life?"

"You brought this on yourself by speaking with her. You opened a Pandora's box."

"Bullshit. Look. Get that lowlife to stop harassing me, Collin. Get her out of our lives!"

"Okay, I'll take care of it. I'll email her."

I watched him type and send the email. This exchange followed:

Collin: Stop harassing my family, or you'll be very sorry. The videos, really, were the final straw. I stand by Jessica and my daughter. We are a family. I am warning you. If you ever contact my family again, you'll be sorry. I will send the videos to your new employer, and you will be living on the street. Proceed at your own risk.

305: Don't you dare threaten me. I'll expose you for who you are—a lying piece of shit, con man. I'll send the videos to your business partners, and instead of just thinking you are a dick, they'll get to see yours up close and personal.

Collin: You've been warned. You know what I'm capable of. Go back to the life you had, or I'll put you back on the streets.

305: You are EVIL. I wish I never met you. You destroyed my life.

After the exchange, Collin said that she went off the deep end when he ended the relationship and started ignoring her, resorting to the latest vengeful behavior. She was unable to come to terms with his choosing me over her, he said. Collin reaffirmed his commitment to me, urging that I let go of the past and look toward our future. Collin had masterfully triangulated us.

The chaos and toxicity had become all-consuming, taking on a life of its own. It was like being in a car with no brakes, going downhill. From the outside, it was easy to judge, but when mired inside, in a constant whirlwind, the brain doesn't easily function. You are untethered from good sense, struggling to right the ship of your life and take bold steps in your self-interest.

This much I knew. My marriage was irreparable. I had to do whatever I could to protect my daughter from these unstable and immoral people.

32

Laura

For Mark's next visitation, I offered to bring Mason to California, knowing he'd snatch up the offer. I told him I wanted to make it easier for him; in truth, I thought it might be safer for Mason, and as a bonus, I got to see old friends. I stayed with my friend, Grace, who lined up a babysitter for my first night so we could hit the town with girlfriends.

We started with a happy hour place we frequented. It was nice to see familiar faces. After our first drink, Grace said she wanted to introduce me to a guy, nodding in his direction across the way. "I think you'll like him. He's a really good guy." I protested, telling her I had "zero interest" in any introduction, that I only wanted "to relax." She smiled and waved him over.

"Andrew, this is my best friend, Laura," she said.

"Hi, best friend Laura," he said, smiling sweetly.

On the introduction, Grace swiftly departed to join others, leaving Andrew and I to share a short, uncomfortable silence. He broke the ice.

"Tell me about yourself," he stammered, not the most inspirational opening. I wanted to nip this in the bud and thought I knew exactly how to do it.

"I'm divorced, I have a baby, and my ex-husband is a full-on psycho." I smiled and raised my eyebrows as if to say, *Heard enough?*

I expected him to bolt. He didn't.

"Sorry to hear that, the last part, I mean, but life has a way of picking you up . . . if, of course, you want to be picked up."

Not bad, I thought. We chatted some more. He was nice, but

I lacked the right frame of mind to engage with him. After several minutes, I said, "It was nice meeting you," and added that I wanted to spend time with girlfriends. He said he understood "entirely." I returned to Grace, telling her I was hungry. We ordered food, and after we ate, I was primed to go home. As we got up to leave, Andrew corralled us.

"You ladies leaving?"

"Yes," I said. "Gotta go."

"Let me give you both a lift," he said.

"Thanks, but we're fine," I said quickly. "We called an Uber."

"We'll cancel it and take the ride," Grace overruled. "Thanks, Andrew." And off we went.

The next day, Grace and I took Mason to play in the park. Being with Grace reminded me how much I missed adult company. Later that afternoon, we stopped at Grace's favorite market to shop for dinner. The six steaks in her cart caught my attention.

"What's with so many steaks?" I said. "Expecting a calvary?"

"We're having people over tonight," she said, bobbing her eyebrows mischievously.

I began to think that coming to California wasn't a brilliant idea after all, and I wasn't ready to socialize outside my existing comfort zone. Nor did I want to be force-fed. But I couldn't push back. Grace was well-intentioned, and who knows? Maybe she had a point. I had to transition eventually.

After we readied for the night's festivities and I put Mason down, I braced for guest arrivals. I was anxious and treated myself to a small pour of wine to get grounded. On the first door knock, Grace called from the kitchen to "please get the door, sweetie." I opened the door to see Andrew, with a bottle of wine in his hand, along with another guy he introduced as Jay. *What is Grace doing?* When I inquired about the invited guests, she didn't mention Andrew, probably because she knew I'd protest. I was a little annoyed.

Of course, the night was fun. The food was delicious, the wine was more than ample, and everyone had a ball. As the night wound down, predictably, Andrew asked for my phone number. The walls were closing in. I hesitated but thought it rude not to indulge. I entered my number into his phone and said goodbye.

Morning came, and the jitters took hold before I rolled out of bed. Mark was set to retrieve Mason at noon. Every time I looked at Mason that morning, I got nauseous. I knew he'd be upset when Mark arrived. He had learned to associate the packing of his diaper bag and cuddle bear with leaving. Mark was like a stranger to him. He never cared for him, even when we lived under the same roof.

Mark arrived on time. When Mason saw him, he arched his back and screamed. On cue, Mark blamed the "shitty mom who can't control" her child. I had become impervious to his inane insults. As I approached his car, I noticed an unfamiliar blond woman in the passenger seat. She could hardly be older than the minimum voting age. I quietly asked who she was, and he said, "None of your damn business."

After they were gone, I sat on the couch for what seemed like an eternity until I felt strong enough to stand. I kept telling myself, *It's only an afternoon. What could go wrong?* Maybe the mystery woman would devote an extra set of eyes and bring a female touch to the childcare. As I wallowed in concern, I received a text. My heart stopped. Already? But it was from Andrew, asking if I was up for lunch. Under the circumstances, the timing was perfect. I responded, "Sure." He arrived twenty minutes later, and we walked to a nearby diner.

We chatted easily, and I slowly let my guard down. It felt good. He wasn't "my type," but I found his soft personality refreshing. Midway through lunch, my phone buzzed. It was Mark calling. I noticed two texts from him. Fingers shaking, I apologized to Andrew for the call; he shrugged to indicate all was good, and I answered.

"Your son has issues, and I'm not going to deal with them," Mark said as soon as the lines connected.

"What do you mean?" I said anxiously.

He hung up.

I shook my head and stared into space. Andrew asked if I was okay. I didn't respond directly, saying only, "Give me a second, please." Andrew excused himself to hit the bathroom.

I scanned my text messages, and pings kept coming in from Mark—each a variation of whether my "boyfriend was intending to be Mason's new father," and, if so, he'd "drop off the hysterical kid." *Boyfriend? Andrew?*

Mark was surveilling me.

Before another thought crossed my mind, I caught Mark pulling into the parking lot outside. Andrew had yet to return to the table. I feared a public scene. I went outside to preempt anything untoward.

"Where is the fucker? He dumped you already?" Mark screamed.

He opened the back door to the car and said, "You get him out." I reached down and unhooked Mason's car seat. He wrapped his tiny arms around me, shaking and crying. I rocked him to calm him down. Mark put the diaper bag on the sidewalk and drove away.

Andrew walked outside as I stood on the sidewalk with Mason.

"Are you okay? Is this your baby?" he said.

"Yes, it is, and no, I'm not okay. My psycho ex-husband paid us a visit. I think he is having me followed."

Andrew looked confused and said nothing. I could see him processing. *Maybe,* I imagined him thinking, *this woman wasn't such a grand idea, too toxic a life.*

"Look," I said, "I'm so sorry, but I need to go. Thanks for lunch." I walked home, leaving him bewildered.

The next month, I worked on getting Mason into a good day care and concentrated on school. Boring had become my new fabulous. I had thirty days until Mark's next visitation. It was like waiting for an inevitable tsunami.

Living with my parents had gotten old. They preferred evenings of watching a Netflix show I had no interest in. They meant well, but I was done joining my parents to watch TV and overeat popcorn. It made me feel like they were summer-camp counselors, and I was their sole camper. I appreciated their enthusiasm, but at my age, a ripe thirty-two, I needed my own space.

Andrew stayed in touch, always concerned about how Mason and I were doing. We chatted about life in general, my life in particular, and his work as an architect. During the most recent call, he said he was coming to Dallas on business. I offered to provide a list of places to eat. He turned that around, saying that, instead, I should take him there.

The weekend came, and I tried to get my mind right for meeting Andrew in the city. I shook off my initial nervousness. We met at the Warwick Hotel lobby and walked to a nearby Thai restaurant. I began to question whether Andrew was the real deal or fake like Mark. My Mark experience infected me with knee-jerk paranoia, and my radar stuck on high alert. In the wake of an abusive relationship, I was mistrustful of men and lacked confidence in my ability to read people and their intentions.

Lively conversation shaped our dinner. But when the waitstaff cleared the plates, I announced, "It's getting late. I should go." He tried to persuade me to hit a jazz bar, but I was unbending and declined with the "can't drink and drive" excuse. We strolled back to my car, and I opened the door to get in.

"I really enjoy your company, Laura," he said.

"Thank you," I said with little enthusiasm.

"Can I kiss you?"

Whoa. I froze. I didn't want to escalate this. A friendship was fine. I wasn't ready for a kiss.

"Um, I'd rather you not, if you don't mind." I got in the car and left him hanging.

The whole ride home, I felt like a jerk, but I had agreed to dinner, not a kiss, and I reasoned that he should appreciate the space I was in. I arrived home to a text from Andrew, asking to let him know I'd arrived safely, to "give Mason a hug" for him, and to thank me for "the amazing evening." I responded, "Safe and sound. Hug administered. Thank you."

Andrew called later that night, which I let go to voicemail. I listened to the message later. He was "checking on" us and wishing us a "good day tomorrow." I didn't respond. A few days went by, and I didn't hear from him. I began to feel selfish and rude and decided we needed a heart-to-heart. I wanted to be up front—that it didn't make sense for us to keep this up because I lived in Texas, and he deserved to know I wasn't interested in a relationship—with anyone. When I called, he was his usual self, smiling through the phone. After I delivered the *how I felt* script, he said, "Laura, you are a sweetheart. I don't want to push you in any direction, but I am here for you and Mason if you need anything." I thanked him for his kindness, and we ended the call.

After I hung up, sadness overcame me. I enjoyed his company, but I was a hot mess, and I'm sure he could do better. My self-esteem had hit a record low, and the last thing I wanted was to burden someone with my troubled existence.

Two weeks later, Mason took his first steps. I was thrilled. He had been slow to develop motor skills. Spontaneously, I texted Andrew, *Mason walked!* He quickly replied, *Yay. Next, he'll be running!* Then, it dawned on me that I shared this milestone with Andrew before anyone else.

He called the next day, and we chatted for two hours. He wanted to visit again, and he did, arriving with a gift for Mason. Mason ran to him, pointing to Andrew, and said, "Dada." Andrew laughed and said, "Hi, Mason. I'm Andrew," and Mason said, "No, Dada." I wanted to laugh and cry at the same time. All I ever wanted was a family, and in his toddler way, Mason felt the same.

33

Jessica

With our relationship restoration project on course, I was desperately trying to stay hopeful that Collin and I could get through this. Collin, out of the blue, mentioned an upcoming business meeting in Chicago with two hedge fund guys (Gary and Miles) to explore a possible new deal. Instantly, Danielle-dread flooded my system.

"Collin, are you going to see *her*?" I said with trepidation.

"Of course not, Jessica. Please stop it. Stop asking stupid questions. I said I'm done with her."

End of discussion.

My trauma-bonded brain begged to believe him. My heart lectured otherwise. I felt trapped between the two voices. I knew believing him was the last shred of hope I had for the family of my dreams. I clung to it, as crazy as it might sound.

As soon as Collin landed at O'Hare, he pinged me on his watch—*Miss you already. XO.* I replied, *Good luck with your meeting today. XO.*

During the trip, he texted and called, providing updates and sending photos of restaurant menus he wanted us to try on our next trip. His final text before boarding the homecoming plane was *Can't wait to get home to my FAMILY. XO.*

Collin returned upbeat about the new business venture. He planned to take Gary and Miles on a fishing trip in the Bahamas to seal the deal in the coming weeks. I didn't give it a second thought.

After he left on the fishing trip, as before, Collin texted constantly, expressing his feelings for me and keeping me abreast of the business dealings with Gary and Miles. We connected like old times. I was included in his business and other important aspects of his life, and he repeatedly told me how much he respected what I had to say.

The night he returned, we grabbed In-N-Out Burger, animal style, and watched a movie together. Old times redux. He chatted about how excited he was to be working again. He had another business meeting in Chicago with his two new partners, a trip that came and went as before.

The night after he returned from the second Chicago trip, Collin said, "Let's take a family trip—me, you, and Alexandra—where I went in the Bahamas. You guys will love it!" I was thrilled.

Weeks later, we were in the Bahamas on a chartered boat. The water gleamed as depicted in travel magazines, clear turquoise bordered by miles of soft white sand.

We bounced from island to island. Alexandra loved playing with the swimming pigs and searching for shells. We let her pet stingrays and watched people swim with sharks. Collin knew how to have a fun time. After island jumping for three days, Collin got a bad sunburn and retired down below. I was making lunch on the top deck when my watch buzzed. To my shock, it was Danielle texting me—messages between her and Collin.

> **305: [Pictures of Collin's ejaculating penis]**
>
> **305: [Snapshot of Collin's email describing how it would be to be inside her]**
>
> **305: [Screen grab of reply to Collin] Why are you contacting me? You are on a "family" vacation.**
>
> **305: Collin: Can't get the vision of your lips on my cock out of my thoughts.**
>
> **305: By the way, he's been on every trip to Chicago with me. Get control of your man.**

I tried to process what was happening. I was making us lunch on a *family* vacation in the middle of nowhere on a boat, and he was emailing this slut while masturbating? *WTF!* I shook from head to toe. I wanted to go home.

After some concentrated breathing to gather myself, I went down below.

"Collin, you are a piece of shit. I fucking hate you!"

"Jesus, Jessica, what now?" he said incredulously.

"What now? What *now*? I'll show you *what now*?" I screamed, thrusting my phone at him. "You are still talking to her, and don't try to weasel out of it this time."

He calmly took my phone and looked at what it showed.

"For crying out loud, Jessica. These are old emails she's recycling. She's a desperate bitch. I told you to block her. The woman isn't stable."

"You need to keep her out of our lives, Collin. I can't do this anymore."

"I have no control over her, Jessica. I don't speak with her anymore. Shit, you speak with her more than I do."

I looked at my phone to double-check.

"The emails are time stamped today. Is she a tech wizard, too? Stop lying! You are sick!"

"Jessica, you are so naïve. There are apps that allow people to alter email headings and the like. She is a millennial. They are good at that crap."

Collin could be persuasive. His demeanor was cool, and his speaking was unruffled. He didn't betray a speck of insecurity or doubt. If he was lying, it was effortless, masterful even. My head ached. I wanted to throw up. I couldn't decide what was true and what wasn't. I was going mad.

"Collin, take us home. Now."

"Jessica, please, get a grip. I chartered this boat for a week, and I'm not going to throw that money out the window because you are unhinged over nothing. If you want to leave, go ahead, and I will stay with my little sunshine. She deserves this trip."

Collin knew there wasn't a snowball's chance in hell that I'd leave Alexandra in the middle of the ocean under his watch. I was imprisoned on the boat.

I spent virtually the balance of the trip with Alexandra, keeping my distance from Collin as best I could. I didn't feel safe around him. I was in a hopeless situation. I had to escape—if not for me, for Alexandra. I had to find a reasonable rental in the neighborhood for the two of us, praying that Collin would go along. I told him what I intended to do, and he didn't comment. On our return, I found a rental home close by. When I told Collin the rental rate, he said, "Go back and haggle the price." I did, and after effort, we arrived at a rate Collin accepted. But when it came to signing the lease, he balked.

We were at a stalemate. We no longer talked. He treated me to his characteristic silent treatment. We lived separate lives. He stayed away often, who knows where. I didn't care. I didn't ask.

One night, after arriving home late, Collin went straight to bed and left his watch on the bathroom counter. His last text was to Danielle—*I'm filing tomorrow.* She said, *If that's true, Collin, I will see you next weekend, but if you're lying, you will never see me again!*

I lay on the bed in the spare room, feeling relieved that he intended to commence divorce proceedings, making it his decision and eliminating another reason to get angry with me. At the same time, I was in emotional pain, knowing this was the end and there was no going back.

The next morning, he entered my room and said, "I'm filing for divorce today." I sat up and said, "Fine, Collin. Please at least leave the house and go live with your hooker. You two are meant for each other, ultimate soulmates."

He filed the papers that day. But he didn't move out. Intolerable.

My mother's birthday was approaching; the last thing I felt like doing was celebrating anything, but she deserved it. Collin announced he would be unable to attend because of another business trip to Chicago. Before leaving, however, he grilled me on every birthday party detail, including when we planned to leave for the party venue. It was odd behavior. I planned an early dinner with some of my mother's closest friends and Alexandra. I left the house a little early to set up the finishing touches on the table. As I backed out of my driveway, I noticed a car about fifty yards away, a four-door silver sedan I had never seen in our permit-only community. After turning right down the street, I glanced in the rearview mirror to catch the silver sedan lagging. I pulled into a gas station to see what would happen. The sedan mimicked. I jumped out of my car as if I intended to pump gas and then jumped back in and left. The sedan followed.

I called my investigator, Hank, and explained the situation. Hank counseled me to proceed normally. He'd send someone—and emphasized that I not drink at the party.

Hank's guy, Cliff, showed up. We exchanged nods. I told my mother we were being filmed. Collin's PI was facing me, one table away, with his phone pointed in my direction. My mother was perplexed and upset, but I encouraged us to continue celebrating her special day. After finishing at the restaurant, I stayed behind, thanking the server, but I asked everyone to go outside to their cars for a few minutes, hoping the sleazebag that Collin sicked on me would leave. On cue, he followed us out, jumped in his vehicle, and waited.

Hank called.

"Jessica, go over to the window of the sedan and tell the guy that you're calling the police to report him as a stalker if he doesn't stop. Cliff will film it."

I was nervous, but I did what he said. It worked; the man in the sedan left.

When I got home, I texted Collin.

Me: Just so you know, asshole, I busted your idiotic, obvious PI. Oh, and by the way, I want you to know how much I admire

that you tried to get the mother of your child arrested on her grandmother's birthday. You are such a lowlife.

Collin: Jessica, you're crazy. You are imagining things.

Me: Stop the bullshit, you phony piece of shit. I have a video of it all.

Collin: Stop trying to ruin my weekend, Jessica.

Me: But of course. I'm so sorry. Please give Danielle my heartfelt best.

I called Hank, and we spoke at length. He suggested I sweep the house for recording devices and my vehicle for a tracker. We set up a time, and Hank and two colleagues came over. Within two hours, they discovered six recording devices and a tracker on my car under the back left bumper. The thought that someone had spent time in my home installing such things freaked me out. But confronting Collin wasn't worth the breath. He'd lie and deny—the two things he excelled at. I had to move fast and be careful. He had executed on his earlier threat to paint me as an unfit mother if I tried to leave him. War loomed on the horizon, and the field of battle was uneven, grossly uneven.

34

If You Knew, Would You Say I Do?

DR. BRENNAN: Welcome back to my podcast, *If You Knew Would You Say I Do?* And welcome back, Laura and Jessica. Let's dive right into what's been going on. You are both having some seriously challenging moments. Laura, as you describe, the abuse and control don't stop even once you are divorced and moved thousands of miles away.

LAURA: Exactly. I felt an initial sense of relief, knowing Mark wasn't living in the same city, but that reprieve was short-lived. It took less than seventy-two hours before his demands and attempts to control me ramped up. Mason was collateral damage—all he had left to control me. He wasn't concerned with his well-being. He wanted to manipulate me and cause me pain.

DR. BRENNAN: The narcissist gets a surge of adrenaline and power when they manipulate and control. Each time they ruin your day, have you jump through hoops, or create chaos in your life, they are invigorated and renewed. Once the relationship is established, the narcissist secures the right to abuse you indefinitely, especially if you have children with them.

LAURA: He tortured me with our child repeatedly, and I had nowhere to turn. The constant harassment and extreme stress terrified me. And it wasn't only how he affected my mental state but also how my body started to break down. Mark went so far as to threaten the careers of my mother and brother. Nothing was off limits. He was willing to stop at nothing to hurt me.

DR. BRENNAN: Unfortunately, once you have a child with a narcissist, even after you break free, you remain a supply source for them. When narcissists reach out to you, they don't come with good intentions. Each move they make is calculated to act upon a self-serving agenda. Unfortunately, the children are unwitting pawns in their winner-takes-all game of life.

LAURA: Looking back, I can't believe I kept my head above water. Each time I turned Mason over to Mark, I feared it might be the last time I saw him. [Laura wipes tears.]**JESSICA**: Sweetheart, it's okay. Here's a tissue.

DR. BRENNAN: Let's take a moment. Laura, we can stop for today.

LAURA: No, no, I'm fine. It's just that my body relives the pain I had then.

DR. BRENNAN: Laura, it sounds like you were and are suffering from *complex* PTSD, an enhanced version of PTSD, from a prolonged period of repeated abuse and trauma.

LAURA: I never realized I was suffering from PTSD in any form. I thought then that it was something only war veterans or sufferers of traumatic accidents experienced.

DR. BRENNAN: Laura, there is no doubt you were traumatized. Living in an abusive relationship is traumatic and often leads to PTSD. The psychological and emotional abuse you endured living with Mark and after leaving him put your body and nervous system into a constant state of flight or fight.

LAURA: That is so true. It has taken me years of working with different therapists to try to overcome PTSD. I finally found an experienced therapist who specializes in trauma and narcissistic abuse, who, it turned out, had lived through narcissistic abuse herself. I felt validation with her. She urged me to listen to your podcast, and I'm so grateful she did. It cleared up so many false narratives and helped me learn that there was a community that has experienced exactly what I went through.

DR. BRENNAN: I am so grateful to both of you for coming forward. My podcast helped you on your journey of healing, and you are now part of that journey for someone else.

JESSICA: I think what the podcast helped me see is that those with NPD suffer from a true personality disorder that embodies who they are, and that is never going to change. The hardest part is realizing there is no hope for a healthy, happy relationship with someone with NPD.

DR. BRENNAN: One of the most difficult things is accepting that the narcissist will never change. No matter how many hoops you jump through, how many sacrifices you make, how hard you try to please them, or how many promises they make, they will never change. Of course, could there be that rare case who commits to intense and regular therapy because of a strong commitment to change? They need the financial means and willingness to invest in the process. I would say, yes, there are cases out there, but I haven't come across one. Healing requires that you accept this. Of course, people stay, but if they do, they must prepare to become a human serving platter, forgoing all hopes, dreams, wants, and needs. Understand that staying with a narcissist means a dark and bleak future.

JESSICA: Listening to your podcasts, I saw how each characteristic and behavior you described for the covert narcissist aligned with Collin. Once my eyes were opened, I couldn't see anything else. At the time, I wasn't at full acceptance because I still believed his lies and gripped tightly to that tethered hope rope.

DR. BRENNAN: Jessica, after prolonged years of psychological abuse, you were securely trauma-bonded and dependent upon Collin emotionally, physically, psychologically, and financially. Collin had both you and Danielle spiraling, with his combined seduction and destruction, to the point where neither of you knew what to believe anymore. You were both willing to accept his rationalizations, fake apologies, and crocodile tears in desperation to keep the attachment. At this point in his game, he convinced you to believe he could change, that he prioritized family, and that his girlfriend was long gone. Unfortunately, unbeknownst to you, he simultaneously seduced Danielle into believing he was leaving you.

JESSICA: The trauma bond was the hardest thing to break; it took years of work to heal myself. I almost equate it to being brainwashed and escaping a cult. He did an excellent job of triangulating Danielle and me. I've come to understand that triangulation for the narcissist is like winning the trifecta. Collin masterfully pitted Danielle and me against each other while blaming me for talking to her. I later learned that Collin nudged Danielle to send their sex videos to me and their other twisted exchanges. He sadistically got pleasure from watching me suffer. He'd tell her how he slept like a baby while I cried all night. Talk about crazy town.

DR. BRENNAN: Oh, yes, Jessica, having two women fight for his love and attention, with the power to control you both, was hitting the narcissist lottery for Collin. The continuous flow of narcissistic supply, both negative and positive, fueled his addiction. He got sadistic pleasure out of torturing and punishing the two of you.

JESSICA: By lying to us both, he worked us into a frenzied state of confusion, intensifying our jealousy and insecurity. Danielle became so unhinged and pliable that she sent me sex videos of her and my husband and correspondence and sexual pictures they had exchanged. I was becoming unhinged. I mean, who wouldn't? The drama and chaos were over-the-top. I am grateful that I got exposed to his double life. Some aren't as lucky and only have their abuser's words to rely on.

DR. BRENNAN: Collin ramped up his abuse and hoovering skills to regain control of both of you. He walked a fine line between hoovering each of you and making you think you were the one. Then he paralyzed you both with the fear of losing the relationship. That way, you'd be willing to go to any length to save it. Know that staying or continuing to go back to the narcissist—which you both did—gave him permission to abuse you, even in crueler ways. They'll never have empathy or compassion for your experience in the drama.

Save your breath and heartfelt conversations. They only have one narrative, and that's their own. They don't care what you have to say.

JESSICA: Collin intensified the triangulation when Danielle and I each threatened to leave. In truth, I was so beaten down that I had virtually lost my ability to make decisions. My fears escalated as I pondered what he might do to Alexandra and me if I filed for divorce. I was also afraid because Collin constantly threatened suicide, which I didn't take lightly. He did the same thing to Danielle, and she believed him as well.

DR. BRENNAN: True to narcissist form, Collin was forever the victim. Exposure and abandonment are kryptonite to the narcissist. When faced with either, they'll go to extremes to alleviate their pain, including fake threats of suicide.

JESSICA: I see now that the threats were a sadistic tactic to manipulate us both. He used my empathy as a weapon against me—playing the victim and making me believe he was suicidal, knowing I'd never walk away from him in that state. Can you imagine how managed down I was? To the point where I was consoling my abusive husband over the loss of his girlfriend while he was crying about ending his life. It was sick, I know, but that is what I learned—that life with a narcissist strips away every ounce of self-worth, dignity, and self-esteem.

DR. BRENNAN: Narcissists can never be the villain. Collin blamed you for why he cheated, and he blamed Danielle for his world spiraling out of control. He lacked all accountability or remorse for the pain and suffering he caused. He never intended to save the marriage or give up his girlfriend. After all, he invested substantial time and energy to groom and secure a good supply. It was clear, however, that you were both in the discard phase, and he wasn't going to let either of you go until he had a replacement supply firmly in place.

JESSICA: He punished us for not serving him in the ways he needed, but no one can meet their needs. The girlfriend voiced needs she wanted met but learned eventually that her needs didn't matter. For my part, I was no longer willing to blindly believe Collin's lies and tolerate his cruel abuse. My eyes were starting to open, and he knew I was peeling away the mask. My dedication, loyalty, love, years of support, and empathy meant nothing to him. I was fungible, and so was his own daughter.

DR. BRENNAN: It is deeply troubling when the narcissist discards a partner when children are at stake. It is scary to see the narcissist lack concern for you or your children and the extremes they will go to punish you.

JESSICA: That he had me followed—for the possibility of getting arrested for a DUI on my mother's birthday—showed a total lack of consciousness. He would regale watching me and our child get escorted in a squad car—all while he was in Chicago, wining and dining with his girlfriend.

DR: BRENNAN: Yes, the wrath is real. But by getting educated about NPD, one can avoid getting blindsided. You learn what to expect when leaving them and can arm yourself with the knowledge and skills to protect yourself and your children. Narcissists can be predictable, and often, they give themselves away once you know how to observe and listen to them.

Thank you both again for sharing the intimate details of your relationships.

I'm your host, Dr. Jules Brennan. Until next time, *if you knew, would you say I do?*

Thanks for listening.

35

Laura

Andrew and I drew closer each day. In little time, he became my rock, and even though we lived in different states, we spent most weekends together and spoke regularly. He treated Mason, then two, with the kind of love and genuine attention expected of a devoted father, which wasn't lost on Mason, who reacted with cheery smiles and called him "Dada."

On the wave of my exciting new life, Andrew joined me in Texas to spend the holidays with me and my family. I picked him up at the airport. When opening the front door after arriving home, I saw Mason in the entryway, tiny arms out, offering me a bright yellow envelope.

"What's this, sweetie?" I said.

He smiled excitedly and said, "For you, from Dada." I looked at Andrew quizzically. He shrugged his shoulders, and I turned back to Mason, taking the envelope. I lowered myself to my knee to get eye level with him and opened the envelope to find a single sheet of paper with capitalized, bold words printed in red Magic Marker.

MOMMY,

ANDREW WANTS TO MARRY YOU.

I HOPE YOU SAY YES.

LOVE, MASON.

I raised up and turned back around to look at Andrew, still behind me, and as I did, Andrew dropped to one knee. "Will you two marry me?" he said, pulling a ring out of his pocket and offering it to me. Stunned, I extended my hand, and he smoothly slid the ring onto my index finger. He then tucked a hand in the same pocket to pull out a tiny gold bracelet, which he delicately wrapped around Mason's wrist.

I said nothing at first, allowing a pool of feelings to rise inside of me—chief among them joy, trepidation, excitement, and fear. I had not prepared for this moment. *Do I want to marry him? Yes. Is it wise to do so at this point? Not sure.* I was overcome. It was too much too soon. My gut said, *Yes, girl, do this.* His love, respect, and desire for family were beyond question, and I felt the same way. *But can I trust my own judgment?* Mark had done a number on my ability to think clearly. My mind had taken a thrashing and was no longer reliable.

I held back tears. Andrew waited patiently for what had to feel like an excruciatingly protracted lull. I finally looked up and into his eyes.

"Yes! Of course," I said, bursting with excitement. I pulled Andrew and Mason toward me, and we enjoyed a long group hug.

That night, the family celebrated with ceaseless smiles, and everyone bubbled with happiness. But as the night wore on, I backslid into doubt. *Is Andrew authentic? What are the odds he harbors a masterfully hidden personality disorder like Mark?* In fairness, not a single red flag had hoisted with Andrew. My gut said, *All good.* I so wanted to trust my decimated intuition. I had shuffled through recent life with confidence-shaking hesitancy, unsure of my grounding, which way was up, which down. I'd learned I was a PTSD victim.

Ignoring the spirit of the MSA (marital settlement agreement) that I live outside California, I decided to join Andrew there. Being close to Mark didn't sit well with me, but all other things considered, I thought Mason would have a better life in Southern California, and of course, that is where Andrew grew up and lived and had established himself professionally.

The relocation went smoothly. Mason enrolled in a new

preschool, and I worked on developing new routines. Seeds of normalcy sprouted. It felt good.

Then shit hit the fan.

After dropping Mason off for preschool, the Thursday of his second week of school, I decided to treat myself to a haircut and pedicure—nothing elaborate, just enough to refresh. I wasn't at the salon for ten minutes when my phone pinged. I dreaded who it might be from. It wasn't Mark. Instead, it was the parent of one of Mason's classmates.

> **Her: Saw Mason was signed out of class today at 11:05 when I went to pick up Charlotte to take her to the dentist. Hope you two are up to something fun!**
>
> **Me: What! I didn't sign Mason out! You sure?**
>
> **Her: Positive. What do you want me to do?**
>
> **Me: Nothing. Thx.**

I called Andrew. "Do you have Mason?" I said frantically.
"Mason? No. Why would I have him? I'm at work."
"Oh, my God!"
"What's wrong?"
"Someone signed him out at school," I screamed and hung up. I called the school. The woman at the front desk clarified that "Mason's father" signed him out, saying that "Mason won't be returning to school today."

I called Mark. No answer. I called again. Nothing. I kept calling. He finally picked up. "Mason, tell Mama bye-bye."

"Bye-bye, Mama," he said in that sweet little voice.

"Mark, what are you doing? Where are you taking him?" I said, demanding.

"Heading to Mexico. We're leaving the country. I'm taking him to where you'll never find me or him. You'll never get him back. It's over. Adios, loser." He disconnected.

I repressed the rising urge to throw up. I tried to control my breathing and summoned the presence to call the police. I gave it to them straight—my ex-husband had kidnapped my son and was trying to leave the country illegally. I insisted that it was an urgent matter, a life-and-death emergency. They were empathetic but kept saying their hands were tied unless I had tangible evidence Mark was not authorized to do what I "alleged" he was doing. Needless to say, on the phone, I couldn't prove anything.

I ran to my car and, before getting in, called the police again, pleading with them to get involved. They put me on hold. My world was falling apart. I was losing my shit. While I remained in phone limbo with the police, Mark called. I disengaged the police call and took Mark's call. I was hysterical. "Mark, please don't do this. Please bring him back." I could not have been more distraught.

He laughed. "You haven't changed a bit, such a drama queen. Could never take a joke. Mason is back at school, you freak. I signed him out for ice cream, and you go apeshit. Calm down."

I didn't respond. I hung up, lowered myself to the ground next to my car, and began to cry. An onslaught of grief washed over me. When my breathing calmed, I stayed motionless on the ground, head bowed, eyes soiled and red. Slowly, my mood altered. My despondency turned into rabid hatred. The depth of the fury I felt disgusted me. I didn't want to feel that way about anyone, even an evil creep like Mark. But hating him came easy. He was that loathsome—impossible to withstand.

I called Andrew and told him what happened in a shrill voice. He'd been trying to call me and was frantic. He asked whether I could drive and offered to get me. I insisted I drive, and he relented. But when I got behind the wheel, I couldn't move my limbs properly. I trembled, and rather than drive off, I sat in place for the next twenty minutes like a museum statue. When I calmed down again, I went to get Mason at school.

I spent the next day dealing with the US State Department

Passport Lookout Tracking System, arranging a travel alert if Mark tried to obtain a passport for Mason to leave the country. If he did, I was to get notified. Mark operated without boundaries or consciousness—no kind of depravity beyond his grasp. He was on a mission to inject chaos into my life, inflict pain on me, and see me suffer. No victory of debasement would placate his penchant for harm. He'd always crave more—an addict. I had an ally in Andrew, someone I loved, who loved me, who was a better father to Mason than Mark could ever be or care to be; this further fanned the roaring flames of his demented persona.

Mark continued to have Mason every other weekend. To prepare, I'd hide Mason's overnight bag to spare him an anxiety buildup awaiting the trip. When Mark would pull up, I'd act surprised, feigning excitement to ward off his innate fear. It never worked. Mason would cry at the sight of Mark and hold me tight until Mark pulled him off me. Each time Mark drove away, I'd implore God to return Mason unharmed. I struggled to find any semblance of peace in a shared custody arrangement. It was torture.

Andrew and I agreed that a traditional wedding was ill-advised. If word leaked about an impending wedding, we feared Mark might dig into his bag of wicked tricks and blow up our special day. An event like this would challenge his ego and churn his stomach. He couldn't stand to see me brimming with happiness. We crafted a creative solution: a surprise wedding, our own little form of bait and switch. The guest invitations announced a surprise thirty-fifth birthday party for me, telling all to keep it mum, dress casually, and be ready to dance the night away.

Andrew and I managed to keep the surprise to ourselves, telling not a soul, including our closest friends and family. It worked like a charm.

At 5:30 p.m., Andrew and I pulled up to the house and entered through the front door. Andrew wore a sharp, light-gray suit, and I wore a blush-colored floor-length dress. Upon our entry, the guests yelled, "Surprise!" and we laughed robustly. Andrew grabbed a microphone, chuckled to himself, and thanked everyone for coming. Barely holding back laughter, he spilled the beans. "Folks, the surprise is on you. You're not here for a birthday celebration. You're here for our wedding." He turned to me and nodded, and together we exclaimed, "Surprise!" The crowd reacted wildly, whooping it up, cheering, and screaming, giving me chills. Mason ran toward us, arms outstretched, and gave us both a hug. That night, we got married.

I harbored some resentment that despite marrying the man I loved, who I wanted to spend my life with, I couldn't shake Mark's insanity. I knew that I was experiencing what other divorced couples with children go through. The MSA gave me 70 percent custody of Mason, which many considered favorable. But Mark persisted. He constantly threatened to file a petition to make it fifty-fifty, a week on and a week off. He knew I couldn't bear, or afford, a legal battle. The specter of his custody maneuvering hovered like darkening clouds, threatening a nasty storm.

I continued to endure physical ailments. I saw a neurologist because of repeated dizziness and other doctors for shortness of breath, severe stomach pains, involuntary muscle movements, and back pain. Doctors were perplexed. Other than defaulting to the stress diagnosis, they couldn't put their finger on anything dispositive. Then, one morning, as soon as I awoke, I vomited. Was it another baffling symptom? Little did I know.

36
Jessica

Collin dragged his feet to serve me with the filed divorce papers, suggesting he was up to no good. It wasn't as if he was trying to repair the marriage in the meantime. In terms of our lives, we were ships passing in the night, barely speaking or acknowledging our respective existences. The house atmosphere was chilly and tense, a powder keg set to explode on the plainest provocation. The whole thing made me ill. I stayed away as much as I could.

One morning, after rising early, I loaded Alexandra into the car, destination unknown. I stopped for gas, and a gentleman pointed out that my front tire was low and missing two lug nuts.

"Is that a problem?" I said.

"Well, if the other lug nuts come loose, the tire might as well. It has to do with pressure on the wheel hub and bearings. It is potentially dangerous." He spoke with confidence.

"Well, par for the course, I suppose. I'm going through a divorce. Maybe my husband is trying to kill me," I said, laughing nervously.

"Yeah, well, I know your husband. He's Collin Worth, and, if you don't mind my saying, I wouldn't put it past him."

I inhaled and exhaled demonstrably and looked at him more closely.

He said, "I'm the dockmaster at the marina where Collin keeps his boat, right?" I stared at him. "Yeah, hey, sorry if that was harsh," he said.

"No, that's okay. I needed to hear that."

"It's just that, at the marina, we call him, 'Mr. Worthless,' because he is such an asshole and cheap as shit. He walks around like he's daddy big bucks, and everyone's beneath him."

"Well, I'd say you're a good judge of character. Thanks for your help."

My mind reeled. *Is Collin capable of doing something like that? Is he that far gone?* I didn't know.

Collin had sixty days to serve me with the papers. On the sixtieth day, literally, at 4:59 p.m., I heard three firm knocks at the door. I opened it to see a gangly process server. I took the papers and closed the door. A range of emotions, mostly sadness, flooded me. I mourned the loss of the family I thought I had. I mourned what had become of me—an emotional wreck, doubting myself, afraid for my safety. I mourned how this mess might impact my daughter. Service of the papers, while anticipated for two months, was a life low point.

For Collin, it was his sweet spot, where he excelled, creating chaos, pain, and fear. We couldn't be more different. I kept rewinding my life. *How did I get here? What mistakes had I made? What should I have done differently?* I called up negativity each time. I couldn't remember the good times. It was as if they had been eternally eclipsed. I was dealing with a man, once the love of my life, to whom I was loyal to a fault, the father of my daughter, who didn't care a whit about me or her. He treated me like a useless, disposable servant and longed for me to fade away, never to be heard from again. I felt lost and erased.

The day came for Collin to move out of the house while we battled in court. He sat down with Alexandra, who had virtually become a stranger to him the past three months, to explain he'd be moving out. Alexandra said, "Okay, bye, but Mommy isn't going with you, right?" Collin took a deep breath, made a grimace, sat down on the couch, and shed some tears, crocodile style, a transparent and pathetic ploy to garner sympathy from his child. Alexandra looked at him bewildered and said, "Daddy, you have your phone, and you will be around the corner." I shook my head in the background. An eight-year-old girl was comforting her father instead of her father reassuring her that everything would be fine. I didn't expect anything more from Collin, but still, it was astonishing to behold.

The next seventy-two hours brought peace to the household. I assumed Collin was in full swing with Danielle. A late-night text blitz dismissed the assumption.

> **Collin: I have no reason to live. You and Alexandra will be fine. Take the house. Take the money. You'll be much happier when I'm gone. It's what you want anyway. Nobody loves me.**
>
> **Me: Stop, Collin. Our child needs a father. Our lives will be forever changed. Please stop talking like this. It doesn't help anyone. You will get through this. We are here for you.**
>
> **Collin: I'm useless to everyone. How did I end up like this? I cry every day. My life has no meaning, no purpose. I am empty without you and Alexandra.**

Minutes later, Danielle shared texts that Collin had sent her. They were identical to the texts he sent me—pathetic ploys of despair and implied threats of suicide. He was playing both ends concurrently, seeking sympathy and control. He wanted his old life back, me at home with his daughter, taking his abuse like a dutiful wife, and his girlfriend hanging on his every word and being his twenty-four seven cheerleader.

The texts continued for hours—him pleading and moaning, me trying to convince him not to take his own life, with dollops of compassion and sympathy. I doubted he'd kill himself, but I couldn't be sure, and I didn't have the constitution or inclination to tough-love him. So, I played along. During the entire exchange, not once did he express concern for the well-being of Alexandra, never mind me.

The suicidal threats kept coming. Most alarming was this thread on the prior night:

> **Collin: I took four Ambien last night with a bottle of wine.**
>
> **Collin: I thought that would be the least painful way to go.**
>
> **Collin: I slept for more than twelve hours.**

Collin: How come I didn't die? I can't even kill myself well. I am a failure.

He had doubled down on his manipulative campaign to gain my support and sympathy. I called his family. His parents dismissed it as nothing to worry about, saying it would pass. I thought of calling 911 but knew that if I did, the authorities would probably commit him, and he'd seek revenge for it later. I was conflicted, but when the threats kept coming, I aligned with his unfeeling parents. He had become the boy who cried wolf. *Have at it. You're on your own.*

When the suicide crusade didn't produce his desired results, Collin tried his hand at financial threats. He cried poverty, that he was in the worst financial crisis of his life and would have to sell his assets. He ranted each day about how I'd bled him dry, and he couldn't even handle the bill for cable TV, which he cut off because I rented movies for Alexandra. I paid little mind, which drove him crazy.

He turned to his most valuable weapon, his daughter. He began asking for more time with Alexandra, which got my attention. The problem was, as my attorney told me repeatedly, I had no legal right to keep Alexandra from her father, and if I tried, I might be guilty of parental alienation and would have hell to pay in the legal system.

I had to give extended time with my daughter to a man who threatened suicide almost daily and spent time with prostitutes and lowlife friends, partying all night in his "man cave." He couldn't take care of a hamster, let alone a child.

During the first visitation, Collin texted that Alexandra wanted me to come for dinner. The last thing I wanted was to spend time with Collin, but my daughter trumped everything, so I went. Once he had me there, he said to Alexandra, "You have to stay here tonight." Alexandra responded, with a degree of innocence only a child can bring, "Okay, if Mommy stays, too." My whole body shuttered. Collin said, "Yes, of course, Alexandra, Mom would love to stay with us." He looked at me and said, "Right, Jessica?"

I wanted to grab Alexandra and run. Collin smirked, pleased with what he had orchestrated. Later that night, I lay in the bed, fully dressed. Collin tried to hold me and tell me how much he loved me, how our daughter needed two parents together, and how breaking up the family would be a huge mistake. His warm breath on my neck made my skin crawl.

The next night, Collin asked me to bring Alexandra to dinner. I declined, saying that Alexandra had an important playdate. Collin argued that no social arrangement is as important as dinner with her father... and on and on. I stood firm, and he ended the debate with this:

"She's my daughter, too, and rest assured, I'll make sure she spends as much time with me as I want and when I want." The battle lines were drawn.

37

Laura

The nausea walloped me for three weeks, prompting a visit to an internist. After a battery of tests, he concluded it was stress. Déjà vu all over again. That night, I lit a candle Andrew bought for me, thinking I'd like the vanilla scent. Five minutes into the burn, I started gagging. Andrew asked if I was choking, and I said no; the odor was making me ill. A light bulb went off, and I told Andrew I had to run out and I'd be back shortly.

I went to Walgreens, grabbed two pregnancy tests, came home, went straight to the spare bathroom, peed on the stick, and watched intently as the pink line emerged. I was pregnant! I ran to the backyard, where Andrew and Mason were playing on the tricycle track Andrew installed. I waved the checkered flag propped up against a chair, bringing them to a halt.

"I won!" Mason said.

"Well, you two will need a bigger track and another bike," I said.

"No, Mommy. Dada has a bike, and I have a bike. Are you going to start riding?"

I laughed. "No, baby boy, but your new brother or sister might want to join the fun!" I said.

Andrew jumped from his seat, grabbed me in a hug, and started to cry.

"Why is Dada crying?" Mason said, looking sad.

"Because he's so happy, sweetheart."

Mason was due to go to Mark the next day. I didn't want him telling Mark I was pregnant, concerned it would fire him up, the last thing I needed. During my last pregnancy, I blamed the stress in my life for some of Mason's learning differences and other abnormalities, like shaky hands and ADHD.

"Mason, Mommy's baby in her belly is our secret for now, okay?" I said.

"Okay, Mama."

It wasn't lost on me that I asked a two-and-a-half-year-old to keep an important secret from his father. I had sunk to a new level in my quest for emotional survival.

Mark and his girlfriend, Tara, arrived to get Mason at 10 a.m. When Mark bounded out of the car, Mason grabbed and pulled my leg to avoid going. Mark scooped him up.

"Daddy is the best, isn't he?" he said as Mason turned away from him to look at me.

Mason didn't answer. Mark asked three more times, each greeted with silence. He gave up and drove off.

An hour later, the following series of Mark text messages landed.

Mark: Looks like Mason is going to have two new siblings!

Mark: Hello?

Mark: Aren't you going to congratulate me?

Mark: Mason's so happy. I told him he should spend more time here so he can be with his brother in a few months.

Mark: Is yours a boy or a girl?

Mark: Hello?

Mark: Congrats.

I didn't respond. I couldn't believe what I'd read. Tara and I were both pregnant, and she was further along.

That night, when Mason came home, I raised the topic.

"Are you excited Daddy is having a baby?"

"Yes, a baby brother. I will share my trucks with him. . . . Mama?"

"Yes, bug."

"I have two mommies now. I call Tara Mommy, too."

I gagged on my food. Sure, Mason called Andrew "Dada." Why not Tara, Mommy? The difference was that Andrew had established himself like a father to him—Tara, he barely knew. Where that came from was plain to me, but I wanted to confirm.

"Do you want to call Tara Mommy?" I said.

"No. I told Daddy I have a Mama, and he said I had to call Tara 'Mommy,' or he would take away my bear."

Wow. That was so Mark, threatening to take away his son's security blanket to embellish his girlfriend, a backhand way of hurting me, trying to dilute my mother status. The man had no bottom.

That night, I lay in bed, staring at the ceiling for hours. Nothing will stop this man from destroying more lives. Not the court system, that's for certain. I sensed more coming.

Sure enough, a week later, I received notice that Mark had petitioned to change the custody arrangement from seventy-thirty to fifty-fifty. A new battlefield threatened down the road.

Andrew tried to be supportive, but most days, I was so exhausted and consumed that I didn't give him attention. He wanted to chat about baby names, and I fixated on how to keep Mark from getting more custody. The preoccupation wasn't fair to him, but I couldn't help myself. Unlike me, Andrew hadn't endured the earlier courtroom debacle, the trailer for the upcoming horror film.

Before leaving for an OB-GYN visit to learn the sex of the baby, my attorney reported that Mark had applied to accelerate the custody hearing. Typical Mark, full-court pressing to make things harder for me, knowing I was pregnant. I cried in sniffles en route to the office while Andrew tried to reassure me that everything would be fine.

We arrived and were ushered into a room. Wiping my eyes, I

lay on the table, and Andrew held my hand lovingly. My mind kept focusing on getting home and working on a rebuttal. "It's a girl!" the doctor said, interrupting my distraction. Andrew smiled and squeezed me tight. I felt ambivalent because Mason would have a brother with Mark with whom he could enjoy boy activities while we were having a girl and wouldn't have the same play rituals. I wondered whether that lament made me a bad person. I mentioned this to Andrew, and he flashed me a what-is-wrong-with-you look, which made me wonder whether Andrew had tired of hearing me complain about Mark. Hard to blame him if true.

I occupied the next few months with attorney visits and legal preparation. My attorney got the hearing delayed—a major relief. I was seven and a half months pregnant and wanted to give birth before the hearing. It looked promising.

I had a C-section birth after rushing to the ER when I felt sick with a fever. The procedure took an hour, and then, there she was, Ruby, adorable as adorable can be. Her cry was soft, her features tiny, and I was in love again. We had taken the next step toward a family foundation.

Becoming a father a second time didn't cure Mark's glaring parenting deficiencies. When Mason was with him, he'd text incessantly, complaining about this or that, often referring to Mason as "your" boy when he couldn't figure things out or got frustrated. I kept telling him that a three-year-old doesn't watch adult movies, drink wine, and eat rare filets—Mark's favorite activities. I suggested he might take him to a playground or trampoline park for "kid fun" and burn energy and engage with him. He didn't get it.

Then came a jolt, not surprising.

"How is your brother?" I asked Mason after a Mark visitation.

"He went away."

"Away? Where?"

"Tara's mommy took him."

"Took him? Did Tara go with her mommy?"

"Yes, Mama."

Something was seriously amiss. I had to find out. I called my attorney and asked him to stall the hearing until we could learn more.

We tracked down Tara. I sent her a text, asking if she was okay. She said no, and I asked if she wanted to talk. She did.

"What's wrong? Is everything okay with your baby?" I said.

"No, no, no one is sick other than Mark, in his head." *Tell me something I don't know*. She unburdened herself.

"He's insane. He doesn't care about either of the children. He only cares about what he wants. Every time I call him on his attitude or behavior, he blames me, calls me a drama queen, and goes on a tirade. Now he is trying to destroy my architectural business, telling everyone I have postpartum depression and am unstable. *He's* unstable."

The pain in her voice was manifest. We bounced back and forth on the details. Her life with Mark was a sequel to mine. The first time she took a long breath, I jumped in.

"Mark has petitioned for more custody of Mason," I said.

"I know. He was giddy about it. He talks about wanting to destroy your life and having Mason adore him."

"How about his drinking?" I said.

"He drinks wine like the rest of us drink water."

"Drugs?"

"Worse. He has a full-blown pharmacy. He's an addict."

"Has he put his hands on you?"

"No. Once, I thought he was going to, but he thought better of it and walked away."

"Consider yourself lucky then." My tone didn't invite follow-up, and she didn't try. Tara had to get off the phone, and I had to get Mason to school. Enough for now. We spoke for two hours. We didn't agree to talk again, but I expected we would.

I debriefed Andrew. We shared a worry about Mark alone with Mason in his current mental state. He was like a wounded animal, making him more dangerous than normal. Andrew didn't hesitate. He hired a PI to keep an eye on Mark during the visitation, the expense be damned. Andrew had a heart and soul of gold. Good people do exist.

The next day, I brought my attorney up to speed. The Tara revelations injected a new dynamic into the judicial proceedings. *Can we get Tara to testify willingly? Will she line up for us?* I knew little about her. My attorney cautioned, "You never know with third-party witnesses, especially in these situations. They can be wild cards. One day, they are warm and fuzzy; the next, they have frigid feet." I crossed my fingers.

Three days later, Tara texted, asking that I meet with her and her attorney without counsel. I checked with mine, who was apprehensive about me going alone. But if we wanted the meeting, we had to oblige. My attorney reluctantly consented.

The next day, I found myself sitting across from Tara and her attorney. The setting brought up mixed emotions.

"Would you like some popcorn and a soda?" the lawyer said.

"Uh, no, thank you. I'm fine," I said. *What an odd thing to offer*, I thought.

"Well, we have a movie to show, and you might be here a while," he said with a chuckle.

Okay, now the popcorn made sense. What kind of movie? I felt unsteady. He dimmed the lights, and the show began.

Mark was inhaling a line of cocaine while Mason sat at a nearby desk playing with crayons. At one point, Mason dropped his crayon to watch Mark. The snorting was hard to ignore.

"My turn?" he said.

"No, Mason, this is special daddy dust. It makes me a superhero," he said, laughing aloud.

"I want to be a superhero," he said.

Mark got up and left the room, leaving Mason alone with lines of cocaine prominently displayed. He climbed down from his seat, went over to the coffee table, examined the cocaine intently for a few seconds—my body shook—and before I could scream, Mason returned to his seat and resumed coloring. I started to cry.

"I can't watch anymore," I said between gushes of tears.

"Are you sure?" the attorney said.

"I don't know. I feel dizzy. Give me a moment, please."

"Of course."

I looked at Tara. She looked sad and sympathetic. I took a long gulp of bottled water and said we could proceed. The attorney said they had more than 2,000 hours of video from inside the Corbin residence. "In terms of your son, you've seen the worst of it. The rest is pretty bad, but mostly it's about Tara. I imagine it is familiar ground to you."

I asked to continue a short while longer. The next clip showed Tara curled up underneath a crib where Mathew, their son, slept. It flashed me back to when I slept with one eye open. Next, I saw Mark enter the room and, with a crazed look, begin to poke Mathew until he started to cry. When the crying awoke Tara, Mark said, "Get up, bitch, and take care of your crying baby."

"That's enough," I said. "I've seen that movie before, except with me in the leading role."

"I know you have a custody battle coming up. I'd like to discuss a possible alliance with your attorney," Tara's attorney said in a somber tone.

"I guess that makes sense," I said.

"Understand, though, that whether we collaborate depends on how we perceive it will benefit Tara."

"I understand."

We adjourned.

Numb and drained, sitting in the car, I rewound what I had seen. Tears rolled down my face. I peeked at myself in the rearview mirror and wondered what would come of all of this, what would ultimately become of me and my son. I had the will to fight most days, but part of me was dying, never to return. The bottom line was this: sharing custody with Mark any more than what the current situation allowed was frightening and not a viable option. Mark endangered the children. He had no business being around them without a real adult present.

While I wallowed in anxiety, Tara called. She was hoping to catch me before I left and wanted to talk. "Of course," I said. A few minutes later, she slid into the passenger's seat.

"You don't seem like the terrible person and mother Mark painted you out to be."

I laughed. "Shocking. How did he describe me?"

"When I first met him, he said you were a raging alcoholic, hooked on drugs, and an unfit mother." I shook my head silently. She continued. "He asked me if I'd consider being a mother to Mason if he could remove him from your life. He made you sound like a total train wreck. He said all he wanted was a family and to be the best dad to Mason, but he constantly worried about you and your addictions. He said you partied all night and slept all day. He was convincing, and I felt terrible for Mason. I wanted to step in and be his mother. I almost hated you."

"Is that why you had Mason calling you Mommy?" I said with some irritation.

"No, no, that was Mark's idea. He said you basically stole his baby and moved to Texas so he couldn't see him." She stopped, implicitly inviting a response.

I exhaled. "I don't know where to start. I really don't. Let me say this. Nothing he told you has a grain of truth. Nothing. His bad-mouthing is him talking about himself—classic projection. The Mark in the videos was the Mark in my life... but much, much worse. He also physically abused me. And understand this, too. *He* wanted *me* out of California. Texas was his idea, not the other way around. The guy couldn't recognize the truth if it bit him on the nose."

"No, I see that now. He is an awful parent and the most selfish person I've ever met. He blamed every hiccup or incident on me. He could do no wrong and could be incredibly insensitive and mean. He is a horrible human being. I can't believe I am with him."

"Don't I know it," I said. "What was it like in the beginning?"

"Heaven. It was the relationship I longed for my entire life. He was the dream companion. Every interest I had, he shared. He was attentive, loving, and sweet. He swept me off my feet, and I fell in love. I noticed he drank a little excessively, but he blamed that on you and the stress from missing his son. He talked about the family we'd build together and how we'd create a lifetime of cherished memories. More like bad dreams to last a lifetime."

"A repeat performance," I said.

"Once I got pregnant, things took a sharp turn for the worse," she said. "I started to see something seriously wrong with him. I think he has an undiagnosed mental illness."

"What do you think it is?" I said.

"No idea. But whatever it is, it's there in full regalia."

We commiserated for another hour about the parallels between our respective lives with Mark. It was as if he had a fixed script and needed to recycle the leading role opposite him in lockstep. I was in script one, Tara script two, there'd be script three soon enough, and who knows how many more over the course of his miserable life. The script repeated, but each prey had a shelf life. As time passed, his mask started to slip, the cracks deepened, abuse replaced the love and attention, and the pedestal we all sat upon became a pitchfork. He had to discard the current object of his desire and find another.

The chat with Tara brought some peace. For the last two years, I couldn't avoid thinking that maybe I bore responsibility for the failure of my marriage with Mark. Tara validated that Mark's physical and psychological abuse had nothing to do with me. It was all about him.

We hugged and said our goodbyes. We'd talk again. For now, however, my main focus was protecting Mason. I dug in my heels.

38

Jessica

Collin turned up the heat, literally. He suspended the electricity service in the home. Then, he sent creepy videos of himself staring into the camera, with no audio, attempting to intimidate me, motioning as if to say, *I'm watching you*. I needed to accelerate the resolution.

In response to my pleas, my attorney arranged mediation. In the first session, they put my attorney and me in one room and Collin and his attorney in another. The mediator, a woman, never addressed or looked at me. After two hours of back and forth, she presented a nonstarter proposal from Collin. It effectively left me homeless, reduced me to the secondary parent, and had other provisions that spun my head. It lacked any semblance of fairness and compromise. I was appalled. My attorney saw things differently.

"If you don't agree to this, you'll give a judge control of your life."

"There is no way I'll sign anything that jeopardizes my daughter, and any deal that anoints Collin as the main parent jeopardizes my daughter. Not negotiable."

I fired him the next day and searched for a replacement.

I retained Doreen Jacobs of the firm Jacobs & Jacobs. She impressed me. She understood what was entailed in dealing with an ill man like Collin. I had a genuine and loyal advocate in my corner. She promptly filed a motion to obtain a temporary parenting plan. In response, Collin moved for the appointment of a guardian ad litem, a volunteer charged with protecting the interests of someone not capable of self-protection, in this case, the minor, Alexandra. In theory, it wasn't the worst thing, so long as the guardian saw through

Collin's bullshit. The concern was Collin seducing any appointed guardian with his charm and sleight of hand. Guardian ad litems were not trained mental health counselors. On balance, we didn't like the idea. Doreen requested instead that the court order a child custody investigator, which, unlike the guardian ad litem, involved professional psychologists.

The court granted our request. It also directed us to set up another mediation with a well-respected mediator. But that went nowhere because Collin refused to provide detailed financial information under oath, essential for any consensual resolution. I was left with exposure to the legal system, precisely what Collin wanted—a war of attrition, a venue where he held most of the cards and could destroy me.

Before that process unwound, the court appointed Ann Harley to conduct a child custody investigation. Ms. Harley explained that the investigation would entail a detailed look into both our lives and include psychological testing. The process went on for months and involved interviews with family and friends. I was skeptical. I knew that having tea with Collin in his mansion would not reveal the true Collin Worth. It struck me as a primitive way to determine parental fitness.

The licensed psychologist to conduct the testing was Dr. Jerome Mitchell. On the day of the testing, Alexandra and I waited three hours for the disheveled Dr. Mitchell to show. When he emerged, he spent the first thirty minutes talking about himself. Red flags went off all over the place. I felt physically ill. He brought Alexandra to another room for a private session. When Dr. Mitchell returned, he asked me a series of questions and then provided me pictures Alexandra had drawn, with commentary. Later, after Mitchell took a break, I photographed what Alexandra produced. When Dr. Mitchell reentered, he said we were done for the day and would reconvene in two weeks.

Not surprisingly, in the days that followed, Collin upped his game as a doting father. He found parenting to be his new religion, as if in competition for Father of the Year. He wanted involvement in each aspect of Alexandra's life and showered her with lavish gifts.

When I met with Dr. Mitchell next, he seemed anxious. Immediately, he observed that Collin was the "most severe narcissist" he'd ever come across. I didn't respond. He also said Collin had a concealed weapons permit, and because I'd earlier expressed concern for my safety, he recommended I leave dated notes around the house that say, "If something happens to me, my husband did it." My mouth dropped open.

First, is he permitted to share his opinion about narcissism at this stage? In other words, did he violate protocol? And second, does he believe Collin posed a serious risk of committing murder? I didn't know what to make of Dr. Mitchell at that point.

The following week, while Alexandra and I were making a cake, Alexandra said, "Daddy and Dr. Mitchell have the same car, and Dr. Mitchell said he loves Daddy's plane." I asked her to repeat what she said. She did, verbatim. I couldn't believe what I'd heard. Maybe I should have. Collin was working with Dr. Mitchell, using his power and resources.

My next meeting with Dr. Mitchell couldn't come soon enough. I was eager to see if his "evaluation" of Collin had undergone a transformation. When the day arrived, I told myself to keep my cards close. But as soon as I saw Dr. Mitchell, I played some.

"Do you normally meet clients outside of your office?" I said, leaning forward eagerly.

"I don't make a habit of it but will under certain circumstances," he said, nonplussed, volunteering no more.

"Well, I mean, did you meet with Collin outside of the office?" I said impatiently.

He paused and nodded. "Yeah, the other evening." He shuffled in his chair.

"*When . . .* in the evening?"

"Um, I think, probably from about eight to midnight.... Is there a problem with that?" he said with a slightly raised voice.

"Well, meeting with Collin until midnight outside of an office setting concerns me. I worry about professional objectivity."

"Well, don't be concerned. He and I are busy. Our time is limited, so we took the opportunity to meet then. It was a matter of convenience."

I had an immediate distrust of Dr. Mitchell. *But am I overreacting?* Possibly. I had long become paranoid when it came to Collin Worth. Trusting my instincts had become a wobbly exercise.

The meeting with Dr. Mitchell was nothing like the last. He stopped referencing Collin's destructive disorder and the dangers he posed to those around him. He focused on what made sense to him as a parenting plan outside the purview of his charge. He had moved away from gathering data for creating psychological profiles. Equally odd, he kept referring to what was in the best long-term interests of "Alexandra and Collin," never mentioning me. It was as if he carried the mantle for Collin. It got even worse. Each time I pushed back on his parenting plan, he got aggressive and frustrated with me, lecturing about what made sense for the "family." At one point, he said, "Jessica, you obviously don't want to cooperate, so let's adjourn for today."

Wow. Collin had seized control over the system. I felt hopeless.

I called Doreen and reported. She found Dr. Mitchell's behavior "alarming." She suggested we wait until the test results were back before she'd inform the social investigator, Ann Harley, who'd do the presenting in court.

For the time being, we had depositions underway, and their results terrified me.

There was the testimony of our neighbor of ten years, Brenda, with whom I had shared countless late-night outpourings about the abuse we both suffered in our respective homes. She always comforted me when I shed torrents of tears over the way Collin treated me and

Alexandra, and more than once, she told me how much she despised Collin. She had confirmed that she was in my corner, had my back, and would testify about all of Collin's domestic horrors.

But when it came time to stand up and do the right thing, she flipped, a full-on 180. She described Collin as a model father and husband. She said she didn't remember our conversations the way I did and that I tended toward the dramatic and emotional excess. She testified that, in contrast to what she'd told me, she and her husband had a "wonderful and well-adjusted relationship that was free of any abuse," and anything to the contrary "was ludicrous." She added that she said certain things to me to "calm" my "frazzled nerves" and often worried that I was "mentally unstable."

I couldn't believe what I was hearing. Judas admitted that Collin offered her use of his plane anytime she wanted to visit her family in Colorado, had taken her and her husband out to a lavish dinner, and began to include the two of them in his high-end, exclusive social circle.

The shocking betrayal, which I didn't see coming, gutted me.

Danielle, his mistress, who swore up and down that she'd provide exhaustive details about how unstable Collin was, suddenly suffered glaring lapses in memory and avoided criticizing Collin. While imperfect, she said, he was a "good and kind human being." She denied, with a straight face, that the gifts Collin gave her affected her testimony or "biased" her.

Next came the psychological evaluation. Collin may have co-opted Dr. Mitchell, but he couldn't (or didn't) corrupt the testing, which revealed Collin as a "malignant narcissistic with sadistic and sociopathic tendencies." I felt vindicated. It also got revealed that Dr. Mitchell embellished Alexandra's handwritten descriptions of Mommy and Daddy and what life was like with each of us, tilting them favorably toward Collin. The drawings Dr. Mitchell proffered were different from the ones I photo'd. For example, one said that Alexandra wanted things to stay the same and live with Mommy, while Dr. Mitchell's court version read, "Every weekend with Daddy." We had nailed Dr. Mitchell's doctoring evidence.

The hearing lasted four days. It was like watching a sequel to *Liar Liar*. Again, Collin pleaded financial ruin. This was someone who boasted a net worth of over 50 million. Now the poor guy was reduced to $300,000. On the witness stand, he expressed dismay that he had to sell his plane and other expensive toys.

Collin had prepared for this scenario for over a year. He transferred all his businesses, stocks, and assets to a trust his father controlled, which explained the delay in serving me with the divorce proceedings. He had a shell game to complete before the judicial process got underway. He even pretended to cry on the witness stand, whimpering Alexandra's name. He left the stand for a few minutes to regain composure.

At one point, the judge asked Collin about the suicide attempts.

"Mr. Worth, about these references to suicide?" he said.

"Oh, Your Honor, you know how that goes. It was a poor joke. I was trying to be funny. I realize now I should be more careful."

"See," the judge said to the entire courtroom, "he was only joking."

When Doreen exposed Collin's lies on the stand, the exchange got heated. The judge interrupted and said, "Come on, counsel, let's move on. You think this is the first time the court has heard lying in family court?" He laughed heartily at his brand of humor.

When Doreen explored the analysis that Collin suffered from not just NPD but "malignant" narcissism, a more severe form of the disorder, the judge, in a fit of palpable frustration, said aloud, as if talking to himself, "Narcissist, shmarshasist."

"Your Honor, to be clear," Doreen said, rising quickly in evident frustration, "the court is dismissing the findings from the very investigation it ordered be done?"

"Counsel, the lives of these parties strike the court as an unseemly web of 'he said, she said.' Who's to say what is the truth? The court doesn't have an eternity to wade through the nuances of the different stories on the remote chance that maybe, just maybe, the actual truth will suddenly burst forth like a biblical revelation. We've already spent too much time on this matter. We need to simplify things, and your attempts to muddy the waters are not helping."

When Doreen explored the depths of Collin's relationship with Danielle—which also disclosed Collin's dalliances with other women during our marriage, "Rita" and "Monica" to name but two—the judge belittled its importance. "Boys will be boys."

The judge also lacked patience with my testimony, showing little interest in the abusive nature of life with a narcissist and how a mentally ill parent endangers children psychologically, emotionally, and physically. He kept badgering Doreen to "move on" and that we were "reaching the point of diminishing returns" and "how much more of this do you have?" He was, however, noticeably enraptured with testimony about hookers, planes, boats, and antique cars.

When the hearing ended, I felt like collapsing onto the courtroom floor, like stone turned to ash from sheer exhaustion. The good news was that the hemorrhaging had stopped, which relieved me. But I was pulverized by how uncaring the judicial system was, and worse, the extent to which it permitted a mangling of the truth, how it allowed falsehoods to coalesce into a narrative that didn't resemble what existed, as if judicial fiat had ordained that the life I had for many years be wiped out and swapped with a disastrous nightmare of someone else's choosing.

We awaited a decision. I expected nothing good.

39

If You Knew, Would You Say I Do?

DR. BRENNAN: Welcome back to my podcast, *If You Knew Would You Say I Do?* And welcome back, Laura and Jessica. Ladies, every week, I am so grateful that you share your stories and allow me and my listeners to reflect on how you lived in relationships with men diagnosed with NPD. But first, Laura, let's talk about getting married!

LAURA: Yes, Andrew proposed to *us*. At that time, I had mountains of doubt about whether getting married again was the right decision not only for me but for Mason. It was a positive light in my life, but true to narcissist form, Mark wasn't going to let me be happy, so the abuse continued. Our secret wedding was beautiful, and soon after finding out I was pregnant, I was elated . . . but not for long because Mark needed to one-up me. Sounds crazy now, but he had me so beaten down that I still believed him when he said Mason wanted to live there because he'd have a brother he could be close to. It worked me into a frenzy.

DR. BRENNAN: Laura, Mark still controlled you because you were still trauma-bonded and suffered from complex PTSD. Also, at that point in the game, you didn't know the depths of NPD, and you had not set boundaries; you were deep in the game. Any reaction to their behavior gives them permission to abuse, which is exactly what happened. You were caught up in the chaos and had not gone without contact.

LAURA: You're right. Mark still triggered and intimidated me. I was afraid for Mason.

DR. BRENNAN: I completely understand, but it didn't matter what you said or did to acquiesce to Mark's commands. The narcissist is never satiated. They constantly move the goalposts, keeping you in a frenzied state of mind. Setting boundaries or acting nonplussed or bored—gray rocking, we sometimes call it—are the only ways to communicate with a narcissist who is your ex. The objective is to avoid eye contact and facial engagement, being as bland as possible, and in the process, provide minimalist reactions, with simple answers that lack emotional content or power. It helps create boundaries and can impede the narcissist's efforts to get the reactions they desperately need to survive—and you want to avoid. If you don't give them what they want, they will move on to another person that will fit their needs.

LAURA: I wish I knew about gray rocking earlier. I can honestly say it took almost ten years to feel at peace and have boundaries. Once I stopped reacting to him, he did move on, and he found a new target that he deemed worthy supply.

DR. BRENNAN: I'm glad you made the commitment to heal. I know the journey wasn't easy, but the work was worth it.

LAURA: Something that helped was speaking with Tara and dispelling the belief that she was better than I was and got the good version of Mark, that maybe I was the one damaged, delusional, and blew things out of proportion. I believed his relationship with Tara was a fairy tale and started to doubt my own memories of the abuse.

DR. BRENNAN: Not everyone gets the opportunity to speak with the next supply, or the next, or the next, but virtually guaranteed, they will describe the same movie, only with a different person costarring with the narcissist. Every relationship is a disastrous failure, no matter how long it lasts. No matter what their relationship looks like, it's a facade, and the next supply will suffer the same fate—whether six months, five years, or twenty years later. There is no love powerful enough to change or fix a person suffering from NPD.

JESSICA: We are both fortunate—if you want to call it that—to have contact with the next supply. It helped take the sting out of watching them idolize their new supply and seemingly be a better version of themselves with them.

DR. BRENNAN: Being replaced and obsessing over the new relationship and new supply is something all survivors experience. The most terrifying is that your narcissist ex will not only love his new supply more, but they will get all the good stuff and none of the bad, leaving you to believe you were the problem all along. I am happy to report that is not the case.

JESSICA: Even though I educated myself about NPD, at the time, I was very much trauma-bonded to Collin and brainwashed. I believed Collin might end his life and was really going broke. Obviously, I later figured out that his suicidal threats were fake, like his financial threats, fake tears, fake love, fake concern, and fake personality.

DR. BRENNAN: Narcissists are inherently weak, fearful people with arrested development, filled with rage, contempt, and jealousy; their greatest fears are abandonment and exposure. You're drawing the line in the sand and moving forward toward divorce, coupled with your communication with Danielle, forced Collin to face his greatest fears. This brought out the worst of Collin's narcissistic, sadistic personality disorder. Collin's threats of suicide to you and Danielle were designed to keep you both supplying him with sympathy and empathy. He calculated that neither of you would abandon him in such a desperate time.

JESSICA: Yes, every day was something new from Collin's bag of manipulation and seduction, from late-night rendezvous with our court-appointed psychologist to seducing our neighbor of over ten years, who I had considered family and who was quick to betray Alexandra and me. He must have had one powerful smear campaign. My neighbor broke my heart. I don't know how I stayed standing. I got TKO'd by Collin daily. He even influenced the judge. I lost all faith in humanity. Even the psychologist minimized Collin's acknowledged diagnosis and altered what Alexandra said about who she wanted to live with. Also, not only did the judge make light of Collin's suicidal threats, abuse, and numerous girlfriends, but he disregarded his diagnosis with NPD as a joke.

DR. BRENNAN: One of the saddest and most heartbreaking aspects of divorcing a narcissist is seeing how easily those you thought loved and cared about you side with the narcissist.

The narcissist employs multiple means to win over others. They smear you and get others to believe the horrible things they say about you. Sometimes, family members fall prey to this tactic. The narcissist won't hesitate to use all available tools, especially money and power, to get what they want. It's not surprising how many people will betray you to align with them for a payoff.

JESSICA: The court process with Collin was a treacherous journey, to say the least. I got thrust into the courtroom fray with a seasoned pathological liar, walking into a broken, unsympathetic system that put the fate of my child's future in the hands of one person—the judge. Unfortunately, the judge connected with Collin and treated him like a buddy at a poker match. He found Collin entertaining. The judge disregarded Collin's diagnosis of NPD with sadistic sociopathic tendencies. He took the bait that Collin was broke and had genuine love for Alexandra and said that his suicidal threats were no more than misguided comedic gestures. In the end, he overlooked the child custody investigator's recommendations for our protection. If I threatened suicide even once, I have little doubt that I'd find myself tossed into a mental institution.

DR. BRENNAN: The system and lying spouses often abuse innocent people, both men and women. Victims are painted as villains. Many judges are not educated about cluster B personality disorders and are unable or disinclined to protect victims. The narcissistic spouse does not need money or power to work the system. They need only to know how to make their way through the cracks—not difficult in a broken system. Rich or poor, narcissists are notorious for exploiting the legal system. They pathologically lie, file frivolous motions, withhold key documentation, delay the process, and mock the law. Narcissists know how to work the system.

JESSICA: My advice is to avoid the judicial system at all costs with a narcissist. When you get there, you'll face the biggest bully on the playground, and you can't count on the judge to protect you or save your future and the future of your children. Well-intentioned or not, they lack the knowledge or training about cluster B personality disorders.

DR. BRENNAN: Ladies, we're out of time, but again, thank you. Our listeners have learned much so far, and I look forward to hearing more next week as we wrap up.

I'm your host, Dr. Jules Brennan. Until next time, *if you knew, would you say I do?*

Thanks for listening.

40

Laura

Andrew was champing at the bit for a report. I first explained that because Tara didn't trust Mark and believed he was trying to undermine her business, she installed nanny cameras throughout the house, an arid taste of his own medicine. Andrew said, "Wow." When I told him what I saw on the video, he put his hands over his eyes and hung his head. He looked up with the saddest eyes I had ever seen, and I nodded and said, "Yeah." At that moment, Mason appeared.

"Dada, don't be sad. Elmo loves you," he said.

Andrew laughed and said, "Thank you, Mason, I needed that. I feel much better."

Mason brought him Elmo and said, "You can hug him and push his tummy." Andrew depressed the button.

"I love you," said Elmo.

"Seeee, I told you that already," he said.

Andrew swept him off his feet, hugged him, and said, "I love you."

Too sweet.

It was Thursday, which meant that Mason was slated for a weekend with Mark. The thought made me cringe. I wanted that day, Thursday, to be forever, a stoppage of time in perpetuity. I wasn't sure how much more worrying my fragile self could tolerate. It helped that we had a PI (John) to track Mark, but John didn't have access to inside the house, where the chaos festered and reigned, and he was only observing and reporting. John wasn't a bodyguard.

Friday arrived despite my pleas. Mark picked up Mason at school, which made things easier so Mason didn't have to see me. Thirty minutes after school let out, John was sitting in his car half a block from Mark's house. I so wanted to be there with him.

An hour later, John reported that four cars had pulled into Mark's driveway, and he was running the license plates. The first two turned up with nothing. Then, after a long delay, John called.

"Ready for this?" he said.

I took a deep breath. "No, but go ahead."

"The other two plates trace to guys with rap sheets that'd choke a horse. Convicted felons, drug trafficking, breaking and entering, and soliciting a minor."

"Oh, my God!" I said, trembling. "What . . . what can we do?"

"Unfortunately, at this point, nothing. Neither has any outstanding warrants. The smart play is to keep monitoring."

I was traumatized, envisioning some drug addict sex offender in a house with my toddler.

The day rolled into the night. John surveilled, and I cried. Andrew tried to console me, but I wanted no one near me. I was mad at the world.

The cars left Mark's at 12:30 a.m.

Frozen in despair and Ruby needing me, I didn't sleep the entire night. I had to pull it together. I was conflicted between trying to be a good mother to my new daughter and grappling with how to protect my son from his father. It was making me insane.

Besides being exhausted, I was on edge all weekend as John periodically reported that Mark hadn't left the house the entire weekend. Unreal.

I picked up Mason at school on Monday. It felt like a reunion—a lifetime in the making. I inspected him head to toe across from the school, hugged him, and drove to get us ice cream.

"How is your daddy doing, Mason?"

"Okay, Mama. His red juice makes him happy."

"You don't drink the juice, do you?"

"No, Mommy." *Phew*.

The next few months, Tara, Andrew, and I worked in concert,

preparing for court. Tara had agreed to appear on my behalf. The thinking of our attorneys was that whatever happened in my custody case would likely affect her situation with Mark, giving us common ground.

The court directed that Mark and I submit to a child custody evaluation, a process that lasted six weeks. Mark and I identified three people as character witnesses for the investigation. The court also directed that we both be tested for drugs, which meant urine tests and hair analyses. I welcomed the drug testing but feared Mark might bribe a lab technician. There was no way he could pass an administered drug test.

The persisting anxiety that Mark would manipulate the truth made me lightheaded and unhealthy. I was shedding a pound a day, my hair started to thin, and my eyes popped out of my head like golf balls from crying and lack of sleep. From my wobbly perch, I had everything to lose while Mark played chess from the killer king role. He had done a good job of killing a part of me. Now he had the chance to finish me off.

The court day arrived. While worried about gross distortion from Mark's side, I was hopeful that the court would see the light. Andrew unloaded the TV monitor we planned to use to show the startling video footage. As we walked through the parking area, Mark zoomed by in a new bright-yellow Ferrari, with a blond woman with shiny bright-red lipstick in the passenger seat. Tara and I looked at each other and shook our heads—next victim up.

Mark pulled his car into a parking spot, and before shutting off the ignition, he revved the engine, presumably to announce his arrival. We watched the two of them walk arm in arm to the courthouse—as if on their way to the wedding chapel. She giggled and looked at him, stargazed.

Mark's attorney spoke first, carrying on about why this "loving and attentive father" should have more time with his son, who "he deeply and unconditionally loves." My rising anticipation to show the video clogged my brain. I couldn't wait. It promised to be a house of tumbling cards.

The first thing my attorney did when his time came was address the video footage.

"Your Honor, we have some revealing and relevant video footage and a third-party witness, a recent ex-girlfriend, to lay its evidentiary foundation. It demonstrates powerfully that Mr. Corbin is an unfit parent."

"Objection, Your Honor, we've not seen this video," opposing counsel said, jumping up as if a bee bit him on the ass.

"Slow down, both of you. I neither want to see the video nor hear from any ex-girlfriend. I have a busy calendar, and we are here to address a single issue: whether Mr. Corbin is clean of illicit substances. If not, he has a problem with the court; if so, he is entitled to equal time with his son. This is not complicated."

"Your Honor, the video is directly on point; it's part of our case. Five minutes. It will shock you. May I make an offer of proof?"

"No, I want to hear from the lab professional."

"But Your Honor—"

"Enough," the court said, "bring in the professional."

I almost passed out. *How could this be happening again?* We condensed countless hours of video into five minutes, working months to prepare and spending a pretty penny. I turned to look at Andrew. He had tears in his eyes. I grabbed a pen, and on the yellow notepad I used to communicate with my attorney, I wrote to the one person left who could save my son: God.

GOD, PLEASE HELP ME!

If you exist, I need you now, please!

"Will Heather Smiton please come to the stand and be sworn in?" the court bailiff said.

Smiton was the "professional" the judge was itching to hear. She worked at the substance abuse center that tested our urine and hair. I had met her. I looked around and didn't see her. Instead, a gray-bearded gentleman rose from the galley and approached.

"Your Honor, my name is George Savion. I am here on behalf of the testing facility."

Mark's attorney shot out of his chair, probably a different bee this time.

"Where is Mrs. Smiton?" he said angrily.

"Your Honor, we relieved Ms. Smiton of her duties at our location. It's a personnel matter," Savion said, directing his comments to the judge.

Mark looked frantic and whispered to his attorney.

"Please take the witness chair, Mr. Savion," the judge said.

After the clerk swore in the witness, the court assumed the questioning, first laying a foundation for the process, all straightforward and professional. I held my breath as the judge moved into the substance abuse.

"Mr. Savion, what did the drug tests reveal?" the court said.

Savion cleared his throat. "Your Honor, first. Mrs. Stambul showed no evidence of drug use.

"And Mr. Corbin?"

"Well, Your Honor, quite different. Mr. Corbin had significant traces of cocaine in his system."

"Any doubt about that?" the court said.

"No, Your Honor, it was quite pronounced, actually. We tested his urine three times. Urine analysis can find cocaine two or four days after usage. Each time, he tested positive, which indicated heavy regular usage. There is no question."

Mark stood up and screamed—another pesky bee doubtless—"I want Mrs. Smiton, not this guy, to report on my test. Something is wrong here!" Mark was frothing.

"Counsel, you need to control your client pronto. He will not address the court unless asked. One more outburst, and I will hold him in contempt."

"Yes, Your Honor." Mark's counsel nodded to him, and Mark,

red-faced but sheepishly, took his seat.

It was all coming to me now. Heather Smiton was a young, attractive woman who Mark had seduced to provide false testimony. I wondered what bounty he used to cajole her and equally wondered how the facility uncovered it, as it apparently did.

Once things settled down, the judge denied the petition to increase Mark's custody rights, ordered Mark to rehab, and ruled that Mark may only see Mason under court-approved adult supervision for at least the next six months.

God showed up that day, big time, and I will never forget it.

My attorney hugged me, then Andrew hugged me, then Tara hugged me. I cried tears of joy. Intertwined in my fingers was a crumpled yellow paper with my prayer. I held it tight and out loud said, "Thank you, God!" Mark stormed out of the courtroom.

I knew what cloud nine meant. Arriving home exhilarated me. Mason handed me a pizza he made from playdough, and I picked him up and squeezed him tight. He said, "Mama, put me down and eat your pizza." I ordered an actual one.

Mason, Ruby, Andrew, and I went to the park the next day. The air smelled different. A dark cloud had lifted. I knew this wouldn't be the end. Mark would rear his ugliness again. But I had a calm in my body that I hadn't experienced in memory and wanted to relish. I had turned a corner, and it felt damn good.

41
Jessica

Less than a week later, Doreen called and informed me that she had heard from the judge.

"Jessica, I don't have good news. I'm sorry. It's such an injustice that I'm considering leaving the law."

I gulped. "What? Please tell me, Doreen."

"Jessica, the judge gave Collin almost everything he requested, disregarding the recommendations of the child custody investigator. Collin only has to attend a single anger management class for four hours and see a therapist once a week for four weeks as opposed to the recommended two years with an appointed personality disorder specialist. He gave Collin more custody time and gave you minimal child support, buying into Collin's tale of financial woe."

Wow. I was beyond stunned. I was nauseous. I didn't say a word while my head throbbed.

"Jessica, are you there?" said Doreen.

"Yeah, thanks. I'll call you later," I mumbled and hung up.

Even though Doreen and others tried to prepare me for less than a perfect outcome, I wasn't prepared for what happened. I collapsed into hysteria. I wanted to die. It was surreal. All that time, money, energy, and mostly undisputed truthful evidence meant absolutely nothing! Even though I was admittedly not an objective observer, there was no question that the judicial system screwed me. There is no way that the result was fair to me or in the best interests of Alexandra. To say I felt defeated and angry would be an understatement.

Alexandra and I had thirty days to vacate the house, limited to taking only personal items. At forty-eight years of age, I was being forced out of my home—with virtually nothing. Not even a pan to cook an egg. I was broke, defeated, drained, scared, and angry.

Alexandra and I started our next chapter in a small two-bedroom rented apartment, which I appointed as best I could to make it feel like home. I was miserable, thinking Alexandra might prefer staying with Collin because she'd lived there for nine years and enjoyed associated memories of playdates, swimming with friends, tea parties, and riding her scooter in the spacious backyard. The "poverty-stricken" Collin began to pour on the "love" for his daughter, adding a tennis court, princess tree house, and jungle gym to the property. For sure, Alexandra loved her father, and that's how I wanted it to stay. I only hoped Alexandra could distinguish between love and theater.

Alexandra loved our new apartment and ironically resisted sleeping at the old house on her own accord. She said she didn't feel safe there. Collin's new girlfriend, Arena, had moved in as soon as we were out, which confused Alexandra. I let her talk through these issues, listening and trying to get her to understand that things will improve in time. I didn't want to bad-mouth Collin, as tempting as that was, and I did my part to stay true to the parenting plan. Unhappy as I was about it, I planned to honor it. I also didn't want Collin to unleash his infamous wrath on Alexandra.

Over time, when Collin realized that showering Alexandra with material things would not work as a substitute for true parental love and attention, he began to lose interest in Alexandra. He receded to the old and real Collin, the invisible man—no longer attending dance recitals, dentist appointments, or any activity where he could embrace the fatherly role. He came late to pick her up and brought her late to dance recitals, where the class awaited and counted on her. It was all about what suited Collin best. It didn't take long for him to steadily reduce the time he allocated to his daughter to a bare minimum. Collin seemed happier not spending time with Alexandra. It freed him to do whatever he liked, right out of the Collin playbook.

For my part, I was lonely, consumed with anxiety and sadness, and financially challenged. In truth, I resented that Collin lived his life without a hitch and that mine was a struggle and a mess. I lost my ability to trust people. I never thought I'd be happy again. This was a deep hole to dig my way out of; it was not easy. I still consider myself in active recovery. I sought out numerous resources to heal from the years of abuse. I donned a mask of bravery for my daughter, friends, and family, but inside, sadness ruled.

I was exhausted and depressed and dealing with different health issues that arose after years of personal neglect. I knew, for Alexandra's future, I should focus on my health. In addition, to try something restorative, I started practicing yoga. In one class, during the last few moments of Savasana, the teacher instructed us to choose a mantra to repeat each day upon awakening and in the evening before sleep. I picked *freedom* and *gratitude*. I was *grateful* for my daughter and my *freedom* from an abusive marriage. I counted my blessings each day.

I repeated the mantra daily, making sure Alexandra's life was stable and happy, and tried to reconnect with family and friends. It wasn't an easy road. Some days, I couldn't face anyone. It didn't help that I walked my dog in front of Collin's new favorite breakfast spot, which was directly across from my new apartment. He'd sit there leisurely, sipping espresso and eating croissants with Arena. His life hadn't missed a beat, ramping up his escapades and living like a rock star while I labored each day to pick up the pieces of a shattered life and glue them back together. Living as Collin's prisoner had isolated me from the people who cared about Alexandra and me. The social estrangement that comes with living with a narcissist is profound. You do what they want when they want and are punished in the end.

No life of comfort—no boat, plane, exotic trip, or future-faking—could coax me into that prison again. The peace I held in my heart was priceless. I was free.

I strive to live by Martin Luther King, Jr.'s quote: "Freedom is never voluntarily given by the oppressor; it must be demanded by the oppressed."

42

If You Knew, Would You Say I Do?

DR. BRENNAN: Welcome back to my podcast, *If You Knew Would You Say I Do?* Ladies, welcome back. Again, please allow me to thank you both for sharing your most vulnerable moments. Your journey and healing will help others realize they aren't alone. You are both strong, courageous women. You did what you had to do to pave a healthy path for your children and yourselves.

JESSICA: Thank you for letting us share our stories, which we hope will help others escape abusive relationships. I wish I knew then what I know now because if I did, I would have never said I do! If I had been educated about the depths of NPD, I could have found freedom much sooner and spared years of pain and destruction.

LAURA: I'm so grateful to be enlightened about NPD. Initially, it's difficult to distinguish love bombing from true connection. Without immersing ourselves in learning about NPD, I assure you that Jessica and I would have stayed vulnerable as targets for narcissists. I don't blame myself anymore because everyone wants to connect, and narcissists are brilliant at playing the role of savior and exploiting that natural desire.

DR. BRENNAN: Thankfully, you won't be fooled again. Life with the narcissist is never what it seems, no matter how wonderful it looks or feels or how alluring the tale the narcissist tells. Each of their relationships is a crazy-making pattern of cruel abuse, with actions that never align with their words. They take no responsibility for the pain they cause and the chaos and drama they bring. They are forever the victim, never the wrongdoer or villain. They twist every narrative to support and advance their goals.

The sad reality is that narcissists don't change. Whoever is unfortunate enough to cross their path learns the hard way how dangerous, deceptive, and evil they can be. No one or epiphany will turn them around—an unfortunate reality we must accept. Don't stay because you are more afraid to leave. Staying is a prison sentence you don't deserve. It's on you to break free from the shackles because, rest assured, the narcissist will never give you the keys to unlock yourself. The cycle can't be broken until you're beyond their reach. There's no other way. If you stay, you will pay . . . *forever.*

I'd like to share a letter we received from a podcast listener living with a person with NPD, sent anonymously because they aren't ready to leave the relationship.

Dear Dr. Brennan,

I have listened to the stories of Jessica and Laura with sympathy and rapt attention. Their stories are my story. I am in a relationship with someone who has severe NPD. I have not summoned the strength to leave. But I wanted to share my thoughts on survival and isolation.

Staying in the relationship helps you understand that you are not part of a couple. You are alone, but not in way where you get to make your own decisions and enjoy life with family and friends in the normal way. No, it's an alone where you cry often, in the corner, in the fetal position, in the dark, or in the cold. The kind where you face obstacles and challenges each hour of each day you are together.

You are forced to accept that you won't receive compassion, empathy, or a modicum of understanding about what you feel or experience. You will not win an argument. On the contrary, your best interests are often served with swift apologies to restore a hint of sanity. Admit you are wrong, and assume you always will be. It is an approach that buys you a few hours of peace and quiet.

You're never in a partnership with a narcissist. You are in a master-captive relationship, living in a figurative prison, chained down, doled out symbolic scraps of food, and brainwashed into being grateful for what you get and the existence they dictate for you.

Your mental health requires coming to terms with the harsh reality that you are under the thumb of a person who doesn't care if you're happy and, worse, repeatedly assures that you never will be. You persist in a forever state of worthlessness, always anxious, feeling shame, and battling unrest—each day spent on edge, deciphering what you did wrong and how you should change your behavior to avoid more pain and punishment.

The adjustments, however—those attempts to find sustained light in darkness—are but a trap, part of the maddening game. As soon as you modify your actions, you face another pitfall designed to take you down. It is the never-ending cycle of life with a narcissist.

JESSICA: That is sad. I can relate. That was my life for many years, and it only got worse over time and became more dangerous. It is still difficult to comprehend that the loving, caring soul who swept me off my feet, who I waited a lifetime for, was a fraud, not only because he didn't love me but because he got pleasure out of hurting me.

LAURA: The seduction is real, and the connection is intense. It's all-consuming, especially when you presume that you've met the perfect partner—only to discover the person you fell in love with never existed.

DR. BRENNAN: Narcissists often have larger-than-life personalities and can be attractive and seductive. They have an air that they're better than the rest of us. Nowadays, however, they've morphed into the common neighbor next door and often present themselves in less transparent, covert ways. Narcissists come in many sizes and varieties—male or female, rich or poor, covert or overt, good-looking or unattractive, successful businesspersons and those who've never worked a day. What they all have in common, however, is a set of criteria, traits, and behavior characteristics of NPD, a serious personality disorder. They lure you with seduction to destruction, with the same tactics, though some are better than others and have more props. They dismantle you with the same motives and devastating patterns of abuse unique to the narcissist. Their sole objective is to control and feed off you until there is nothing left for them, and then they will discard you while shaming you for being a shell of yourself. They are in constant need and continuously search for a new supply without which they feel they are dying. Don't be fooled by the wolf in sheep's clothing—whether it's a custom-made suit or sweatpants and flip-flops. They can be your husband, wife, partner, sibling, boss, friend, coworker, parent, and even your child. NPD is a dangerous mental health disorder that brings severe damage to unsuspecting victims around the world.

Thank you, Laura and Jessica. You've made this a powerful series to help create awareness about narcissistic personality disorder and its long-lasting effects on those who have experienced it. Hopefully, your contributions and insights will prevent others from a path of destruction. You both will forever hold a special place in my heart.

I'm your host, Dr. Jules Brennan, and I hope, now that you know, you have to go.

Until next time, *if you knew, would you say I do?*

Thanks for listening.

EPILOGUE
Collin Worth and Mark Corbin

Collin's life underwent rapid change. Liam Worth refused to return the various assets Collin transferred to him during his ploy to avoid judicial scrutiny in the divorce with Jessica. His father took the view that Collin should pay the piper for his nifty legal ruse. Collin got to keep assets away from Jessica, and he—the patriarch who put himself at risk—deserved the spoils, a perverse quid pro quo.

The unexpected setback sent Collin into a tailspin. He became estranged from his family, forcing him to restore his financial footing anew. Before too long, he formed a hedge fund—The High Worth Fund—that generated unprecedented investor returns. The fund quickly became a small investment empire.

After going through several romantic relationships, Worth settled down with a former model named Stella Simmons, a woman half his age, and the two began a life together—at least that's what Stella thought.

Collin's financial services brand was flamboyant pitches to potential clients, staging road shows on his yacht, followed by raucous parties where would-be investors enjoyed the company of hired escorts and indulged in a wide range of drug use.

It was during an investment party that Collin met Mark Corbin, who a friend had invited to hear the High Worth investment pitch. The two hit it off.

Corbin's life took an odd turn. By the time Worth and Corbin met, the Corbin family had quietly eased Mark out of the retail business, no longer willing to tolerate his unchecked drug and alcohol abuse. Mark responded by becoming a drug purveyor in

Southern California, building an exclusive high-end clientele. He limited his inventory to designer drugs, which mimic the effects of popular controlled substances, effectively a synthetic version, without the characteristics that allow detection and classification as illegal. The ready availability of those drugs for Collin's investment parties and the potential client network for Corbin from party guests was a match made in heaven for both men.

And that is how Collin Worth and Mark Corbin became business partners.

Meanwhile, Stella Simmons discovered that the man who'd professed his undying love for her and waxed incessantly about building a future together had been indulging himself with two other women, much like Worth did with Jessica, Danielle, and others. Rather than confront Collin for answers and contrition—she knew he'd swarm her with a legion of lies and blame her—she elected another approach.

Two days after the discovery, she boarded an early United plane for JFK and, upon arrival, grabbed a taxi to 26 Federal Plaza, rode the elevator to the twenty-third floor, strolled with determination to the receptionist, and asked to speak with the FBI duty agent.

The law enforcement research and planning that followed took two months.

On Monday, July 25, 2022, between 4 and 6 a.m., a cadre of FBI in Los Angeles, armed with search and arrest warrants, raided the homes and business offices of Collin Worth, members of the High Worth management team, and Mark Corbin, as well as Collin's yacht.

The federal government charged Collin Worth, among others, with multiple counts of money laundering and wire, bank, and securities fraud built on the foundation of an elaborate Ponzi scheme. The feds also charged Collin with aiding and abetting prostitution.

The charges against Corbin included multiple counts of possession of scheduled drugs and drug paraphernalia, drug dealing and trafficking, drug manufacturing, and tax evasion.

The FBI agents took both Worth and Corbin into custody and booked them at the *Los Angeles* Metropolitan Detention Center.

At the bail hearing, the court confiscated each of their passports, set bail at $3 million for Worth and $4 million for Corbin, and, pending the posting of bail, which both later did, placed them under house arrest, with electronic monitoring ankle devices. Both pled not guilty.

The criminal cases against both remain pending.

Laura and Jessica

Laura is flourishing, living with Andrew, Mason, Ruby, and their two dogs in the great state of Texas. She is a consulting agent for a restaurant group. Laura also volunteers at a local domestic violence shelter, where she helped develop a violence prevention curriculum for youth. She advocates for women and children who go through the judicial system. She remains in therapy to continue her path of recovery from PTSD. She offers thanks each day that she got her life back on track and can raise her children in a healthy environment so they can become productive citizens.

Jessica rebuilt her business from scratch and is consistently ranked in the top 5 percent of real estate agents in Orange County. She lives with her fiancé and Alexandra, sharing their passion for international travel and documenting their amazing journeys. She holds monthly speaking engagements to educate others about NPD and assists them in leaving unhealthy, abusive relationships. She is forever focused on her healing journey.

Mason

Mason became a youth activist for violence prevention. He will graduate from medical school. His first question to new patients is "Are you safe at home?" He is his mama's biggest fan.

Alexandra

Alexandra thrives in high school with an excellent group of friends. Her school passion is computer science, and she intends to study business in college. She cofounded a school club that supports awareness of teen dating violence, designed to educate youth about healthy relationships. She is also the captain of the varsity lacrosse team.

Ruby

Ruby is a happy-go-lucky kid who is fixated on reading and ballet. She keeps talking about becoming a famous ballerina and writer.

Forever Friends

That once-in-a-lifetime chance meeting on that LAX flight to NYC formed an unbreakable sisterhood. Laura and Jessica reside in different states, but the distance has changed nothing. They are each other's first call most mornings. They thrive on an indestructible bond and feel blessed their paths crossed. They hope their healing journeys bring hope to others living under similar conditions.

Acknowledgment

We would like to express our deepest appreciation to our mentor, Michael Coffino, who not only helped us throughout this process but was also our rock, which gave us the courage to see our vision through.

www.ingramcontent.com/pod-product-compliance
Lightning Source LLC
LaVergne TN
LVHW091714070526
838199LV00050B/2389